THE
BONE BOX

Center Point
Large Print

**This Large Print Book carries the
Seal of Approval of N.A.V.H.**

THE
BONE BOX

BOB HOSTETLER

CENTER POINT PUBLISHING
THORNDIKE, MAINE

Hostetler
Bob

This Center Point Large Print edition
is published in the year 2009 by arrangement with
Howard Books, a division of Simon & Schuster, Inc.

Copyright © 2008 by Bob Hostetler.

The text of this Large Print edition is unabridged.
In other aspects, this book may vary
from the original edition.
Printed in the United States of America.
Set in 16-point Times New Roman type.

ISBN: 978-1-60285-366-9

Library of Congress Cataloging-in-Publication Data

Hostetler, Bob, 1958-
   The bone box / Bob Hostetler.
      p. cm.
   ISBN 978-1-60285-366-9 (lib. bdg. : alk. paper)
   1. Archaeologists--Fiction. 2. Fathers and daughters--Fiction.
   3. Excavations (Archaeology)--Fiction. 4. Mareshah (Extinct city)--Fiction.
   5. Caiaphas, High priest, 1st cent.--Fiction. 6. Large type books. I. Title.

PS3608.O836B66 2009
813'.6--dc22

2008042405

Dedicated to
Robin
None compare

ACKNOWLEDGMENTS

Thank you to Dave Lambert and all the fine folks at Howard Books for believing in this book, making it better at every point in the process, and being unfailingly delightful to work with.

Thank you to Lissa Halls Johnson for her erudite and thorough editing work on the manuscript. You made it better, saved me from embarrassment . . . and look, we're still friends!

Thank you to Steve Laube of the Steve Laube Agency for his able representation on this project, as always.

Thank you to Dr. Steve Weiner at the Weizmann Institute of Science in Israel for his kind response to my queries, and his helpful guidance. Thanks also to Daniel Ben-Natan, vice president for development and international relations at the Israel Museum in Jerusalem, and to Dr. Edwin M. Yamauchi of Miami University (Ohio) for his counsel in the early stages of the manuscript's preparation.

Thank you to my church family at Cobblestone Community Church, and to the leadership team for believing not only in my pastoral ministry but my writing ministry as well.

Thank you to my daughter, Aubrey, for her insights and edits, which added tremendously to the book's quality and authenticity.

Thank you to the lovely Robin, my wife, who continues to believe in me despite all counterindications.

PROLOGUE

TaLPIOT, SOUTH JerUSaLeM

The bulldozer operator slammed the twin levers backward with both hands, as if he could pull the machine back from the brink by using all the power in his thick, hairy arms.

He studied the ground with constantly shifting eyes as the earthmover rolled backward down a gentle slope. The pastel colors of the sunset shone over the ancient city to the west as the dust he had raised with his work settled to the ground. Finally he reached what he judged a safe distance. Then, cutting the engine and climbing down from his perch, he walked gingerly forward, looking a little like a circus bear balancing on a rolling ball. He stepped to the edge of the hole that had appeared in the ground beneath his machine moments ago, and peered down. He whistled.

He waved to several others in the work crew and called to them in Hebrew. The men were breaking ground for a new water park in the Peace Forest, south of Jerusalem, designed to entertain Jerusalem residents and tourists who were flocking to the *tayelet*—or promenade—that stretched for half a mile and provided a commanding view of the Old City and the Judean desert. The project had

9

ignited controversy among both Jews and Arabs, but for different reasons—from the destruction of green space to upsetting the delicate balance between the Arab and Jewish populations in the area.

The workers dropped their tools and strode to the bulldozer operator's side. He pointed to the gaping hole in the ground.

They leaned forward and gazed through the opening below their feet. Even in the waning light of day, the men could discern two sealed stone boxes in the middle of the stone floor. Pieces of other stone boxes lay broken and strewn about the hole. The men lifted their heads and looked at one another. They had uncovered an ancient burial cave.

WE LOOK NOT TO THE THINGS THAT ARE SEEN
BUT TO THE THINGS THAT ARE UNSEEN.
—PAUL THE APOSTLE

1

R and Bullock stumbled through the flap door of his tent and paused in the predawn darkness surrounding the excavations. One hand held a duffel bag stuffed with rumpled clothes; the other gripped the handle of his laptop computer's carrying case.

He looked around at the shadowy camp. Mareshah was an amazing place, an archaeological complex in the heart of the Shephelah, the region of Israel between the coastal plain and the mountains of central Judea. It was also a shopping mall of ancient civilizations, from the Israelite fortifications of the eighth to the sixth centuries B.C. to the caves cut to shelter Jewish rebels during the Second Jewish Revolt against Rome in about A.D. 132–135. The Hellenistic settlements of the third century B.C. featured an underground labyrinth of caves and corridors, including subterranean olive presses, pigeon cotes, temples, and tombs. It was an incredibly well-preserved—and intriguing— site. And, thanks to Yigal Havner's reputation and expertise, it was one of the best-staffed and best-run digs Rand had ever worked.

Long before the *Indiana Jones* movies, most people who thought they knew anything about archaeology "knew" all the wrong things. Even his own wife and daughter had occasionally joked about Rand's profession with some remark about "digging up dinosaur bones." But Rand, like most archaeologists, had never unearthed a dinosaur bone; the only dinosaurs he'd seen were in museums he had toured in the company of his wife and daughter. Most people also imagined archaeology to be a glamorous and exciting profession: opening ancient tombs, discovering buried treasure, fleeing from elaborate booby traps, and eventually becoming rich and famous. Few things could be further from the truth. Archaeology is usually a tedious exercise, and most archaeologists never find anything spectacular. The vast majority enjoy adding even the tiniest detail to the world's understanding of past civilizations, and usually the "treasures" they discover are valuable only for what they reveal about the people who left them behind. As Yigal Havner loved to say, "It's not what you find but what you *find out* that matters."

Rand let out a heavy sigh and watched his breath dissolve into the air before putting his head down and walking toward the car parked a few yards from his tent. He tossed his clothes and computer into the passenger seat and folded his six-foot frame into the tiny car. He reached for the key in the ignition.

"Huh?" he muttered. He pulled his hands away from the steering wheel and searched the floor of the car. Then he craned his neck to look at the steering column.

"I know I left them here," he said. He twisted awkwardly and patted the seat behind him but found nothing. Then suddenly he spun around and faced forward again. He peered through the windshield . . . and groaned.

He was in the wrong car. His dusty white Fiat 500, a different model and color from the car he occupied, sat several yards away in the fog of the not-yet-morning.

"Story of my life," he said. He gripped his computer and duffel bag, one in each hand, and wrestled himself out of the car, shaking his head. He had been that way for months, ever since his wife had died. His life and his career had become a shambles, and he couldn't seem to rally himself. He'd spent the first days and weeks after his wife's funeral in a stupor, feeling numb both mentally and emotionally. He had pretty much abandoned his well-funded excavation on the island of Crete (and with it, he felt sure, abandoned his career as well), thinking he should stick around the house for the sake of his daughter, Tracy, who would have to graduate from high school without her mom. But the great gulf that seemed to separate him from his daughter had only widened in the weeks following the funeral, and Rand had nothing to fill the gap except drinking, crying, and sleeping an average of twelve hours a day—until his friend Yigal Havner

15

had called, inviting him to join the excavation at Mareshah.

He had done so, but still had been unable to emerge from his fog. It was more than grief, he knew. Joy's death had left a hole the size of a crater in his life. Though he had neglected his marriage and family for years while he crisscrossed the globe from one archaeological dig to another, Joy had always been there, the only meaningful relationship he had—the only meaningful relationship he'd ever had. And now, in addition to having to deal with his overwhelming loss, he felt a hundred deficits in his life, a hundred vacancies, a hundred desires for love and friendship and relationship . . . and he had not the first clue about how to fill those needs.

He strode to his car, opened the door, and tossed his bags inside. This time, however, he didn't get in. He ran a hand through his short brown hair and scratched the back of his head. "Get it over with," he told himself. He left the car door open and headed down the row of tents, finding his old friend just where he'd expected: alone at his table under an awning, poring over a stack of papers and notes.

Havner barely looked up as Rand approached. "Shalom," the balding archaeologist said. He wore only an undershirt and boxer shorts despite the chill that still hung in the early morning air.

"I'm leaving," Rand said.

Havner lifted his gaze to Rand's face, his expression showing no surprise, only sadness. He said nothing.

"I want to save you the trouble of asking me to leave," Rand said.

"I am planning to ask you to leave?" Havner asked.

"If you aren't, you should be." He paused. "I'm grateful for everything you've done for me. But we both know I haven't been pulling my weight here." Havner opened his mouth, but Rand anticipated his objection. "You haven't shown any impatience or disappointment, and I'm grateful for that, too. You've been nothing but kind. But I won't ask you to lift the load for me any longer, and you should not have to pay for—for what I'm going through."

Havner came out from behind his table and approached Rand. "I . . . I do not know what to say." He squeezed Rand's elbow with his right hand and frowned, as though he were choosing his words carefully. "I suppose I should have asked you first."

"Asked me?" Rand said. "Asked me what?"

"It is just that I found out only last night, and did not want to disturb your . . . sleep."

My drinking, you mean, Rand thought. But he said, "Found out what?"

"You know how Jerusalem is. Every building project, no matter how small, becomes an archaeological site." He shrugged. "A park project in

17

Jerusalem resulted in a cave-in, and someone is needed to evaluate and excavate it."

The two men stared at each other for a few moments.

Havner continued, "It would be a favor to me, if you do this thing." He kept speaking, talking in circles, but as he spoke, some of the fog seemed to lift from Rand's sleep-laden mind, and he opened his mouth slowly, working to mesh words and thoughts.

"This," he began, interrupting Havner, "this is not a favor to you. I'm not helping you out—*you're* helping *me* out, aren't you?"

Havner's eyes blazed. "A moment ago, you tell me you are grateful for all I have done for you. If that is true, then here is a way to thank me." He peered into Rand's eyes and tightened his grip on his friend's elbow. "Whatever you find in Jerusalem, it is a good opportunity for you, I think. A beginning. A chance to—to regain—yes, to regain some of what you've lost."

Rand stared defiantly at his mentor for a few moments.

"The site is Talpiot," Havner said, his voice low. "Ask for Sergeant Major Sharon."

After a moment, the hint of a smile appeared on Rand's face. "Sharon," he echoed. He gripped Havner's shoulder. "Yigal," he said, "what have you gotten me into?"

The famous archaeologist embraced his tall American friend. "Shalom," he said.

2

Tracy Bullock stood with her friend Rochelle in the crowded airport terminal.

"I can't believe you're seriously leaving," Rochelle said. A large group of Hasidic Jews stood directly behind them, talking loudly and rapidly in a language neither of the girls understood. Tracy waited in line to show her boarding pass and identification to the uniformed woman who would admit her to the long, snaking line that led to the security checkpoints and into the gate area.

Rand Bullock's nineteen-year-old daughter tried to smile through her tears. She and Rochelle had been college roommates at Rothan College, a private college near Chicago. They had been nearly inseparable since they had met at freshmen orientation the first week of college.

"You should at least *try* to appeal your expulsion," Rochelle insisted. "Maybe they'll change their minds."

"No way," Tracy answered.

"Heather Underwood only got probation, and she was the one who *bought* the beer."

"Yeah, because her *daddy* went to the dean."

"So call *your* dad," Rochelle pleaded. "Get *him* to talk to the dean."

"Yeah, right. I can hear it now. 'Tracy *who?*'"

"Come on, Tracy," Rochelle pleaded.

"Come on yourself," she argued, feeling the sting of hurt and anger commingling in her eyes. "Why should he have time for me now? When my softball team went to the state championships, he was in Greece. The night of my senior prom, he was in Crete."

"But, Tracy—"

"The night *my mom died,* he was . . ." Her voice quivered. "I don't even know where he was."

"He's an *archaeologist,*" Rochelle whispered, her index finger drawing small circles on Tracy's back.

"I know," Tracy said. "Believe me, I know that. That's about all he is. He sure isn't much of a father."

"Then why are you going?"

Tracy dabbed her tearful eyes with the back of her hand, mindful of the thick mascara she wore. "I've got nowhere else to go."

Both girls glanced at the line. Tracy's turn would come next. She signaled the person behind her to go ahead, and people quickly began to flow around her.

Rochelle's eyes clouded with tears. "I'm just so worried," she said. "You going all that way by yourself, and he doesn't even know you're coming."

Red rings formed around Tracy's eyes. "He'd just tell me not to come."

Rochelle wrapped her arms around Tracy and hugged her tightly. "I'll miss you, girl. Promise me you'll be careful."

Tracy inhaled sharply as she returned Rochelle's hug, trying but failing to disguise a sob. "I promise," she said, wanting to tell her friend how scared she was. But she said nothing more as she turned to reclaim her place in line and thrust her boarding pass and ID at the security guard.

3

Baka, South Jerusalem

The car window next to Randall Bullock's head suddenly cracked, splintering the glass into a web of jagged lines. He started, slamming his head into the ceiling at the junction of the roof and windshield.

He cursed loudly, reflexively releasing his death grip on the steering wheel and lifting his right hand to his forehead. He felt the warm wetness at his hairline, then lowered his hand and held it in front of his face, staring at the blood on his fingertips. He shook his head and wiped the blood on his khaki pants, then gripped the steering wheel again.

He had left Tel Mareshah more than an hour earlier, taking Highway 35 east, then north on 60 all the way to Jerusalem. He had rolled the window up only moments before, as he approached a crowd of Palestinian protesters lining the road, shouting, shoving, and shaking their fists. There had been no chance to turn around on the narrow road, and if he had not rolled up the window when he did, the thrown rock that had fractured his car window might have fractured his skull. He began to fear that worse might happen—very soon.

He cursed again, this time invoking the name of Yigal Havner. "You could have mentioned," he complained to his absent friend, "that I might run into a tiny war!"

The Israeli-Palestinian conflict was not new to Rand, of course, but like many Westerners— even well-traveled ones like him—he had only a passing familiarity with the issues that seemed to keep the hostility alive between Jews and Arabs in the area. Though the bad blood had flowed for millennia, the modern conflict started after the Second World War, when Jewish immigrants began pouring into the area. In 1947, the United Nations tried to partition the land into Arab and Jewish states, but the Arabs refused, and war broke out. The Jews established the State of Israel in 1948, and fought a decisive war for independence that ended with armistice agreements among Israel, Egypt, Jordan, Lebanon, and Syria in the first half of 1949 . . . and created almost a million Arab refugees. Wars broke out again in 1956, 1967, 1973, and 1982, along with an ongoing campaign of terror raids and suicide bombings against Israel, and Israeli reprisals against Palestinians.

Like most visitors to Israel, Rand had frequently been struck by the numerous contrasts and contradictions. American news reports portrayed Israel as one big war zone, yet most of the country appeared at least as safe and secure as his own home in Ohio. Divisions between Jew and Arab went back thousands of years and persisted over issues such as water, jobs, and land, but Jews and Arabs seemed to work, shop, and eat side by side, as far as he could see. Most of the time, life and business in Israel seemed to go on without incident, but it was always a bit striking to see armed soldiers riding public buses and heavily armed security forces in all but the smallest private businesses. Overall, Rand knew that one could expect an abnormal normality when living and traveling in Israel.

He continued to inch the car forward along the pitted street and through the angry crowd, hoping for some sign of his destination. He wished fervently that he could open his windows, but it was obviously safer to keep them shut. Beads of sweat collected in his eyebrows and rolled down his nose as the bright sunlight and stifling heat filled his car. Wide circles of sweat colored his blue cotton shirt;

he fluttered the shirt front with his thumb and forefinger, hoping to circulate the air against his chest, but the cloth was already too wet and sticky. He licked his lips.

Then suddenly the attention of the crowd seemed to turn . . . to him. Rand watched in horror as the protesters turned his way. Someone pointed at him, and instantly the car was surrounded, making further progress impossible. Protesters pressed against his car on all sides. They began pounding on the roof and sides of the car, shouting at him as though he were responsible for the millennia of conflict between Arab and Jew.

"Oh, no," he muttered. "No, please, no." Fear clutched his stomach and tied it in knots as the mob began to rock his car from side to side. He repeated his prayer several times as the engine stalled. The crowd grew denser on all sides until he wondered if it would be possible for them to crush his car from the mere press of the people. He lifted his arms and pressed his hands against the roof, as if to preserve the shape of the car with only his muscles.

Rand could see nothing except angry faces and clenched fists—no sky, no landscape, no buildings. He turned to the passenger window of his car and watched as the face of a boy—no more than fourteen or fifteen years old—flattened against the glass like a child in a toy store window. Their eyes met momentarily, and the boy seemed to grimace in pain, until his eyes became glassy and seemed to roll back into his head.

"Stop!" Rand shouted at the crowd, slapping the window and screaming at the others who flattened the boy against the car. "You're crushing him!" He pointed to the boy, whose face had begun to pale.

Rand reached across the passenger seat and tried to roll the window down, still pleading with the crowd. He gritted his teeth with determination, but the crank wouldn't budge. He shifted in his seat to get better leverage, and the crank broke off in his hand. He tossed the crank to the floor and pressed both hands against the window, framing the unconscious boy's face, hoping that someone in the crowd would see, hoping that someone would care.

Suddenly the sound of gunfire mingled with the noise of the crowd, and Rand watched in relief as the press of the mob around his vehicle seemed to abate. As the crowd began to fan away from the Fiat, the boy's limp form slid down the window and the side of the car.

Rand looked out the windshield and saw a phalanx of Israeli soldiers approaching, their weapons pointed in the air. The protesters were retreating slowly to the east, turning occasionally to hurl rocks and curses toward the soldiers.

He turned back to the driver's side door, unlocked it, and opened it as the soldiers split into two groups. One group formed a line between the car and the retreating crowd, while another group, of three soldiers, jogged to the passenger side of Rand's car. The soldiers loomed above the boy, who had regained consciousness. They shouted angry phrases at the boy, kicking him and beating him with the butts of their rifles.

"No!" Rand shouted as he unfolded his six-foot-tall frame and tumbled out of the car. He raced around the front of the car and thrust himself into the trio of soldiers. "No, stop! He's just a boy!"

One of the soldiers turned and raised his rifle in the air as if he were prepared to bring the butt down on Rand's head. Rand reached out a hand, gripped the rifle butt in his hand, and glared at the soldier.

"Go ahead," he said in English, his voice tight but quiet. "Beat both of us."

The two men stared wordlessly at each other for a long, silent moment until Rand released the weapon.

The soldier relaxed his grip and lowered the rifle slowly, never breaking Rand's gaze. "We saved your life," the soldier said in a thick accent, nodding in the direction of Rand's car.

"I know," Rand answered. He knelt beside the boy, who lay in a fetal position on the road. The boy flinched; he had understood none of Rand's words. *And I think I've just saved his,* he thought.

4

EL AL FLIGHT 106

Tracy unwrapped a stick of chewing gum and popped it into her mouth. After a lengthy delay, during which everyone sat in the stuffy cabin of the huge plane, the captain had finally announced that they were cleared for takeoff, to the cheers of the passengers and crew.

She sat in an aisle seat. A little girl, whom Tracy estimated to be four years old, fidgeted across the aisle from her in the middle section of seats, her short legs barely extending over the edge of her seat. A woman Tracy assumed to be the girl's mother sat on the little girl's right, busying herself with another, even younger child in the seat on the other side of her.

"Would you like some gum?" Tracy asked the girl. She pulled the silver-wrapped stick slightly out of the pack of twenty wrappers and extended it in the girl's direction. "It'll keep your ears from popping."

The four-year-old stared at Tracy, then glanced at her mother. Tracy noticed that the woman had turned her attention in their direction the moment Tracy had spoken, and she blessed the transaction with a smile and a nod.

The girl took the gum, popped it into her mouth, and began chewing it vigorously. Tracy smiled, leaned her head back against her seat, and closed her eyes.

She was awakened twenty minutes later by an overweight man who bumped her elbow on his way to the lavatories at the back of the plane. She opened her eyes, shifted in her seat, and reached for a magazine from the pocket in front of her.

There were two magazines: the airline's in-flight publication and a thick, fragrance-laden magazine called *Gorgeous*. She chose the latter.

"Whatcha readin'?"

Tracy looked up from an article titled "Fresh Hair Looks You'll Love." A blond twentysomething guy in a perfect haircut leaned on the seat back in front of her. She flipped the magazine closed and turned the cover toward her questioner.

"*Gorgeous*, huh?" Perfect Haircut said. He studied her face, then dropped his eyes appreciatively to her torso and crossed legs. He grinned. "You don't need to read that. You should be *writing* it!"

She cocked her head. "Do I really look stupid enough to fall for that line?"

"Well," he said, suddenly flustered, "uh, yeah. I mean—"

Perfect Haircut straightened suddenly as a flight attendant guiding the service cart bumped into him from behind. He stammered an apology to the flight attendant, lowered his head, and shuffled down the aisle without another word to Tracy.

Tracy smiled wryly and tucked the magazine into the seat pocket, noticing as she did that the mother across the aisle had extended a facial tissue to the little girl.

"Put your gum in this," the woman said.

The girl shook her head emphatically.

Tracy turned to watch the drama between mother and daughter.

The mother repeated her instruction, and again the girl refused. When the girl spoke, her eyes were wide with anxiety. She pointed to Tracy. "She said if I don't chew the gum, my ears will pop off!"

Tracy and the mother exchanged surprised glances over the girl's head. The mother laughed, and then explained to her daughter what Tracy had meant. Reluctantly, then, as if still uncertain that her ears were safe, the girl surrendered her gum to her mom and then faced Tracy.

"I'm going to see my daddy," she whispered.

Tracy forced a smile. "You're a very lucky girl," she answered, turning her gaze immediately toward the front of the plane.

5

*I*t had worked.

A Roman soldier, an emissary of the governor, Valerius Gratus, stood before him, awaiting a response. The slightest of breezes wafted through the graceful limestone house in the wealthy Upper City district of Jerusalem. The day was only a few hours old, but the coolness of morning had already departed.

"Tell His Excellency," he said, his face expressionless, "I accept." He watched as the soldier nodded, turned his back on the newly appointed high priest of the Jews, and left. He stood for a moment, rooted to the spot, savoring the moment. This appointment had come at a steep price. First, his marriage to an unhappy woman, who quite often gave him reason to think she was mad. Then, with the influence of her father, who had once been high priest, an appointment to the legation that traveled to Rome the previous year to discuss provincial finances at the court of Caesar. Since then, regular—and transparent—bribes had been paid to the Roman governor, until he feared his wife's money would run out before he had anything to show for it.

But all his efforts and sacrifices had worked. He would soon be installed as high priest, the fourth since his father-in-law had been deposed soon after Gratus had arrived in Judea only three years earlier.

He strolled to the veranda of his home and looked past the sprawling olive tree in the yard to the distant, gleaming facade of the Temple, atop Mount Zion, where he had served the God of Israel all his adult life as a priest, inspecting and offering the daily sacrifices for the sins of the people and, in recent years, overseeing the smooth administration of the Temple and its ministry. No priest of Israel had worked harder than Joseph bar Caiaphas. It will be worth it, *he told himself.* It will soon be worth it all.

"So, you are high priest, then?" It was his wife's voice.

He turned. She stood in the doorway, draped in an expensive gown and reeking of too much perfume.

"Yes," he said. "Your father will be pleased."

"Perhaps," she said. "If you fare any better than Simon. Or Eleazar. Or Ismael." A taunting smile creased her face.

They stared at each other, and then she turned and walked back into the house, the names of the recently deposed high priests hanging in the air. Valerius Gratus had quickly installed Ismael, son of Phabi, in place of Annas, her father. The next

31

year, Ismael was likewise removed and replaced with Eleazar, son of Annas. Just as quickly, Eleazar was out and Simon, son of Camithus, was in . . . until today.

He walked back into the house and called for his servant Isaac. He would begin immediately. He would waste no time. He must make sure that he would not share the fate of his predecessors.

6

TaLPIOT, SOUTH JerusaLem

Rand watched the ambulance race up the road toward Hadassah Hospital, carrying the wounded Palestinian boy, and for a moment a familiar hardness formed in his gut, a grief that surfaced less frequently than it once had but which was just as bitter when it did.

For a moment his mind took him back to West Chester, Ohio, to a scene that had repeated itself many times in his imagination—two scenes, actually. The first was a grisly slow-motion depiction of his young wife's Camry being smashed by a drunk driver who crossed her route to some women's meeting at the small church she attended. In the next scene, she was being whisked to the hospital in an ambulance, desperately calling her husband's name. But the scenes existed only in his imagination, because he had been nowhere near West Chester at the time of the accident. He had been half a world away, and had learned of the accident when some doctor he'd never met managed to reach him on site at an archaeological excavation on Crete. By that time Joy had been dead almost twenty-four hours.

He made it back to Ohio for the funeral. The trip home had been interminable, the agony of grief that pierced his heart every waking moment compounded by the physical impossibility of getting there quickly, to see her, to confirm firsthand that it had really been her in that car, to finish all the sentences he'd started in nearly twenty years of marriage to her. When he arrived, after thirty-four miserable hours in planes and airports, he was in no mood for Joy's talkative Uncle Herbert, who met Rand at the baggage claim.

"Where's Tracy?" Rand asked. He'd tried to reach her on her cell phone while at the airport in Athens, and again in Frankfurt and Chicago, but had managed only to reach her voice mail. He had left multiple messages, and had hoped to have a message waiting on his cell phone at each layover on the interminable trip from Greece to Ohio, but she hadn't called.

"She's doing just fine," Herbert said in a cheerful tone that struck Rand as wildly insensitive.

"I tried to call her," Rand said. "I haven't even talked to her since . . ." His voice trailed off.

"You don't have to worry about a thing. Tracy's been staying with us the past two nights, and everything's taken care of. They do a great job, those funeral people. Though it's a creepy job, I don't know what possesses a person to decide, 'Hey, I think I'll run a mortuary,' you know? Somethin' sick about it. Of course, they've got a college of mortuary science here in Cincinnati, not far from the funeral home, in fact. I drive by it every once in a while, they've got a big ol' sign out front saying what it is. Maybe people drive by that place and Junior says, 'Mommy, what's mortuary science?' And she has to explain, and the kid thinks, *That's what I'm going to be when I grow up.* Still can't see it as anything other than sick, though."

He nodded as Herbert rambled, but the monologue barely pierced Rand's clouded mind. He let the man go on as they claimed the luggage, walked to the parking lot, and exited the airport in Herbert's station wagon. Ten minutes later they crossed the river, and by that time Herbert's discourse had taken a number of hairpin turns without slowing down.

"And you know, whenever you try to call some company nowadays, you have to listen to one recording after another—"

"Who's doing the funeral?" Rand asked. He'd been polite enough, he decided, and the only way to ask Uncle Herbert a question was to interrupt.

"Paul Leeland. Seems nice enough. At least he doesn't dye his hair. I hate it when a preacher dyes his hair, it just doesn't seem right . . ."

Rand gazed out the window then, and let Herbert talk the rest of the way. Paul Leeland, the pastor of the church he and Joy attended, was at least a decade older than Randall and Joy Bullock, but they were good friends. Almost from the first moment they met, Paul had always seemed able to look Rand in the eye . . . and see straight through into his mind and heart. Rand didn't know if Paul still had the touch after all these months. He hoped not.

His reunion with his wife took place in front of her casket in the funeral home, moments before the funeral was scheduled to begin. The world seemed to spin beneath his feet as he looked down at the now lifeless form of the only woman he had ever loved. He stood for a long time beside her casket, crying, touching her cold hands, combing her hair with his fingers, seemingly rooted to the spot, unable to consider leaving her side. His *world* lay in that casket, and nothing else mattered to him, nothing else existed . . . until his daughter, eighteen-year-old Tracy, appeared at his elbow.

He turned and draped an arm over Tracy's shoulder, and immediately felt her back straighten and her shoulders stiffen. He gazed at her face then, out of the black hole of his own despair, and was shocked at her expression. Whatever he had expected to see, it wasn't this—a mask. A wall. He waited for her to look at him, but she didn't. She stared, seemingly impassive, at her mother's form in the casket.

He was unaware at first that it was Paul Leeland who eventually guided the two of them to a chair on the front row, unaware that a roomful of mourners had watched his silent reunion with his daughter, unaware even that everyone else in the room stood and sang and listened at Paul's behest. He learned these things later, when the short service had ended and the funeral director, a leprechaun of a man who, but for his black suit, seemed a wholly unlikely mortician, stepped to the coffin and invited the guests to offer their "last respects."

Rand stood and waited for Tracy to accompany him to the casket, but she sat, unmoving, staring at the floor at her feet. He whispered her name; she shook her head. He reached out to take her arm, and she moved away from his grasp. He stood a moment longer, not knowing what to do or how to reach across those few but infinite inches that separated him from his grieving daughter.

Finally, he turned away from Tracy and stepped to the casket, where he resumed his silent, tearful vigil. The others in the room waited patiently, respectfully, until Paul draped an arm around Rand's shoulder.

"Let's go, Randall," he said. "I'll walk you to the limousine."

Rand shook his head. When he spoke, his voice was thin. "I want to stay here," he insisted.

Paul squeezed Rand's shoulder sympathetically. "I know," he said. "But others are waiting to see her, too."

Rand spoke, his gaze still fixed on his wife's face. "How long have they been waiting, Paul? A few minutes? It took me almost *three days* to get here. I've waited in cabs, boats, airports, planes, and all I've wanted is to see her again." His face melted, then, into a paroxysm of grief. *And she's not here!* he thought. *I'm looking at her, and I keep looking at her, I can't bear to look away, but . . .*

"I know, Rand," Leeland said. "But she's not here." Then, a pause before adding, "She's with God."

Rand's expression changed, and he turned to Paul, stone-faced. "I should hit you," he said. He looked at the front row of seats, saw that Tracy's chair was empty, then walked slowly around Paul Leeland and left the funeral home.

He stayed in Ohio after the funeral, attending Tracy's high school graduation and planning to take her to college at the end of the summer. But he felt utterly isolated from her, and alone in his grief. She had several good friends, for which he was glad, but he felt laughably inadequate to understand her, let alone help her in any way. So when his friend Yigal Havner had called to invite him to join the excavation at Mareshah, Rand had accepted, hoping that returning to the activity he loved would clear his mind and get rid of some of the things he'd been thinking and feeling since the funeral . . . and before, to be honest.

"That really worked, didn't it?" he muttered, still staring after the departed ambulance, which had disappeared over the crest of the hill. He swiped his palm across his sweaty face and sighed wearily, though it was not yet noon. He turned back to his car, noting that the Israeli soldiers still watched him warily. He opened the door, then paused.

He locked eyes with one of the soldiers; it was the same man he'd locked horns with earlier. "I'm looking for Talpiot," he said matter-of-factly.

The soldier slowly rotated his head and shoulders. He pointed up the slope.

Rand followed the gesture. A cluster of construction equipment and building supplies crowned the hill; he could see a number of people walking around in the dusty haze of late morning in Judea. The road between his current position and his destination was clogged with a string of cars.

He sighed and scanned the rocky countryside all around him. There was nowhere to go, nothing else to do but wait. "Could be worse," he said without cracking a smile. "But not by much."

He nodded to his former adversary and ducked into the car.

7

You know, of course, that Shimon son of Hillel will preside until you are installed." Annas reclined on a low couch at the table of his son-in-law Caiaphas, the newly appointed high priest. The two men—the corpulent Annas and his younger, handsome host—ate together at the low, circular table in the elegant room. The only other occupant of the room was a male servant, who stood just inside the doorway that opened into a breezy courtyard.

Joseph bar Caiaphas nodded patiently and slid a large grape between his lips. The table before them was spread with an assortment of fruits, vegetables, sauces, and wine.

"They will ask you two things."

Caiaphas chewed for a moment. "Yes, I know. I was present for the investiture of the others."

"Still," Annas insisted, "it is important how you answer."

"The council all knew my father and grandfather. They know our ancestor Zechariah's name is recorded in the archives of Jeshana at Zipporim," he said, referring to one of the family's primary claims on the high priesthood.

"They must ask also of any infirmity or uncleanness."

Caiaphas nodded again. "I have been exceedingly careful, I assure you, to avoid all defilement. 'Zeal for your house consumes me.' "

Annas reached for his wine cup. "I don't care about your ceremonial purity, you know that. But you cannot take a careless attitude in to the council. Your answers must be careful."

The younger man sighed and smiled. "You must not worry, Father. I am not mocking when I say, 'Zeal for your house consumes me.' I know Rome has made me high priest—"

"And your wife's father."

Caiaphas nodded. "Yes, and many bribes and schemes as well. But I do not intend to be high priest in Rome's eyes only. I will be high priest of the Jews, and I will serve my nation while there is breath in my breast."

Annas studied his son-in-law. "You will succeed where I have failed?"

"With your help, yes."

"You have great faith in your own abilities."

"Yes, but not in my abilities alone. I have faith, too, in Hashem, and in the One who is to come."

Annas laughed, a single syllable. "You are not that One."

"No," Caiaphas admitted. "But I am high priest. And when righteousness has been restored in Israel, he will come."

"And how will you do this?"

"Slowly. Little by little. But it will start when I am anointed as high priest before the Sanhedrin."

"Anointed?" Annas's tone was incredulous.

Caiaphas nodded slowly.

Annas seemed momentarily dumbstruck. He turned his cup around in his hand, then seemed to find his tongue. "You—you are high priest by investiture. There has not been a high priest by anointing since . . . since before the exile! You know that many think such anointing must be reserved for the Coming One, the Messiah."

Caiaphas wore a solemn expression. "It must be so now. It is fitting for us to restore all righteousness."

The older man's mouth opened and closed several times, as if he were speaking, but no sound came out. He returned his cup to the table and shook his head. "The council will not stand for it! It is insane."

"I have already spoken to a majority on the council. They will not protest."

"Surely Shimon, and Gamaliel—"

"They were the first I spoke to."

"And the others?"

"There will be no dissent. I assure you. The votes are all but counted."

"But—but who will anoint you? Not Herod! He is an Idumean!"

"No, not Herod," Caiaphas said.

"Then . . . who?"

Caiaphas was smiling now. "You," he answered.

8

TaLPIOT, SOUTH JerUSaLeM

He parked his car next to a dusty dump truck and got out, estimating that it had been nearly an hour since the boy had been taken away in the ambulance. He touched the junction of his forehead and scalp again; the blood had dried, at least. *All in all,* he thought, *a pretty unpleasant start to my day.*

He walked a few paces from his car to a young woman in a uniform of khaki shorts and shirt who stood with her arms crossed, apparently observing the lumbering movement of a bulldozer near the top of the hill. A large belt and gun holster hung on her hips.

"Excuse me," he said. She turned and met his gaze; he estimated her age at twenty-six or twenty-seven. He fished in his shirt pocket and withdrew a scrap of paper. "I'm looking for Sergeant Major Sharon," he said, pronouncing it to rhyme with "alone," as the Israelis did. "Can you tell me where I might find him?"

"I think I can help you." The woman's English bore the slightest accent. "What is your business with Sergeant Major Sharon?"

He smiled patiently at the pretty young woman.

"I'm Dr. Randall Bullock. I'm here to take charge of this excavation. Now, if you'll just show me where he is, you can go back to doing whatever it is you were doing."

She nodded. "We have been expecting you," she said, unfolding her arms and propping her hands on her hips. "Actually, we expected you earlier."

"Yes, well, I was nearly killed in a riot just down the street."

She started walking toward the top of the hill. Rand fell into step beside her.

"Yes. I am afraid you have walked into a sensitive situation."

"That sounds like an understatement," Rand said. "I could have been lynched back there."

"Are you better now?" the woman asked.

Rand studied her quickly. She wore no makeup. Her black hair was gathered at the back of her head in a comb. Her dark, deep brown eyes sparkled from an elegant face, tanned but not dry, and he couldn't shake the suspicion that she laughed at him behind that beautiful face. He broke her gaze, and looked away as he spoke. "What's it all about?"

"What do you mean?"

"The violence. The protests. The mob that broke my window and nearly crushed a young boy to death against my car."

She nodded again, and swept her arm to indicate the construction area that surrounded them. "They are protesting."

"I saw that. But what are they protesting?"

She shrugged, as though she couldn't be less interested. "It is what they do."

They arrived at the scene of the cave-in. Yellow tape, wrapped around fence stakes, cordoned off the area. "Come," the woman said, ducking beneath the tape.

Rand followed, and felt his senses snap to attention like soldiers in review. He assumed a new sharpness, a new intensity in his demeanor, though the change may not have been perceptible to a casual observer. He crouched near the edge of the cave-in, where the earth had slid into a tomb. The forenoon sun washed the cave with sunlight.

Four limestone ossuaries, or bone boxes, lay in the central chamber of the cave. Two of the ossuaries had been broken, each into several large pieces. Two others appeared to be intact, still covered.

"As you can see," the woman said, "we are not dealing with the best circumstances here. The Antiquities Authority wants this to be completed as quickly as possible."

"How quickly?"

She shrugged. "In a situation as sensitive as this, 'as quickly as possible' means as quickly as possible."

Rand wiped his sweating forehead with the heel of his hand and tore his eyes away from the woman to survey the site again. "I have to have a time

44

frame. That will dictate nearly every decision I make. So what are we talking about? Weeks? Months?"

She shook her head. "Days."

"You can't be serious," Rand said. He felt his face warm, and not from the Judean sun. He waved a hand in the direction of the tomb. "This appears to be a Jewish tomb dating to the Second Temple period. That seems likely from the presence of ossuaries," he said, referring to the small stone boxes used by Jews primarily from the end of the first century before Christ's birth until about A.D. 70, when the Second Temple was destroyed by the Romans. After a body had been buried long enough for the flesh to decompose, the bones would be gathered together and placed in an ossuary, usually made of limestone and sometimes decorated with carvings and inscribed with the given name or family name of the deceased. "There looks to be at least four of them," he continued, "and possibly more—which we won't know until we get down there."

"Yes," she said. "I see that." She crossed her arms on her chest. "But I am afraid there is nothing else we can do. Like many things in Israel, this is not a simple situation. As you may know, every time we turn a shovel in Israel, we disturb history. This part of Jerusalem, in particular, is littered with tombs, and thousands of these bone boxes have been discovered. And I know archaeologists like you want to carefully excavate every piece of stone or bone or pottery. I understand that. But those are not the only concerns. We oversee hundreds of salvage excavations a year here in Israel, and we must constantly balance the political, religious, and economical realities with the archaeological. It is complicated. Like everything in Israel."

Rand searched her face. "I will need a team."

She smiled. "*You* are the team."

"You're joking," he said flatly.

She shook her head.

"It can't be done. There just aren't enough hands. There's not enough time."

She stared back at him, her expression unsmiling but not unsympathetic.

Bullock shook his head. "What about Sergeant Major Sharon? When will he be getting here?"

She thrust her hand in his direction. "He is here," she said. She shook his hand. "I am Sergeant Major Sharon of the Israel Police."

He blinked a few times, and only then noticed the insignia on her arm: a three-striped chevron topped by an oak cluster. "You're—you're Sergeant Major Sharon," he said, blushing. "I—I'm very sorry. I had no idea. You see, I—I didn't—"

"Expect a woman?"

"No, it's not—it's not that," he stammered. "I just, well . . ." He sighed, and stopped. "I've embarrassed myself, haven't I?"

She nodded. "You are not the first," she said. "If you can believe it, Israeli men are even more chauvinistic than Americans."

He opened his mouth to protest but shut it quickly, and smiled instead. "I'd like to start over," he said. He extended his hand. "Sergeant Major Sharon," he said as he shook her hand. "I'm pleased to meet you. My name is Rand."

She still didn't smile. "Dr. Bullock," she said, pronouncing each syllable distinctly. "I am Sergeant Major Miriam Sharon."

9

TALPIOT, SOUTH JERUSALEM

Rand set to work immediately, descending into the cave through the hole in the roof, while Sergeant Major Sharon remained above.

The coolness of the cave was a welcome relief from the heat of the day. It had been carved into the soft limestone bedrock that was characteristic of the eastern slopes of the Judean desert. A lowered portion of the floor, called a standing pit, indicated the original entrance to the cave on the east; the standing pit had allowed ancient mourners to stand up in the low-ceilinged cave.

Rand pointed to three openings in the cave's west wall. "Loculi," he said, using the archaeolog-

47

ical term for the burial niches. "Another indication that this is a Jewish tomb." The Jews of Jesus' day would bury a corpse, wrapped in layers of linen and perfumed spices, in a loculus about six feet long and a foot and a half high. A stone would then be used to block the loculus opening, as well as a larger stone to block the entrance to the tomb itself. A year later, when the corpse had sufficiently decomposed, the family would open the tomb and collect the bones from the loculus into an ossuary. These practices, which began fairly suddenly and ended even more suddenly (when Jerusalem was destroyed in A.D. 70 and most of the residents were killed or dispersed), were almost unique to Jerusalem and the surrounding area. As a result, the vast majority of ossuaries have been discovered in and around Jerusalem (some have been found in Galilee, where many Jews fled after Jerusalem was destroyed, but those are typically made of clay instead of limestone).

The loculi carved into the west wall appeared to be empty. A fourth opening, along the south wall, however, contained two ossuaries, sitting side by side. His gaze rose, and he saw that the chamber roof was decorated with a large, intricate rosette design carved into the stone ceiling. "Nice," he said.

"Did you call?" Sharon stood peering down at him through the hole in the roof.

"No," Rand answered. "Just talking to myself. I

do that a lot. I was saying . . ." He stopped when he realized she had moved away from the opening, and resumed his monologue while studying the rosette design in the ceiling. "Could be an indication of wealth and status, along with the overall size of the room." He nodded slowly, considering. "You could have something here, Randall. This could actually be important."

He inhaled slowly. Yigal Havner's words, spoken only hours ago, came back to him: *Whatever you find in Jerusalem, it is a good opportunity for you, I think. A beginning. A chance to—to regain—yes, to regain some of what you've lost.*

"All right, then," he said. "No time to lay out a grid. I'll just have to get everything marked and measured, and then get the best photos I can manage. Once that's done, I can start dusting things off and moving them out."

Rand worked feverishly and continuously for the next six hours, taking photographs and making observation notes on every detail of the site. In addition to photos of the cave from every possible angle, he also "tagged" every artifact—down to the smallest identifiable stone chips—with a number and a scale stick to indicate the size of each object being photographed. He snapped multiple photos of every artifact and logged the location of every item and feature in the cave on a clipboard of forms. The smaller items—several ceramic oil lamps, a clay water jar, and a small bottle that probably had been used to store ointments or perfumes, as well as numerous pottery and limestone shards—he bagged and labeled in ordinary paper sacks, both lunch size and grocery-store size. He worked quickly but carefully, slowing down or stopping only when necessary.

With his hands occupied, his mind roamed from Talpiot to Yigal Havner's dig at Tel Mareshah, and from there to Cincinnati, where his wife was buried, and then on to Chicago, where his daughter, Tracy, was in school. He hadn't always felt so distant from his only child, so powerless to understand or reach her. He remembered the look on her face that time he had surprised her by flying home in time for her performance as Mary in the Christmas pageant at church; her eleven-year-old eyes sparkled with almost as much adoration of him as they did for Brad Warner, the boy who had been chosen to play Joseph that year. *It's hard to believe,* he reflected, *but that was probably the last time Tracy looked at me like that.* Through her teen years, Rand had seemed to do nothing right in Tracy's eyes, and every semester he stayed home it seemed he spent his time trying to atone, unsuccessfully, for his most recent absence. And every time he left for the field, he knew he was creating more resentment than he would be able to reverse during his next sojourn at home. That's when the drinking started. In fact, that's when everything started.

I should have found a teaching position somewhere, he thought. *I should have been there for Tracy long ago. If I had been there when she was twelve and thirteen, maybe I could have been there for her when—when Joy died.*

As he worked, he mused that the tomb seemed an apt metaphor for his own life and relationships. When he was satisfied with the recording phase of the work, he ascended from the cave. Sharon leaned against her patrol car, her arms crossed on her chest.

"I think I can begin clearing out the contents of the cave tomorrow," he reported.

She nodded.

"As long as nothing goes wrong," he added, "it could be done in less than a week."

"Sooner," she said.

He shook his head. "I don't think that's possible. It's very time-consuming. Everything has to be removed very carefully. As it is, I will need some sort of help getting the larger pieces out of the cave."

"What kind of help?"

"You know, lifting and carrying."

"I can help you," she said. "But I cannot leave my post."

"All right," he said. "I'd appreciate anything you can do."

She nodded and turned her gaze down the roadway.

He pulled his cell phone from his pocket and dialed Yigal Havner's number. "Shalom," he said when the older man's voice sounded on the other end. "I have a favor to ask."

Just then, Sergeant Major Sharon stepped in front of him in such a way as to interrupt his call and command his attention. "We have trouble," she said.

10

Tel Aviv

Tracy stepped off the plane at Ben-Gurion International Airport in Tel Aviv into a cacophonous crowd of travelers and greeters, people hugging each other, chattering loudly, and a group of veiled women calling in a high-pitched warble that sounded to Tracy like the wail of some animal or bird. She was surprised to find that the terminal seemed much more modern than the airport she had left behind in Chicago, and directions were posted in Hebrew, Arabic, English, and—she assumed—French.

She had begun to feel sick on the plane, but not from the motion of the flight. Fear had clutched her almost from the moment her flight left Chicago's O'Hare International Airport. All sorts of fearful possibilities had occurred to her, and she had begun to wonder if this trip had been a bad idea from the beginning. She didn't know anyone in Israel except her father, and he didn't know she was coming. She didn't speak or read Hebrew. What if she got lost? What if her money was stolen? What would she do?

"You're here now," she told herself as she followed the signs to baggage claim and customs. She had made it, safe and sound . . . mostly. She felt her spirits rising as she politely skirted slower travelers headed her way. She had actually done it! She was in Israel, about as far away from Rothan College as she could get, though her stomach still felt a little queasy. "I just need a little fresh air," she said.

Her heart dropped, however, as she entered the baggage claim area. Hundreds of people crowded the luggage carousels, and even more waited in long, snaking lines for their passports and bags to be checked by customs. It would be a long time before she could get some fresh air.

She inhaled deeply and was immediately sorry she did. The unfamiliar richness of smells—human and otherwise—added to her discomfort.

11

*T*he journey had been long and hot. The new high
priest, with an entourage of twenty cavalrymen
and a select company of officials, had left
Jerusalem two days earlier. Passing Beth-horon on
the main east-west highway to the sea, they had
journeyed twenty miles each day, spending the first
night in Lydda and the second in Apollonia, on the
way to the Roman capital on the coast of the
Mediterranean.

The city had arisen on the site of an ancient
anchorage that had long been called Strato's
Tower, for a Sidonian king. It had been conquered
by the Roman general Pompey eighty-one years
ago and had ever since been a non-Jewish city.
The Roman emperor Augustus had awarded the
site to Herod the Great forty-eight years earlier,
and Herod had created an entirely new city and
gave it a new name—Caesarea, to honor his bene-
factor, Caesar Augustus. It was one of Herod the
Great's greatest achievements. Construction on the
Temple in Jerusalem dragged on, year after year,
and continued still, long after Herod's death, but
Caesarea of Palestine sparkled like a diamond

54

between much lesser gems, the port cities of Ptolemais to the north and Joppa to the south.

The contrast between the congested, sweaty streets of Jerusalem and the breezy, expansive environs of Caesarea could not have been more pronounced. Caiaphas's entourage approached from the south, the Great Sea always in view and the great city sprawling over 164 acres to the north, east, and south. As they entered the Cardo Maximus, the broad street stretching eastward from the sea, the horses' hooves clopped on the massive granite slabs that paved the way, and long rows of marble columns lined mosaic sidewalks that stretched as far as the eye could see.

They passed innumerable shops, palaces, and temples along the way, and marked the largest structures as they went: the hippodrome, the amphitheater, and—gallingly—Herod's massive Temple of Roma and Augustus, overlooking the harbor from a commanding height and flanked by a stately colonnaded porch. If any man in the group had doubted Caesarea's wealth, status, or paganism, there was no doubting any of it by the time they arrived at the governor's palace.

To Caiaphas, the glimmering beauty of the city was like an exquisite shroud on a corpse; dress it up however you will, the stench of death and decay could not be disguised. Far from being impressed, he hoped for the day when the prophet's words would be fulfilled throughout Israel, and this city built on bloodshed and crime would be filled with the knowledge of the glory of the Lord, as thoroughly as the waters cover the sea. He hoped, too, that it would come to pass during his high priesthood. And he hoped today's audience with the governor would begin to lay the necessary foundation for it.

Caiaphas knew he was attempting the impossible. He knew that Rome corrupted everything it touched; he had seen it in his father-in-law, Annas. He knew he would have to cooperate with Rome, even compromise in some ways, and he wasn't sure he could avoid contamination any more than the others before him. But he was determined to try. He knew that if righteousness were restored throughout Israel, Messiah would come. Until then, Rome must sleep, and Caiaphas would sing her lullabies.

A servant met the legation at the gate of the great palace on a thin finger of land poking out beside Caesarea's man-made harbor. After commanding other servants to see to the travelers' horses and baggage, he escorted Caiaphas and his delegation into the grand courtyard. To their right was the governor's templelike audience hall, and ahead was the massive palace of granite and marble surrounding a colossal swimming pool shaded by towering palm trees. Caiaphas closed his eyes, smelling the salty air and absorbing the music of the waves against the shore.

"He will make us wait, of course," the rabbi Gamaliel, grandson of the Great Hillel, said, referring to Valerius Gratus, the Roman governor of Judea.

"Of course," Caiaphas answered.

Both men—and the others with them, Ismael and Alexander, and Caiaphas's young brother-in-law, Jonathan, all members of the Sanhedrin—were surprised, therefore, when the servant returned only minutes later.

"The governor welcomes you to Caesarea," the man said. He swept his hand to indicate the doorway into the palace. "He will receive you now."

Neither Caiaphas nor his four companions moved toward the doorway. As devout Jews, they could not enter the dwelling—no matter how palatial—of a gentile. The governor knew this, of course; his invitation to enter the palace was clearly intended to present the new high priest with the choice of compromising the requirements of his religion or offending the man who had just appointed him to his office. When Caiaphas spoke, however, his voice flowed like the long, silky fabrics he could see fluttering inside the governor's palace.

"We would not disturb His Excellency's important business. Please tell him we will content ourselves to enjoy his gardens until he chooses to refresh himself with a stroll."

The servant studied the priest's face for a moment before nodding slightly and disappearing into the building.

12

TALPIOT, SOUTH JERUSALEM

Rand ended his call to Yigal Havner with a promise to call back right away, as four dusty cars roared to a stop at the edge of the cordoned area marking the excavation zone. Every car door seemed to open simultaneously, and a procession of men in beards and black hats marched toward Rand Bullock and Sergeant Major Sharon.

Sharon bellowed commandingly to the crowd of more than a dozen men, each wearing a long black coat despite the heat. The men stopped at the yellow tape where she alone blocked the way to the dig, but their red faces and angry tones made Rand doubt that they would be controlled for very long.

He strode slowly to her side, but with absolutely no confidence that he would be of any use if the herd decided to stampede. He watched as she faced the group. She seemed to have planted herself directly in front of the apparent leader or spokesperson, and gazed, unflinching, at him while he ranted. The men surrounding him shook their heads almost in unison at the man's words, sending the curly forelocks of hair at their temples into a whirling dance.

When the man finally stopped his tirade, Sergeant Major Sharon spoke in low, measured tones. Rand could not understand any of her rapid Hebrew after her initial "Shalom," but whatever she said seemed to inject some control into the situation . . . until she turned her back on them and began walking toward her blue-and-white car.

"*Assur!*" they began shouting immediately. "*Assur!*" Forbidden.

Rand caught up to her and walked beside her, while the crowd behind them chanted in unison, as loudly and angrily as before.

"What's going on?" he asked as they walked. He was sure the men would pour through the yellow tape at any moment and overtake them. "Where are you going?"

"To my car," she said, her jaw defining a straight line from throat to chin.

"Why? What for? Are you leaving?"

She didn't answer, but opened the trunk of her car and pulled out a carbine rifle.

"These men are *hevrat kadisha*," she explained. She shut the trunk. "A sort of society for proper burial practices among the Haredi, the most Orthodox Jews. They believe it is forbidden for us to disturb the dead. When they find out that a Jewish tomb has been discovered, they will protest

59

violently, with their lives if necessary, until they are allowed to reinter the remains and seal the tomb."

"You're joking." Rand had heard of these people but knew next to nothing about them.

"Oh, no, this is very serious."

"But they can't do anything about it, right?"

"Actually, Israeli law is on their side," she said, starting back toward the mob. "According to the law, human remains that are found during emergency excavations must be turned over to the Ministry of Religious Affairs for immediate reburial."

He gripped her arm, and they stopped walking. "Immediate? How immediate?"

She slowly removed her arm from his grip. "I believe immediate means right away."

Rand shook his head. "So you're telling me, if there are bones in any of the ossuaries in that tomb, I can't take them to a lab for testing."

"If there are human remains anywhere in that tomb, they must be turned over for immediate reburial."

"How immediate?"

"I believe you've already asked that question."

"You can't be serious," he insisted. "I mean, this is a tomb! There are likely to be bones in that cave, and given the presence of ossuaries, they're likely to be two thousand years old! And those bones are likely to tell us something—maybe something important. You can't possibly expect an archaeologist to pull bones out of an ancient tomb and simply hand them over to a bunch of freaks in frock coats!"

She answered him only with a passive glance from her dark brown eyes.

"You must understand," he attempted, "how important any remains would be from an archaeological standpoint."

"Dr. Bullock," she said, "if I understand, or if I do not understand, it does not matter. It is the law."

"I can't believe it," Rand said. He ran a hand over the short brown hair on his head, and stood shaking his head, helpless.

"I am sorry, Dr. Bullock," Sharon said. "I do not like to make your job harder."

"Yeah, I know. You're just doing your job." He sighed. "Can I at least examine them on-site?"

She nodded. "Yes, but any human remains must be preserved as they are. There must be no damage or modification of the remains."

That would mean no carbon-14 dating, Rand knew—among other things. "There has to be someone I can call," he insisted. "Like, that Ministry of Religious Affairs you were talking about. Maybe I could talk to someone there."

Sharon glanced at the clot of Haredi Jews, still shouting and chanting in the direction of the tomb. "That would be our friend in the black hat," she said.

"What? He's with the government?"

She smiled. "The Ministry of Religious Affairs oversees the burial societies in Israel. There are hundreds of them. And they are paid by the government for every Jewish body they rebury."

"Unbelievable," Rand said.

"As I said, Dr. Bullock," Sharon said grimly. "Nothing is simple here. Nothing is easy."

13

TeL aVIV

You don't understand," Tracy told the man at the Avis counter in the sprawling Ben-Gurion International Airport. She had stepped into a strikingly different world after finally making it through the crowd and confusion of baggage claim and customs, and traversed the most modern, most expansive airport she'd ever been in, filled with more shops, restaurants, and fountains than an American mall.

The man at the counter smiled broadly. "It is you who do not understand," he said in his heavily accented English. "You must be twenty-five years of age to rent a car. You are"—he looked at her Ohio driver's license—"nineteen?"

"But . . . but can't I rent it in my dad's name or something?"

"Is your father here?" the man asked, still smiling.

Tracy shook her head. This was crazy. She had been living on her own since her mom died. Except for the credit card her father had given her for tuition and books, she had been living an adult life with adult responsibilities, so she hadn't even considered the possibility that she wouldn't be able to rent a car at her destination.

She leaned across the counter at the still-smiling man. "Isn't there some way you can help me? I have to get to Mareshah today."

"Mareshah?" the man repeated.

That's right, Tracy remembered. *Mareshah is the name of the site. He probably wouldn't know that.* She dug in her shoulder bag. "It's near a . . . a kibbutz," she said. She pulled out a scrap of paper and turned it over. "Beit Guvrin."

The line behind her grew as she talked to the man. Several people started chattering in Hebrew, and the man directly behind her groaned, *"Yallah,"* which she assumed meant something like, "Move it!"

The man at the counter pulled out a map so ragged Tracy thought it might have crossed the Red Sea with Moses. He studied it for a few moments, then finally pointed to a spot southwest of Jerusalem. "Beit Guvrin," he said.

"Yes," Tracy said, recognizing the name at the tip of the man's finger. "How do I get there?"

The man sighed loudly. The smile was gone. He shrugged. "Bus or taxi." He craned his neck and looked at the person behind Tracy. "Next."

14

TaLPIOT, SOUTH JerusaLem

Rand redialed Yigal Havner's number on his cell phone. The first two calls failed to complete, despite what appeared to be a full signal. The third call, however, connected.

"Shalom."

"Yigal," Rand said, neglecting the customary "Shalom" in return. "I need your help." He turned his back to the men in black hats and Sergeant Major Sharon, who stood with her feet slightly apart and both hands resting on the rifle that hung from her shoulders.

"I hope it is help I can give," Havner told Rand. "I cannot possibly get away right now."

"Sure, I understand that. But can you send someone?"

"I am short of hands here myself, Randall. What is it you need? What have you found?"

Rand sighed, and explained the situation to his old friend, including the appearance of the hevrat kadisha.

"That is not good," Havner said. "It is horrible,

just horrible, the state of archaeology in Israel. And yet every time they try to fix the situation, the Israeli Knesset only makes matters worse. There are so many factions and—"

"Can you help me?" Rand interrupted.

"What is it you need?"

"A hoist would be a nice start. And a generator and a couple work lights and stands would be good."

"I should be able to do that," Havner said. "I can send those things up to you first thing in the morning."

"Good, thank you! And look, I know you're shorthanded, but can you possibly send Nadya for a day or two?"

"Nadya? So you have bones, then."

"Don't know yet. But I might."

"I'm sorry, Randall. I thought you knew that Nadya left several days ago. Her mother—"

"Oh, right," Rand interrupted. "I knew that. Is there someone else?"

"Another osteoarchaeologist?"

"Someone," Rand pressed. "Anyone. If there are bones in that cave, Yigal, they'll have to be analyzed on-site—in the cave, in fact."

"Because the moment you bring them out, they will have to be turned over to the hevrat kadisha."

"Apparently so."

Havner sighed loudly on the other end. "I wish there was something I could do for you, Randall.

But with Nadya gone, there is no one here with any more expertise than you or I."

Rand went silent for a few moments. "Well," he said finally, "I'll have to do the best I can."

"That is always a good spot to be in," Havner said.

The two men exchanged a few pleasantries and a final "Shalom," and Rand pocketed his cell phone. He turned around and met Sharon's gaze. He nodded to her. "I'll be getting some more equipment," he said. "But it won't be here until morning."

"Are you staying somewhere nearby?" she asked.

"Staying somewhere?" he said. It took a moment for her question to sink in. "Oh—I don't know. That is, I—I haven't given that any thought."

She nodded.

"What about you?" Rand asked. "You've been here all day. You probably have to go home soon."

She looked at the hevrat kadisha. "While you were on the telephone I radioed my shift supervisor to tell him about the situation here. He said to expect someone to relieve me for the night." She turned her gaze back to Rand. "I don't."

Rand nodded, catching her meaning: she didn't expect the promised relief at the end of her shift, which meant they were both stuck there, on-site, for the night. He looked slowly around himself, then. He scanned the construction site, the clustered buildings on the opposite side of the road, the boys kicking a ball behind a chain-link fence, the dome of a mosque beyond the boys, and the setting sun beyond Teddy Kollek Stadium, Jerusalem's twenty-thousand-seat soccer arena, two or three kilometers away. "So," he said finally, nodding at the men in black, "will they leave for the night?"

She shook her head. "No more than a few of them. They will be here as long as you are here."

"And it looks like you're going to be here as long as they are here," he said.

She shrugged. "If I leave, they will not be restrained by you."

"Good to know," he said. They stood a few moments in silence, until Rand spoke again. "Are you hungry?"

Another shrug. "I ate yesterday." A tiny smile.

"Yeah," Rand said. "Me, too. I'm starving. Would they let me through? In my car, I mean?"

She patted her rifle. "I could talk them into it."

"Well, then, why don't I go get us something to eat?"

"I would like that," she said, with the same small smile. "There is a place called New Deli not far from here." Her eyes seemed to brighten as she said this. "Just drive on this street for two blocks, then turn north and go to Efek Refaim. It will be right there, number 44."

"Would they still be open?"

She smiled broadly. "Knock loudly on the door. Tell them you have an order for Miri."

"Miri?"

"Yes. It is short for Miriam."

"Miri," he repeated.

Her smile turned sardonic. "I would like the grilled lamb sandwich. And a Dr Pepper."

Rand was smiling broadly. "You got it . . . Miri. Grilled lamb and Dr Pepper."

15

a.d. 18
caesarea of palestine

Valerius Gratus, procurator of Judea, approached Caiaphas and his party. Without his elegant robes and patrician bearing, he may have appeared to be an ordinary, stocky, middle-aged man whose hair was rapidly graying. But Caiaphas knew he was not ordinary, of course; he had taken the measure of the man during previous encounters, and gauged him to be someone who would not be flattered but could be impressed. He also knew that the governor enjoyed exercising his considerable power, subject only to the approval of Tiberius Caesar, the successor to Emperor Augustus.

Gratus, shadowed by the servant Caiaphas's party had already met, stopped on the top step of his palace. His gaze seemed to take in the vast horizon of the Great Sea, before settling on the five Jewish officials before him. "Joseph bar Caiaphas," he said, speaking a flawless and formal Greek dialect, attesting to his refinement and education. "Welcome to Caesarea."

Caiaphas nodded and smiled serenely. "You are most gracious, Your Excellency. I hope we do not intrude on your important business on behalf of the emperor."

The governor did not reply directly, but let his gaze roam over the faces of the others, dark as nomads compared to his typically pale Roman face.

Caiaphas took the hint. "Your Excellency, I present Rabbi Gamaliel, son of Shimon and grandson of the Great Hillel."

Gamaliel bowed slightly. "Strato's Tower," he said, purposefully calling Caesarea by its ancient name rather than the name of the emperor, "is indeed a fitting capital for Your Excellency's governorship."

Gratus's eyes narrowed, and the corners of his mouth twitched. Caiaphas thought the governor recognized Gamaliel's artistry in speaking—honestly—words that could be construed as a compliment or an insult.

"Alexander, treasurer of the Temple," Caiaphas continued, "and Jonathan, son of Annas." He saw the recognition flash in the governor's eyes and knew Gratus was not only marking Jonathan as the son of the still-powerful Annas, but also as Caiaphas's own brother-in-law.

"And," Caiaphas concluded, "Ismael, son of Phabi, whom I believe you know."

It lasted only a moment, but a look of shock crossed Gratus's features as he connected the name and the face. Ismael had been the first high priest Gratus had installed after becoming prefect, only to replace him a few months later, when Eleazar offered an attractive series of bribes.

"Yes," Gratus said, quickly recovering his composure. He locked gazes with the former high priest, a much older man than Caiaphas. "I am surprised to see you."

"Pleasantly surprised, I hope," Ismael answered. "It is my honor, Your Excellency, to congratulate you on the wisdom of your latest appointment."

Gratus blinked at the words, not knowing that they had been given to Ismael, word for word, by Caiaphas himself. "We shall see," he said. He turned his gaze on Caiaphas. "What brings you to Caesarea?"

"Your generosity," Caiaphas said. He deftly produced a small bag from the folds of his clothing, and extended it toward the governor. Immediately the servant stepped forward and received it, opened it, inspected it, and showed it to Gratus. "I am grateful, Your Excellency, for the confidence you have placed in me and my ability to serve my people as high priest. This is a small expression of my ongoing gratitude . . . and that of my entire family." The reference to his family was purposeful; Gratus knew Annas still owned most of the lucrative concessions that sold goods and exchanged money in the Temple courts. His words were intended to signal to Gratus that he could expect a periodic commission from the enterprise, while Caiaphas remained as high priest.

Gratus waved a hand to the servant, who disappeared into the palace with the bag. "You—and your family—are wise to show your gratitude," he told Caiaphas. "Enjoy your visit to Caesarea."

Caiaphas ignored the governor's effort at dismissal. "Your Excellency, there is one thing more."

"More?"

"A small thing for Your Excellency to grant," Caiaphas said. "Since the time of Herod, when Your Excellency fought so valiantly with Quintillius Varus, the vestments of the high priest have been stored in Fortress Antonia, as you know. When we require the vestments for ceremonial use, we make a formal request to the captain of the garrison, and the request is always granted, of course. So it would be a small change, but a great encouragement to the house of Caiaphas—and my entire family—if the care and keeping of the vestments were entrusted once again to the Temple officials."

Gratus studied the face of Caiaphas, as though searching for more information.

"As I say," Caiaphas prodded, *"it is a small thing for Your Excellency."*

"Hardly worth your attention," Gamaliel injected.

"A simple order signed by Your Excellency is all I seek," Caiaphas added.

Gratus paused a moment, then turned and called for his secretary.

16

HIGHWAY 1, ISRAEL

Tracy leaned forward and felt her sweat-soaked blouse peel off the rear taxi seat. The trip from Tel Aviv's Ben-Gurion International Airport had begun hot and sticky, and had recently changed—to hot, sticky, and dusty, as the car turned off the modern four-lane highway that stretched from Tel Aviv to Jerusalem. The new road was two lanes, and though it was still paved, the dust and fumes of the van in front of them rolled in the half-opened rear windows of the taxi and mingled potently with the diverse smells and textures of the car's interior.

She and the driver had exchanged no words since she had told him where she wanted to go. She was in this strange land for the first time, and she was alone. She had been relieved to arrive in Israel, but now all her fears and misgivings rose inside her like bile. As she gazed out at the varied scenes that passed by her windows—farms and fields, shopping centers, housing complexes, war memorials, shepherds tending sheep, armed soldiers waiting at bus stops—her sense of isolation and vulnerability increased. What if the driver had misunderstood her? What if they weren't headed to Beit Guvrin? He could take her nearly anywhere he wanted, and she wouldn't know the difference . . . until it was too late. She began to wonder if she should ask the driver to stop the car so she could get out, but what good would that do? Was being alone by the side of the road any better than being alone in a strange, foreign man's taxi?

As the sun began to set and the driver took another turn, Tracy found it hard to hold back tears of panic. The scenery had become less green and more brown and gray. Her surroundings were becoming less populated, more remote. And the day was waning, making Tracy wonder what she would do if it got dark before she'd reached her destination—*if* she reached her destination. Finally the car topped a rise in the road, and not far ahead she recognized a seemingly haphazard conglomeration of tents around a flat-topped hill as an archaeological site—like many her father had told her about.

"There!" she said. She pointed. "That's the place." She had to bite her lip to keep from bursting into tears.

The driver shook his head and pointed farther down the road, speaking rapidly in a language she assumed was Arabic.

"No," she said. "Here."

He pointed and spoke more emphatically. "Beit Guvrin," he said slowly. "Beit Guvrin."

"Oh," she said, suddenly understanding. He was pointing to the kibbutz. "Yes, that is Beit Guvrin. But I am going to Tel Mareshah." She pointed to the side. "Take me there, to Tel Mareshah."

The driver frowned, as though he had never been so inconvenienced, but he guided the car up the dirt drive to Tel Mareshah.

"How much?" she asked as the car rolled to a stop.

He turned in his seat and spoke a heavily accented answer, which Tracy did not understand until he repeated himself. "Two hundred," he said.

"What?" Tracy said. She was sure she had heard wrong. "How much?"

"Two hundred *shekel*," he said.

"Oh," she said, gasping with relief. She opened her small bag. "How much in dollars?"

The driver took no time to compute his answer but answered immediately. "Fifty American dollars," he said.

Fifty dollars, she thought ruefully. She drew two twenties and a ten from her bag and held the bills over the grimy vinyl bench seat in front of her. The driver took them without speaking or smiling.

Tracy lugged her bags toward the expansive assemblage of tents and trucks that surrounded the mound known as Tel Mareshah. She wiped her cheek on the shoulder of her shirt and approached the first person she saw, an ebony-skinned woman with high cheekbones who sat on the ground beneath an awning, her arms folded on her knees, her head balanced on her arms.

"Hi," Tracy said pleasantly. "I'm looking for Dr. Randall Bullock."

The woman lifted her eyes and looked at Tracy, then shook her head slowly, speaking a phrase in a language Tracy did not recognize. She pointed down the dusty lane before returning to her former position.

Tracy stood uncertainly for a moment, then started in the direction the woman had pointed. At last she reached what appeared to be the mess tent, where she found two men and a woman, in shorts and T-shirts, sitting around a table. She dropped her suitcases into the dust and stepped into the shade of the tent.

The trio stared at her for a few moments. Then one of the men stood.

"I'm looking for my father," Tracy said, suddenly feeling very shy, though she wasn't sure why. "Dr. Randall Bullock."

The man who had stood glanced at the others, then stepped toward her, wiping his palms on his shorts. "I am Yigal Havner," he said, his voice deep and thick. He shook her hand. "Your father is a friend of mine."

A wave of relief washed over her, and she felt her skin tingle with the emotion. Her eyes filled with tears. She had done it. She was safe. "Can I see him?"

Again he glanced at the others. "He is no longer here," he said.

17

*J*oseph bar Caiaphas emerged from the Hall of Polished Stones, the chambers of the Sanhedrin at the southwestern corner of the massive Temple complex. There he had stood before the Great Sanhedrin, patiently and decorously responding to the council's inquiries regarding his qualifications for the office of high priest. The first question, as expected, regarded his genealogy, and when he answered that his ancestors' names were inscribed in the archives of Jeshana at Zipporim, no further question on that score was posed.

The second area of inquiry, however, was a lengthy one, as Caiaphas knew it would be. He was asked scores of questions about his physical features. For example, did he have a missing or *deformed limb? Did his face lack whiskers? Even whether his nose was too long or too short (a question he was prepared for, and one he answered by placing his little finger alongside his nose, from forehead to tip, to indicate the desired proportion). After these questions followed more: Had he practiced idolatry? Was he intoxicated? Had he been involved in the burial of a close relative? Were any of his priestly garments lacking? Were any garments unkempt or unwashed? and so on.*

Finally, however, the questioning was complete, and the entire council stood to their feet and recited, "Blessed be God, blessed be He, that no disqualification has been found in the sons of Aaron. Blessed be He who chose Aaron and his sons to stand and serve before Him in His most Holy Temple."

Then, slowly and solemnly, the Temple guards pushed open the great doors of the hall, and Caiaphas, wearing only a simple white linen tunic from his shoulders to his ankles, walked into the sunlight, followed by the council. He strode to the brass laver in the Court of the Israelites and washed his hands, then ascended the steps of the sanctuary and knelt facing the waiting crowd. Annas stood before him and, dipping a finger into a brass bowl of fragrant oil, slowly drew on Caiaphas's forehead a form like that of the Greek letter χ. Then he stepped behind the kneeling priest, lifted the bowl into the air, and poured the oil, in a long stream, onto Caiaphas's bowed head.

When the oil had run down Caiaphas's hair, into his beard, and onto his garments, he rose. One by one, members of the Sanhedrin came forward with the "golden vestments" of the high priest, so called because each of them, unlike the robes of ordinary priests, contained the symbol of purity and splendor. First came the meil, a dark blue robe (shorter than the linen tunic) fringed with golden bells and blue, purple, and scarlet tassels shaped like pomegranate blossoms. Next came the ephod, the embroidered vest of gold, purple, scarlet, and blue threads. A third council member placed the mitre, the turbanlike headpiece bearing a gold band engraved with the words "Holiness to the Lord." Finally, Shimon son of Hillel came forward and draped on his chest the ziz, the golden front-piece inset with twelve precious gems representing the twelve tribes of Israel.

When he stood, arrayed in the common clothing of ordinary priests and the unique garments of the high priest, Caiaphas struggled to control his emotions. There was much still to be done before the sun set that night—sacrifices to offer, prayers to recite, incense to light—but the moment he had long awaited had finally come. He was Kohen haGadol, *the anointed one, the high priest of Israel, the holy nation, the people of God.*

He let his gaze rise over the glistening white walls of the Temple, to the clear sky over Mount Moriah, this rock where Abraham's son Isaac had been spared by the sacrificial ram, where David had longed to build a Temple, where countless offerings of bulls, lambs, and goats had been made to Adonai. He imagined the God of Abraham, Isaac, and Jacob looking down with pleasure on this day—on him.

18

TEL MARESHAH

The relief Tracy had felt just moments earlier had vanished when Yigal Havner had told her, after an overnight flight to Tel Aviv, after wrestling her way through baggage claim and customs, and after arranging transportation to the site where she *thought* she would find her father, that she still hadn't completed her journey. "Where is he?" she asked.

"He left early this morning for an emergency excavation in Talpiot, outside Jerusalem," Havner explained. "It is not far from here."

She started to cry, though she couldn't have said whether her tears flowed from fear, or disappointment, or stress, or the cumulative effects of all that had happened in the past few days, from the time since she was a student at a safe midwestern college to now, a nineteen-year-old alone in a foreign land searching for a father.

Havner guided her to a bench by a table, and the woman brought her a plate of food and a glass of water.

"I can try to call your father," Havner said. "We spoke not long ago."

"No," Tracy answered through her tears. "No, please don't. He'd just be mad, and that would make it worse."

"But he will want to know where you are, yes?"

She shook her head and lifted the glass of water to her lips with a trembling hand. She drank, then set the glass down on the table. "No," she said, her gaze downcast. "He thinks I'm still in school. I have to see him first. I have to explain things. It's—it's complicated."

Havner nodded slowly, and exchanged a worried glance with the woman. "You can stay here tonight," he said.

"You can stay in my tent," the woman offered.

"And in the morning," Havner said, "I will be sending some equipment to your father. I can send you, too."

She looked up. Havner and the woman were both smiling at her. She inhaled through a few short sobs. "I guess—I guess that would be all right."

"You can leave right after breakfast, then."

She nodded. "Okay."

"Good," Havner said. He stood. "Now eat, and when you have finished, Rachel here will take you to your tent."

She wiped the tears from her cheeks with her hands. "Thank you," she said.

"It's nice to meet you, Tracy," he said. "Welcome to Eretz Israel."

19

TaLPIOT, SOUTH JerUSaLeM

Twilight in Jerusalem is like nowhere else on Earth. When Rand returned to the excavation site with food and drinks from the New Deli, the sun had set, the hevrat kadisha apparently slumbering in their cars. The floodlit walls and sparkling holy places of Jerusalem's Old City—where shops close each night, massive gates swing shut, and a calm descends in place of the day's dust and din—shimmered in the distance.

He climbed onto the hood of his Fiat 500, leaning his back against the windshield and extending his long legs over the hood, and invited Miri Sharon to join him. When she did, he emptied the paper bag of its contents and they ate their grilled lamb sandwiches and tomato and cucumber salads together.

"Do you know a boy named Mansour?" she asked.

"Mansour?" he echoed. "No. Why?"

"He asked for you," she said. "While you were getting the sandwiches."

He shook his head. "Did he say what he wanted?"

She took a bite, in no apparent hurry to answer. When she finished chewing, she answered, "He said you saved his life. He wanted to thank you."

Suddenly Rand knew. He told her about the riot he had encountered that morning, and how the boy had been crushed against his car. He left out the part about the threats of the Israeli soldiers, and simply told her that the boy had been taken away in an ambulance.

"He seemed to be fine," she said, eyeing him with interest.

"Good," he said. "How did he know I was here?"

She shrugged, and dropped her apparent inspection of his face. "He asked for the American who drives a white car."

"That makes sense." He smiled, nodding. "Thanks for telling me. I'm glad he's okay."

They had finished eating, but the conversation continued, shifted to learning a little of each other's background. Rand was the younger of two brothers in his family; Miri was the only child born to Sephardic Jews Yakob and Sylvia Sharon, who settled in Israel after the 1948 War of Independence. Rand was raised in the farming community of Brookville, Kansas; Miri grew up in the Tel Aviv suburb of Ramat-Gan. Rand attended the University of Chicago, and Miri pointed to the lights of her own alma mater, Hebrew University, on Mount Scopus, to the northeast of where they sat.

Before long—too quickly, Rand thought, though it was predictable enough—talk turned to the subject of his wife's death, and he told her, his voice breaking several times, about his wife and daughter, his failures as a husband and father, and the circuitous path that had brought him to Israel and Jerusalem as a nearly broken man of forty-two.

Miri said nothing while he spoke, and when he finished, he apologized. "I'm sorry. I know you didn't ask to hear all that."

They sat in silence for a few moments, until Miri gathered her food wrappings and empty soda can and slid off the hood. She held out a hand, obviously offering to take Rand's trash.

"Let me do that, please," Rand said. He slid off the car and took the trash from her hand, and their hands touched. He met her gaze and, without moving his hand away, said, "I'm sorry I've talked so much. I wish I had learned more about you."

She quickly released her trash into his hands. "Do women in your country not take care of their own rubbish?"

Her response seemed unnecessarily sarcastic to him, until he suddenly remembered the word Israelis called native-born Israelis such as Miri Sharon: *sabra*, the name of a cactus plant that is rough and thorny on the outside, sweet on the inside. He smiled. He suspected she was a perfect sabra. "Good night, Sergeant Major Sharon," he said.

She gazed back at him evenly. "Shalom," she responded. Then she turned and walked to her patrol car.

20

TeL MareSHaH

Tracy Bullock lay awake on a narrow wood-frame cot. Her luggage lined the foot of her cot like so many sentinels. She could tell by Rachel's breathing that her tentmate had fallen asleep long ago. She stared at the canvas of the old tent and wiped sweat from her forehead with her wrist; the fabric was so thin she could see the flicker of several bright stars in the sky.

She wasn't happy at the prospect of spending the night; she had hoped to see her father that day. After all, she had calculated, by morning she would have been in Israel for more than twenty-four hours before seeing him. But contrary to her nature, she did not argue when Yigal Havner had said her journey must end here, for the night at least. Instead, she congratulated herself for what she had accomplished so far. She had flown alone to the opposite side of the world, rented a cab, and managed to locate her father from nothing more than the name of an archaeological dig. She supposed that was something few nineteen-year-olds could have done. Besides, she reasoned, she was tired, and a night of sleep before her reunion with her dad wouldn't be so bad.

But now that she was in this tent, lying on a cot, dressed only in shorts and an oversized T-shirt tied above her midriff, sleep would not come. She wondered what her reunion with her father would be like.

"Of course he'll be happy to see you," she said aloud into the night. "He's your father."

But her words rang hollow against the walls of the tent. She closed her eyes and pictured their reunion in the morning. She would drop her bags and run to him, laughing, and throw her arms around his neck. His mouth would hang open in surprise, and he would wrap his arms tightly around his grown daughter, and a tear would flow down his cheek, evidence of his joy.

Suddenly it was as if she heard her friend Rochelle's voice: "Girl, what have you been smokin'?" She smiled wanly. More likely, she figured, her father's face would register shock, then annoyance. "What are you doing here?" would probably be his first words to her. Or, "Why aren't you in school?" Or maybe even, "What have you done now?"

What it all came down to, she realized, was that

she had no idea what to expect. She honestly didn't know how her father would react. Because she honestly didn't know her father.

21

*D*id you see?" he asked his wife, Salome, who met him at the door of their home.

She arched her eyebrows imperiously. "See what?"

He pushed past her and strode into his private chamber, where he carefully removed the priestly ankle-length tunic in favor of a shorter, lighter robe. He knew without turning around that she had followed him and was watching him. He knew better than to suppose that she would be impressed or attracted, though for a man of thirty-two years, he felt proud of his broad chest and athletic form. But Salome had not desired him since her latest miscarriage just over two years ago. "Your husband is now high priest by anointing," he said. "I would think you would have wanted to see such an honor bestowed on your family and household."

"If it was an honor," she said.

He turned. "If it was *an honor? Do you not feel honor, as wife of the Kohen haGadol, to benefit from the twenty-four priestly gifts we will receive? The* pidyon ha ben*? The* challah*? The* bikkurim*? Do you not wish to share in these blessings?"*

She shrugged. "I share in them already as daughter of Annas. Or have you forgotten how you became high priest?"

He wound the rope girdle around his waist and tied it, sighing and shaking his head. "No, Salome, I have not forgotten. How could I? You won't let me."

"No," she said with a growl. "I won't let you forget, Yehosef bar Qayafa*! What is the house of Caiaphas compared to the house of Annas? It is nothing. You could not even buy this house without my father's money, let alone the high priesthood! And yet here you are! You have the house, you have my father's position, you are even anointed . . . and I have nothing!"*

"I have told you, wife, we are both young. We can still have a son."

She glared at him for a long moment before turning and storming out. Joseph Caiaphas watched her go, and felt the familiar sadness wash over him. He had endured many such conversations with Salome, until he felt like he knew what her next words would be even before she spoke.

It hadn't always been so between Joseph Caiaphas and Salome. When they were betrothed, Salome seemed attracted to Joseph, and he was entranced by her. Once the two were married, the trouble started, however. Salome wanted nothing more than to have a son, like her sister-in-law Miryam, the daughter of Shimon and wife of Salome's brother Jonathan. But each conception had ended in miscarriage, and the last had been so painful, physically and emotionally, that she had abandoned hope of bearing a child . . . and with it, had also abandoned all pretense of loving or respecting her husband.

It grieved Caiaphas, not only because he longed for a son, too, but also because he knew Salome's words were true: the house of Caiaphas was nothing compared to the house of Annas. And without a son, it would always remain so, for Joseph Caiaphas had no brothers and no uncles. If Salome never conceived, the name Caiaphas would die with him.

22

TALPIOT, SOUTH JERUSALEM

Rand awoke before sunrise, his legs and back impossibly cramped from the hundred different positions he attempted through the night while trying to sleep inside his Fiat. As he maneuvered his six-foot frame through the car's passenger door, like a butterfly emerging from a cocoon, he sensed before he saw the presence of Sergeant

Major Miri Sharon, who stood with her hands on her hips, watching.

With great effort, he straightened and stood. "Morning," he said.

She wore a mocking smile. "You did not sleep in that," she said.

He turned a quick glance at the car, then looked back at her. "What do you mean?" he said. "Of course I did."

"The whole night?"

"Yes."

"Why?"

He held out his hands, palms up. "Where else would I sleep?"

Her smile broadencd, and she walked to her car, picked up a blanket from the ground near the cave entrance, where she had spent the night. She opened her car trunk, rolled the blanket, and placed it in the trunk. "I am sorry," she said. "I should have offered you one of my blankets."

He watched her, knowing she was enjoying herself at his expense, but feeling oddly okay with that.

Moments later, Rand was in the cave. He fumbled around in the predawn light, preparing everything for the arrival of the lifting and lighting equipment from Tel Mareshah. He made repeated trips up and down the ladder, taking the bags filled with smaller artifacts to his car. On his third such trip, as the sun was peeking over the mountains of

Moab in the distance, he noticed that the men in the black suits and hats had awakened and were once again very angry. Sharon was walking toward him as he set down a handful of bags by the Fiat.

"They insist that I inspect the bags you are bringing out of the tomb." Her tone was apologetic. "To make sure there are no human remains."

Rand nodded, stifling a yawn. "Sure," he said. "Knock yourself out."

Two of the four ossuaries in the center of the cave floor were broken in pieces. Rand had inspected them yesterday, and determined that they bore no designs or markings and were looted long ago of any contents.

The two other bone boxes, however, remained intact . . . and the time had come to remove the lids and see what was inside.

23

TeL MareSHaH

Yigal Havner introduced Tracy to Carlos, a staff member from Turkey. "Carlos knows his way around very well," Havner said. He nodded to the young man, who looked as if he might be a few years older than Tracy, and whose deep tan evidenced his four months spent toiling in the Judean sun for the renowned archaeologist. Carlos hefted

Tracy's much-traveled luggage into the back of an open-topped Land Rover, next to a few assorted pieces of equipment that Tracy judged to be about as old as she was. "And he is a good driver. He will probably get you to your destination in one piece."

"'Probably'?" Tracy echoed.

Havner nodded without smiling. "He is from Turkey," he said.

Tracy looked back and forth between Carlos and the old archaeologist. "What does that mean?"

Carlos smiled and shook his head, sending his curly locks of black hair bouncing about his ears. "Nothing," he said. "Absolutely nothing." He climbed behind the wheel of the vehicle.

"You must hurry," Havner said. He shook Tracy's hand and helped her into the Land Rover. "Abir called."

Carlos nodded, reached forward, turned the key in the ignition, and the vehicle's engine roared to life. Havner slapped the side of the Land Rover as Carlos stepped on the accelerator and the Land Rover's wheels kicked up the dirt and gravel of Tel Mareshah and spun away from the camp.

"Abir?" she shouted, holding her hair in place with one hand and bracing herself against the door with the other. "Who's Abir?"

"He is a friend."

"I don't get it. What's going on? Why do we have to hurry?"

"It is nothing."

"Then why not tell me? If it's nothing—"

"You will just worry, and there is nothing to worry about."

"You keep saying it's nothing and there's nothing to worry about, but I believe you less every time you say it! Why don't you just tell me and let me decide whether to worry or not?"

Carlos shrugged. "Abir is a friend with connections in the military."

"Okay. And . . ." Tracy prompted.

"He sometimes tells us when border crossings into or out of the Palestinian-controlled areas are going to be closed."

"Okay. And . . ." she repeated.

"We will be driving through the Palestinian area."

She waited this time.

He shrugged again. "Abir says the crossing at Bethlehem is going to be closed soon."

"Why?"

"It could be the threat of a suicide bomber. Or some other kind of attack."

"If it's dangerous, shouldn't we go another way?"

"Not really. Some people think Israel does it just to frustrate the Palestinians."

"So, what does that mean for us?" Tracy asked.

Another shrug. "It means we want to get there before the crossing is closed."

"And . . . what if we don't?"

He wagged his head slightly back and forth.

"Are you saying we could be stuck somewhere?" she asked.

He flashed an engaging smile. "No. Not stuck. Delayed."

24

TaLPIOT, SOUTH JerusaLem

The ossuaries in the center of the room were empty.

Rand had gingerly removed the fitted, beveled lid from each limestone box and gazed inside at nothing but dust and air. "Well," he said, "that simplifies things." He knew, of course, that thousands of these bone boxes had been found in and around Jerusalem over the years, and that the vast majority had virtually nothing to distinguish them: no inscription, no decoration, no bones, nothing. He also knew that such nondescript ossuaries were very easily and cheaply obtained on the antiquities market. Whether viewed from an archaeological, scholarly, commercial, or personal perspective, the two ossuaries he had just examined were virtually worthless.

Still, his training demanded caution. The ordinary ossuaries would be removed and preserved carefully. He wondered how much longer he would have to wait for the arrival of the lighting and lift equipment from Mareshah. There was really no safe way to get these ossuaries out of the cave until the equipment arrived, so Rand turned his attention to the remaining two ossuaries in the loculus along the south wall.

He had saved examination of these ossuaries for last because they seemed the most promising to him. They remained in the loculus, the only ossuaries in the tomb that were so situated, which could mean that they had been undisturbed by looters, for whatever reason, and still contained their original contents. And they both possessed complete and secure lids, which apparently were still in place.

"Sure could use those lights," he muttered. The sun was higher in the sky by this time, but it was still very early in the morning and it would be almost noon before the last shadows in the cave dissipated. He slid one of the ossuaries slowly out of the niche and, turning it slightly to gain a better grip, lifted its forty-five pounds and carried it to the center of the tomb. Before he even set it down, he recognized one key difference from the other boxes he had already examined: something was etched into one of the long sides of the box.

25

*C*aiaphas groaned in pain.
   "*Of course it's no surprise,*" he told the rabbi Gamaliel.

The grandson of the Great Hillel was in many ways an odd ally for Caiaphas. He was a Pharisee; Caiaphas, of course, was a Sadducee. The Pharisees and the Sadducees were the domi-nant religious and political parties of the day, and were usually at odds with each other. The Pharisees had preserved Jewish life through the Captivity, redefining it as a religion that revolved around study of the Torah. The Sadducees had restored the sacrificial system and revived the priesthood and Temple worship as the central facets of Judaism. Pharisees revered the written Scripture and the oral traditions of the rabbis; Sadducees recognized only the five books of Moses as Torah. Pharisees believed in angels and spirits, and the resurrection of the dead, which the Sadducees denied. Generally speaking, Pharisees were more popular but Sadducees were more pow-erful; Pharisees were righteous, and Sadducees were rich.

Caiaphas and Gamaliel, though they were Sadducee and Pharisee to the bone, were not only allies but also friends. Each longed for the appearance of the Messiah, and each hoped to usher in Messiah's reign with righteous leadership. And each needed the other. Caiaphas the high priest needed Gamaliel, who, though not yet thirty years old, was already being called rabban, even while his father lived and exercised leadership on the Sanhedrin. And Gamaliel certainly needed the high priest as an ally if the Sanhedrin and the nation of Israel were ever to return to righteousness and see the glory of the God of Israel.

The two men sat in the courtyard of Caiaphas's opulent home, in the shade of a sprawling olive tree. Caiaphas rubbed his temples with both index fingers. "Valerius Gratus has been writing the emperor incessantly, begging to be returned to Rome. He has been able to talk of nothing else for the past several years."

It was no surprise, then, when the news reached Jerusalem that Valerius Gratus, with whom Caiaphas had so carefully and expensively nurtured a cooperative working relationship, had been recalled to Rome and a new governor had been appointed. But the news had nonetheless given the high priest a painful headache as he contemplated having to start over with someone new.

"Eight years," Caiaphas said with a moan.

"I suppose we should be grateful. His tenure was

much longer than that of Annius Rufus or Marcus Ambivulus."

"Yes, but do you know how hard I worked and how much I paid to build Gratus's trust and assuage his greed?"

"Hmm," said Gamaliel cautiously. He and Caiaphas vehemently disagreed on the issue of paying bribes and sharing revenue with the Roman authorities. "What do you know of the new governor?"

Caiaphas answered without lifting his head or opening his eyes. "He is said to be from an eminent equestrian family, like Sejanus. His wife is Claudia Procula, granddaughter of Augustus and daughter of Claudia, Tiberius's third wife."

Gamaliel grunted. "A powerful man, we must assume."

Caiaphas nodded, and moved his fingers, pressing them into his eye sockets as though he intended to blind himself. "And it is said that she is coming with him."

"She is coming here?" Officials' wives seldom left the comfort and amusements of Rome for the discomfort and danger of the provinces. "That is unusual. I'm not sure whether that indicates his influence with the emperor . . . or his wife's interest in his career. Perhaps both."

Caiaphas raised his head and fixed his friend with a weary gaze. "Gamaliel, my friend, I am afraid we must prepare for a stony path ahead."

The rabbi stood. "Then I must buy new sandals,"
he said. He turned to go, but stopped after just a
few steps. He half turned. "What is the new gov-
ernor's name?"

"Pilate," Caiaphas said. "Pontius Pilate."

26

BETHLEHEM

Carlos slowed as they approached the checkpoint at Bethlehem.

Their short trip from Tel Mareshah had been uneventful. As they entered Bethlehem, Tracy smiled at Carlos. "This is *not* what I expected," she said.

"What did you expect?"

She sang. "O little town of Bethlehem, how still we see thee lie."

"Your singing is pretty," he said.

She rolled her eyes. "I thought Bethlehem would be, you know, more like a village."

He smiled. "I think it has a population of about twenty thousand."

She nodded and turned her gaze out the window. "So many shops are closed."

"Since Israel built the wall to keep the terrorists out, the traffic and tourism into and out of Bethlehem is much less than it was." Suddenly his forehead wrinkled. "Uh-oh," he said.

Tracy turned her attention from Carlos to the road ahead and saw what appeared to be a line of cars waiting at a checkpoint of soldiers and metal barriers, with a second checkpoint beyond that. A car would have to stop for the checkpoint, then weave slowly around a concrete barrier jutting into the roadway, and then weave back into the proper lane before continuing to the second checkpoint. "What's happening?" she asked.

Carlos studied the scene ahead for a few moments before answering. "I think it's all right," he said. Five or six rifle-toting soldiers manned the checkpoint. As cars approached, two soldiers would question the occupants of the first car, while other soldiers approached the second and third vehicles. Trunks were opened, buses were boarded, and trucks were pulled over to the side for more careful inspection. In most cases, after a visual search of the car's occupants and contents, the cars were permitted to pass through. "It looks like they haven't closed it. The cars seem to be getting through."

"How long will this take?" Tracy asked.

He shrugged. "Not too long," he said. "You'll need to get your identification ready."

"Identification?"

He nodded. "Yes, you know, your visa or passport."

"It's in my luggage," she said, reaching for the door handle.

"No!" Carlos said. "Stay there!"

Tracy released the door handle as if it had stung her. She stared back at Carlos.

He inhaled slowly. "I'm sorry, I did not mean to frighten you. The soldiers would not like it if you got out of the car and tried to pull something out of the back."

"Oh," she said. "I see what you mean. They might think I was—dangerous or something."

He nodded. "Or something."

"So what should I do?"

"Just wait. When the soldier asks for your identification, explain that it is in your baggage, and he will go with you to get it."

It happened just like Carlos said, and a few moments later, he and Tracy continued their drive up Highway 60.

"How much farther?" she asked.

He smiled at her. "Just a few minutes."

27

TaLPIOT, SOUTH JerUSaLEM

Rand was desperate for more light. He angled the ossuary on the floor of the cave to get the best possible light shining on the scratches he had felt with his fingers. He knelt, and peered closely at the etchings while tracing their outline with the middle finger of his right hand.

The letters were in two lines, running from the bottom up the side of the box instead of parallel with the lid, making it seem likely that the inscribing had been done after the box had been placed in the niche in the chamber wall. Whoever scratched the lettering would have had to reach into the space between the ossuary and the wall, and Rand thought it likely, given the position of the lettering relative to where the ossuary had been placed, that it had been done by a right-handed person; while someone writing in English would most likely have written on that side in a line stretching from top to bottom, because Hebrew and Aramaic were both written from right to left, the inscriber apparently wrote from the bottom to the top.

Beyond those assumptions, however, Rand couldn't make heads or tails of the lettering. But he immediately thought of Sergeant Major Sharon; if the lettering was in Hebrew, she might be able to read it. He hoped that the crudity of the lettering (which was most likely scratched in the soft limestone with a nail or something similar, with no more care than a twenty-first-century scribe would use to write a phone number or e-mail address) would not be too great a hindrance to translation.

He grabbed his clipboard and pencil and did his best, in the light of the tomb, to mimic the scrawl on the side of the ossuary. Then he ascended the ladder, exited the tomb, and squinting against the morning sun, looked around to locate the Israeli policewoman.

At that moment, however, a dusty, black Land Rover approached the yellow-tape barrier around the construction site and pulled to a stop beside the clot of black-clad hevrat kadisha. Rand quickly recognized Carlos, the driver, from Tel Mareshah, and waved, at the same time noticing Sharon's approach.

"That's my equipment!" he called.

Then the passenger door opened, and someone stepped out.

28

TALPIOT, SOUTH JERUSALEM

Tracy didn't know what to do. She had seen her father notice the Land Rover, and then watched his eyes as he seemed to recognize Carlos as he got out of the vehicle. She found herself wishing she could stay in the car and observe from a safe distance, but forced herself to grab the door handle and step out.

It was going to be awkward, she knew. She saw her father turn his gaze in her direction, and watched him as he saw her and then looked from her to Carlos, and back to her again. She tried to force a smile. She told herself to just walk up and give him a hug. But her feet weren't working properly, and she seriously considered getting back into the Land Rover.

Her father walked slowly toward her, and she couldn't tell from his expression whether he was confused or—no, she was sure he was confused. But she didn't know what else was in his expression. Was it anger? Or frustration? It sure didn't look like joy, or love, or anything very positive.

She opened her mouth. She thought she might say, "Hi, Daddy," but he spoke before she could get the words out.

"What are you doing here?" he said.

His tone wasn't angry, but she was disappointed nonetheless. "IIi, Daddy," she said finally.

"I—I don't understand," he said. "What—what are you doing hcre?"

Okay, I get the message, she thought. *You're not exactly glad to see me. But you don't have to keep saying the same thing.* "I, um, I wanted to see you."

"What about school? How did you get here? What's going on?"

"Can't you even say you're glad to see me?" Tracy said, her voice rising. "Did it ever occur to you to hug me or ask me if I'm okay?"

"I am glad to see you," he protested. "Really. I'm just a little shocked—"

"Look, forget it, okay? Tell me where to put my luggage and I'll get out of your way."

"Tracy, would you listen to me—" Rand reached out for her but she stepped away and headed to the Land Rover, where she started yanking her bags out of the back. Suddenly Carlos was beside her.

"Can I help with those?" he said softly.

"No!" she said. Then, not quite so harshly, "I can get it."

"I'd like to help," he said.

Tracy braced herself against the back of the vehicle. "You probably have to unload the rest of the stuff, right?"

"I suppose I could do that."

She picked up two bags, leaving two others sitting behind the Land Rover. "I'll come back for these," she said.

Carlos ignored that, picking up the bags and falling into step behind her. "Are you always this stubborn?" he asked.

She shot him a glance. "Look who's talking," she said.

Rand watched his daughter pull her luggage out of the Land Rover, still wondering what she was doing here and how she got here while simultaneously realizing that her arrival confronted him with a whole new set of questions: Where would she stay? How long would she stay? And how would he complete the excavation while making whatever arrangements needed to be made?

"Where do you want me to put these?" Tracy once

again stood in front of him; he hadn't changed position since the first words he had exchanged with her.

"Here," he said. Still holding the clipboard he had carried since exiting the cave, he took one of the suitcases from her and turned, talking over his shoulder to her as he led her toward his Fiat. "I just got here yesterday morning, and haven't had time to think about getting a room. We can put your bags in the car, and then we can talk about—"

"Wait," she said, stopping in her tracks a few feet from the car. "There's no place for me to stay?"

He looked from her to Carlos to the men in black to Sergeant Major Sharon, who had been watching the drama unfold from her post facing the hevrat kadisha, and finally back to Tracy. *Just one or two crises at a time would be nice,* he thought, suddenly remembering Sharon's words, which were sounding a lot like a prophecy: "Nothing is simple here. Nothing is easy."

29

a.d. 26
THE HALL OF POLISHED STONES, JERUSALEM

*S*ilence!" *Caiaphas hammered the stone floor with the sturdy staff in his hand.*

The entire Sanhedrin had gathered, on short notice, in the chambers at the southwestern corner of the Temple complex. Gamaliel was there, as was his father, Shimon, the aging son of the Great Hillel. Also Jonathan, becoming more influential by the day. Alexander. Nicodemus. Ismael. Eleazar.

"It's an abomination!" shouted Joseph of Arimathea.

"A disgrace!" bellowed another.

"An outrage!"

"A provocation!"

Joseph of Bethany stepped forward and tore his robe from the neckline to the waist. "Idolatry!" he roared, and the room again filled with shouts and angry ululations.

Most of the men in the room had known that Pontius Pilate, the new governor of Judea, had ordered the Augustan cohort to relieve the Jerusalem cohort for the winter. There had been no reason to think the move was anything but a routine rotation of troops. The previous governor, Valerius Gratus, had periodically rotated troops throughout the province of Judea with some regularity, primarily to stave off boredom. But when the troops arrived the night before, they had erected new standards—bearing the image of Tiberius—all around Fortress Antonia, which overlooked the Temple precincts from the north.

The sudden appearance of the banners emblazoned with the prominent profile of the emperor greeted the day's first worshipers at the Temple at sunrise. A crowd formed almost immediately, and *before long a riot appeared imminent. The iconic images of the emperor transgressed the commandment of God against graven images.*

Caiaphas banged the floor again with the staff, and raised a hand. The room quieted somewhat. He motioned to Annas, who stood slowly from his seat on a bench in the front row. The crowd quieted further.

"Annas will speak," Caiaphas announced.

Annas's first words were soft—intentionally so, Caiaphas knew. He had watched his father-in-law do the same thing many times.

"Let him speak!" called a voice from the back row. "I want to hear what Annas is saying!"

"Though His Honor Valerius Gratus and I had our differences," Annas began, prompting a round of knowing laughter from the room, "he came to understand and respect the demands our faith places upon us. He kept the Augustan cohort stationed at Strato's Tower. This new governor may not be as informed regarding our customs."

"Or he is inciting rebellion!" someone shouted, stirring the council to fresh outbursts.

"Let him finish," Caiaphas said, lifting a hand. "Let Annas speak."

Annas nodded wearily to his son-in-law. "We have done well in recent years to keep dogs out of the house of Hashem," he said, earning more laughter and approval with his reference to the Romans. "But if we act carelessly in this matter, the dogs will come running, and they will rip with their claws and tear with their teeth."

"But we cannot let these Roman idols stand!" Alexander protested.

"No," Caiaphas agreed. He nodded to his father-in-law, who sat down. "But Annas is right. We must give the governor no provocation. Whether he is merely ignorant of our faith or whether he seeks to incite rebellion, the effect is the same. We cannot let the standards remain, but neither can he simply remove them."

"Why not?" someone asked.

"Because he is a Roman governor, and a new one, at that. To remove the standards now would be a show of weakness, and he cannot afford to look weak. And the very reason we object to them— because they bear the image of the emperor—is another reason he cannot simply remove them, because to do so would be an insult to Tiberius."

"They are an insult to Hashem!" someone cried.

"Tear them down!" several shouted.

"We will fight!" another said, while others lifted similar cries.

"Rulers of Israel, listen to what I am saying! We will fight, and we will prevail, but not with swords and spikes! We will fight with prayer. We will fight with righteousness. We will fight with Hashem on our side."

30

TALPIOT, SOUTH JERUSALEM

Rand struggled to quiet the conflicting questions and competing priorities in his mind. He reminded himself that he had repeatedly missed opportunities to show Tracy that she was more important than his work, and didn't want to make that mistake again. But just a few feet from where they stood was a hole in the ground with two-thousand-year-old artifacts—maybe routine, maybe Earth-shattering, who knew?—that could mark the difference between professional ruin and resurrection for him.

He couldn't just drop what he was doing and focus on Tracy; Sharon had made clear that his time was sorely limited, and there was no telling what she and the hevrat kadisha would do if he took a day or two off to spend some quality time with Tracy.

He placed the suitcase on the ground by the Fiat and placed his clipboard on the car's roof.

"Tracy," he said, taking a deep breath and gripping her shoulders in his hands, "I am in the middle of something here—"

She stiffened.

"No, wait," he said. "I am glad to see you. I

109

really am. And I—I want to . . ." He felt like he had to choose his words so carefully, but Tracy seemed to withdraw further from him with every word, every syllable he spoke.

"Let me start again," he said. "I just got here yesterday morning, and I found out I had only a few days to excavate this site. It's a tomb, probably two thousand years old, and I've been trying to catalog and record and excavate and all the rest by myself, so the only meal I've eaten was last night and I slept in the car—or tried to, anyway—and I had no idea you were coming, so I haven't had the chance to make any arrangements for you, but I can do that, I *want* to do that, just as soon as I—"

"I got expelled," Tracy blurted.

Rand dropped his hands from her shoulders. "What?"

Her eyes started to fill with tears. "It was really stupid, okay? It was Jennifer's idea, but Heather and I went along with it." She continued, telling Rand about the party, the school's policy about underage drinking, and the firestorm that erupted after the party was broken up by police and news got back to the school's administration. "I wasn't the only one who was expelled, but they could all get their parents to come pick them up."

"So that's why you came here."

She nodded. "With Mom . . . gone . . . I didn't know where else to go."

"Why didn't you call?"

110

She wiped a tear from her cheek. "I don't know," she said. "I knew you'd tell me not to come."

"So," he said, forming his words slowly, "you bought a plane ticket, and flew to Israel, by yourself?"

She nodded again. "I packed a few things and put most of my stuff in storage off campus."

"And you went to Mareshah."

"Yeah," she said. "I thought that's where you were."

"It was, until yesterday. How did you get there from the airport?"

She smiled sheepishly. "A cab. I tried to rent a car, but they wouldn't rent it to me, because I'm only nineteen, so I had to take a cab. It cost fifty dollars."

He nodded, and they stood in silence for a few moments. Carlos still stood behind Tracy, holding two bags, and Sergeant Major Sharon still faced the hevrat kadisha, impassive. "So," he said at last, "what do you . . . what do we do now?"

She shrugged. "I don't know. I didn't know what else to do."

"Well," he said, scratching his head, "we can't sleep in the car. I found that out last night."

Sergeant Major Sharon turned and stepped over to stand beside them, her carbine slung over her right shoulder, the muzzle pointed at the ground. "It is none of my business," she said. "But I do have a suggestion."

31

All eyes turned to Sharon. "That hill right there," she said, pointing to the northeast, "is called Ramat Rachel. There is a kibbutz there, and they operate a very nice hotel. And it does not cost a lot of money to stay there."

Rand nodded and thanked her for the suggestion. "Oh," he said, "Tracy, this is Sergeant Major Sharon, with the Israel National Police. She has been here since before I arrived." He turned to Sharon. "This is my daughter, Tracy."

The two women shook hands. "Call me Miri," Sharon told Tracy.

Rand then introduced Carlos and Miri to each other, and then turned to Carlos. "If Tracy and I take our luggage to Ramat Rachel, could you set up the equipment in the tomb?"

Carlos nodded.

Rand lowered his voice. "Everything that is in the tomb right now must stay there until I get back."

"Sure," Carlos said. "It will take me a while to set up the lighting and the lift, anyway. I won't do anything else until you return."

"Good," Rand said. He picked up his clipboard

from the roof of the Fiat and turned it toward Miri. "Before we go, can you tell me if you recognize these letters?"

Sharon looked at Rand's clipboard. "What is this?"

"Letters," he said. "They are scratched into the side of one of the ossuaries in the tomb. I assume they're Hebrew."

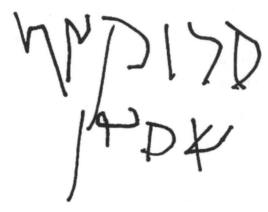

She took the clipboard from him. "Not like any Hebrew I've ever seen." A pause. "No, wait. I guess that could be a *kof* . . . or a *mem*," she said, referring to letters of the Hebrew alphabet. "And that's probably a *reysh*, and then a *yod*, and . . ." She looked up.

"What?" Rand asked, as Carlos and Tracy still looked on.

"Is this some kind of joke?"

"Joke? No. Why?"

"This writing—this was really what is written on one of the bone boxes in the cave?"

"Yes, of course," Rand insisted. "Why? What's the matter?"

"Well, I cannot be sure, but it looks like—if this is Hebrew—then the first line could be my name."

"*Your* name?" Rand asked. "What are you talking about?"

She shrugged and pointed at the marks on the clipboard. "I cannot be certain—the writing is . . . I am not sure how to describe it. Childish. Or crude, that is a better word."

"It's—it's scratched on the side of a limestone box, probably with a nail. It didn't come out of a computer printer."

"Then it is possible it is the name Miriam. It is a fairly common Jewish name."

"Miriam," Rand echoed.

"That's pretty cool," Tracy said.

"What about the rest of the letters?" Rand asked. "What do they say?"

She looked at the page again. After a moment she frowned and shook her head, pointing to the last scrawlings on the top line of Rand's transcription. "I do not know what that is. It does not make any sense to me." She studied it for a moment longer. "I suppose that," she said, indicating the first letter on the lower line, "could be *shin*, and that could be another mem, but the rest of it just looks like . . . like scratches to me."

"It could be another name. That's often the case with tomb inscriptions. You know, maybe, 'Miriam, daughter of so-and-so.' "

She gave the page another look but shook her

head. "Sorry." She offered the clipboard back to Rand.

He hesitated, then took it. "No, thanks, you've been a big help," he said. "That's more than I had before."

"If I looked at the inscription itself," she offered, "it might become clearer."

He smiled. "That's true."

"I could look at it when you bring it out of the cave."

Of course she had to stay at her post, he realized. He nodded. "I haven't opened that ossuary yet, and there's still one left in the loculus on the south wall." He lowered his voice again. "If there's anything notable inside either of them, it's probably going to be a while before I bring them up. But when I do, I'll have you take a look."

She gave a slight nod, and shot a glance at the hevrat kadisha. Several of the men held prayer books in front of them and bobbed back and forth in the rhythmic manner of Orthodox Jews at prayer. "They will not be patient much longer," she said.

"What will they do?" Rand asked.

"They will put me in an impossible position," she answered.

"Impossible how?"

"When they get tired of waiting, they will just come."

"Come? Come where?"

"Here," she said. "To the tomb. They will rush the tomb and dare me to shoot."

"And will you?"

The beautifully feminine contours of her face suddenly became harsh. "They know that an Israel National Police officer who shoots an Orthodox Jew trying to uphold halacha will face severe repercussions."

"What does that mean?" Rand asked.

Her expression softened into an ironic smile. "It means, the longer this takes, the worse the situation becomes."

32

a.d. 26
THE HALL OF POLISHED STONES, JERUSALEM

First," Caiaphas said, basking in the attention of every man in that room, including his father-in-law, whom many still regarded as the high priest of God, "we must send an embassy to the governor to explain the affront he has caused—in the most diplomatic terms, of course—and help him see that we are not merely being difficult or cantankerous."

"Who will lead the delegation?" someone asked.

"Caiaphas, of course!" another answered. "He is high priest."

"What about Annas?" someone said. "He should go."

"Annas?" said another. "The journey is too long for Annas! Do you want to kill him?"

"The rabban, then," someone else said, referring to Gamaliel. "What about the rabban?"

Caiaphas fixed Gamaliel with a meaningful gaze. "I think the rabban would be a fine choice to lead the delegation."

"It will take days for the delegation to reach Strato's Tower!" someone protested. "What happens until then? The images cannot be allowed to remain one minute longer!"

"The people will not stand for it," Jonathan warned.

"They're ready to storm the fortress!" said a man in the second row of seats. The council had calmed considerably since Caiaphas had begun speaking, and all but six or seven were now seated—though he knew from experience that, like the nation itself, they could become agitated again in an instant.

"Yes, I know," Caiaphas said, "but we all know that would be suicide—for them and for the nation. So we must instruct the people who remain in Jerusalem to avert their eyes when they are in the vicinity of the fortress, and give the most agitated a way to occupy themselves and burn off some of their frustration in constructive ways."

"What do you mean, 'constructive ways'?"

Caiaphas smiled. "When the delegation leaves tomorrow for the palace of Pontius Pilate, the word will have been spread among the city's most volatile citizens that a peaceful show of numbers will help to persuade the governor."

"You will send the most 'volatile' Jews and expect them to be peaceful?" one of them countered.

"And others will certainly join them," said another. "You know they will. The crowd will become larger as word spreads."

"Certainly," Caiaphas allowed. "But the journey to Strato's Tower will take several days, more for those on foot. That may be enough time for some of their anger to cool."

"And if it isn't?" the man asked.

Gamaliel stood, then, and spoke for the first time. "The counsel of Caiaphas seems good to me," he said. "It may succeed in removing the idolatrous standards without the shedding of blood. But if not—if violence is unavoidable—is it not better if it occurs outside the city of our God?"

Suddenly, for the first time that morning, the Hall of Polished Stones fell silent as seventy-one rulers of the Jews agreed with Caiaphas's strategy.

33

ramat rachel, south jerusalem

She seems nice," Tracy said.

Rand turned his gaze from the desk clerk in the expansive lobby of the Ramat Rachel Hotel and looked around. "Yeah, this is a beautiful place."

"I don't mean her," Tracy said, indicating the woman at the counter. "I mean the police lady."

Rand blinked at her. "Oh," he said.

Tracy rolled her eyes. "Oh, go ahead."

"What?"

"Okay, whatever. Pretend you haven't noticed how hot she is."

"Who? Sergeant Major Sharon?"

"Oh, please," Tracy answered sarcastically, "in her hot little uniform with the sexy shorts."

Rand shook his head as the desk clerk returned his credit card and handed him the room key. "Don't be ridiculous."

"All right," Tracy said. "Whatever."

On their way to the room, they passed the entrance to a large dining room where a long line of tour bus passengers waited to pay the cashier. They marveled at the spa, health club, swimming pools, and synagogue included in the hotel's amenities.

"I need to hurry back," Rand said the moment

they had deposited their bags in the room. "Do you want to stay here and rest, or would you like to come back to the site with me?"

"You don't want me there," she said, slumping onto the end of one of the beds.

"Why? What makes you say that?"

She shrugged. "I'd just be in the way."

"Tracy, I know you've come a long way, and if you need to rest, I understand. But I could use your help at the site, too."

She bit her lip. "I don't know."

He stood in the doorway, irritated by her hesitation. She was his only child, and he had only yesterday been wishing for a way to undo all the years he'd neglected her. And yet, not much more than an hour after she had unexpectedly shown up in Israel, for crying out loud, he found himself already annoyed by her little-girl ways. *She's nineteen,* he reminded himself, but she's playing the part of a nine-year-old. She was there when Sharon explained that the urgency of this excavation increased with every passing moment, and yet she delayed.

It wasn't just her, he knew. Somewhere in his racing mind, ever since Tracy showed up, he had realized—calculated—that it was only a matter of time before he blew it royally again, and ended up hurting the only person left in his life to love. He felt backed into a corner. If she had arrived forty-eight hours earlier, things might have been completely different. Maybe he would have waved good-bye to Mareshah and Yigal Havner and taken the opportunity to spend time with Tracy and show her all the amazing sights to be seen in Israel—Masada, the Dead Sea, Bet Shean, the Sea of Galilee, Caesarea, not to mention Jerusalem. They could spend a week in the narrow, crowded streets of the Old City together and never get bored.

But she didn't show up forty-eight hours ago; she arrived *this morning*. He couldn't just drop everything. He'd already done enough damage to his career; he couldn't bury it totally. Especially if there was a chance—and there still was—that something was in that tomb worth finding. He could know that soon. He could finish then. And maybe reclaim a little self-respect.

But he couldn't do all that *and* give his daughter the attention she needed. Deserved. Craved, even. And so he was trapped. Between the living and the dead.

34

TALPIOT, SOUTH JERUSALEM

By the time Tracy and Rand returned to the Talpiot site with lunch from the New Deli for the four of them, Carlos had the light stands (powered by a small generator) illuminating the cave. He also had a small scaffold, platform, and winch in place to act as an elevator, more than sufficient to get the larger and heavier pieces out of the cave.

"You did all this by yourself?" Rand asked as he and Tracy unpacked the food and distributed it among them all.

Carlos smiled and nodded, glancing at Tracy more than at Rand. "It was not hard," he said.

Rand patted him on the back. "Maybe not," he said, "but it's a job well done!" He peered down into the cave, then snapped his fingers.

"Is something wrong?" Carlos asked.

Rand shook his head. "No, I just realized I should have asked Yigal for a camp table."

Carlos dashed off, reached into the Land Rover, and returned, carrying a folding table by a strap handle. "Do you mean like this one?"

"I guess I should ask," Rand said, smiling broadly, "if you pull rabbits out of hats."

Carlos's smile disappeared. "I do not know what you mean."

"It's an expression, Carlos," Tracy said. "He means you're a magician."

"Oh," Carlos said. Then he smiled again. "I did not know."

Rand clapped him on the back again. "Well, now you do," he said. "Why don't we use this table to test the lift?"

Moments later, they had the table set up in the

well-lit cave, with the ossuary Rand had removed from the southern loculus set on top. In the light, he compared the scrawls on the side of the ossuary to his transcription on the clipboard. "I could have made that line a little longer," he commented, indicating a vertical scratch on the lower line of letters, "but otherwise I think I copied it well, in what light I had at the time."

"What next?" Tracy asked.

Rand glanced over to the south wall. "I think we'll get the other ossuary onto the table, and we'll go from there."

The moment Rand touched the bone box, he knew this one was different. Once he had placed it on the table, Carlos and Tracy—from different perspectives—called attention to the writing on two of the sides. This ossuary contained words on both the back of the box and one of the ends. The front of the box bore an intricately carved design, two rosette wheels inside a rectangular pattern of palm branches bordering two circular designs. The ossuary's arched lid—the only decorated lid Rand had discovered in the tomb—was edged with a series of double-rimmed rectangles.

"Wow," Rand said. "This is magnificent."

"What does this one say?" Tracy asked.

Rand shook his head. "I don't know. But I sure hope to find out."

Once Rand had painstakingly copied the inscriptions onto a fresh sheet on his clipboard, he climbed out of the tomb, followed by both Tracy and Carlos, who clearly didn't want to miss a thing. With a wary eye on the men in black, he presented the clipboard to Miri Sharon. "It's from two sides of one ossuary," he explained.

She studied the page. "If this is Hebrew," she said, "it is not like today's Hebrew."

"The only letters that look familiar to me"—she pointed—"is this one, which could be *kaf*, and that one, which looks like *kof*."

"*Kaf* and *kof*?" Rand echoed. "They sound the same."

She shrugged and pointed to another shape. "I suppose that could be a *peh*."

"If they are those letters," Rand attempted, "what do you think it spells?"

She shook her head. "I don't know."

"Can you guess? It's very likely a name in there somewhere."

She sighed, still shaking her head. "I—I cannot say."

He nodded. "All right."

"I'm sorry." She handed the clipboard back to Rand.

Another nod. "No, that's all right. You've still been helpful, and I would have to get a linguistic analysis anyway. I was just hoping for a shortcut."

"Are you almost finished?" she asked.

He lowered his voice to a whisper. "I have the last two ossuaries to open. It all depends on what's inside."

"You must hurry," she said, with the tiniest nod in the direction of the hevrat kadisha. "I think they are gathering reinforcements."

35

Back in the cave, Rand ran two fingers along the deep scratchings on each of the ossuaries. "I sure would like to know what these inscriptions say," he said.

"I could take your drawings to Dr. Havner," Carlos suggested.

"He knows his Hebrew," Rand said.

"And his Aramaic, and his Greek . . ."

"You probably should be returning anyway, right? I'm sure Yigal didn't intend to loan you to me; he's pretty shorthanded."

Carlos dropped his gaze. "Yes, that is true."

"Okay, then—"

"Wait," Tracy said. "I have an idea. We could use my phone."

"Your phone?" Rand said.

She pulled a cell phone from her pocket. "I got it when I landed in Tel Aviv. It's a camera phone. We could take pictures of the actual inscriptions, and I could send them to Mr. Havner."

"Doesn't he have to have a camera phone to receive them?" Rand asked.

"Yeah," Tracy answered, "but maybe he does. And that way Carlos could stay—you know, to help."

"I will call Dr. Havner," Carlos suggested.

Before Rand could object, Carlos had ascended the ladder and was gone. Rand looked at Tracy.

"What?" she said, as though he had accused her of something. "I'm trying to help."

A few awkward moments passed between them until Rand said, "You bought that phone in Tel Aviv?"

"Yeah," she said. "A guy on the plane told me even if my old phone worked at all, it'd be a lot cheaper to buy one from here, because of the long-distance charges, I guess. Why?"

"Do you want me to have the number? In case I need to call you?"

"You mean, from the other side of the cave?"

"No," he said, flashing her a look that said, *Don't be a smart aleck.* "You know what I mean."

"Okay," she said. "Sure." She pressed a series of buttons on her phone. "Here it is," she said, showing her father the number, which he immediately programmed into his phone.

At that moment, Carlos reappeared, and descended the ladder into the tomb as quickly as he had left. "He said he can receive photographs, and he would try to help."

Rand smiled. "All right, then. Let's get going."

Rand and Carlos moved the ossuaries around in the lighting, and Tracy experimented with different angles and distances before Carlos gave her the number to call while she recorded the digits in her phone.

When Tracy had left the cave to take her phone to the surface for better reception, Rand asked Carlos, "Did Yigal ask you to return to Mareshah?"

"No," Carlos answered.

"Did you ask to stay here?"

"I told him there was much to be done here."

"And he gave his permission?"

A pause. "He said there is also much to be done there."

Rand hesitated, but when he spoke, it was decisively. "Carlos, you have been very helpful, and I thank you for that. But I don't want to take advantage of my friend's kindness. He has done too much for me. He has loaned me this equipment, and sent my daughter here with one of his vehicles and one of his volunteers. I would be the worst kind of friend if I encouraged you to stay here when he needed you there."

Carlos nodded, and seemed to be studying the floor of the cave when Tracy returned.

"I sent the pictures," she announced.

"Good," Rand said. "Thank you."

"I must be going now," Carlos said.

Rand and Tracy both turned sharply to face him.

"What?" Tracy said.

Carlos blushed. "I am needed back at Tel Mareshah."

"But," Tracy objected, "that's the whole reason I . . ." She frowned, blinking repeatedly. "I mean, I thought that's why we sent the pictures."

Carlos flashed an enigmatic smile at Tracy and reached out to shake hands with Rand. "I would like to come back to pick up the equipment when you are finished with the excavation."

"Of course," Rand said. "We could never fit it in my Fiat, could we? I'll, uh—I'll tell Sergeant Major Sharon you're leaving."

"I'll do it," Tracy said.

A moment later, they were gone.

36

a.d. 26
THE UPPER CITY, JERUSALEM

Caiaphas paced back and forth in front of Gamaliel, who sat beneath the olive tree in the courtyard of the high priest's home.

"It is a good plan," Gamaliel insisted.

"I am afraid it's too risky," Caiaphas said.

"You did not ask me. I offered."

"Yes, but Gamaliel, my friend, if the nation should lose you—if I should lose you—it would be a catastrophe!"

"Is it not better for one to die—or even hundreds—than for the whole nation to perish?"

"One can take that reasoning only so far," Caiaphas suggested, still pacing.

Gamaliel smiled. "Yes, I suppose that's true. But

I am willing. If I am to be a martyr, I will go like a sheep to the shearers. I am ready to play my part. And only you can play your part."

A young male servant with curly black hair stepped into the courtyard and waited for Caiaphas to acknowledge him. "The bags are packed and the horses are ready," he reported.

"Thank you, Malchus," Caiaphas said. He stopped his pacing. "Where did you get the horses?"

"They are borrowed from a merchant," Malchus answered. "They are adequate but unimpressive."

"Good. And the baggage?"

"Your Excellency will not be recognized. Unless his dignity and nobility betray him."

Caiaphas allowed himself a mirthless smile. "Thank you, Malchus," he said. "We will leave shortly." When the servant disappeared, Caiaphas turned back to face the rabban. "We don't know this man, this Pilate. We met him only a few months ago. Who can tell if he will even receive me, or if he will greet my embassy the way Hanun son of Nahash received David's delegation?"

Gamaliel sighed and shook his head. "Who knows?"

"That is exactly right, my wise friend. Who knows if he will listen to me? Or if he can be reasoned with at all? Who knows if he is even sane?"

Gamaliel stood, and placed a hand on each of Caiaphas's shoulders. "The God of Israel," he said. "He knows. And one way or the other, he will teach us what he knows."

37

hanks for bringing me here," Tracy said to Carlos. They had just informed Miri Sharon that he would be leaving the site. They walked to the Land Rover Carlos had driven that morning from Tel Mareshah.

He smiled. "It has been very nice to meet you."

"I wish you could stay and help."

He shrugged. "I would like that very much. But Dr. Havner has lost a few key people at Tel Mareshah in recent weeks, and it has been very hard on him. I have probably stayed too long already."

They looked at each other, and Tracy quickly became embarrassed. She wanted to keep the conversation going, but felt at a loss for what to say next.

Carlos opened the door of the Land Rover. "Perhaps I could come on my day off."

"Oh," Tracy said, "that'd be great! When's your day off?"

"I do not know," he said. "That is, it changes, and I do not know when my next day off will be. But perhaps I could find out and then I could come and see you—and your father, I mean. I could come and help you and your father." His tanned complexion was suddenly crimson.

Tracy smiled. "I'd like that." She brushed a windblown wisp of hair off her face. "And I think my father would, too."

Rand had been waiting for Tracy's return. He was surprised at her demeanor as she descended the ladder into the tomb; she seemed cheerful. He had noticed a spark of interest between her and Carlos, and thought she would be morose once Carlos left. But that seemed not to be the case, and Rand was relieved. He asked her how everything had gone with Carlos, and she shrugged and said, "Fine."

"I could use your help with this lid," he said. He indicated the first ossuary he had pulled out of the southern wall. "I think we're ready to open it and see if there's anything inside."

She nodded, and poked the fingers of each hand under the lip of the arched lid that sat atop the bone box.

"We'll lift it slowly," Rand instructed, "and then move it to your left and set it flat on the floor of the cave. Ready?"

She nodded, and a moment later the two of them were peering into the box. Rand had mentally started calling it the "Miriam" ossuary.

"Wow," Tracy said. Then, after a pause, she added, "That's really kind of creepy."

The ossuary contained bones. "Okay," Rand

said, "we have to move the other ossuary off the table, so I can put these bones on the table."

"You're going to touch them?"

Rand smiled at his daughter and nodded. They placed the other bone box, still covered with its lid intact, on the cave floor, and Rand began carefully removing each bone from the limestone form that had been its home for the past two thousand years.

He started by lifting a fully intact skull from the box. Almost immediately, however, he frowned and turned the skull on its side.

"What's wrong?" Tracy asked.

He lifted the skull to eye level. "There's something inside." He poked into the skull from the bottom and drew out a coin. "Tracy, would you grab my camera? I should have asked you to start recording as soon as we had the lid off."

He placed the skull where it had been earlier, then directed her to photograph the inside of the ossuary. When that was done, Rand held the coin in his palm, and Tracy took a photo of each side of the coin while it lay in his hand. On one side was a semicircle of Roman letters beneath the figure of an umbrella, and the reverse had a clear image of three stalks of wheat or barley.

"So why was the coin inside the skull?" Tracy asked.

Rand cocked his head to one side. "Good question," he said. "I'm not totally sure. If this was first-century Greece instead of Judea, it would be obvious. The Greek custom was to place a coin in the mouth of a corpse, kind of an admission fee to the afterlife. The Greeks did it as a payment to the god Charon for ferrying the dead person across the River Styx."

"Guess I should have paid more attention in mythology class."

"But here, in a Jewish tomb of the Second Temple period . . . I don't know. Maybe it indicates some overlap of Jewish and pagan burial customs."

Rand set the coin on the table, then reclaimed the skull from the ossuary. He turned it around in his hands. "Looks like a female," he said.

"How can you tell?" Tracy asked.

He held the skull in his left hand and pointed with his right. "It's a combination of things." He paused, rewinding the mental tape that had produced his earlier deduction. "The size of the cranium is one thing; in females, I guess you could say, it's smaller and pointier. The mandible, or jawbone, is another indication; female mandibles tend to be rounder, while male jaws are more squared." He pointed to the bone over the eye sockets. "The supraorbital margin," he said, indicating the ridge above the eyes, "is sharper in women, while the superciliary arch"—he turned the skull sideways so Tracy could see the ridge above the nose—"protrudes less than in males. And, in general, teeth and sinus cavities are typically smaller . . . and the whole skull is both smaller and smoother in females than in males. Among other things." He smiled.

"You really like all this stuff," Tracy said. It wasn't a question.

Rand cocked his head and gave a tiny shrug. "Yeah," he said. "I do."

"You're good at it, too, aren't you?"

He dropped his gaze to the skull. "Used to be," he said.

He felt her studying him as he resumed the task of unloading the bones from the box. He placed them on the table in a rough estimation of how they would appear in an intact skeleton. Before setting the pelvic bone on the table, he showed it to Tracy, who continued to snap pictures each time a bone was added to the assembly. "This is a clear indication that this is a female skeleton. The pelvis is much different in females, as it has to be for a baby to survive the journey through the birth canal. The pelvic outlet is oval instead of heart-shaped, the subpubic arch is much wider, and the pubic symphysis is more flexible than rigid."

Moments later, after placing the femurs on the table, he added that the femur in women tended to be shorter in length and smaller in diameter than the male femur. As he was placing the last bones on the table, the tiny bones of the fingers and toes, his cell phone vibrated.

"You can get calls down here?" Tracy asked.

He shook his head. "No, but for some reason it looks like a message will ring in. You keep taking pictures, and I'll go up top and check the message. Okay?"

He climbed the ladder and immediately pressed the voice mail number on his phone's keypad. The message was from Yigal Havner.

"Rand, my friend," he had said after identifying himself, "I received your photographs and had them printed out—in black-and-white, but the resolution is just fine. In fact, I have already managed to finish a rough translation. So call me back as soon as you get this message. And be sure that you are sitting down."

38

TALPIOT, SOUTH JERUSALEM

I'm sitting down," Rand told Havner, though he was actually propped on the hood of his Fiat.

"For the sake of clarity," Havner said, "let me just make sure: the photos you sent were from two ossuaries. Is that correct?"

"Yes," Rand said, nodding unconsciously. "There was one inscription—on two lines—from a single ossuary, and two inscriptions from two sides of another, more elaborate ossuary."

"What do you mean when you say 'more elaborate'?"

"I mean it's the most beautifully decorated example of the stonecutter's art I've ever seen." He described the carvings on the front and on the lid of the second ossuary he took from the south wall.

"I see," said Havner.

"Is that significant?"

"I will let you decide after I tell you what the inscriptions say."

"I'm all ears," Rand said.

"The inscriptions are in Aramaic," Havner said.

"Aramaic?"

"Yes. Of course, it's very similar to ancient Hebrew in its appearance, though quite different from modern Hebrew. It was the language in Israel at the beginning of the Common Era."

"Uh-huh," Rand said patiently. He knew that, of course, but didn't want to slow Havner down.

"It's an early form. First century, I'm reasonably confident."

"All right. What does it say?"

"I'm no paleographer."

"Of course," Rand said.

"My translation should not be considered conclusive."

"Of course."

"But I believe it is safe to say that the first inscription reads, 'Miryam berat Shimon.' Or, 'Miryam, daughter of Shimon.'"

"Miryam," Rand echoed.

"Yes, daughter of Shimon."

"Hold on for a minute, would you, Yigal?" Rand cupped the phone in his hands and summoned Miri to come closer. "You were right," he told her. "The name I showed you really is Miryam."

She smiled.

"Could I ask a favor of you?"

She nodded.

"Would you ask my daughter to bring my clip-board?"

Miri nodded and stepped over to the cave. Rand put the phone back to his ear.

"Okay," he said, "so the first inscription is 'Miriam, daughter of Shimon.'"

"That's correct."

"What about the others?"

"I think the other inscriptions are intended to be identical."

"Intended?"

"Yes," Havner said. "There are calligraphic distinctions in the two inscriptions."

"They're not identical."

"I believe the words are, but there are some slight anomalies between them."

"Anomalies," Rand repeated.

"May I assume these two inscriptions were on different sides of the ossuary? I couldn't tell from the photos you sent, because of course they were focused on the writing and were much too narrow a view for me to see the setting. But am I correct in assuming that one inscription was made on a short end of the ossuary and the other on a long side? The back side, perhaps?"

"Yes, that's exactly right," Rand said.

"I thought so. That could explain the differences."

Tracy appeared from the cave with the clipboard. She walked over to Rand and handed it to him while Miri returned to her post a few yards away. "Write this down," he said to Tracy. "Just a minute, Yigal. My daughter is here taking notes for me." His tone changed. "Write down, 'Miryam, daughter of Shimon.'" He spelled Shimon for her.

"All right, Yigal," he said when Tracy was done. "I'm back."

"Your daughter arrived safely, then."

"Yes. Thank you so much. She made it just fine. And thank you for sending Carlos. He is on his way back, by the way."

"Splendid," Havner responded.

"So what do the inscriptions say?"

"I think we are dealing with a family name," he said. "And not just any family name."

"Oh?" Rand said.

"The family name looks to me like Qayafa." He spelled the name.

"Qayafa."

"Yes. The full inscription, with a minor variation on one side, looks like 'Yehosef bar Qayafa.'"

"Hold on." This time Rand claimed the clipboard from Tracy and wrote the words himself, balancing the phone between his shoulder and ear. " 'Yehosef bar Qayafa.' "

"That is correct," Havner said. "Joseph, son of . . . Caiaphas."

"Caiaphas," Rand echoed. "Caiaphas. That name sounds familiar."

"It should," he said. "It's the name of a priest, referred to by the Jewish historian Josephus as 'Joseph, who was called Caiaphas.' "

"I'm still not placing the name, for some reason."

"I'm sure this will help," Havner added. "Caiaphas was not just any priest. He was the high priest who presided over the trial of Jesus."

39

TALPIOT, SOUTH JERUSALEM

Rand hung up the phone. The name of Caiaphas took him back many years. Of course, he knew the stories of Jesus being tried by the authorities and sentenced to die on a cross. He had heard them first from his mother, he supposed, probably before he was old enough to go to school.

He had grown up in the little farming community of Brookville, Kansas, population 700, not counting the cows, which would have been many times more than the human population. His mother had taken him to Sunday school and church every Sunday, in a white clapboard church with a white steeple. His father stayed home, which had always seemed perfectly normal to Rand, no matter how many of the other kids' fathers suffered through the long, hot services. His father had always seemed absent even when he was in the same room. Rand could not recall him ever expressing love or support to him, and seemed able to go days and even weeks without speaking a complete sentence to his son.

By the time he was a teenager, Rand had stopped attending church, and though he loved his mother, all her pleading words and hopeful looks did nothing to change his mind.

He also had attended a few church services after his marriage at age twenty to Joy Stevenson, a classmate at the University of Kansas. Old habits of indifference, even antagonism, toward churches and Christianity quickly returned. When his young wife had professed to being "born again" at a church on the University of Chicago campus, where Rand was pursuing graduate studies, he had warned her not to expect him to change. "I'm perfectly happy just as I am," he had told her at the time. The stories of Jesus and his crucifixion were only *stories,* he told himself; they had nothing to do with him and his life.

Yet right at this moment he stood yards away from an ancient casket that might bear the name of Caiaphas, the high priest who had presided at the trial of Jesus. Could it be the same person? Could there have been more than one "Yehosef bar Qayafa"? And could the bone box in that cave possibly contain the two-thousand-year-old bones of a man who supposedly helped to send Jesus to his death?

"Daddy," Tracy said, "are you all right?"

He nodded, then inhaled slowly and exhaled even more slowly. Still holding the clipboard, he pushed himself off the hood of his car and walked slowly over to Miri Sharon. "How are things going?" he asked.

She answered without removing her gaze from the hevrat kadisha and the ribbon of road beyond them. "Three more men have arrived since dawn. I sense they are expecting more."

He nodded. "If I find bones, what is the procedure for turning them over to those guys?"

"*If* you find bones?" she asked.

"That was my question."

The tiniest smile appeared at one corner of her mouth. "You will then have a few options. You may bring the bones to the surface in their original bone box, and the hevrat kadisha will transfer the bones to bone bags and remove them from the site. Or you may take some of the men into the cave with you, and they will remove the bones from where you found them. Or you can simply turn over the cave to them when you have removed everything except human remains."

"I think I would like to bring the bones to them," he said, "in their original ossuaries."

"*If* you find bones," she emphasized.

"Right," he said. "*If* I find any."

He and Tracy returned to the cave. "We have to work quickly," he said, "but we can't sacrifice accuracy."

"What do you want me to do?" she asked.

"Keep taking pictures," he said.

"Are you going to tell me what the names mean?"

He blinked at her for a moment. "Oh, yeah," he said. "Sure." He began carefully returning the bones to the Miriam ossuary. "These bones may belong to someone named 'Miriam, daughter of Shimon,' or Simon, as we would pronounce it."

"Okay," she said. "Who is she?"

He shook his head. "Don't know." He picked up a leg bone. "The bones appear to be fully developed, and the epiphyses of the long bones are fused to the diaphyses"—he pointed to the end of the femur where it connected to the shaft—"with no evidence of fusion lines, which indicates that she was an adult."

"Okay, I guess I'll take your word for it, because I don't understand a thing you just said. How old was she?"

"I don't know," he said. "I'm hoping an osteoar-chaeologist will have enough information in the photographs to answer that."

"So that's all we know?" Tracy asked.

"Except," he said, "for the possibility that she was a member of the Caiaphas family."

"The Caiaphas family?"

He smiled. "Yeah," he said. "That's the big sur-prise. According to Yigal Havner, the inscription on that other ossuary reads 'Joseph, son of Caiaphas.' "

"Okay," she said. "So who's that?"

"Here, help me get the lid back on this one," Rand said once the bones were all back in the Miriam ossuary. "It could be the guy who was the high priest in Jerusalem when Jesus Christ was crucified."

"Jesus Christ?"

"My sentiments exactly," he said.

40

a.d. 26
caesarea of palestine

C aiaphas stood before the new Roman governor. After a strenuous horseback journey of roughly eighty miles, he and Malchus had arrived near Caesarea the night before. And, though they had lodged in the finest available quarters, the spacious seaside home of Yochanan the Blind, Caiaphas had enjoyed little rest. He considered it likely, after his audience with the procurator, that he would no longer be Kohen haGadol, high priest of the Jews. And, just as likely, the week could well end with the unraveling of his scheme and the death of Gamaliel . . . and many others.

Pilate sat enthroned on a dais of white marble in the audience hall, a pavilion in the court of his palace. The entire area was rimmed with elegant statuary and flowering plants of every kind. A refreshing breeze from the Mediterranean wafted through the pavilion, almost constantly cooling the procurator as he sat as Caesar's judicial, executive, and legislative representative over the provinces of Judea, Samaria, and Galilee.

Caiaphas signaled to Malchus to stay behind as he approached the man, who was attired in his white patrician tunic with vertical scarlet stripes. Over his shoulders he wore the purple and gold robe of his office, and around his neck hung a medallion suspended from a golden chain bearing the profile of Tiberius. A laurel of gold leaves rimmed his head.

"Your Excellency," Caiaphas said, bowing his head slightly.

Pilate nodded. "Greetings, noble rabbi."

Caiaphas nearly corrected the governor by explaining he was not a rabbi, but a priest. But he

145

caught himself. "I bring you the good wishes of all Jerusalem and the hopes of the entire nation of the Jews for your health and well-being."

Pilate ran his tongue along the inside of his lips and smacked loudly, as though trying to dislodge a morsel of food from between his teeth. "You have my thanks."

"I come on a matter of some . . . sensitivity."

"Is this sensitive matter related to the Jewish mob that is strewn out along the Via Maris?"

"Yes, Your Excellency," Caiaphas answered. "It is directly related to that."

Pilate waved a hand imperiously. "Speak," he said.

"Mine is a secret embassy," he said. "I hope to be of service to Your Excellency . . . and to my people."

A servant entered, bearing a platter of dates and other fruits, and carried it to Pilate. He picked a gold and orange apricot and waved the servant away simultaneously.

Caiaphas continued, speaking slowly and choosing his words carefully. "A delegation of the Sanhedrin is coming to request the removal of the Augustan cohort from Fortress Antonia."

Pilate shifted in his seat and leaned forward. "For what reason?"

"The standards of the Augustan cohort," he explained, "bear the image of the emperor."

The governor leaned back again and bit into the

146

juicy fruit. "I am aware of that," he said, juice trickling down his chin. "They earned those ensigns for their bravery and distinction in the service of the emperor."

"Yes," Caiaphas said. "But the delegation will request their removal nonetheless."

Pilate shrugged. "I will refuse." He took another bite.

"Of course. That is why I have come."

"To hear my refusal?"

"To prevent a tragedy."

Pilate sighed. "I am weary of you, rabbi." He took another bite of the apricot and then summoned the servant with the platter, who took the fruit from Pilate's hand and handed him a towel. Pilate vigorously wiped his hands with the towel before returning it to the servant, who disappeared.

"Your Excellency, we Jews follow the Law of God, which forbids graven images. There are tens of thousands of Jewish men in Jerusalem who will die rather than disobey that law."

"Then they will die," Pilate said, with no more passion than he had displayed in eating the apricot.

"More will join them," Caiaphas insisted.

"More will die!" Pilate said impatiently.

"Your Excellency, I am not here to oppose you. But I do not wish to see the shedding of blood, either Jewish or Roman." He cleared his throat and further lowered his voice. "The emperor's cohorts here in the province of Judea are well armed and well trained. However, they are auxiliary forces, and combined, they number just a few thousand. And with the governor of Syria, Lucius Lamia, still in Rome at the emperor's insistence, any reinforcements from Syria would come too late to save lives and . . . reputations."

Pilate stood. "Do you threaten me?"

"No, Your Excellency. I assure you, if the offended crowd that is now strewn out all along the Via Maris had remained in Jerusalem, they would have stormed the five hundred troops stationed in Antonia Fortress by now. That is why I sent them out of Jerusalem."

"So you plan to storm my palace instead of Fortress Antonia?"

"No!" Caiaphas unconsciously glanced at the soldiers flanking the governor's dais. "That is not at all what I intend. You see, the crowd that is coming behind the Jerusalem delegation will have had more than eighty miles of walking to calm them down. They will still be irate, but they will be more inclined—after waiting days already—to await the results of Your Excellency's deliberations."

"And will they walk calmly back to Jerusalem when they learn that the ensigns of the Augustan cohort will certainly remain in place?"

Caiaphas bowed his head for a moment. If his

next steps were not directed by the Lord, he would be walking into calamity. "They will not," he said bluntly. "But"—he lifted a hand in a conciliatory gesture—"that is why I have come, alone, to seek Your Excellency's wise assistance in averting a bloody rebellion . . . only months after your arrival."

He watched the governor closely. The last phrase seemed to find its mark. It would be a severe blow to the new governor's reputation and standing in Rome if a large-scale insurrection broke out so soon in his tenure. Rome would crush the rebellion, of course, and the Pax Romana would be restored, in time—but the damage would be done. And procurators had been recalled for lesser blunders, Pilate knew.

And now he knew that Caiaphas knew it, too.

41

TaLPIOT, SOUTH JerusaLem

Tracy felt chills despite the glaring floodlights in the cave. She should have recognized the name Caiaphas without having to ask her father. She remembered now, though. Of course she remembered. Some of her earliest memories were of curling up in her mother's lap listening to her read stories from the Bible. She loved them as a little girl, especially the stories of Ruth, and Esther, and Daniel in the lion's den. But more than all, she had been fascinated with the story of Jesus, the gentle teacher and miracle worker who rode into Jerusalem on Palm Sunday, though he knew the week would end with his death. Oddly enough, she reveled in the story of the Last Supper, the betrayal in the Garden, the series of trials—before the Sanhedrin, before Pilate, before Herod—and even in the dreadful climb to Calvary and the Author of Life's gruesome death between two criminals.

Even as a girl, she wondered if there were something wrong with her because the other children exulted in Easter eggs, clothes, baskets, and pageants, while she had always thought of Easter as an exclamation point; it only served its purpose if everything leading up to it merited such a climax. She wouldn't have put it quite like that as a child, of course, but she always sensed it in one way or other.

When she got to middle school and high school, and started playing trumpet in band, she'd discovered she felt much the same as a crescendo and a forte; whether the crescendo was molto (a lot) or poco a poco (bit by bit), it always seemed to her that the power of the climax was determined by the path taken to get there. But by that time, the story of Jesus and his steadfast, sacrificial love for the whole world had taken a backseat to more important things: becoming liked by boys, becoming popular among girls, and becoming anything but one of those "Jesus freaks" who seemed to take pride in being weird. It wasn't that she'd lost faith, as much as she stopped looking for it.

So now, to come halfway around the world to find her father and also find the tomb of a man who played a key role in that story—well, she didn't know quite what to do with that, but it did kind of take her breath away for a moment.

Her reverie was interrupted by her father asking her to grab one end of the Miriam ossuary and move it onto the floor. When that was done, she helped him lift the other bone box—presumably the one that once belonged to Caiaphas—and place it on the table.

"Ready?" he asked her. "Let's see what's inside."

The lid of this ossuary was not only more elaborate, but also taller and wider than the other. It extended to the edges of the box on all sides, and the quality of the carving and fit made it harder to gain a purchase under the rim. It took a few moments to maneuver her fingers under the edge on each side. When she did, Tracy could tell immediately that this lid was also slightly heavier than the other.

When the lid was safely settled on the floor, Tracy turned her attention to the bone box, unconsciously holding her breath while she focused her gaze on the open container. The first thing she saw was a skull.

42

TALPIOT, SOUTH JERUSALEM

Rand lifted the skull from the bone box slowly, even reverentially. He turned it around in his hands several times, inspecting the various characteristics he had explained to Tracy when analyzing the skull from the other ossuary.

"So?" Tracy said. "What is it?"

"It's a skull," Rand said without a trace of sarcasm.

"No duh," Tracy answered. "I mean, is it a man?"

"Looks like it. Large, rounded cranium, prominent supercilary arch. Square mandible. I'd say it's male."

"So it could really be him?"

He pointed to the teeth. "Definitely adult. Could have been fairly advanced in years."

"You mean he was old?"

He didn't respond, but set the skull down on the table and turned back to the box. He gingerly lifted out the pelvis and examined it closely. "Judging from the auricular surface and pubic symphysis . . ." He frowned. "This is why I really need an osteoarchaeologist. Nadya could perform a lot better on-site analysis than I can."

"You can't tell how old he was?"

He pursed his lips. "Not with any confidence."

He looked at her. "That's why your photos are going to be absolutely critical. I mean, it looks to me like our patient is going to turn out to be an older adult—fifty years old or more—but I can't be any more precise than that. And that's really just a guess at this point."

"But still," Tracy insisted, "it could be him."

He set the pelvis on the table. "Let's not jump to any conclusions." He reached into the box and began carefully withdrawing the contents, one at a time.

"But so far, so good, right? You said it's definitely a man, and he was probably old. So it could be him."

He stopped what he was doing and propped his hands and forearms on the sides of the open ossuary. He looked at her. "It's possible. But I've seen too many people jump to conclusions based on incomplete evidence and analysis. I don't want to make a mistake. This could be important, Tracy, and if it is, we don't want to rush it. We can't afford to be careless—"

Suddenly a voice called his name from above. It was Miri Sharon. She didn't sound relaxed.

"Yes?" he said, taking a step or two closer to the ladder.

"Dr. Bullock, could you come here for a moment?"

He shot a glance at Tracy. He didn't like the tone of Sharon's voice. "Get all the pictures you can," he said. "I'll be back in a minute."

Before he even got to the top of the ladder, he heard the voices. Angry voices. Chanting. Cursing. The men in black were suddenly shouting and shaking their fists again, like they had at the beginning.

Miri was waiting, her rifle in hand, at the top of the ladder. Before he straightened into a standing posture, she said, "How much longer is it going to be down there?"

"Why? What's going on?"

"How soon can you finish?" Her voice was suddenly sharp. Her eyes flashed.

"I don't know," he said. "What's happening?"

"They will not wait much longer," she said.

"You mean today? You expect me to finish today? I just got the last ossuary opened."

She glanced meaningfully to the western sky. "They will not wait for Shabbat."

"What?"

"Shabbat is coming. Sabbath. They will not stay here through Shabbat."

"So that's good, right? They'll be gone when the sun goes down."

"You do not understand," she said. "They will not simply go away. They think you have bones in that cave, and they will make sure it is empty before Shabbat."

"So what's that supposed to mean? I'm supposed to finish before they have to go to church?"

A rock landed a few feet away from where they

154

stood, and Sharon shouted a few words he couldn't understand. Far from being pacified, the mob turned up the volume of their shouts.

"You seriously think they're going to cross that tape?"

She turned a hard look on him. "What do you think?"

"Listen," he said. He turned his back to the hevrat kadisha and lowered his voice. "I do have bones in there, and I am going to turn them over— all of them. But I need more time. I just now opened what may be the most important ossuary in the whole tomb, and I haven't had any time to analyze them or photograph them. Is there anything you can do?"

Another rock landed nearby. Then another. They were either out of practice or not yet trying to do any damage. Rand assumed the latter.

Miri gripped her carbine more tightly, and frowned in the direction of the men in black. She consulted her wristwatch. "Sundown is just a few hours away. But they will not wait for sundown."

"How long *will* they wait?"

"Nu," she answered, shaking her head and using a multipurpose Hebrew term that in such a situation might be translated "Who can tell?" or "What's the difference?"

Rand didn't know the word, but he understood her answer. "What if I bring out the first ossuary? Will that buy me any time?"

"I can tell them you will be bringing human remains to the surface in thirty minutes," she suggested. "That might help."

"How long will it take them to do whatever it is they do?"

"*Nu,*" she repeated. "I do not think it will be more than fifteen minutes."

"So that would buy me an hour . . . max."

"How much can you get done in that time?"

"Not enough," he said.

43

TaLPIOT, SOUTH JerusaLeM

Rand thanked Miri for her help and turned toward the cave while she approached the noisy group of protesters. He scrambled into the cave and quickly updated Tracy on his conversation with Miri. Within a few moments they had the Miriam ossuary placed on the lift.

Once the ossuary was on the surface, the shouting men in black quieted. Rand and Tracy carried it together, and set it on the ground within a few feet of the crowd behind the yellow tape. He turned to Miri.

"They must not damage the ossuary in any way," he said.

She nodded. "I will make sure."

By the time he and Tracy had traversed the few yards to the cave entrance, the men had formed a circle around the box and seemed to be preparing for a ceremony. In the tomb, he set about removing the skeleton, piece by piece, and reassembling it on the camp table.

While he worked as rapidly as he could, he occasionally stopped to make a remark and jot a note on his clipboard. Only when he paused did Tracy halt her photo-snapping. However, after removing a femur and both tibia bones from where they had been grouped against the long inner wall closest to him, he stopped suddenly.

"What is it?" Tracy asked, lowering the camera.

Rand's jaw hung open in an expression of astonishment. He gingerly placed the tibia in his right hand on the table. Tracy watched his movements closely; instead of positioning the tibia in its proper place in the skeleton, between the femur and the foot bones, as he had done with all the other bones as he removed them from thc caskct, he placed it absentmindedly alongside the reconstructed frame.

"What is it?" she repeated.

He started to reach his empty right hand into the ossuary but thought better of it and withdrew it. He looked at his daughter. "Take pictures of this," he said.

The box was nearly empty. "Of what?" she asked.

He circled the table and stood next to her. He

pointed to the seam between the side and bottom of the ossuary. "There," he said. "Take pictures of that."

Then she saw it. A long, dusty shape. It looked like something cylindrical, encased in old leather. The creases in the leather indicated where once it had been tied with thin cords, though now only wisps of the binding remained. "What is it?" she asked.

He stared, as if expecting it to move or change or disappear at any moment. "I'm not sure," he said. "But it could be a—a scroll."

44

a.d. 26
caesarea of palestine

A tense moment passed between the high priest and the Roman governor. Caiaphas waited what he hoped was a prudent amount of time before breaking the silence.

"I rely on Your Excellency's reputation as a shrewd man who came to these shores to administer peace and justice to the emperor's subjects."

Pilate stared haughtily at Caiaphas and then resumed his seat on the throne of judgment. "Let's hope that your thinking is as sound as your words are smooth."

Caiaphas smiled appreciatively. "Thank you, Your Excellency. I know removal of the Augustan cohort's standards would be an unacceptable concession."

The governor inclined his head, as though trying to view the Jew from a different perspective. "It would be an affront not only to the cohort but also to the emperor himself."

Caiaphas nodded. "Yes. And, of course, a new governor in such an unstable province as Judea cannot give even the smallest appearance of giving in or backing down."

Pilate's eyes narrowed. "Go on," he barked.

"So when the Jerusalem delegation comes, you will of course have to refuse their request."

Pilate's response was a slow, interested nod.

"But these men cannot back down, either. They cannot abide images of man or beast in the city of our God. It is unthinkable to them. Intolerable."

"No one is requiring them to worship these images!" Pilate suddenly protested.

"Many years ago, when our people were camped in the wilderness of Paran, a horde of venomous snakes overwhelmed the camp, and many were bitten by the snakes. Many died. So our deliverer, Moses, was instructed by God to create a bronze serpent and place it on a pole so the whole camp of Israel could see it lifted above the tents. Whoever looked on that serpent was miraculously healed from the venom, and the plague ended. A

great many years later, one of our kings, a right-eous man named Hezekiah, had to destroy that bronze serpent because the people had turned it into an object of worship."

Caiaphas paused, but he saw no understanding in the governor's eyes.

"You see," he continued, "that is why we Jews must be careful to avoid graven images. It is the nature of man to turn an image into an idol. That is why, in the last days of Herod's life, when he erected a golden eagle over the entrance to the Temple, some of our scholars tore it down, at the risk of their lives."

"What manner of people would act in such a way?"

"We love peace," Caiaphas said, "but we love God more."

Pilate frowned, and glared at the priest.

"So," Caiaphas explained, "the delegation—and the crowd that is coming from Jerusalem—will insist that the standards be removed. They will not be pacified until that occurs."

"Then you are wasting my time!" Pilate shouted.

"Please forgive me, Your Excellency. I have not finished. When the delegation makes their request, Your Excellency may suggest that your decision will be announced in the theater." Caiaphas unconsciously nodded behind him and to the right, in the direction of the theater just beyond the elegant courtyard.

"Why in the theater?"

"There the crowd—even if it numbers in the thousands, which I suspect will be the case—can be easily and unobtrusively surrounded by your soldiers."

Pilate watched with rapt attention.

"When you announce that the standards will not be moved, the people will protest. They will insist further. And they will go on insisting."

Fascination and—perhaps—respect commingled in the governor's expression.

"When tensions threaten to explode, you could offer the women and children safe passage out of the theater. Some will go. Most will stay. Of course, all will understand you to mean that the people of Jerusalem will either accept your decision . . . or die. You will then command your soldiers to unsheathe their swords and await your order."

"You are mad." Pilate's tone was not uncomplimentary.

"At that point, it is probable that someone—Gamaliel, perhaps—will step forward and offer to be the first to die. Others will follow suit."

"You are proposing that I ruthlessly slaughter thousands of the emperor's subjects."

Caiaphas shook his head. "No. No, not at all, Your Excellency. At that point, you could—perhaps—announce that you are exceedingly moved by the Jews' devotion to their God, and so you are inclined to spare them. And, though you will not remove the emperor's image from the standards, nor deprive the Augustan cohort of the honors they have earned, it would please you to transfer the Augustan cohort to Caesarea, where you may gaze with appreciation on the image of the emperor on their banners."

The governor studied Caiaphas in silence for a few moments. At length, his eyes narrowed again. "What makes you think I will not assemble your people in the theater"—he waved a hand—"and kill them?"

"Your Excellency's reputation as a wise judge and cunning ruler," Caiaphas answered, though he had received no such information about Pilate. "A reputation that will grow when you untie this knotty situation . . . and peace prevails throughout your province."

Pilate studied the priest, rubbing his clean-shaven jaw with a manicured hand. At last he ran his tongue along the inside of his upper lip. "You know, of course, that the emperor's prefect will do what he thinks best for the empire."

"Of course," Caiaphas answered.

"That is all," Pilate said.

Caiaphas bowed slightly and left the audience hall, silently praying that he had not just delivered his people—and Gamaliel among them—into the hands of a butcher.

45

TaLPIOT, SOUTH JErUSaLeM

A scroll?" Tracy echoed.

Rand nodded, still staring. Moving slowly, as if the form in the box were a coiled snake and he had to be careful not to arouse it, he reached over slowly and picked his pencil off the clipboard. Using it as a probe, he poked the pencil into the cylindrical form and gingerly pried back the outer cover to expose the brittle yellow texture of an ancient papyrus scroll.

He knew this was highly unusual. A tomb excavation invariably uncovered all sorts of other items: pots, jars, clay lamps, vases, writing tablets, carvings, textiles (usually garments or shrouds), and so on. Many of these sorts of things even appeared occasionally inside the ossuaries, along with jewelry and coins (such as the Herod Antipas coin he'd already found in the Miriam box). But as far as he could remember, of the thousands of ossuary listings in *Levanon's Catalogue of Jewish Ossuaries*, not one mentioned a scroll having been found inside an ossuary.

Jewish burial customs during the Second Temple period were thoroughly practical and fairly well defined. The vast majority of inscriptions followed

163

a predictable pattern, either identifying the deceased by name and patrilineage, or by a title or some distinguishing characteristic (such as "Yochanan the Leper" or "Yo-ezer the Scribe"). On occasion, an ossuary revealed some commingling of Jewish and pagan burial customs, as may have been indicated by the coin discovered in the Miriam ossuary, or a combination of Jewish and Christian elements.

In every case, however, there would have been a certain logic for specific objects to have been included in a tomb or an ossuary. Lamps were enclosed in Egyptian tombs to light the dead person's way to the afterlife. Vikings were buried with their weapons, along with food and drink to supply their journey into the next life.

But a scroll? Scrolls—or scroll fragments—had been found in monasteries and libraries, and in ruins of homes throughout the ancient world. A scroll was found beneath a synagogue floor at Masada, where the Great Jewish Revolt against Rome had ended with nearly a thousand Jews killing themselves rather than letting themselves be taken by the Romans. And, of course, scrolls had turned up in caves—most famously, the Dead Sea Scrolls, discovered in a network of caves near Qumran, which had housed an ancient community of ascetic Jews. As hard as he tried, though, Rand could not think of a single discovery of a scroll in a Jewish tomb—Egyptian and Chinese, sure—let alone inside an ossuary.

What would be the reason? Why would a Jewish family—perhaps the family of Caiaphas, the high priest, though it was far too soon to be sure of that—place a scroll in this ossuary? Was it buried with the corpse in the primary burial, laid alongside the newly deceased person when he was placed in the tomb, and then transferred to the limestone box when the bones were gathered? Or was the scroll included only later, at the time of the secondary burial?

And what did the scroll contain? Was it a portion of Scripture, like the Great Isaiah Scroll of the Dead Sea discovery? A treasured possession of the deceased? Something related to the manner of this person's burial? Or did it have something to do with how he died?

Rand shook his head. Such thoughts were more like Agatha Christie than the *Journal of Near Eastern Archaeology*. But the presence of a scroll in the Talpiot tomb did raise many questions— fascinating questions. The vast majority of archaeological artifacts were no more dramatic than broken bowls or chipped arrowheads. Sometimes those small discoveries, strung together like beads on a necklace, added a small piece to the world's knowledge of a past civilization or ancient culture; more often, however, they were the archaeological equivalents of discovering a penny on a sidewalk. But scrolls do not turn up every day—papyrus and leather scrolls deteriorated rapidly in all but the driest climates of the world, and the use of scrolls—the "books" of the ancient world—began to decline in the first and second centuries A.D., giving way to codex, or booklike, manuscripts. So if the Caiaphas inscription had increased his expectations, this new development had raised the stakes even higher—and made the hasty way he was having to work that much more maddening.

"Dad!"

Rand was shaken from his reverie by Tracy's voice. He focused on his daughter's face, which registered impatience.

"The police lady," she said. "She's calling you."

46

TALPIOT, SOUTH JERUSALEM

They will be finished any moment," Miri Sharon reported to Rand, who had left Tracy photographing the ossuary, scroll, and skeleton in the cave.

"All right," he said, thrusting his hands into his pockets. "What happens then?"

"That is what I want to ask you."

He stared at her for a few moments, dumbfounded. "I don't know what you mean."

"Will you be finished when they are finished?"

He pulled his hands from his pockets and ran a hand over the top of his head. "Do I have a choice?"

She shifted the rifle and slung it over her shoulder, muzzle down. "I do not like being difficult, Dr. Bullock. But I have no choice. Shabbat is coming, these—men—have been waiting almost since you arrived, and the security of your site and your operations is becoming more"—she sighed—"more unrealistic with each passing moment. I am willing to help you in any way I can, but I must insist that whatever human remains you have in your possession must now be turned over to the hevrat kadisha."

He rubbed his heavily whiskered face with both hands and then fastened her with a weary gaze. "I have a male skeleton laid out on the camp table in the cave. The last ossuary is open on the table, and it must not be disturbed—must not even be touched. I can't put the bones back in the ossuary to bring them up to them, so if you would tell them to come on down to the tomb and remove the bones from there, I guess that will have to do."

She nodded solemnly. "Thank you," she said. "I will tell them."

He thrust his hands back in his pockets and turned back to the cave.

"Dr. Bullock," she called.

He turned.

"When they are gone, I will stay to help you."

He shook his head. "That's really not necessary."

She responded with a mirthless smile and turned back toward the hevrat kadisha.

He suddenly realized that once the tomb was emptied and the on-site excavations were complete, Sergeant Major Sharon would have finished her assignment. She would go home, and he and Tracy would return to the Ramat Rachel Hotel.

Of course that's what would happen.

Of course.

What else, he asked himself, *did you think would happen?*

47

a.d. 26
Lydda

The arduous horseback journey from Caesarea to Jerusalem was a torment for Caiaphas. He spoke nothing except the most curt, cursory instructions or questions to his servant, the faithful Malchus. At times he trembled violently, and by the time he and Malchus arrived at the inn at Lydda, he could not stop his heart from beating so wildly he thought his chest would explode.

The inn, near the intersection of the Via Maris (way of the sea) and the Emmaus road, presented a natural stopping place on the journey between

Jerusalem and Joppa. The courtyard of the inn pulsed with travelers of all shapes and sizes—malodorous caravan drovers, boisterous Roman soldiers and officials, shifty buyers for the Egyptian markets, along with Jews from the coastal cities of Apollonia, Joppa, and Ashdod coming and going to worship at the Jerusalem Temple—and their stock of horses and asses, along with the chickens, sheep, and goats belonging to the inn itself, all of which were outnumbered by the flies that buzzed everywhere. The cacophony of languages—Latin, Greek, Egyptian, and Aramaic, among occasional others—and surfeit of smells from meals cooking over multiple fires made for a nauseating combination when a person was feeling well. But Caiaphas was not well.

The familiar pain started soon after his audience with the governor. As usual, it began as a dull ache, little more than a suspicion, which at first was indistinguishable from his vexation and worry over what he had just accomplished—or failed to—and whether disaster was imminent for him and his people. By the time he and Malchus left their lodgings in Apollonia, his worry had given way to a constant, pulsing pain at his temples and behind his right eye—and frequent nausea that had forced him to stop twice that day on the second leg of his journey.

"The Sabbath is coming," Malchus whispered as he helped the high priest settle on a bed of pillows under an awning. "It will do you good to rest tomorrow."

"Rest?" Caiaphas muttered. Sweat beaded on his forehead and upper lip. "Who can rest? Here, of all places."

"I will bring you water from the well."

"Malchus, don't leave me!" He pressed his fingers deep into his eye sockets. "I am not thirsty! Stay here."

Malchus returned a moment later with a bulging goatskin pouch. Caiaphas opened his eyes long enough to watch the servant douse a scarf with the cool water from the skin. After slightly wringing the water from the scarf, he placed it gently over the priest's eyes and forehead. "You must rest," he said. "You have had a hard journey."

"It is not the journey," Caiaphas said. "I am afraid, Malchus. For Gamaliel. For my people. For the whole nation." He groaned loudly, as though his groans could somehow dispel his pain. "What if we fail? What if I've led them all into Sheol? What will I do?"

The prospect of spending the Sabbath in this foul, noisy caravansary, a mere thirty miles from his lavish home, was dreadful. But even worse was the knowledge that he may not know for days whether his stratagem had succeeded or failed. There was little he could do but wait for word from Gamaliel and the others.

What if Pilate delayed, or dissembled? What if

170

he simply refused to receive Gamaliel and the others? Or what if the mob refused to follow Gamaliel's lead and fought back? What if—

What had he been thinking? And how could Gamaliel have been so foolish as to go along with the plan—even after Caiaphas had begun to have misgivings, even after he had recognized it as being too risky? There were just too many what-ifs. They should never have gone through with it.

Caiaphas propped himself up on his elbows. He could not breathe. He could not get air into his lungs. He was going to die here, in this wretched place.

48

TaLPIOT, SOUTH JerusaLeM

The scene was surreal.

Tracy watched from above, standing next to her father, while the group of black-hatted men crowded around the camp table in the cave. The skeleton from the last ossuary lay on the table. Two of the men in black, the older ones, stood nearby at ground level; Tracy assumed they were not capable of descending the ladder into the cave.

The proceedings began with the men swaying back and forth, and one of them chanting words

Tracy could not understand, to which the whole group responded "Amen."

After a few moments, Tracy took a few steps over to Miri, who stood slightly apart from the action. "Do you know what they're saying?"

Miri flashed a tiny smile and nodded. "It is called the kaddish. It is a part of the Jewish funeral ceremony."

"What is it?" Tracy asked. "What are they actually saying?"

Miri paused for a moment. Tracy wasn't sure if she was listening or remembering.

"It starts, 'May his great Name grow exalted and sanctified in the world that he created as he willed.' And then it goes on, 'May he give reign to his kingship in your lifetimes and in your days, and in the lifetimes of the entire family of Israel, swiftly and soon.'"

"What are they saying when they all chant together?" Tracy asked.

"There are two parts they all say together. The first one is, *'Y'hei sh'mei raba m'varakh l'alam ul'al'mei al'maya.'* This means 'May his great Name be blessed forever and ever.' And the second is much shorter. It is simply *'B'rikh hu,'* which means 'Blessed is he.'"

Tracy smiled. "It's pretty cool that you know all that."

Miri shrugged. "I am a Jew."

"Do all Jews know that stuff?"

"I do not know. If they live in Israel? Maybe. Jerusalem? I think yes, definitely."

Tracy nodded. She could no longer see the men in the cave from where she and Miri stood, but she could still hear them. "How long will they be down there?"

"Twenty minutes more, I think."

"And then they'll go?"

Miri nodded. "They will take the bones you and your father discovered, and place them in pine boxes and bury them in a Jewish cemetery somewhere."

"Even after all these years, huh?"

"Honoring the dead is very important to religious Jews."

"What do you mean, 'religious Jews'?" Tracy said. "I thought being Jewish *was* a religion."

"To some, yes. But it is also a nationality. And a race, an identity. But not always a religion."

"Are *you* religious?"

Miri hesitated, then tried to explain that, like most Jewish Israelis, she wasn't an observant Jew. Her parents, Yakob and Sylvia Sharon, had looked to the new nation of Israel as a political haven for the Jewish people, not as a fulfillment of prophesy, like the Hasidim. In fact, she detailed how she considered religious Jews to be almost as big a threat to the security of Israel as the Arabs.

"The modern state of Israel is like a walker on a tightrope," she concluded, "forced to balance forever on a cable called Judaism, strung between Islam on one end and Christianity on the other. I must walk the tightrope because I am Israeli, but it is not a position I like."

"So," Tracy said, "you're not religious."

Miri smiled sadly. "I am not a fan of religion—whether Judaism, or Islam, or Christianity. But I sometimes wish I could find what my religious friends seem to have found—some connection, some relationship, some *communion* with . . . something. Something higher than themselves. Someone, perhaps."

Tracy nodded, and Miri turned her attention back to the cave.

"They are finishing," she said.

49

TaLPIOT, SOUTH JerusaLem

The day was rapidly waning as the hevrat kadisha climbed out of the cave and solemnly streamed toward their cars, taking the bones from the "Caiaphas" ossuary with them. Rand called to Tracy to join him, and then began to descend the ladder to the tomb.

"It shouldn't take us too long to pack everything up," he told her. "The biggest task will be taking apart the scaffold and the lift, but once that's done, maybe we can get a bite to eat and actually sleep in a comfortable bed tonight."

"Where will you put everything?" Tracy asked.

Rand paused. "I don't know. I guess we'll stack the scaffolding somewhere on site. The ossuaries and artifacts can't be left here, though." He knew his tiny Fiat wouldn't afford much help. "I suppose we'll just take it all to our room."

"Even the scroll?" Tracy asked.

Rand shrugged. "I don't know what else we can do, with the Sabbath starting tonight."

"Aren't these, like, valuable? Aren't you supposed to turn them over to somebody?"

He shrugged. "I'm the sole archaeologist on this project. It's my responsibility to excavate and categorize and analyze everything, and then the Israel Antiquities Authority decides what to do with it all. But for now, I pretty much have to store and secure everything."

"So we just pack up and go to the hotel?"

"I guess so."

She smiled. "We could swim. Or watch movies in the room."

"Sure," he said. He gestured for her to help him move the ossuary from the camp table to the lift. "I could download all your pictures into the computer, and start the process of cataloging my notes. I'll also need to send the osteo photos off for analysis as soon as possible, and get started on writing my summary."

Tracy's smile had disappeared. "Yeah," she said. "Sounds like fun."

He folded the table and placed it on the lift with the ossuary. "I'm sure we'll have plenty to do."

It took three trips in his tiny Fiat, but by the time the first star had appeared in the sky, Rand had carted off all the ossuaries and equipment, leaving behind only the scaffolding and lift platform, which he planned to return to Yigal Havner at Tel Mareshah as soon as possible. He also had taken Tracy to the hotel and had saved the Caiaphas ossuary—and the scroll it contained—for last.

"Thank you for your help," he said, shaking Miriam Sharon's hand.

"I did the best I could," she answered, letting go of his grip. "When the hevrat kadisha learn of a tomb being excavated, the options . . . become less."

"I understand," he said. "It's such a shame. From an archaeological point of view, that is."

She nodded.

He nodded.

They stood awkwardly for a moment, until she gave him a sad smile and turned to her patrol car.

"I don't . . ." He started over. "I don't know how to get in touch with you."

She opened her car door. "Why would you need to contact me?"

"Oh," he said, "I don't know, I just thought—

something might come up. You know, related to the excavation."

Her deep brown eyes locked onto his. "The excavation is over."

50

He heard the commotion outside his darkened sleeping room. Someone was arguing outside. Without opening his eyes or lifting himself from his mat, he strained to listen.

Malchus. He heard Malchus's voice, protesting, resisting, and then another voice, older, smoother. Or perhaps that voice was only in his mind. Perhaps both voices were in his mind. It had been hard to tell these past few days—if days it had been. He was sure—though he didn't know how he was sure—that it had been more than a day since he and Malchus had completed their journey from Caesarea, and his faithful servant had lowered him onto the comfortable pillows of his own bed in his own home. But he had been overcome with delirium before leaving Lydda, and he couldn't recall how Malchus had managed to bring him the last thirty miles to Jerusalem. Had he enlisted help? Had he borrowed a cart? No, Caiaphas was

177

sure he recalled being on horseback for at least part of the last leg of the trip. But how Malchus could have conducted him safely home after that dreadful Sabbath spent tossing and turning in that wretched inn at Lydda, Caiaphas could not guess, and certainly could not remember.

The voices rose, and came closer, and suddenly the door of his room swung open and let in light, the cursed light that caused him such pain. He threw his forearms over his closed eyes and groaned.

"Shut the door!" he bellowed, punctuating his cry with more groans. "Go away! Whoever you are, just go away!"

He felt a shuffling beside him, and then a quietness, a stillness seemed to envelop the room, which was dark once more. He lay still and listened. The door had closed but someone was in the room with him.

"Please," he whispered. "Please go."

He was aware of . . . sound. Like the softest whispering. He relieved the pressure of his arms against his face, then slowly removed them and let them rest on his chest.

Suddenly he knew what it was. He opened his eyes and saw the form of a man kneeling nearby, hands outspread in front of him, rocking slowly back and forth. The man was praying. His words would have been completely inaudible if they had been unfamiliar to Caiaphas. But he heard them because he knew them. He had often—countless times—spoken them himself.

"Barukh atah Hashem, rofeh ha'cholim." *Blessed are You, Source of healing. And, over and over again, as he rocked, the tassels of his* tallith *were swaying pendulously:* "El na refa na lah." *Please God, bring healing.*

Caiaphas lifted himself from the mat and propped himself on one elbow. "Gamaliel!" *he cried.* "Gamaliel, is that you?"

The man turned, and it was *Gamaliel.*

Caiaphas extended his hands like a grandfather summoning a child, and Gamaliel gripped the priest's forearms in his hands. "You live!" *Caiaphas said, and relief washed over him in a tidal wave of emotion. He hung his head on his chest and sobbed convulsively.*

When his sobs finally subsided, Caiaphas summoned what dignity he could. "Forgive me, my friend," *he said.* "I have not been well. I have done little except lie on this bed and pray for relief. And Hashem has heard my prayers, for here you are! I was so afraid for you, and for our people."

Gamaliel released his hold on the priest's arms, but clapped a firm hand on Caiaphas's shoulder. "Your prayers have indeed been heard," *he said.*

"And the others? The others who went with you?"

"They are well," *Gamaliel replied.*

Caiaphas sighed loudly and closed his eyes. "So

179

the prefect received you?" He opened his eyes again to watch his friend as he answered.

"The governor delayed for a few days," the Pharisee said, "but otherwise followed your plan down to the last jot and tittle. The ensigns of the Augustan cohort no longer fly in the Holy City. And you, my friend, have earned the friendship of the prefect, Pontius Pilate."

"Ha!" Caiaphas said. Curbing the laughter that tried to rise within him, Caiaphas corrected his friend. "No," he said. "Not friendship. Never friendship, we can be certain. But tolerance, even cooperation? We can hope, my friend. We can hope!"

And then the high priest let go. He lay back on his mat and let the laughter roll out of him in one wave after the other, until the laughter was replaced with sleep.

51

ramat rachel

Tracy let the water from the showerhead stream over the top of her head, forming a canopy of water and hair over her face. The hot water—almost too hot to stand—felt good. A good, hot shower was one of her favorite places to think, and while she would have liked better water pressure than the shower in her hotel room afforded, it was still a welcome activity after the long day.

It was hard to believe that she had left Tel Mareshah only that morning. So much had happened since then . . . and yet nothing had changed, really. She had managed to toil beside her father all day in the cave, breaking only for a late lunch, and yet they'd hardly talked. Oh, they'd exchanged plenty of words. But it had been so urgent to get the tomb cleared out and the bones examined and turned over to those creepy men in black suits, they had talked only about that.

What was he thinking? Had her arrival changed anything? The day had passed pleasantly enough, but she still didn't think he wanted her there. That was clear when he had talked only about the work he had to do now that the tomb was empty, and didn't seem at all interested in catching up with her or spending time with her.

She shut off the shower, and stood for a few moments, letting the drops of water roll off her body and down the drain. She opened the thin shower curtain and groped for the towel.

This is a mistake, she told herself. *It seemed exciting and maybe a little exotic to leave the States and fly all the way to Israel to find your father. But now you've found him. Now you're here. You did it. Now what? What did you think would happen once you got here? Did you think he would take you in his arms and twirl you around*

181

and make you feel like a little girl again? Did you think he would drop everything and spend time with you? Pay attention to you? Get to know you?

She finished drying her hair and wrapped the towel around her body, still dripping from the shower. A peek into the hotel room revealed that her father still wasn't back from his latest foray to the cave, so she padded into the room and made quick work of dressing, throwing on jeans and two T-shirts. Once she was dressed and her father still hadn't returned, she reached for the television remote and turned it on, then sat on the end of the bed and crossed her legs.

The television came on to a news channel broadcasting in English. Then another news channel, also in English, followed by yet another news channel, but this one, she assumed, was in Hebrew. The next choice was some kind of documentary. An old black-and-white movie, subtitled in Hebrew. Something that looked like a soap opera, but the actors were speaking—she was surprised—Spanish. The next channel was showing a commercial, and the one after that showed a police drama set in New York City. And that was it. She was suddenly back at the first news channel she had encountered, which turned out to be CNN International.

She turned the set off and looked around her. She picked her cell phone out of her jeans pocket. She thought of calling Rochelle; she really missed her friends. "Probably costs way too much," she concluded.

Shoving her phone back into her pocket, she returned to the bathroom, tied her hair into a knot, picked up her plastic room key off the desk, and left. Arriving at the bank of elevators, she noticed that the call button for the elevators was already lit, so she waited.

And waited.

After a few minutes, she looked up to see what floor the elevator was on, and watched in frustration as it stopped at every floor, without exception, on its way to her. It arrived, she stepped in, and pointed her finger at the "L" on the control panel. It was already lit. In fact, every number was lit.

She groaned. *Stupid kids,* she thought.

Several minutes later, the elevator finally delivered her to the ground floor. She stepped off and turned toward the main lobby. The sound of raucous singing, dominated by male voices, assaulted her ears, growing louder as she walked toward the lobby. Halfway there, she reached the source of the noise: the large cafeteria she had passed several times that day. She entered.

Her eyes widened at the sight. The room was filled with people seated shoulder-to-shoulder at the long tables. The men were dressed in black suits. The women wore dresses. Young children in "church clothes" roamed—and sometimes ran—back and forth between the tables and along the edges of the room. And most of the adults—all of the men, seemingly—sang. Lustily. Loudly. Some even tilted their heads back and opened their mouths wide so their voices bounced off the distant ceiling. Some banged their fists or cups on the tables as they sang. In one corner, three men draped their arms across each other's shoulders and danced as they sang,

Hinei ma tov uma nagim, hinei ma tov uma nagim,
Shevet atjim gam yajad, shevet atjim gam uajad,
Hinei ma tov uma nagim, hinei ma tov uma nagim,
Hinei ma tov, hinei ma tov; lajlajlai, lajlajlai.

The song went on and on. The volume rose and fell. Through it all, a person would occasionally rise and walk over to correct a child who'd become too rambunctious, or simply move to a different position to stand and watch. When the song was over, the room began to buzz with conversation, until a man near the front banged his cup on the table. Most people stopped talking and turned their attention to the man, who spoke in Hebrew for a few moments. When he finished speaking, someone in the crowd began singing, and the room quickly erupted in a new refrain.

She felt rooted to her spot on the periphery of this strange scene. Then, from the corner of her eye, she saw a figure in a black suit and white shirt break off from a group of others. She turned. It was a boy—a young man, really, whom she judged to be about her age. Maybe not. It was hard to tell. He wore a beard, which may have made him seem older. But the hair of his beard was fine and thin, which may have made him seem younger.

He walked directly toward her.

"You are American?" His accent was thick, but she had no trouble understanding him.

She glanced at her T-shirt, wondering what had identified her as an American; she had forgotten that she had donned a solid shirt with no design. "How did you know?"

He smiled. "I can tell."

He's cute, she decided. She turned her gaze back to the room. "What's going on?" she asked.

"What do you mean?" he said.

"What's all this about?"

His smile disappeared and his mouth opened in an "O." "Oh, you are not Jewish."

"No," she said. "Why?"

He seemed disappointed. "It is Shabbat. Sabbath."

"Oh," she said. "Like church."

His face became a mask. "No," he said. "This is the meal."

It looked like everyone had finished eating, but no one seemed in a hurry to go anywhere. A young boy came running toward her; when he turned to taunt the three boys who chased him, he ran into her legs, and she caught him just in time to prevent a fall. He blinked at her and, without a word, ran off. She turned back to the young man who had approached her . . . but he had left. She looked around, and saw that he had rejoined the group from which he had earlier detached himself.

The singing in the room had stopped again, and an old man with a long, gray beard had been talking for some time, and seemed likely to go on. She had no idea what the man was saying, but she felt intensely interested nonetheless. She hungered to know more about these people. She thirsted to grasp what was going on. She wasn't sure why she wanted those things, why she could barely tear herself away, and why she suddenly felt so . . . what was it? She couldn't come up with a word. But it was a little like how she had felt soon after her mom's funeral, when she awoke one morning and, instead of slowly and painfully remembering that her mother had died, struggled to remember what it had been like to have a mother.

She turned to leave. As she walked numbly toward the elevators, she heard the rowdy singing start again. When she reached the elevators, one door stood open. She entered, and pointed a finger to press the number for her floor, but saw that once again all the numbers were lit.

She leaned against the back wall of the elevator and resigned herself to a slow ride back to her floor.

52

Wait!" Rand said.

He strode to the open door of Miri's patrol car. She sat behind the wheel, gripping the door handle, and slipped her long, tanned legs under the steering wheel.

He wasn't sure what he was doing, but he knew he wanted to do something. He wanted to delay her departure, if nothing else. No, more than that: he wanted to prevent her from going—somehow. "What if," he said, the words coming out slowly and measured, "I need your help?"

"What kind of help would you need from me?" she asked.

"All sorts of help," he answered, though he was momentarily stunned by her question. He stammered for a moment before an answer occurred to him. "I don't know my way around Jerusalem. I'm going to need help getting around."

"There are maps," she said.

"I'll need to know where the Israel Museum is; I have to get some analysis done there."

"It is located on Avraham Granot Street. Off Ruppin Boulevard. On Givat Ram, near Hebrew University."

187

"All right," he said. He decided to try a different tack. "What if I wanted to get a drink with someone?"

"I'm sure the desk clerks at Ramat Rachel can help you with that," she said.

He ran a hand over his hair and then down the back of his head and across the back of his neck. "You're—you're intentionally being difficult. Why?"

"You are in Israel, Dr. Bullock," she answered. "Nothing is easy here."

53

raмaт racheL

What a mess, Rand thought. And he wasn't just thinking of the hotel room, cluttered as it was with ossuaries, various artifacts in paper bags, equipment from the excavation site, suitcases— and Tracy's dirty clothes and bath towel. Rand reflected that she had apparently dropped each article of clothing exactly where she had removed it.

When he had returned to the room the previous night, after loading the Caiaphas ossuary into his Fiat and saying his awkward good-bye to Miri Sharon, Tracy had been curled up in bed with the lights out. He had considered rousing her to ask if he could bring her something to eat, but decided against it. Instead, he had eaten a late dinner alone in the hotel's lobby café (rather than the cafeteria, which was full) and then, returning with a few brownies wrapped in napkins in case Tracy woke up, had done a little work before going to bed himself.

Now, however, with Tracy still asleep in the next bed, he had been to breakfast and back, and still saw no signs of life in her sleeping form. He decided to do as much work as he could without disturbing her.

The room's small desk was largely occupied with the Caiaphas ossuary and its scroll, still in situ, so he chose the only other writing surface in the room, a round table accompanied by two upholstered chairs. He talked to himself as he outlined on paper the tasks before him.

"First," he said, "I have to bring some order to this mess and catalog everything I pulled out of the tomb." The ossuaries, he knew, would be numbered in the order of their discovery; the Miriam ossuary would very likely become number five, and the Caiaphas ossuary would be labeled number six.

Then would follow his analysis of the ossuaries themselves. While he didn't expect any surprises, it would still be prudent to inspect the boxes and inscriptions, and jot a summary of each. He would then deliver the ossuaries to a laboratory for oxygen isotope analysis of the inscriptions, which would give an approximate date and age of the inscriptions, as well as a more precise dating of the limestone boxes themselves, thus revealing—among other things—whether Miryam berat Shimon was buried before or after Yehosef bar Qayafa.

"After that," he continued, transferring the next item from his mental list onto paper, "will be to get a full osteopathic analysis of the bones done from Tracy's photos." He would try e-mailing them to Nadya and asking her to give it a shot. He decided to make that a priority, so Nadya—if she agreed—could be working on that analysis while he was moving forward in other areas.

"I can take the ossuaries and inscriptions to the Israel Museum tomorrow," he figured. The business week in Israel extended from Sunday to Thursday, and some offices conducted business on Friday mornings, but Friday and Saturday constituted the "weekend" in Israel. Other than essential functions, such as hospitals, and support systems, such as hotel services, Arab businesses closed on Fridays and Jewish enterprises and government offices on Saturdays.

Most important, of course, would be authentication of the Caiaphas inscription, and preservation and analysis of the scroll. For the latter task, he knew he would need to call on the experts at Israel's world-class Center for Conservation and

Restoration, which also was housed in the sprawling complex of buildings at the Israel Museum.

If that all panned out—if the inscription turned out to be authentic, if the tomb really did belong to the high priest who was involved in Jesus' trial and crucifixion, and especially if the scroll turned out to be more significant than an ancient shopping list or dry cleaning claim ticket—he would have scholarly papers to write, interviews and lectures to give, eventually even a book to release, or maybe several. It wasn't the Dead Sea Scrolls, of course, but any archaeologist worth his salt should be able to make a career out of something as important as the tomb of the high priest who sent Jesus to the cross. People such as Asher Goldman and Yigal Havner, both world-famous archaeologists, had done just that sort of thing.

"Oh, yeah," he said. "I need to get the equipment back to Yigal as well." He grabbed his cell phone and dialed Yigal Havner's number.

FAITH IS THE ASSURANCE OF THINGS HOPED FOR,
THE CONVICTION OF THINGS NOT SEEN.
—THE WRITER TO THE HEBREWS

54

GIVAT RAM, WEST JERUSALEM

In December 1949, soon after Israel's War of Independence had formally ended with armistice agreements between the new nation and its Arab neighbors, plans were laid to establish a government district in the city of Jerusalem. The site chosen for this complex of government buildings was Sheikh Badr Hill, which the Israelis renamed Givat Ram. The Israel Museum, which had been planned from the nation's earliest days, was founded in 1965, and encompasses the Shrine of the Book (created to house the Dead Sea Scrolls), a sprawling and detailed model of the city of Jerusalem at the time of Jesus, as well as a fine-arts museum, the Bronfman Archaeology Wing, and state-of-the-art library and research facilities.

Rand's first task was to deliver the scroll to the Center for Conservation and Restoration at the Israel Museum. Knowing the delicacy of such artifacts, he still had not removed the scroll from the setting in which he found it—the bottom of the Caiaphas ossuary. He left the Miriam ossuary locked in his car while he carried the Caiaphas ossuary and scroll into the modern museum complex. After leaving the scroll with someone for preservation and analysis, he would then take the ossuaries, one at a time, to the archaeology wing, where someone in their research department—he hoped—could perform an oxygen isotope analysis.

After consulting numerous information desks and museum directories, he made it to the Conservation Laboratory. An attractive woman in a light green blouse looked up from her station at the reception desk. As he approached, she removed MP3 player earbuds and draped the cord around her neck.

"Shalom," he said, gently setting the ossuary on the edge of the desk.

"We don't accept antiquities here," she said. Her tone was perfunctory.

"I would like to see the head of the Paper Conservation Laboratory," he said. "I have a scroll from an emergency excavation."

She eyed him carefully, then picked up the phone receiver on her desk. She spoke in rapid Hebrew for a few moments, then held the receiver away from her face and addressed Rand. "He is not in."

"May I ask his name?"

She paused for just a moment. "George Moore," she answered.

"Is there someone else I could speak to? I need to have a document preserved, translated, and analyzed."

She hesitated, then spoke into the receiver again.

After a few bursts of Hebrew, she hung up the receiver and stood. "Follow me."

Rand shadowed the woman down several hallways until they approached a door labeled "Paper Conservation Laboratory."

"There it is," the woman said. She turned and walked away. Rand watched her press the buds back in her ears before she turned a corner.

He entered the room and encountered three twentysomethings, a man and two women, in lab coats, leaning over a table. They all looked up as he entered.

He set the ossuary down on the table as carefully as possible. "I have a scroll for preservation and analysis," he said.

In unison, the three technicians looked into the ossuary. "How old is it?" one of the men said.

"Possibly two thousand years."

"Where did it come from?" asked the woman.

"I just finished an emergency excavation in Talpiot on Friday," he said. "It was apparently a Second Temple Period tomb."

"Who are you?" asked the third technician.

"Dr. Randall Bullock," he said. "I've been working at Tel Mareshah with Yigal Havner."

They blinked at him, then looked at each other.

"We should call Dr. Elon," the woman said.

55

The size of the crowd astounded Caiaphas. People blanketed both banks of the Jordan, and as he approached with his small entourage, it seemed that streams of people—hundreds of them—flowed from all directions, from Jericho and Gilgal, Bethany and Heshbon.

He had traveled from Jerusalem with his servant, Malchus, and Alexander the treasurer, along with Eleazar, to see for himself the man everyone seemed to be talking about: Yochanan the Immerser . . . John the Baptist. The man had recently appeared from nowhere, it seemed, and began preaching in the wilderness around the Jordan, urging the people to repent from their sins and turn to righteousness. It was a message Caiaphas welcomed.

"Could he be a prophet?" Caiaphas had asked Eleazar, who had actually witnessed the man in action. They had been reclining around a low table under an awning in the packed inn at Jericho.

Eleazar seemed to hesitate. "Some think so," he said quietly. There were others around who might hear if he spoke too freely, and he knew it was the high priest's desire not to be known. "He certainly has the appearance. He wears garments of camel hair and a leather belt around his waist."

Caiaphas felt the hair on his arms stand up. "Like Elijah the Tishbite," he said.

Eleazar nodded. "And he is found preaching at Bethabara."

"The place of the crossing," Caiaphas said, referring to the crossing of the Jordan by Joshua and the Israelites—but also by Elijah and Elisha.

"And where Elijah ascended in a whirlwind," Eleazar added.

"And he calls the people to teshuvah," Caiaphas said, using the familiar word meaning return, or repentance.

"I hear," Alexander inserted, "he tells tax collectors to go on collecting taxes for Rome."

"But to collect only what is right," Eleazar said.

Alexander glared at Eleazar. "And he tells soldiers not to extort money and not to accuse people falsely!"

"That would be a start," Caiaphas allowed.

"But only a start!" Alexander complained. "If he were a true prophet, would he not condemn both tax collectors and soldiers?"

"He says 'The ax is already at the root of the trees,'" Eleazar argued.

Caiaphas adjusted his girdle, the cloth belt that circled his waist, which had grown so much in his nine years as high priest that even the short trudge across the rocky loam from Jericho winded him. "And you think by that he means—"

"Messiah is coming," Eleazar said. "The change we have long awaited, the reversal in the order of things, is coming soon."

A slow nod. Then, "Is it him?"

"No!" Alexander shouted. "It cannot be! By the heavens, his miqva is the Jordan! Will he build a temple there, too?"

Caiaphas ignored Alexander. "Does he preach against Rome?"

Eleazar shook his head. "No. At least not yet."

Caiaphas nodded approvingly. "Do those who are immersed become his followers?"

Eleazar thought for a moment. "Some," he said. "Most return to their towns."

"Does he give them any instruction when they depart?"

"I don't know," Eleazar said.

Caiaphas had pondered this for a long time that night, and was mulling it over again as they approached the banks of the Jordan, a ribbon of water bordered by thick green vegetation running through the rocky Judean wilderness. So far he had liked nearly everything he heard. Alexander's points about tax collectors and soldiers were well taken, but he wanted to avoid making a snap judg-

ment. He would see the man himself. He would soon be able to judge firsthand.

But he sincerely hoped the man was right, and the ax was already at the root of the trees.

56

гамат racHeL

Tracy woke remembering the scene from two nights ago. The cafeteria filled with men, women, and children. All ages, eating and singing, drinking and talking. Little boys and girls running around the room. Here and there, a baby crying or nursing or sleeping. It was like a family reunion, she thought with fascination, except not like the few reunions she had attended: everyone seemed to want to be there for this one. But it suddenly occurred to her: that was it. It was like a family. Not like any family she'd ever seen before, but more of a family than she had ever known.

She rolled onto her back and quickly pulled the covers over her head. *Too much light.* It was morning. Her father was gone. She had spent a crazy amount of time sleeping yesterday . . . but then, there hadn't been much else to do on a Sabbath in a Jerusalem hotel, and the seven-hour time difference from back home had her constantly feeling like she felt a headache or a cold coming on. She'd been bored out of her mind since they'd cleared out of the cave, and the more bored she became, the more she resented her father for not noticing. He spent the whole day counting and tagging and arranging and writing stuff down. From time to time he had asked her if she needed anything, but what good would it have done to tell him what she needed? How would he have responded if she had said, "Yes, a little attention would be nice," or "I need you to stop working and pretend that you care about me"?

She remembered hearing her dad moving around in the room, and was pretty sure he had left the room once or twice that morning while she still dozed. Suddenly she bolted upright in bed. *What day is it?* She rubbed her face with her hands and tried to think. *Yesterday was the Sabbath, that's Saturday. So today is Sunday.*

She threw the covers off and sat up, looking around the room. There, on the bedside table. The digital clock radio read 9:40.

9:40 Sunday morning.

She thought hard for a few moments, trying to clear her sleep-addled brain and remember something from yesterday. *No, not yesterday, the day before. No, it was yesterday. That's right. Yesterday. I was still in bed and Daddy was on his cell phone. He called Yigal Havner at Tel Mareshah.*

She hadn't been paying attention, just wishing her father would stop talking so she could get back to sleep, and then she heard him mention Carlos's name. That's when she listened more closely, and her father said something about meeting "him"—Carlos, she assumed—at the excavation site at ten o'clock on Sunday.

In twenty minutes.

Carlos would be at the cave in twenty minutes. He may already be there. And if she didn't hurry, he would load up the equipment and be gone.

She jumped up from the bed and dashed into the bathroom.

57

GIVAT RAM, WEST JERUSALEM

Dr. Jacques Elon, head of the Restoration Laboratories and Center for Conservation at the Israel Museum, eyed the encased scroll in Rand's ossuary. "This," he said, speaking English in a mix of accents that sounded strange to Rand and made the man difficult to understand, "is not totally what we do in this place."

"What do you mean?"

Elon stroked his black goatee and cocked his head to one side without taking his eyes off the scroll. "We do not ordinarily operate laboratory services for objects that are not owned by the museum's collection."

"Oh," Rand said. "But you've done work for Yigal Havner, so I assumed—"

"Dr. Havner is a museum board member, so we make exception for him."

"Oh, I see."

A pause. "This was found in Jerusalem?"

Rand nodded. "Talpiot," he said. "A construction project caused a cave-in."

"I think I know where you speak." He leaned in closer to the scroll. "It was just so when it was found?"

Rand could tell the man was clearly intrigued by the scroll. "Yes," he answered. He decided to take a gamble. He grabbed the ossuary with both hands and picked it up. "I'm sorry to have bothered you. Can you recommend a laboratory where I might get the scroll analyzed?"

Elon looked up with something approaching terror in his expression. He looked as though he might just have a stroke right then and there. "It is not bother," he said quickly. "Truly. It is not bother."

"Oh, but since this isn't the sort of work you do here—"

"Ordinarily," the man said very slowly. "But we sometimes make exception, yes? Maybe this is one of those sometimes."

"Oh, I wouldn't want to put you out," Rand said, pressing his advantage. "I'm in a bit of a hurry, and I'm sure you have a lot of work to do."

"Yes, yes," Elon said. "But it is not rare to discover a scroll, no?"

The ossuary was not getting any lighter, but Rand didn't want to set it down just yet. "No," he said. "I mean, yes. It *is* rare to discover a scroll. And especially in a Jewish tomb. Inside an ossuary. I think that's very rare."

Elon nodded. "I think that, too. So we are men of science, yes? And something that is rare, we want to discover carefully what it is, yes?"

"Yes, of course—"

"There are good people here, the best in Israel, many the best in the world."

"So," Rand said, "you would like to analyze the scroll yourself?"

Elon reached across the table, placed a hand on each end of the ossuary, and with Rand's cooperation, guided it back onto the table. "It will be safe here."

Rand released his grip on the ossuary. "I'm sure there are forms to fill out."

"Yes, yes," the man said. "I will get them for you. And then we will make safe the scroll."

"I have a few other ossuaries, too," Rand said. "Some of them with inscriptions, like this one. I wonder if I can have some oxygen isotope analysis done?"

"Yes, yes, of course, of course," Elon said.

"Where should I take them?"

"Right here," he answered. "I am chief head of

restoration and conservation for all laboratories."

"So you'll be able to do the analysis on the ossuaries, too?"

"Yes, yes. Don't worry. I will go to my office and I will come back with forms to fill. Yes?" He strode to the door. "I will be back."

Rand breathed a satisfied sigh as the man left. He was getting somewhere. Then he glanced at his watch. It was 10:00 A.M. He was late.

58

A.D. 28
BETHABARA, ON THE EAST BANK OF THE JORDAN RIVER

The Immerser's voice rolled over the country-side in waves, like thunder. Caiaphas and his companions stepped carefully along the rocky terrain, and picked their way through the brush that clung to the banks of the river. He could discern the preacher's words before he saw the man himself.

"Hear, O Israel!" he shouted. "Hear the voice of one calling in the desert,

> *'Prepare the way for the Lord,*
> *make straight paths for him.*
> *Every valley shall be filled in,*
> *every mountain and hill made low.*

The crooked roads shall become straight,
the rough ways smooth.
And all mankind will see God's salvation.'"

The high priest's heart leaped as he heard the words. The Immerser quoted Isaiah's great prophecy. His booming voice prompted an echo in Caiaphas's heart, and the priest found himself murmuring, as if he were speaking to John, "You who bring good tidings to Zion, go up on a high mountain. You who bring good tidings to Jerusalem, lift up your voice with a shout, lift it up, do not be afraid; say to the towns of Judah, 'Here is your God!'"

Indeed, the moment the high priest peered past the thick circle of onlookers and located the speaker's form in the shallows of the Jordan, it seemed as though John looked straight at him—as if Caiaphas had spoken the words aloud. It sent a shiver up the priest's spine, and he started to step back—he, the Kohen haGadol!

"Eleazar," he called, after only a moment of hesitation. "Alexander. Come." He shouldered his way through the crowd, pulling the others with him as Malchus did the best he could to follow. They finally made it close to the west bank, opposite Bethabara.

The Immerser was stripped to the waist, exposing a barrel chest covered with hair. He was not tall, but he stood in the water like something made of granite—solid, immovable, irresistible. He continued speaking, sometimes facing the east bank and sometimes turning to face the west bank, farther from where he stood, waist deep in the water. "The day is coming—no, it is already here—when

> *'The Sovereign LORD will come with power, and with a mighty hand.*
> *His reward will be with him, and judgment will accompany him.*
> *But his flock he will tend like a shepherd: He will gather the lambs in his arms carrying them close to his heart, and gently leading those that have young.'*

"Do you think, O Jacob, that your ways are hidden from the LORD? Do you think your cause is disregarded by him? I tell you, no! But you must all repent, and produce the fruit of repentance, for the kingdom of heaven is approaching.

"And do not say, 'We have Abraham as our father.' God can raise up children for Abraham from the stones that lie all around you. But let your actions show that you are children of Abraham. For the ax is already at the root of the trees, and every tree that does not produce good fruit will be cut down and thrown into the fire.

"So let all you who confess your sins, and turn from them, come and be immersed by me."

As he finished speaking, a stream of people waded out to him. He received them one at a time, speaking privately to most and occasionally turning to say something to the crowd. Then he would place a hand on the person's head, and guide them in squatting into the water, as if they were descending the stairs of a miqva bath, the ritual cleansing every Jew submitted to before worshiping at the Temple.

Caiaphas watched John closely, transfixed. Caiaphas had met many ambitious men, even charismatic men. But this Immerser seemed different. He greeted every person who came to him to be immersed as a father would welcome his own child, and yet he seemed strangely detached from the people. The crowd seemed almost ready to worship him, but he appeared to be unaffected by the crowds who hung on his words.

Caiaphas called Eleazar and Alexander to come close to him, where he could whisper to them without anyone in the press of people hearing his instructions. They nodded obediently and moved to the edge of the water.

Eleazar called to the Immerser, who halted and turned slowly toward the Sadducee's voice. "Who are you?" Eleazar shouted. "Where do you come from?"

"Are you the one the prophets spoke of?" Alexander asked.

"I baptize you with water," John answered,

though he clearly spoke to everyone in the crowd. "But one is coming who is more powerful than I am, one whose sandals I am unworthy to unlace. He will baptize you with the Holy Spirit and with fire. His winnowing fork is in his hand, to clear his threshing floor and gather the wheat into his barn. But the chaff he will burn up with a consuming fire."

Caiaphas could not help himself. "Are you Ha Mashiach?*" he shouted.*

"I tell you, I am not the Christ," he said adamantly.

"Then who are you?" Eleazar asked. "Are you Elijah?"

"I am not."

Someone on the opposite bank joined the questioning. "Are you the Prophet?"

"No," he said.

"Who are you, then? Give us an answer to take back to those who sent us. What do you say about yourself?"

"I have told you; I am the voice of one calling in the desert, 'Prepare the way for the Lord.'"

The voice from the other bank spoke again, and Caiaphas identified the familiar sound of the voice just before he located its source, standing amid a group of phylacteried Pharisees: Nicodemus, a distinguished member of the Sanhedrin and friend of Gamaliel. "Why then do you immerse people," Nicodemus asked, "if you are not the Christ, nor Elijah, nor the Prophet?"

"I baptize with water, but among you stands one

you do not know." John swept his hand to indicate the crowd that lined the banks. "He is the one who comes after me, the thongs of whose sandals I am not worthy to untie."

"I told you," whispered Alexander, who had sidled up to Caiaphas again, "we've come all this way for nothing."

Caiaphas found it hard to tear his gaze away from the man, but did finally turn back toward the Jericho Road. He wished he could be alone to think, to pray. But they all had a long return trip to Jerusalem ahead of them, and he felt confident he had seen enough. "I'm not sure of much at the moment, Alexander," he said. "But I'm sure of this: it hasn't been for nothing."

59

TaLPIOT, SOUTH JerUSaLeM

Tracy had brushed and washed and dressed hastily, then applied a few touches of makeup before pulling her hair back and tucking her room key and cell phone inside the pockets of her jean shorts. She was on her way to the excavation site before 10:00 A.M.

Her knees ached by the time she had walked down the steep driveway from Ramat Rachel and turned toward the cave. Walking briskly along the dusty sidewalk, she was able to take in her surroundings much more thoroughly than she had while careening through traffic with Carlos or her father at the wheel. She was struck by the familiarity of the business signs on the buildings she passed—Mazda, RE/MAX Realtors, Pizza Hut, even a kosher McDonald's—but with Hebrew, Arabic, and English lettering. Streets were narrower than at home, and buildings were stacked up against each other.

She reached the tomb. Construction workers swarmed the site. The rhythmic beep of a large truck backing up sounded nearby. Dust swirled in the air. The yellow tape barrier was gone, but the hole was still there, partially covered with a slab of plywood. She wondered if they would completely fill in the cave, or just give it a new roof and pave over it somehow. A few of the workmen stopped what they were doing and glanced in her direction. One of them wiped his forehead with a cloth, whistled, and shouted something, seemingly at her.

She suddenly worried that her shorts were too short and that her ribbed T-shirt clung too tightly and her neckline dipped too low. She turned away, trying to ignore the men, and saw the spot where she and her father had left the equipment. It was gone. The scaffolding, the lift, the generator. They were all gone. She looked all around, but there was no trace of them anywhere. Was she remembering wrong?

No, it had been right there, not a dozen feet from the entrance to the tomb. And now it was gone. That could mean only one thing.

She pulled her cell phone from her pocket. Except for the photos her father had asked her to send to Yigal Havner, she had assumed it would be too expensive to make calls or send texts over here, but she still kept the cell phone with her at all times—out of habit, mostly, but also because she used it as a clock. It was 10:14. Carlos had been here. He must already have been here. He must have loaded up the equipment . . . and left.

She had missed him.

60

TALPIOT, SOUTH JERUSALEM

Tracy wasn't sure what to do.

She glanced down the street and up the hill in the direction of Ramat Rachel. Her eyes welled with tears. It felt just like the day she left Chicago. She had no place to go . . . except to her father. Nothing to look forward to . . . except more rejection. Nothing to do . . . except to feel lonely.

She dropped her gaze to the dust at her feet. "If I wanted to feel like this, I could have stayed in Chicago," she said.

Someone shouted not far away. She lifted her

gaze and saw the workman who had whistled to her earlier walking briskly in her direction. His chest and arms bulged with muscles. His bald head glistened in the sun. And he looked more than capable of breaking her in half with one hand—or worse.

Her heart raced. The other workmen who had watched her with interest moments earlier now seemed utterly disinterested; none of them seemed inclined to protect or defend her. If she turned back toward the hotel, she would shorten the distance between her and the man who seemed intent on pursuing her. So she turned in the other direction, away from the construction site and away from Ramat Rachel.

The man wasn't deterred. He quickened his pace, so Tracy quickened hers. She scanned the route ahead of her. She didn't see a likely escape route. There were buildings on either side of the street. Maybe she could duck into a shop and find protection there. Or maybe she would be trapped if she did that.

He shouted again, more urgently it seemed, calling to her to stop, but she knew her options would shrink the moment she let him catch up to her, so she walked even faster, so fast she was practically running.

Suddenly a large vehicle skidded to a stop in front of her, throwing dust and gravel everywhere. It came so close to her, she stopped and screamed, covering her face with her hands.

"Tracy!"

She dropped her hands.

"Tracy, stop!"

The voice was familiar. It had said her name. She looked behind her. The construction worker was nearly upon her, and she was momentarily trapped between the vehicle and her pursuer.

Then her eyes landed on a familiar face, though it took her a moment to recognize it: Carlos. He appeared on the side of the Land Rover and approached her, smiling broadly. "It is you!" he said. "What are you doing here?"

She cried out in relief, and threw her arms over Carlos's shoulders and embraced him.

"What are you doing here?" he repeated.

She stammered out a few disjointed syllables, but before she could finish, the workman from the construction site was just feet away, and she screamed and sought refuge behind Carlos.

"What is going on?" he asked.

Tracy wasn't sure whether Carlos addressed her or her would-be attacker. She only hoped he would be strong enough to protect her. The man from the construction site seemed a lot bigger and stronger than Carlos.

The man spoke, then, and Carlos answered him, in Hebrew. Tracy watched over Carlos's shoulder. They seemed to be talking civilly to each other. She looked at Carlos's face; he was actually smiling.

Carlos nodded, and said a few more words, and the man turned back toward the construction site.

"What's going on?" Tracy said, still speaking over his shoulder. "How did you do that?"

"Do what?" Carlos asked.

"He was running after me," she explained, moving around to face him. "He was going to attack me!"

"Attack you? What makes you think that?"

"I saw him! He whistled at me, and yelled, and then he started to come after me—"

Carlos laughed. "Tracy, he was not going to attack you."

"He—he wasn't?"

"No! He recognized you from the excavation. He wanted to tell you that the workers had moved the equipment."

She blinked at him.

"He said he called to you, but you ran off, and he could not catch up to you . . . until I arrived."

"Oh," she said.

"Why did you think he was going to attack you?" His smile seemed iridescent to Tracy. But it annoyed her.

She felt herself blushing. "It's not funny," she said.

"No," he said. "It is not." He stopped smiling. But he looked like he wanted to.

61

*C*aiaphas sat on the low wall that rimmed the *rooftop of his home. It had been an excessively warm day, and the roof offered a welcome sanctuary from the heat and provided a striking vista of the city and the Temple. Caiaphas loved this view, especially at times like this, as the sun sank in the western sky, lighting up the walls of the Temple mount before entrusting the night to the moon, which would soon rise over the place of God's presence. It never failed to thrill his soul. Finally, though, he managed to turn his attention to his companion. "You say it happened the day after I was there?"*

"The next morning," said Nicodemus, the Pharisee Caiaphas had seen questioning the Immerser that day by the Jordan River. "The people were still wondering in their hearts if this Yochanan could be the Messiah. His words seemed so powerful and compelling, how could he not be the one?"

"He does seem to inspire many," Caiaphas said. He wasn't sure about this Nicodemus. He knew Gamaliel thought highly of him, but he seemed to

Caiaphas—what was it?—gullible, perhaps. Too quick to listen. Too willing to believe.

"Yes, but that morning a man entered the water while Yochanan was still speaking—"

"Before the immersing had begun?"

"Yes."

"Where did he come from?" Caiaphas asked.

Nicodemus looked puzzled. "Where did he come from? I don't know. I suppose he had been standing among the reeds at water's edge, like everyone else. I first noticed him as he waded out to where Yochanan stood, and the Immerser stopped him."

"What do you mean?"

"He held out a hand while the man was still several paces away, and fastened his blazing eyes on him and said, 'I need to be immersed by you, and do you come to me?' "

"The Immerser said that?"

"He did."

"And what did the other man say?"

"I can't be positive. He spoke much more softly than Yochanan, but I asked some who were closer, and their understanding matched mine."

"What did the man say?" Caiaphas insisted. Pharisees were far too concerned with words. Caiaphas didn't care about the words themselves; he simply looked for signs that Messiah was coming.

"He said, 'Let it be this way, for it must be so, in order to fulfill all righteousness.' "

Caiaphas's eyes widened, and he jumped up from his seat on the wall. "He said that? 'In order to fulfill all righteousness'?"

"Yes," Nicodemus answered. " 'In order to fulfill all righteousness.' "

Caiaphas turned his back on his guest and crossed his arms on his chest, gazing at the sunset-lit walls of the Temple. "What did he look like?" he said. "Describe him to me."

The Pharisee shrugged. "He seemed like any other man. In fact, I took him for a Galilean."

Caiaphas spun and stared at Nicodemus. "A Galilean!"

He shrugged. "He was a rustic. Nothing would have caused anyone to remember him, except for what happened next."

"Yes, yes, tell me about that."

"After Yochanan told him to let it be, the Immerser placed his hand on the man's head, and he disappeared beneath the water." He stopped.

"Go on," Caiaphas urged.

The Pharisee seemed to avoid the priest's gaze.

"What is it?" Caiaphas asked.

"I don't know," Nicodemus said. "I'm not sure how to explain this. Or even what it is I am trying to explain. I only know that, in that moment, it felt like—like everything stopped. Like the breeze that had been blowing suddenly died, and the sun started to go out. Like all sound and time and space were about to collapse." He paused, as if *listening to his own words, and then shook his head slightly, as though he didn't even believe himself. "And then," he said, "in one great motion, the man came up out of the water, as if leaping from a great depth!*

"It shocked everyone, everyone standing there. Some even cried out, they were so surprised. I mean, who comes out of a miqva like that? And the very sky seemed to open, and bathed his face in light, shimmering light, like—like fluttering wings, it seemed to me, accompanied by thunder in the sky."

Caiaphas studied his guest. "Thunder," he said dismissively.

Nicodemus looked helpless beneath Caiaphas's gaze. "Yes."

"Flashes of light and thunder."

Nicodemus sighed and spread his hands out, palms up. "It was like nothing I've ever witnessed."

Caiaphas sat on the wall again and placed his hands in his lap. "What did he say?"

Nicodemus blinked.

"The man who was immersed," Caiaphas clarified. "What did he say after he came up out of the water?"

"Nothing."

"Nothing?"

Nicodemus shook his head. "No. He stood there for a few moments, his arms spread wide, his lumi-

220

nous face lifted toward heaven, his eyes closed, as though he were listening, or waiting . . . or praying."

"Did he say nothing to the crowd?"

"No. He simply walked to the bank—and the crowd parted for him, as the Jordan had parted for Elijah, and he walked through them."

"Where did he go?"

The Pharisee shrugged. "I don't know."

"Well, then, what did the Immerser say? Surely he said something!"

"He did."

Caiaphas was losing his patience. "Well, what then?"

"He said, 'Behold, the Lamb of God who will take away the sins of the world.'"

62

rUPPIN BOULEVarD, WEST JErUSaLEM

By the time Rand had completed the paperwork and turned over the scroll and the ossuaries to Dr. Elon, he was hopelessly late. He jumped into his Fiat and dialed Yigal Havner's number on his cell phone.

"Shalom, Yigal," he said when his friend answered. "Does that young man have a cell phone with him? I need to call him. I'm running late."

"I think he does," Havner said. "But his number is in my cell phone, and I am afraid I do not know how to keep you on the line and look up his number at the same time."

"I understand," Rand said. "I'd have to do the same. Can you call me back with the number? I don't want to miss him."

"I could just call him for you, and tell him you are on your way."

"Oh," Rand said. "I guess that makes sense."

"How long will it take you to get there?"

Rand swerved to avoid a donkey cart. "It shouldn't be more than ten or fifteen minutes."

"I will tell him to expect you."

"Thank you," he said. "I just keep relying on your kindness, Yigal."

"Shalom," Havner said.

"Shalom," Rand answered. He pocketed the phone and sped toward Talpiot.

A few minutes later, Rand's cell rang again. It was Yigal.

"I just spoke to Carlos," Havner explained. "He said he's already loaded the equipment, and there's no need for you to come there."

"Oh," Rand said. "Really. Well—"

"Is there some reason you needed to be there?"

"I guess not. I just wanted to make sure everything was returned properly."

"According to Carlos, he has everything we loaned you. He said he will bring it to me tomorrow."

"Tomorrow?"

"Today is his day off. He offered to pick up the equipment in exchange for the use of the Land Rover."

"Well then," Rand said. "I guess I don't need to go by there. I'll head back to the hotel room."

"How is the work going?"

Rand filled him in, telling him for the first time of the scroll's discovery and relating the reaction of Jacques Elon at the Israel Museum.

Havner chuckled when Rand mentioned Elon's name. "He is a different sort of person," he said. "But if it is the tomb of Caiaphas you excavated— and especially if that scroll has any archaeological significance—Jacques will be of great value to you. And you will wish there were more like him."

"What do you mean?"

A grim laugh answered Rand's question.

63

TALPIOT, SOUTH JERUSALEM

Tracy climbed onto the passenger seat of the Land Rover. "You didn't tell him anything about me, did you?"

"No," Carlos answered. "Why would I say something about you?"

They had placed the last piece of scaffolding in

the back of the vehicle moments before, and Carlos had offered to give Tracy a lift back to her hotel.

"No reason," she answered.

They sat together in silence. Carlos pulled the vehicle into the street and turned toward Ramat Rachel. Finally Tracy turned sideways in her seat and faced Carlos.

"Do you have to go back to Tel Mareshah?"

He shook his head. "It is my day off." He glanced at her, then turned his gaze back to the road.

"Let's do something," she said.

"What would you like to do?"

"I don't know. Something fun. I've been bored stiff since I got here. What is there to do around here?"

"Many things," he answered.

"Like what?"

"I will show you," he said. "Do you wish to call your father?"

She shrugged. "He won't even notice I'm gone."

"He will not worry about you?"

She dropped her gaze and played with a wayward string on her shorts. "If he does," she said, "it might do him good."

64

Caiaphas had let the Pharisee string him along with his fantastic account of the Galilean's immersion, but he vowed never to let it happen again.

Nicodemus was a fool. If it was true—if the man whose immersion seemed to halt time for Nicodemus was truly from Galilee—then there was nothing further to interest Caiaphas. He was no Pharisee, with their insane devotion to Torah and their veneration of the Prophets and the Writings as well as the books of Moses. But one didn't have to be a Pharisee to know the prophets. And the prophets all made it clear that Messiah would come from David's descendants, and would come out of the city of David, Bethlehem.

"You would think they would have learned from the example of Judas," Caiaphas muttered as he prepared to retire for the night. "Judas the Galilean," as he was most often called, because he was from the town of Gamala in Galilee, incited a rebellion roughly thirty-five years earlier, during the reign of Augustus, when the governor at that time launched a census to level new taxes on the

population. Judas had gained support and the rebellion had spread, but when the high priest Joazar had proven ineffective in ending the revolt, the governor of Syria, a man named Quirinius, intervened and conducted the census. The rebellion was quashed, Judas was killed, and Israel was further demoralized.

Though Judas's influence outlived him, in the faction of Jews who called themselves Zealots, Caiaphas nonetheless found it hard to imagine any Jew—even a Pharisee—being so stupid as to consider, much less follow, a "Galilean Messiah."

And the Immerser's final words merely added to Caiaphas's disappointment and disinterest. Lamb of God? *Who would want to be proclaimed* Lamb of God? *What kind of man would allow himself to be called that? And who would follow him if he did? Hadn't the Jews been sacrificial lambs long enough? Hadn't enough of them been led to the slaughter by Assyrian, Babylonian, Greek, and Roman masters? What they needed, what they longed for, what they* prayed *for, was a deliverer like Moses, a righteous judge like Gideon, a king like David.*

Whatever Nicodemus had witnessed at the Jordan, it was nothing like that. "And therefore," Caiaphas concluded, pulling his tallith *over his head to say evening prayers, "it is nothing I need to concern myself with."*

65

гамат гаснеL

The first thing Rand noticed when he entered the hotel room was the blinking light on his computer, informing him that a message awaited him. The second thing he noticed was that Tracy seemed to be gone.

"Tracy?" he called. The bathroom door was open, so even as he put his head in the doorway and called again, he knew she wasn't there. He scanned the scene. The bed was unmade, clothes littered the floor, and her suitcase lay open in the corner. He looked around for a note but found none, so he opened his cell phone and dialed her number.

"Hi, this is Tracy." Voice mail. Then it dawned on him. He checked the time on the clock radio: 11:01.

"Of course," he said aloud. She must have awakened not long ago, and gone down to the cafeteria for something to eat.

He relaxed, then, and sat down to his computer on the table. Several e-mails had logged in, but he was interested in only one.

It was from Nadya Stanishev. The subject line read: "preliminary analysis." She wrote:

rand, it is good to hear from you and to learn you are doing well. i am well also and my mother is not improving but she is comfortable at least. thank you for asking.

the photos you send are good quality but as you know using photographs is a poor way to try to do an osteological analysis, but i understand it is the best you can do under the circumstances. i will write a complete report of my observations but of course you understand that very little can be considered conclusive or final, since photographs are all we have to work with.

my initial impression is that preservation of both skeletons appears to be excellent. surfaces look like they are very well preserved. i would grade them both 0-1 (as far as i can tell). we will just have to assume that phrase ("as far as i can tell") is attached to every part of my analysis.

The e-mail went on to describe the specifics of the Miryam skeleton, identifying a nearly complete adult female skeleton likely to have been 1.62 meters—approximately 5 feet, 4 inches—tall. She characterized the person's age at death as being in the "old adult" range, meaning fifty years or older.

But it was Nadya's analysis of the other skeleton that most interested Rand. He read slowly:

skeleton [2] comprised most skeletal elements, enough to be considered complete. the only bones that seemed to be missing were both patellae and some facial fragments. i estimate it at 90% complete.

based on the morphological features displayed in the skull and the pelvis, skeleton [2] looks to be an adult male. judging from the diaphyseal length of the left femur and tibia, I would say skeleton [2] is likely to have been roughly 1.8 m or approaching 6 feet tall.

the auricular surfaces and the pubic symphyseal face suggest an older adult. stage 5 or stage 6. I'm sorry, that's the best i can do. if you are a gambler, bet on 60 or a little older.

Nadya's report went on from there, and Rand read it all the way through. But it had already told him all he needed to know. Well, not all, since the bones had been lost to any scientific analysis. But still, there were no glaring contradictions.

It was possible.

He stood from his chair. He walked to the window and gazed out at the gigantic hotel swimming pool, and a wedding gathering at an overlook in the other direction. He crossed his arms on his chest, then lifted his left hand to rub his bristly chin.

It was possible. He had no idea who Miryam had been, but according to the osteo analysis, and given the strong provenance of the discovery, it remained possible that Dr. Rand Bullock had recently handled the two-thousand-year-old bones of the high priest who sentenced Jesus to death.

66

ramat rachel

Rand turned from the window. Would a kosher hotel in Jerusalem have a copy of the Bible, like hotels in America?

He stepped to the table between the beds and opened the drawer. It was empty. He looked around, and saw that the desk had a drawer. He opened it.

"God bless the Gideons," he said.

He sat at the desk where earlier that day the Caiaphas ossuary and scroll had sat. He knew enough about the Bible from Sunday school not to begin at Genesis, but it took him a few moments of thumbing through names that sounded foreign to his ears—Ezra, Obadiah, Habakkuk—before he found what he was looking for: the Gospels. He wondered what his saintly mother would say if she knew her younger son knew more about the Gospel of Thomas and the Dead Sea Scrolls than he did about the Scriptures she had probably read every day of her life.

He turned to Matthew, the first of the four Gospels, and began scanning the pages slowly, searching for the names of Miryam and Caiaphas, the two names discovered in the tomb. He stopped scanning at chapter six, and read aloud, in mumbling tones, the familiar lines of the Lord's Prayer, which he had learned as a child in his small-town Kansas church. From that point onward he became absorbed in the words and sayings and stories. By the time he reached the first mention of Caiaphas's name, in the twenty-sixth chapter, he had been reading for nearly two hours. He held his breath as he read the account of "the chief priests and elders of the people" assembling in the house of Caiaphas to plot how they could arrest Jesus without prompting a riot on "the feast day"—whatever that meant.

Later in that same chapter, Rand read the riveting account of Jesus being arrested and taken to the house of Caiaphas, where the chief priests, and elders, and all the council accused him and taunted him and found him worthy of death. He continued reading, mesmerized, into Matthew 27, where the chief priests remanded Jesus to Pontius Pilate, the Roman governor. He noted that Caiaphas was not mentioned by name in the twenty-seventh chapter.

"Where'd you go, Caiaphas?" he whispered. "Did you fade into the background once Jesus was convicted in your presence? Or were you just part of the group after that?"

He turned back to the twenty-sixth chapter. "You're clearly in charge in chapter twenty-six," Rand said. He flipped again to Matthew 27. "So I wonder why you're not specifically mentioned once Jesus goes to Pilate . . . and is crucified."

He continued reading, then, into Matthew 28, the last chapter of that first Gospel. He absorbed the account of Jesus' resurrection, and how, afterward, the "chief priests"—was Caiaphas among them?— received the report from the soldiers, who told of an earthquake and an angel rolling the stone away from the tomb. He finished the chapter, with its accounts of Jesus appearing to the disciples and commanding them to go and spread the news, and then stood and stretched his back, leaving the Bible open on the desk.

Strange, he thought. *It's strange to be in Jerusalem, where these things supposedly happened. It's even stranger to be reading about an earthquake that opened a new tomb, what—two thousand years ago—when less than a week ago, a bunch of heavy equipment prompted a man-made earthquake that opened an ancient tomb. One that belonged to one of the characters in that story.*

"Don't get ahead of yourself, Rand," he said out loud. "All the evidence isn't in yet. Take it one step at a time."

He sat again. "One step at a time," he reminded

himself as he picked up the Bible from the desk. He moved to the bed and propped himself in a sitting position on the bed pillows. He read the last three chapters of Matthew several times again, slowly, before moving on to Mark's Gospel, which he read straight through in under an hour, noting by the time he finished that this author never once called Caiaphas by name, but mentioned only "the high priest."

At that, he stopped reading again. An unfamiliar feeling started to rise in him. He stared at the open book for a few moments. Something was happening. Something new. Something foreign. What was it?

He got up from the bed and walked over to the desk. He set the Bible down on the desk, open to the end of Mark's Gospel. He stood for a few moments, gently smoothing the pages of the Gideon Bible, pondering. He tried to identify what he had been feeling or thinking. It took a while, but he finally recognized it.

He had heard Bible stories before. He had even read some of them as a kid. He had tried to pay attention when parts of the Bible were read at weddings and funerals. But what he had been doing for the past couple of hours, he had never done before. He had encountered these words he'd been reading, but never like this.

Adam and Eve, David and Goliath, Jonah and the whale. Lazarus. Zacchaeus. Jesus. The crucifixion. The resurrection. These were fairly familiar stories to him, or had been, once. But they had always been just that: stories. He had equated them with the rest of the tales he'd heard as a child: Hansel and Gretel, Little Red Riding Hood, the boy who cried "wolf."

But for the past two hours, he had been reading these words in a different way, a totally new way. He had not been reading them as stories. Because he had excavated that Talpiot tomb and seen with his own eyes that Caiaphas inscription, and handled with his own hands bones that could be the bones of the high priest described in these pages, he had been reading these words and sentences and paragraphs as evidence. As—well, as data, like the data he had spent all day yesterday recording in his laptop.

He had never considered the possibility that the stories of Jesus might be true.

67

a.D. 28
THe Temple MOUNT, Jerusalem

Caiaphas had just exited the Hall of Polished Stones with two of his wife's brothers, Jonathan and Alexander, trailing him, when the commotion seemed to subside. As the three men turned a corner and entered the great Court of the Gentiles, bounded on three sides by colonnaded porticoes, Caiaphas stopped as suddenly as if he had walked into a wall.

The place was a shambles.

The once-orderly line of cashier's tables had been thrown into disarray; tables were askew, upended, overturned. The money from the tables seemed to be everywhere on the pavement; it would take countless hours to separate Temple coins from Roman coins and restore a profitable order to it all.

A few dazed merchants wandered aimlessly, while others frantically tried to round up flapping doves, bleating sheep, and bellowing cattle or reclaim their broken cages and reassemble broken stalls. A growing crowd formed around the court, some amazed, some jubilant, and some merely curious.

And in the center of it all: one man.

He stood amid all the broken cages, overturned tables, scattered coins, and stunned people, with a braided rope dangling from his hand. He calmly surveyed the scene, like a foreman inspecting a job site.

"Take these things away," he said, his voice stentorian. His eyes blazed, not with madness, but with authority and passion, and he commanded the attention—amazement, even—of everyone in that broad court. "Do not make my Father's house into a marketplace."

"Where are the guards?" Caiaphas asked, looking all around for a Temple guard to command. *"Why aren't they doing their jobs? Why are they not arresting that man?"*

Alexander stepped in front of his brother-in-law. *"Wait,"* he said.

"Wait? Don't be ridiculous," the high priest blustered. *"If I have to, I'll arrest him myself."* He started to go around Alexander, but this time Jonathan joined in the effort to hold him back.

"Alexander is right," Jonathan said. *"Just listen. Everyone knows those tables and stalls belong to you and our father, Annas."*

"All the more reason to have him arrested!"

Alexander shook his head slowly. *"No. Look at the people."*

"What?" Caiaphas said impatiently.

"Look at the people," he repeated.

Caiaphas gritted his teeth and looked past his wife's brothers at the crowd that now ringed the court on three sides. He scanned their faces. They were pleased. Some laughed. As he watched, one old woman even shook her fist at a retreating cashier. And then he saw a face he recognized: the Pharisee, Nicodemus, who stood in the shade of Solomon's Portico and watched the man in the center with what looked like admiration.

Of course, Caiaphas thought. *It wouldn't break a Pharisee's heart to see this.* The Pharisees worshiped at the Temple like any righteous Jew, but they nonetheless favored a strict form of observance that emphasized Torah study in the synagogues. As the Temple was the Sadducees' power base, the Torah formed the basis of the Pharisees' authority. But the crowd was not comprised primarily of Pharisees.

"Look how many there are," Jonathan urged. "They think this man has done a brave thing. A righteous thing."

"How can they think that?" Caiaphas complained.

The brothers exchanged glances. When Alexander spoke, it was in the manner of a man with unpleasant news.

"The merchants cheat the people," he said.

"What?" Caiaphas said. He looked from one to the other, his anger growing. "The Temple merchants? In the courts of our God?"

Jonathan nodded. "We have tried to stop them."

"We cannot watch them constantly," Alexander explained.

Caiaphas glared at them. They were the sons of Annas, all right. When Caiaphas had become high priest, he had worked hard—but carefully—to introduce reform. He had not abolished the profitable Temple system; there was really no way to change the reality of things. Worshipers coming from a distance needed to be able to purchase animals for sacrifice rather than bringing a lamb or a bull from home. And by no means could offerings in the Temple be made with Roman coins, which bore the images of emperors or governors. But, of course, those obvious necessities had opened the door to great abuses during the tenures of Annas, Ismael, Eleazar, and Simon. Merchants charged exorbitant prices for sacrificial animals. Priests inspecting the animals that worshipers brought with them to the Temple seldom failed to find some blemish that made the animal unfit for sacrifice, forcing the worshiper to buy from the Temple merchants, who paid concessions from their profits to the high priest's family. The fees charged for exchanging Temple coins for Roman money were split between the money changers and the priesthood.

Caiaphas thought he had changed all that. He limited what the merchants and money changers could charge, and enforced the observance of the Levitical guidelines for the inspection of sacrificial animals. He knew he could not completely erase the scheme that enriched him and his wife's family, but he had hoped to make the necessary sacrificial system more fair and just while retaining its profitability. But he knew now that his brothers-in-law had actively circumvented his reforms and surreptitiously returned things to the way they were.

His gaze moved to the man who had produced that discovery. He must be some new rabbi—they were always springing up all over the countryside, like lilies of the field. Most of them incited interest *for a while—the people were always looking for something new, someone to follow, some ray of hope in their otherwise miserable lives.* But this one, *Caiaphas surmised,* this one seems to be different somehow. Cunning. *He nodded his head slowly. That was it. This new rabbi was smart. He had not done this insane thing out of mere emotion. He was not just picking a fight with the Temple authorities. He wasn't simply putting on a show. He had known exactly what he was doing. He had done what he did to gain the attention of the people, here a few days before Passover, when the news would spread rapidly, and the vast crowds of pilgrims would seek him out and gather around him to hear him teach.*

"We will speak of this later," he said finally to Jonathan and Alexander. "For now, go ask this man if he performs any miraculous signs to demonstrate his authority to do what he has done. And have the courts cleared of people, and this mess cleaned up."

He watched the sons of Annas walk away, and determined he would learn more of their intrigues, and of the clever man who had caused all that commotion.

68

THE OLD CITY, JERUSALEM

Tracy followed Carlos as closely as she could through the narrow alley. "Why are you walking so fast?" she asked.

"I have something to show you," he answered without slowing.

Tracy had no idea where they were, except she knew Carlos had parked the Land Rover outside the walls of Jerusalem's Old City, and they had been wandering in an endless maze of streets and shops and alleyways ever since. They walked on streets paved with rugged cobblestones, crowded with shops and stalls, people and handcarts. Many of the streets were too narrow to accommodate a motor vehicle other than a motor scooter, but somehow the merchants managed to truck in a vast variety of food, textiles, electronics, and tourist trinkets. Often Tracy not only lost all sense of direction but also couldn't decide whether she was outdoors or indoors as the awnings and roofs stretched over long sections of street.

"You're going too fast!" she complained.

"We are almost there," he said.

Finally Carlos slowed his pace and reached behind him to take her hand. He led her up a short series of steps and then around a corner, and suddenly Tracy stood on a balcony overlooking a broad, open square teeming with people. The square was bounded on two sides by buildings, and on a third side by a great stone wall. Beyond the wall rose a blue building with a shimmering gold dome.

"Oh," Tracy said, "I've seen pictures of this."

Carlos smiled, apparently pleased at her reaction. "It is the Western Wall, a very holy place for Jews. It is believed to be the only remnant of the Jewish Temple that was destroyed by the Romans."

"That was part of the Temple?" Tracy asked.

"No, not the Temple itself. That wall was part of the whole Temple complex. The Temple building actually stood where that building with the golden dome is now."

She nodded.

"Many Jews go to the wall every Friday afternoon," Carlos explained, "to pray and lament the destruction of the Temple. That is why some call it the Wailing Wall. It is also a popular place for weddings and bar mitzvahs."

"It's amazing," she said. "What's the deal with the fences?" The part of the square closest to the wall was enclosed by three-foot-high barriers.

"It is for the protection of the wall . . . and the people praying," he said. "There have been attacks."

"Really?"

"Yes. And the fence down the center of that area separates the men's side from the women's side. Jewish men and women pray separately."

They stayed for a few moments longer, and then Carlos asked if she was ready to go.

"Where to?" she asked.

He shrugged. "We will see!"

A few moments later they were once again weaving their way through narrow cobblestoned streets. As they turned down one lane, they were greeted by a dazzling array of multicolored tapestries, scarves, rugs, and clothing hanging over their heads and from the walls on both sides.

"Are we inside or outside?" Tracy asked.

"Yes," Carlos answered.

A heavily accented male voice called out, "Hello! Hello, Americans. Come see my store. I give you good deals."

Then another, "Come, come, I want to give you a present."

Tracy took Carlos's arm in both hands. "No, thank you," she said.

"Lo toda," Carlos said, echoing Tracy's "No, thank you" in Hebrew.

"Come, come," the shopkeeper insisted, blocking their way and pointing to his store. "My wife had a baby today and I want to celebrate."

"Lo toda," Carlos repeated as they skirted the man and kept walking.

"Come, let me rip you off!" Another shopkeeper

242

stepped out of his store, smiling broadly. "I cheat you good!"

Tracy laughed, released Carlos's arm, and darted into the store. She scanned the shelves of brass menorahs, wood carvings, and brass knickknacks, and spied a rack of skirts. The salesman followed her closely, jockeying to get closer to her than Carlos, but Carlos held his own. She pulled a long, green skirt from the rack.

"You like?" the salesman asked. "It will look beautiful with your eyes."

"How much?" she asked.

"For you, twenty-five dollars."

"Too much," Carlos said.

"No, no," the salesman insisted. "It is good price, for a very pretty lady."

Tracy shrugged and returned it to the rack. "I don't think so."

Carlos leaned close and whispered in her ear. "If you see something you like, don't say so. Just touch your nose or your ear, so I'll know."

She swallowed. His lips had brushed her ear, and it was the closest he'd been to her. "Okay," she said quietly.

She picked up another skirt, like the first, but blue. She glanced at Carlos and lifted a hand to tuck her hair behind her ear, the one Carlos had whispered in.

He gave her a tiny smile and took the skirt from her. "It is not the right color."

"This one I give you for twenty dollars," the salesman said.

Carlos frowned. "I can get it cheaper in Bethlehem."

"Bethlehem! It is not the same quality. Eighteen dollars."

Carlos shook his head and returned the skirt to the rack. "We'll keep looking." He took Tracy's hand and started to walk out.

They hadn't made it to the door of the shop when Tracy felt a hand on her shoulder. She turned. The man was pursuing them, with the skirt in his hand.

"Fifteen dollars," he said. "It is best price anywhere."

Carlos ignored the man and kept walking. Tracy followed him into the street.

The salesman wasn't giving up. "Okay," he said, "okay, I give it to you for twelve. Last offer."

"Lo toda," Carlos said, still walking away.

"Ten dollars!" the man pleaded. He had stopped, and now stood a few yards from his door with the skirt in his hand.

Tracy halted. "Oh, give me a break!" she said.

Carlos finally stopped, turned, and came back to stand beside Tracy. She turned and faced the salesman. "Ten dollars?" she said.

"Yes, yes, come," the man said. "Ten dollars. I never take so little."

She reached into her pocket, but Carlos put his mouth to her ear again. "Let me pay, okay?"

She flashed him a scornful expression. "Thanks, but I can pay for myself."

Their faces were almost touching as he whispered his response. "It's not just about the money, okay? It's a matter of honor with them, to drive a hard bargain and make a sale. It is like an arm-wrestling match—it is better to win against a man."

Tracy rolled her eyes. "That sounds totally chauvinistic."

He smiled. "It is."

She smiled back. "Well, okay," she said. "If it makes you both feel like big, strong men."

Carlos pulled out his money and turned to the merchant, shaking his head. "It is still too much," he said. "You drive a hard bargain." He handed the man ten dollars.

"Ach!" the salesman said. He took the money and turned over the skirt to Carlos.

Carlos handed the skirt to Tracy, who draped it over her arm as they turned to walk away. She looked behind her. The man still watched them. "Thank you," she called.

"You come back tomorrow," the salesman called back, smiling broadly. "I cheat you good!"

69

RAMAT RACHEL

Rand rubbed his eyes with both hands, as though waking from a dream. *What time is it?* Even as his eyes focused on the digital clock on the bedside table, his heart started beating a quick rhythm inside his chest.

Where is Tracy? Where has she been all this time? He'd assumed that she'd gone downstairs for a late breakfast, but she still hadn't returned, and he'd been too absorbed in his reading to mark the passage of time or . . . or give her a second thought.

He cursed, and berated himself as a selfish jerk. He grabbed his cell phone and dialed her number, but after several rings, his call went to voice mail. He tried again, with the same result, prompting another curse.

"Where could she be?" he said out loud. "If she did get up and get dressed . . . maybe she went to breakfast. Then what?"

He remembered: there was an Internet computer terminal in the hotel lobby. She might have gone to use that—and maybe lost track of time, as he had. "Please let that be where she is," he said aloud as he left the hotel room and headed for the elevator.

She wasn't there. He searched the dining room, largely empty except for an old couple in one corner who sat at a table and stared blankly out the windows. He checked the pool area, walking three times around the pool itself as he tried to make sure he didn't overlook a single swimmer or sunbather, but she wasn't there.

He walked back into the hotel, reasoning as he did that she could be back in the room by now, while he wandered the grounds looking for her. He reentered the hotel and followed the directional signs to the gift shop and beauty salon. He inquired at the spa and sports center. He stopped at the reception desk in the lobby and asked if there had been any messages left for him. Finally he walked out the hotel's front entrance and, standing at the edge of the circular drive, stared vacantly at his surroundings. After a few moments of that, he turned and went back into the hotel. As he traversed the long lobby, he pulled his cell phone from his pocket, dialed Tracy's number again, and listened as it rang.

"Hi, this is Tracy." It was her voice mail greeting—again. He hung up and headed for the elevators.

If she wasn't in the room when he got there, he didn't know what he would do. What if something had happened to her? What if she had gotten lost? What if she was alone, or in danger?

She would call, he thought. *She would call if she*

needed me. But what if she couldn't call? What if her phone battery was dead? Or what if she couldn't get a signal? Or . . . what if she was hurt or unconscious? Or . . .

I could use a drink, he thought. Fear rose in him, but not even the kind of fear he was accustomed to. It was a new feeling for him. For most of his daughter's life, he had been no more than a "secondary parent." Joy had always taken care of things on the home front while Rand was pursuing his career—and making a decent living, he reminded himself. When Tracy fell off her bike, Joy was there. When she got hit with a bat in softball practice, Joy was there. When her boyfriend broke up with her, Joy was there. When her mother died . . . no one was there.

Just a small drink, Rand promised. He wasn't sure he could think, otherwise.

He opened the door to the room. Tracy still hadn't returned. He strode to the phone on the table between the beds and punched the "0."

"Yes, shalom," he said when the operator or desk clerk answered. He paused for a moment. Thinking. Wrestling with himself. Finally he said, "I need the number for the police. I need to locate a Sergeant Major Miriam Sharon."

70

*Q*uickly! Come quickly!"

Caiaphas pried open his sleep-heavy eyelids and sat up on his luxurious mat. "What?" he complained. "What is it?"

His wife stood over him, a clay lamp in her hand. The flame from the oil-soaked wick in the lamp quivered as though it, too, wanted only to be left alone and allowed to return to darkness. "It's our sister, Miryam," she explained, referring to her brother's wife with the term Jews applied to close female relatives. "Come quickly!"

He groaned and lifted himself off the mat. He pulled a cloth off a wall peg, draped the cloth over his shoulders, and lumbered from his bedchamber. His wife, leaving the lamp burning in a nook in the wall, led him across their courtyard and through the gate.

"Slow down, wife!" he called out in the cool night air.

The Upper City that surrounded them housed the wealthiest citizens of Jerusalem in comfortably large homes enclosing luxurious courtyards. And except for the few Romans who lived close to the

249

governor's palace along the western wall of the city, Caiaphas and his father-in-law, Annas, were the wealthiest. Nearly as wealthy, however, was Jonathan, the eldest son of Annas, and it was his home that Caiaphas and Salome now entered.

"She is here," Salome said, leading the way into Jonathan and Miryam's bedchamber.

Jonathan sat cross-legged on the floor beside his wife, who lay on her sleeping mat. Jonathan didn't rise as Caiaphas and Salome entered, and didn't even acknowledge their arrival. He simply reached into the basin next to him and drew out a thin rag, wrung it out, and traded it for the cloth he removed from Miryam's forehead.

"Her fever," Jonathan said, as he dropped the cloth into the basin of water, "it gets worse. The moment I put the cloth on her forehead, it is no longer cool; the fever steals the moisture from the cloth like a—like a draft steals the flame from a candle. And yet the fever is no better, it only gets worse."

"Has the doctor come?" Salome asked.

"And left," he answered. He pulled back the thin sheet that covered her naked legs to reveal at least a dozen leeches attached to her thin limbs. "He said the leeches would suck the fever from her body." He covered her again. "But still she gets worse."

"Has she spoken?" Salome knelt beside her sister-in-law and felt her cheek.

"No," Jonathan said. "Even her dreams seem to

have stopped. She hasn't made a noise, not even the slightest groan, since you left. She hasn't moved. She—she hasn't moved at all." He reached back into the basin.

Salome looked at her husband, who had moved no closer since entering the dim room, lit only by the moonlight streaming in the square window at the top of the wall past Miryam's head. "What can be done?" she asked, her tone not pleading, but angry. "There must be something."

Caiaphas stared at his wife for a long moment, then turned his gaze on Miryam. As he looked at her still form, for some reason he thought of the rabbi, the man who had cleared the Temple courts less than a week earlier. Caiaphas had sent Malchus to watch him and find out what he could about the man, but there had really been no need. He was the talk of the town. All of Jerusalem had been buzzing about the teacher—from Galilee, it turned out!—who had "cleansed" the Temple. That's what they were saying: that he had cleansed the Temple, when in fact he had done no such thing. The merchants and money changers were back in operation the next day, protected by a full contingent of the Temple Guard. No one talked about that, however; the people were amazed that the rabbi had done such a thing and escaped arrest or punishment of any kind.

But that was far from the only thing Caiaphas had learned from Malchus. It was reported that *this rabbi not only taught with great authority, but also that he had performed miracles, right there, in the shadow of the Lord's Temple. Malchus said he had seen the man take a sick baby, crying and flushed with fever, from a mother's arms and lovingly cradle the child until the crying stopped, the fever abated, and a healthy color returned to the child's face.*

A strange mixture of hope and dread suddenly came over Caiaphas as he stared at his prone sister-in-law, recalling not only the incident at the Temple and Malchus's subsequent report, but also the words of the prophet Malachi:

"See, I will send my messenger, who will prepare the way before me. Then suddenly the Lord you are seeking will come to his temple; the messenger of the covenant, whom you desire, will come," says the Lord Almighty.

"But who can endure the day of his coming? Who can stand when he appears? For he will be like a refiner's fire or a launderer's soap . . . he will purify the Levites and refine them like gold and silver. Then the Lord will have men who will bring offerings in righteousness, and the offerings of Judah and Jerusalem will be acceptable to the Lord, as in days gone by, as in former years."

Caiaphas felt cold, clammy. Perhaps he had been mistaken. Perhaps the reported healings were real, and Malchus had observed the power of God at work. Had not the prophet also said, "The sun of righteousness will arise with healing in his wings"? Could that truly be happening? What if the man who had come to the Temple with such a vengeance and healed people with such tenderness was Miryam's only hope? What if he could heal her, even after the doctor had given up?

"Husband!" Salome's imperious voice shattered his trance. "Can nothing be done?"

Miryam's situation was grave, he knew that. But he was not only her close relation; he also was the high priest of the Most High God. He had a grave responsibility to the flock of Israel. He couldn't just invite this so-called healer into his sister's bed-chamber. What if the man was a charlatan? What if word got out that Caiaphas had called on him to work a miracle for the daughter-in-law of Annas, the wife of Annas's son? People would say the high priest was among the man's followers! Such a thing could have dire consequences. The whole nation could be led astray.

He exhaled slowly, only now realizing he'd long been holding his breath. "No," he said, flatly. He met his wife's imploring gaze. "Nothing can be done."

71

THE OLD CITY, JERUSALEM

I'm hungry," Tracy said.

"I am, too," Carlos said. "And I know the perfect place. But I would like to show you one thing more."

"Aren't we lost again?" she asked. They had twisted and turned through the labyrinthine streets of the Old City all afternoon, and Carlos had several times admitted that he wasn't sure which way to go. But each time, they had continued wandering until Carlos found his bearings, and they resumed their journey.

"Yes," he answered, "but we will soon be found again."

They held hands as they walked. It had started as Carlos leading Tracy up steps and through alleys, as he showed her the Church of the Holy Sepulchre (the traditional site of Jesus' tomb), the Ecce Homo Church (where they saw stones from a Roman street Jesus may have walked on), and "the Cardo," the main street of Jerusalem during Roman times. But sometime during the afternoon, he had simply stopped releasing her hand when they reached their various destinations.

They had eaten a pizza lunch in the Jewish

Quarter (one of the four divisions of the Old City, along with the Christian Quarter, Muslim Quarter, and Armenian Quarter). At one point when they had turned a corner and entered a narrow street, Tracy spied the side of a cow hanging beside her at the same moment she felt her feet slip on the stone pavement and looked down into a stream of bloody water. She covered her mouth, struggling to control her nausea, and noticed chickens, sheep heads, and other grisly displays of meat lining the street.

Heroically, Carlos wrapped his arms around her shoulders. "Close your eyes," he said, "and put your head on my shoulder." He spun them both around and headed back in the direction they had come, explaining calmly but apologetically that he hadn't realized they were so close to the Butchers' Street, and he was sorry for leading her that way.

Tracy recovered quickly, but her appetite had disappeared for the rest of the afternoon . . . until now, when she realized she was hungry.

"Can you wait another hour for dinner?" Carlos asked.

"I think so," she answered.

A few moments later they were leaving the Armenian Quarter through the Zion Gate, which still bore countless bullet marks from the intense battle around the gate in Israel's 1948 War for Independence. A moment later, Carlos was paying someone for admission to a limestone building.

"What's this place?" Tracy asked.

"It is an ancient house in what used to be called the Upper City of Jerusalem."

"How do you know all this?"

He shrugged and squeezed her hand. "I pay attention."

"So why was it so important for you to bring me here?"

"Dr. Havner said one of the inscriptions in the tomb may refer to Caiaphas, the high priest at the time of Jesus' trial and crucifixion."

She nodded. "Right," she said tentatively.

"Well, you know those stone steps outside, the steps we walked down to get to this building?"

"Yes," she said.

"They were almost certainly used by Jesus on his way to and from this place."

"Wow," she said. "What is this place?"

"It is not what it *is,* but what it *was,* that is important."

"All right, then," she said, feigning frustration. "What *was* this place?"

He smiled and gestured to the walls surrounding them. "The house of Caiaphas," he said.

72

гамат гаснеL

Rand paced the lobby, waiting for Miri Sharon to arrive. His call to her had been awkward, especially as he had struggled to explain that Tracy had been gone for hours.

"When did you discover she was gone?" Miri had asked.

"I came back to the room this morning, a little after ten."

"She was gone then?"

"Yes," he had said. "But I didn't think anything of it because I had assumed she'd gone to eat breakfast or something like that."

"When did you realize you were mistaken?" she had asked.

That's where Rand seemed to lose all coherence, as he tried to describe the process of becoming immersed in research and losing track of time and then searching the hotel for her and the more he talked the more he felt like the worst possible father. He was sure, from Miri's silence on the other end of the line, that she agreed.

She finally pulled up in her blue-and-white police car and parked in thc circle, behind a tour bus that had disgorged its passengers moments earlier. He met her at the door.

"Thank you so much for coming," he said.

She scanned the lobby and indicated a set of chairs. When they were both seated, she crossed her tanned legs and leaned forward. "I am willing to help you," she said, "but I am not an investigator."

"That's okay," he said. "I wanted you."

"Why?"

He blinked. "Why?"

"Why?" she repeated.

"Well," he said, "I suppose . . . because I know you. I didn't know who else to call."

She nodded. "All right. Do you have a photograph of her?"

He reached for his wallet and froze. "No," he said. "I don't think I do."

"On your computer, perhaps?"

He shook his head ruefully. "No."

"Perhaps one of the photographs taken at the excavation site?"

He cocked his head and thought for a moment, then slowly shook his head from side to side. "No," he said. "Once she arrived, she took all the photos."

A pause. "Do you know where she might have gone?"

He shook his head.

"Do you know what she was wearing?"

He ran a hand over his short-cropped hair. "No," he said. "No idea."

"What things did you talk about most recently?"

He searched his memory. "We really haven't talked since . . . since we last saw you."

Her eyebrows arched. "That was . . . nearly two days ago."

"She was asleep when I got home that night, and I worked all day Saturday. She slept a lot." He couldn't bring himself to look her in the eye. "I think the jet lag finally caught up to her."

"If you don't have a photograph, and she didn't discuss going anywhere, and you don't know where she might have gone . . . where do you suggest we start?"

He propped his elbows on his knees and dropped his face into his hands. "I don't know," he said. "I'm sorry, I don't know what to tell you."

She reached out a hand and touched his forearm. Neither of them said anything for a few moments until Miri broke the silence. "Does she have any friends or family in Israel? Someone she might visit?"

He shook his head without raising it from the cradle of his hands.

She lifted her hand from its position on his forearm and leaned back in her chair. They sat in silence.

Finally Rand lifted his head. "I'm sorry for dragging you out here like this," he said. "I just don't know what to do."

73

THE OLD CITY, JERUSALEM

Tracy and Carlos entered the Armenian Tavern at number 79 on Armenian Orthodox Patriarchate Road in Jerusalem's Old City.

As they descended a short staircase into the restaurant, Tracy felt again the sensation she had experienced several times that day: of leaving the twenty-first century and stepping back in time. The restaurant's vaulted ceiling soared overhead, evidence of the structure's history as a Crusader church. A large chandelier hung from the ceiling, and an aged water fountain gurgled in the room, the stone walls of which were decorated with colorful Armenian tiles. The unmatched tables and chairs looked like they could have been crafted centuries earlier.

When the waiter had helped them order their meal from the Armenian fare on the menu, Tracy leaned across the table and said, "Explain to me what I just saw."

Carlos thought for a moment. "Okay, yes," he said. "Some Armenian food is similar to Turkish food, but not if you are Turkish or Armenian."

"Not the menu," she said. "I meant the house of Caiaphas."

"Oh," he said slowly. "Right. What do you want to know?"

"Was it really the house of Caiaphas?"

He shrugged. "Very likely. At various times through history, the people of this area marked a certain spot in that area as the house of Caiaphas. Some years ago, a construction project uncovered the remains of that house we were in today."

"Like a construction project uncovered the tomb."

He nodded. "It happens very often around here. Jerusalem has been on the same site for thousands of years. And the city has been destroyed many times over those years, and each time it was destroyed, people rebuilt it on the ruins of the former city. So there are layers upon layers of civilization beneath our feet. If you were to dig through this floor, right here, right now, you would certainly discover some remains of people who lived and died here long ago."

The waiter filled a small water glass for each of them from a glass pitcher. "But," she said, "when that house was discovered, how did people know it was the house of Caiaphas? Just because it was in the general area where people said Caiaphas used to live?"

He shook his head. "No, it was because the archaeologists also discovered the remains of an ancient church, called the Church of the Apostles, that historical records say once existed on the site of the high priest's house. Many pilgrims to the

Holy Land reported visiting that church in the first two hundred years or so after the time of Jesus, and they describe a church built over the place where Caiaphas once lived."

"And tell me again, when we went down those stone steps—"

"That was the dungeon Jesus would have been kept in the night he was interrogated by Caiaphas and the Sanhedrin."

"There were no steps back then, right?"

He nodded again. "That is right. No steps and no lights. The hole at the top was very likely the only way a prisoner could get in or out, by being lowered or lifted with a rope."

Their food began to arrive. It seemed to arrive in waves, until their small table disappeared under a multitude of dishes and bowls. The conversation suspended for a few moments, and the waiter introduced each dish, in a heavily accented voice that Tracy struggled to understand. When the waiter left, Carlos reached across the table and laid his hand on top of Tracy's hand.

"Would it make you uncomfortable if I gave thanks for our food?" he asked. When she smiled shyly and shook her head, he wrapped his fingers around her hand.

She closed her eyes and bowed her head as he prayed, "Thank you, our God, for the food that is ours to enjoy . . . and the . . . and the lovely woman I have to enjoy it with. Amen."

She lifted her head and gazed at him. He still hadn't released her hand. "Who *are* you?" she asked.

He blinked. He removed his hand from holding hers and moved his napkin from the table to his lap. "I do not know what you mean."

Neither of them had touched their food yet. "I'm not used to this," she said.

"What are you not used to?"

"You've been so nice to me. You're so polite. And it's like you know everything, like you're . . ." She shook her head and pursed her lips. "It's like you're too good to be true."

He smiled. "I'm sorry," he said teasingly.

"I mean it," she said. "I don't think I've ever met anyone like you."

"Is this a bad thing?"

"Every time in my life when something seemed too good to be true, it always was."

"Do you mean it was not good? Or not true?"

"Both," she said.

His expression changed, and his countenance became serious. "If you will eat your food," he said, "I will tell you the truth about me. And you can decide whether it is good . . . or not."

74

ramat rachel

Rand suddenly stood and faced Miri Sharon as a large group of Japanese tourists flowed past him in the lobby. "Where would she go?" he asked. "Where *could* she go? She doesn't have a car, so if she left the hotel grounds alone, where could she have gone?"

"She could go anywhere," Miri answered.

"No," he said. "You don't understand. I mean, what direction would a nineteen-year-old American girl—on foot—take? How many realistic choices would she have? Is there a—a mall or shopping district nearby? Is there—I don't know—someplace she would go to get her hair done?"

"There is a salon in the hotel," she reminded him. "And shops. There would be no reason for her to go somewhere else."

His eyes flamed. "But if she did"—he pointed out the lobby doors, his voice rising—"if she did leave the hotel, where would she go?"

"There is no way to answer that question, Dr. Bullock. You have driven to this hotel many times. You know it is on top of a hill. The roads to Ramat Rachel come through residential neighborhoods, and a nineteen-year-old American, like anyone, would have to walk for a kilometer or maybe two kilometers before finding anything that is not available in the hotel."

"But there has to be some way to figure this out!" he insisted loudly. He ran a hand over the top of his head. "I don't know where my daughter is!"

Miri planted herself directly in front of him. "Dr. Bullock," she said sternly. Though she was four inches shorter than he, she intentionally reinforced her authority by stepping closer until their bodies almost touched. She glared into his eyes without blinking. "Please sit down."

He leaned slightly backward and blinked for a few moments, surprised at the change in her demeanor. Finally, however, he frowned and, glaring back at her, said, "All right." He sat in the same spot he had risen from a few moments earlier.

"I will do my best to help you," she explained calmly. "And I understand you are worried, but—"

"I want to find my daughter," he said. "I feel like I need to go looking for her."

"That is the last thing you need to do. You need to be here in case she returns."

He considered that. "You're right," he said, casting a wishful glance toward the front doors.

She snapped her fingers, as though an idea had suddenly occurred to her. "Have you looked in your room for her passport?"

His face registered surprise. "No," he said. "You think she may try to leave the country?"

"No," she answered. "I mean, for the photograph."

"Oh, of course," he said.

"Go to your room," she said. "I will wait here to watch for her. If you can find her passport, I will alert the hotel management to help us by showing her photograph to every employee. Perhaps she is still in the hotel, and someone will recognize her. Or perhaps someone saw her leave."

"Good," he said. He started for the elevators.

"Oh, and Dr. Bullock," she said.

He turned. "Yes?"

"May I have your cell phone?"

"My cell phone?"

"Yes," she answered.

"Why?"

She smiled patiently. "I promise to give it back."

He pulled the phone from his pocket and handed it to her. "What do you need it for?"

"It will take time for me to explain and, right now, time is more important than an explanation. Do you agree?"

"Yes, okay," he said. "Of course." He turned and headed quickly in the direction of the elevators.

75

*J*onathan the son of Annas was never a cheerful man, but since the death of his wife, Miryam, the previous year, he had become increasingly morose, and even more unpleasant to be around than he had been before. So when Caiaphas saw his brother-in-law approaching across the Court of the Gentiles, he braced himself for a long and gloomy harangue about the state of the sheep pens or the condition of the sheep pool.

Instead, Jonathan brought news. *"The Galilean rabbi you are so interested in,"* he said. *"He is at the Pool of Bethesda."*

The Pool of Bethesda, though not visible from where they stood because of the porticoes that surrounded them on every side, was nonetheless close by. The pool, surrounded by five colonnaded porches in the style of the same Herodian architects as the Temple precincts, was a popular gathering place for multitudes of sick, blind, lame, and paralyzed people. Many people believed that the waters of the pool, which was fed by underground springs, had healing powers. If a true miracle worker wanted to display his powers, there could be no better place to go than the Pool of Bethesda.

Caiaphas opened his mouth to speak, but reconsidered. He chose his words carefully when speaking to Jonathan, especially since the death of Miryam. Jonathan knew that Caiaphas awaited the coming of Messiah, but made no secret of his disdain for such optimism. "What is he doing?"

Jonathan sneered. "Nothing," he said. "I watched him for a good long while. He just stood there, with his talmidim *surrounding him, looking at all those miserable people like a shepherd tending his sheep."*

"He has not healed anyone?"

"On the Sabbath? No. He gave no sign that he planned to do anything."

"Then why is he there?"

Jonathan shrugged as if to say, Who knows?

Caiaphas nodded slowly, trying to hide his impatience. He had sometimes contemplated the scene at the Pool of Bethesda and thought, When Messiah comes, he will make these people whole! He will fulfill his word through Jeremiah when he said, "I will restore your health and heal your wounds. . . . I will restore the fortunes of Judah and Israel and will rebuild their cities." He will instantaneously turn the crippled and blind into warriors of righteousness! He will destroy those who attacked us, and exile those who sent us into exile! *If the man from Galilee were truly sent from God, of course he would go to the pool!*

"I am finished here," he told his brother-in-law. "I think it's time that I go see this man for myself."

Jonathan fell into step behind Caiaphas as he started toward the porch and the marble staircase leading to the Sheep Gate. He had barely gone ten steps, however, when he noticed a clot of people, Pharisees mostly, engaged in animated conversation. This was no surprise, for the Pharisees seemed always to be engaged in animated conversation.

But it was some of their words that reached his ears that made him stop. He turned his attention toward the group.

"It is the Sabbath!" one of them was saying.

"You profane the Law of Moses!" another one added.

Caiaphas moved in closer to see what the commotion was about, and he saw a little man standing on scrawny white legs in the middle of the circle, holding a sleeping mat under his right arm.

The man with the bedroll stared up at them with a dazed expression. "The man who healed me said to me, 'Pick up your sleeping mat and walk.' "

"Who?" several demanded at once.

"Who told you that?" another asked.

"I didn't ask him for his name," the man said.

"No one would say such a thing as that," one of them said.

Caiaphas stepped into the group. He felt his skin tingling as he approached the man. "Do you know who I am?"

His eyes widened as he took in the rich clothing Caiaphas wore. "You are the Kohen haGadol," he answered in an awed voice.

"It is as you say." A full six inches taller than the man, Caiaphas looked on him with sympathy. When he spoke again, his tone was like a man speaking to a child. "The man who healed you—did he heal others?"

He blinked. "I don't know."

"If you saw him again, would you recognize him?"

"Oh, yes. I could never forget him."

"Good," Caiaphas said. "If you see him again, would you come to me, or to this man"—he indicated Jonathan, standing over his left shoulder—"and tell us who he is?"

The man nodded slowly, looking at the faces all around him before returning his gaze to Caiaphas. "Yes," he said.

"But you are not simply walking through the Temple courts to get to the other side, are you? You know it is disrespectful."

"The Temple of Hashem is not a convenience for travelers!" one of the Pharisees scolded.

"Oh, no, Your Excellency," the former cripple said, ignoring the scolding and addressing himself to Caiaphas. His expression had changed from dazed to passionate. "I have come to the Temple to give thanks to Hashem, blessed be he."

"Amen," Caiaphas said as a few Pharisees joined in the obligatory answer.

270

"But you must not carry your bed," one of them said. "It is a disgrace."

"It is a sin!" someone else added.

The man peered around at the circle of faces. "For thirty-eight years," he said, his voice thick with emotion, "this mat has carried me. Sabbath or not, it is not the slightest burden for me to carry it instead."

76

THE OLD CITY, JERUSALEM

I am from Turkey, you know that already," Carlos said as Tracy dived in to her dinner. "My name is not originally Carlos."

"It's not?"

"No," he said, shaking his head. "I was born as Kiral Ergul in the village of Elkondu, in the Sivas Province, which is the second-largest province in all of Turkey. My earliest memories are of my mother waking me before dawn to take our family's cows to pasture, wherever there was much grass, and of returning home every evening in time for my father to beat me before it was time for bed."

Tracy stopped chewing and hid her mouth with her hand. "Every night?" she asked, her tone incredulous. "He beat you every night? Why?"

271

Carlos shrugged. "Because his father beat him, perhaps. Or it may have been because I was the only son he would ever have—my mother could have no more children after me—and he wanted more sons. Or better sons. I do not know which."

"Did he drink?" Tracy asked.

"Oh, yes. And he was often drunk. But sober or drunk, it didn't matter. He beat me just the same."

"That's so horrible, Carlos."

Another shrug. "For many years I simply thought this was how all fathers treated their sons."

"How old were you?"

"This happened from the time I was too young to remember."

Tracy shook her head slowly. "Wow," she said. "That's so sad. I mean, I've never had much of a relationship with my father, but at least he never beat me." She lost herself in thought for a few moments, wondering if she should feel some gratitude, at least, for the father she had. Though he was pretty much a stranger to her, at least he was a benign stranger for the most part. She thought maybe she should feel some appreciation for that fact, but couldn't seem to summon any.

"Eat," he reminded her. "It is good food, no?"

"It is very good," she agreed as she dipped her fork in her food.

"I ran away when I was ten years old," he continued. "I had hidden away some food and clothes in the cow shed, and one night when my father came home drunk, I took money from his pocket and left Elkondu forever."

"Ten years old?" Her phone chirped as she was asking the question. She picked it from her shorts pocket and read the display. She rolled her eyes and returned the phone to her pocket. "Where did you go?" she asked.

"Sivas, the city that is the capital of Sivas Province. I was so hungry by the time I arrived in the city, but young as I was, I knew if I spent my money on food, I would have nothing to buy more when the food was gone. But I had enough to buy a pack of American cigarettes, which I sold on the streets and in the cafés, one by one. When the cigarettes were all sold, I bought more, and sold them."

"What did you do for food?"

He smiled. "For the first few weeks, I ate only what the street vendors and restaurants threw away. But little by little, I began to do better, until I was selling cigarettes, newspapers, and water in the streets near the train station in the mornings and in the government district in the afternoons." He paused. "You have stopped eating again."

"Oh," she said, shaking her head slightly. "I'm sorry. I just can't believe all this."

"You do not believe me?" he asked.

"No, I believe you," she said. "I mean it's—I don't know, it's just—I mean, I'm so sorry you had to go through all that."

"Oh, do not be sorry," he said. "I mean, I know

it is a terrible thing for a father to mistreat his son as I was mistreated. But I am not sorry. If my father had not treated me so poorly, I would not have run away. If I had not run away, I would not have gone to Sivas. And if I had not gone to Sivas, I would not have met Dr. Carlos."

77

*H*is name is Yeshua."

Caiaphas turned. It was the man who had been carrying his sleeping mat. Though only an hour or two had passed since their first encounter, Caiaphas would not have recognized him. He seemed transformed. Caiaphas thought he may even have grown by several inches!

"Yeshua," the high priest said.

"Yes. Yeshua of Nazareth."

Caiaphas considered that. "Thank you," he said. "So you have seen him?"

"Yes, Your Excellency. He found me in the outer courts and told me, 'Now that you are well, stop sinning, that nothing worse will come upon you.'"

He thought for a moment, then said, "And your sleeping mat? Have you lost it?"

"No, Your Excellency." The man bowed his

head, as though embarrassed. "I left it in the Temple as a thank offering."

Caiaphas smiled. The man's sincerity was touching. "And Yeshua—where is he now?"

The man turned slightly in the direction of the Royal Portico behind him. "He is on the teaching steps near the Triple Gate."

He thanked the man and headed toward the Royal Portico without hurrying. The high priest of Israel did not hurry.

78

ramat rachel

Rand finally located Tracy's passport in the side pocket of a suitcase. He had no reason to doubt that it was hers, but nonetheless flipped it open and checked the photo before heading out of the room. Moments later, waving the passport like a flag at a Fourth of July parade, he approached Miri Sharon in the lobby.

"You received a call," she told him. She held his cell phone in her hand.

"Tracy?" he asked.

"No," she said. "It was from someone at the Center for Conservation and Restoration."

"The Center for—oh," Rand said. It had to be Dr. Jacques Elon, about the scroll.

"I asked him to call back and leave a message on your voice mail," she explained.

"Okay, sure," he said. "That's fine. What about Tracy?"

"Is that her passport?"

He only then realized he still held her passport. "Yes," he said. He thrust it at Miri, who traded him the passport for his cell phone.

She opened the passport. "I will give this to the hotel manager and ask him to make copies of her photograph and send as many staff members as possible around the hotel—in the restaurant, the swimming pool, the spa, everywhere—to ask if anyone has seen her."

"Good," Rand said.

"While I am doing that, you try to call her. I tried to reach her a few minutes ago, using your phone, but there was no answer. I would like for you to call her number every three minutes."

Rand watched her long-legged stride to the lobby desk, then opened his phone and pressed Tracy's number. It rang three times before switching to voice mail. He closed it and noted the time on the phone's digital display. As he did, the phone vibrated and displayed the notification box indicating that he had just received a voice mail message.

He ignored it.

79

D r. Carlos," Tracy repeated.
"Yes," he answered. "From the beginning, I was so much happier in Sivas than I had been in my village. For the first time in my life I knew the pleasure of going to bed without a beating and going to sleep without pain. For the first time in my life I felt that I was going somewhere instead of taking the cows out each morning and bringing them in each night, one day after the other, with no purpose and no hope."

"But you were ten years old!" Tracy protested. "You should have been, I don't know, going to school and playing tag and riding bikes."

He smiled. "Yes, perhaps. But instead, my friends were merchants and imams and government officials, people much older than I was, and they taught me many things, more than I could ever have learned in a village school. And that was especially true after I met Dr. Carlos, the man who introduced me to the love of God."

Tracy felt a tiny tingle at the base of her neck but said nothing. She felt Carlos watching her even more closely than before. "Was he a . . . minister?"

He shook his head. "He was a doctor. He bought

277

newspapers from me. He learned my name. He asked where I was from. And little by little, I told him my story. And little by little, he told me his story. And little by little, we became friends, Dr. Carlos and I."

Tracy's phone chirped again. She pulled it impatiently from her pocket and read the display. "Sorry," she said. She set it on the table beside her plate. "Go on."

He nodded at the phone. "It is okay."

She picked it up, flipped it open, and turned it off. "There. No more interruptions," she said.

He smiled. "What was I saying? Oh, yes, Dr. Carlos. He told me about God, and his love for me. And he taught me how to read, using the Bible. Because of him, you understand, I became a follower of Jesus in Sivas. So why would I ever be sorry for coming to Sivas? You see?"

Tracy nodded.

"And when I learned to read, I started to read also the newspapers I was selling, because newspapers sell better when you tell people what is inside, when you give them a reason to buy. And when I started reading the newspaper, I learned that there were universities all over Turkey where a person could study many things, and I decided, *That's what I want to do.*"

"You were living on the streets and selling cigarettes to feed yourself, and you thought, 'Gee, I think I want to go to college'?"

278

"No, not exactly like that." He smiled.

"How old were you then?" she asked.

He cocked his head thoughtfully to one side. "Perhaps twelve," he said. "Yes, I think that is right. Twelve years old."

"But doesn't college cost money in Turkey?" she asked. "It costs *a lot* in America."

"Oh, yes, it costs money." He leaned closer to her. "I did not know how much, but you understand, I had been learning more and more about how to make money and how to save money and how to use money to make more money. So with help from Dr. Carlos, I put together a plan. There is a university in Sivas, but I decided not to go there. I decided I wanted to go to Istanbul, it is the largest city in Turkey, about seven hundred kilometers from Sivas, a great distance for a twelve-year-old boy to travel.

"But, you understand, I had been selling my cigarettes and newspapers and water at the train station for more than two years by this time, and I knew many people, many friends. So instead of buying an expensive train ticket to Istanbul, I was hired to assist the cabin stewards, and was also allowed to sell my American cigarettes to passengers during my breaks."

Tracy laid down her fork and lifted her water glass.

"Are you finished with your dinner?" he asked.

She nodded as she drank.

"Then it is time for dessert!" he announced.

"No," she protested, setting down her glass. "I couldn't possibly eat anything more."

He reached across the table and took her hand in his. "I have talked too much."

"No," she said. "I'm fascinated. I want to hear more."

"But our meal is coming to an end."

"I don't care. I can't believe you could possibly make enough money to go to college by selling cigarettes."

He shrugged carelessly. "It was not cigarettes alone, and it grew to become much more. I started in Istanbul the same way I started in Sivas, investing all the money I had saved into merchandise, and spending almost nothing on myself. I knew it would be hard to learn enough to pass the entrance exam, but even if I managed to do that, I knew it would be even harder to make enough money to pay for tuition and books. But I was determined. I made up my mind that I would go to university even if it took me ten years to become accepted." He smiled. "It took me four."

"Four years?"

He nodded. "I made good money in Istanbul, and saved almost all of what I earned. So I was able to enroll at Istanbul University when I was sixteen years old."

"Sixteen?"

"It took me longer than other university students

to finish, because I had to keep my businesses going while I was also studying. I had time to sleep only four hours a night most of the time. But when I finished university, I was able to sell my businesses and leave the country for a paid internship with the great Yigal Havner."

"Your *businesses?*"

Tracy thought she sensed a little sheepishness when Carlos answered, "Yes. At the time I finished university, I owned a small store—very small—and three street carts. That is how I paid for my books and classes."

She shook her head and gazed at Carlos with open admiration. "You're amazing," she said.

"I have tried very hard to make you think so," he answered, smiling.

80

a.d. 29
THE TEMPLE MOUNT, JERUSALEM

Yeshua from Galilee was not the only rabbi seated on the steps at the southern entrance to the Temple, but he was surrounded by the largest—and most contentious—crowd. Caiaphas approached, slowly and cautiously, hoping not to draw attention to himself.

"You admit to healing on the Sabbath!" a

Pharisee—one wearing particularly long tassels on his tallith—shouted angrily.

"Why do you perform work on the Sabbath?" asked another.

"My Father never stops working," the rabbi responded, "so neither do I."

The words stopped Caiaphas in his tracks. The Galilean had referred to Hashem—he whose name is too holy to be uttered—as his Father! He shook his head with frustration. If the man was truly healing people, and not a mere pretender, why would he say such a thing?

Caiaphas stepped closer, and saw the teacher on the steps. It was, as he had assumed, the man who had attacked the merchants and money changers at last year's feast. Since that time, the priest had heard regular reports of a new rabbi and miracle worker, but the reports were mixed. He had heard of a man who had healed many people and performed exorcisms, but some reports also said he had healed the son of one of Herod's officials. The same man, supposedly, had begun assembling talmidim—student followers—like any rabbi, but one of them had reportedly been a tax collector! He had caused no small sensation teaching in the synagogues all around Galilee, but had been forcibly driven out of the synagogue in his hometown of Nazareth—and very nearly stoned—for his inflammatory words, something about Hashem showing kindness to Gentiles. And worst of all, *this was happening in the hinterlands of Galilee.*

None of it made any sense to Caiaphas. It seemed that the news that came to him about this man from Galilee simultaneously raised his hopes and dashed them. The man confirmed Caiaphas's expectations . . . and then immediately contradicted them. One report had Caiaphas believing that the Day had come, and the next had him exasperated at the man from Galilee's penchant for saying and doing exactly the wrong thing.

Now that same man (Caiaphas was reasonably sure) sat on the Temple steps, surrounded by the rustics Caiaphas assumed were his talmidim, curious onlookers, and a gaggle of sneering Pharisees like the group that had crowded around the man from the Pool of Bethesda.

"I give you my word," Yeshua was saying, "the Son can do nothing by himself. He acts in unison with the Father, and does exactly what he sees the Father doing. What the Father does, the Son does. For the Father is in such loving unity with the Son that he tells him everything he is doing, and the Son will do much greater things than healing this man. You will be amazed at what the Son does. He will even bring the dead to life, just as the Father does."

Standing on the fringe of the crowd in his elegant robes, Caiaphas could not believe his ears. These were not the words of a respectable rabbi. This was not at all how the rabbis taught. This man seemed to be saying things no sane man would ever say. Was he speaking of himself—or someone else?

"In fact, I give you my word," he continued, "that all those who listen to what I say and believe in him who sent me have been raised from the dead. They have escaped condemnation and entered into eternal life, passing from death into life."

Caiaphas bristled. Sadducees didn't believe in an afterlife; they believed men needed to make the most of this life, because it was all they were given. This rabbi obviously didn't care about gaining the support of the powerful priestly party.

"And I give you my word also that the day is coming—in fact, it is here—when the dead will hear my voice, the voice of the Son of God. And those who listen will live. The Father is pure life, and he has granted his Son to hold life in his hands, and has given him authority to judge all the living because he is the Son of Man."

Caiaphas felt his heart beating wildly, and knew he was not alone in his extreme reaction to the rabbi's words, as the Pharisees—and some of the others—erupted in exclamations of shock and indignation.

"Don't be so surprised!" the man from Galilee said, calmly but authoritatively. He swept his hand to indicate the tombs that proliferated throughout the Kidron Valley below them. "In fact, the day is *coming when all the dead in their graves will hear the voice of God's Son, and they will rise again. Those who have done good will rise to eternal life, and those who have continued in evil will rise to judgment. But I do nothing on my own; I judge as I am told, and my judgment is perfectly righteous, because it comes out of my unity with the Father, who sent me."*

Someone in the back of the crowd shouted something. Caiaphas didn't hear exactly what was said, but apparently Yeshua did, for he seemed to lift his chin and speak in the direction from which the voice had come.

"If I am the only one offering testimony on my own behalf, then of course my testimony would be invalid; everyone knows that. But there is another who is testifying about me, and I can assure you that everything he says is true. Not only that, but let me remind you of John the Immerser. You sent messengers to listen to him, and what he said is also true. But the greatest testimony about me is not from a man—I simply remind you about John's testimony so you might not continue in darkness. John was a lamp that lit the way for you, and you recognized and rejoiced in that light. But I have even a greater witness than John, the witness of my teachings and my miracles, the things my Father has assigned for me to do, and they testify that the Father has sent me—which he himself confirmed, but you could neither hear his voice nor see his

form, and so you do not have his message in your hearts, because you do not believe me—the one he sent to you.

"You search the Scriptures," he continued, his tone becoming plaintive, "because you believe they hold the secret of eternal life—and they do, because the Scriptures all point to me! But you refuse to come to me, and so cheat yourselves out of eternal life."

At those words, the Pharisees in the crowd became derisive, hurling loud protests and objections not only at the rabbi, but also at those who stood around, mesmerized, as Caiaphas was, by this man's words. But their vehemence seemed not to move the teacher at all; he simply watched them, serenely waiting for their vitriol to abate. When it did, he continued.

"I'm not trying to gain your approval, because I know you don't have God's love in your hearts. After all, I have come to you on my Father's behalf, and you reject me, even though you readily accept others who come only on their behalf. No wonder you can't believe! You go to great pains to honor each other, but you care nothing at all for the honor that comes from God alone.

"I won't even be the one to accuse you of this before the Father; Moses himself will accuse you!"

Caiaphas's jaw dropped open, and the Pharisees were so enraged they seemed sure to attack the rabbi right there, in front of the crowd and the Temple itself.

"Who do you think you are?" they shouted.

"You transgress the Law of Moses, and you dare to accuse us?"

"He is a lawbreaker!" another said.

"He calls Hashem his Father!"

"And breaks the Sabbath!"

"How dare you speak to us of Moses!"

But he continued, while they still shouted, raising his voice now to be heard over their outrage. "Yes, I speak to you of Moses," he said, "whom you say you regard so highly. But if you truly believed Moses, you would have believed me, because he also testified about me. If you don't believe what he said, how will you believe what I say?"

The shouts and protests erupted again, and Caiaphas turned away from the verbal melee the man from Galilee had instigated. His head was spinning, and he needed to think, away from the crowds, away from the Temple, away from it all.

It was maddening, the way this man spoke. He spoke with such authority, and such clarity, that it was clear he was not mad. And when he had spoken of John the Immerser, Caiaphas suddenly knew that it was this man Nicodemus had seen immersed in the Jordan. And apparently his miracles had been witnessed by many.

Caiaphas shook his head in consternation as he traversed Brook Kidron and ambled into the *garden called Gethsemane. If this man was from Hashem, if the stories of his miracles were true, wouldn't he be uniting the Jews instead of dividing them? Wouldn't he be preaching against Rome instead of accusing Pharisees? If he were truly sent from God, he would certainly have much more sense than to tell a crowd of Pharisees, to their face!, that Moses—Moses, whom Pharisees and Sadducees alike revered, but Pharisees more so because of their fanatical adherence to the Law— would accuse them! It was ludicrous. It was dangerous. It would be like . . .*

Caiaphas searched for a fitting parallel. It would be like . . .

And then, suddenly, he knew. Yes, he thought, turning and facing the gleaming white limestone facade of the majestic Temple Mount. It would be like coming into the Temple courts . . . and telling a group of Sadducees that they have demeaned the House of God by making it into a marketplace.

81

ramaT racHeL

"W hat?" Miri said into her cell phone. "Where?"
Rand stared at her as she held her cell phone to her ear, listening and every few moments responding to the caller with a statement or question.

"Are you sure?" she said. Then, "How long ago was this?" Then, after another pause: "All right, keep me posted. Let me know the moment anything changes."

She closed her phone. "Let's go," she said.

"Go?" Rand answered. "Where?"

She was already striding toward the lobby doors. She answered by calling back to him over her shoulder without breaking stride. "Get in the car," she said.

Rand followed her to the blue-and-white Israel National Police cruiser, and moments later they were careering down the winding drive from Ramat Rachel. "What's going on?" Rand asked as Miri turned into the evening traffic on Emek Refaim Street.

"She's not far from here," Miri said, turning on the cruiser's siren and emergency lights.

"What? You know where she is?"

Miri nodded.

"How?"

"Her cell phone."

"What do you mean?" Rand threw up his hands to shield himself from an imminent collision with a panel van, but Miri darted around it and swerved back into traffic just in time to miss another collision with traffic in the oncoming lane.

"I gave Tracy's cell number to our techs. They were able to locate her cell phone and determine her position using GPS. As long as she still has her cell phone with her, we know where she is. Or at least where she was a few minutes ago."

Rand shuddered. Until Miri mentioned it, he hadn't even considered the possibility that Tracy could have become separated from her cell phone—or the possible reasons that could have brought that about. He shook his head involuntarily, to dispel those thoughts. "Where is she?"

"The Old City. The Armenian Quarter. Very near the Jaffa Gate."

"The Old City?" he echoed. "Why would she be there?"

"I have a fair guess," Miri offered. Again the car swerved, narrowly missing the bumper of a public bus that had pulled to the curb but still stuck out into traffic at the rear.

"What?" Rand asked. "What's your guess?"

"A restaurant," Miri said.

"A restaurant?"

She nodded. "Most of the Armenian Quarter is actually the enclosed grounds of a very large monastery. It has been there for centuries. Apart from the monastery, nearly everywhere a visitor would go in the Armenian Quarter—except for several churches—is clustered around the Jaffa Gate. And very near the Jaffa Gate"—she slammed on the brakes suddenly to avoid a donkey cart driven by a withered old man who was either deaf or had no regard for police sirens—"is a popular restaurant called the Armenian Tavern."

"That's where she is?"

"That is where I think she is."

Rand held tightly to the dashboard in front of him with both hands as Miri navigated the car through a hairpin turn at the top of the street, and slammed the car to a stop at a row of concrete pillars that separated the buses, trucks, vans, cars, and carts on the street from the pedestrian traffic coursing through the Jaffa Gate.

She led the way through the gate at a trot, and just inside the gate turned right toward the Armenian Tavern.

82

THE OLD CITY, JERUSALEM

Rand entered the Armenian Tavern immediately behind Miri Sharon, who descended the narrow staircase to the restaurant and turned the corner to peer into the restaurant. Rand stopped beside her, shoulder to shoulder, and looked for Tracy.

"Do you see her?" Miri asked.

The restaurant was dimly lit; even so, all but one or two tables could be seen from where they stood. "No," he said. He took a few steps forward so he could see the tables around the corner to his right, but she wasn't there, either. "She's not here," he said.

Miri pulled Tracy's passport from her shirt pocket and approached a young woman in a white shirt and black skirt. She flashed Tracy's photo and spoke a few rapid words of Hebrew. The girl nodded enthusiastically and pointed at a table in the corner.

It was empty.

83

a.d. 30
THE UPPER CITY, JERUSALEM

Caiaphas saw Malchus appear in the courtyard and stand patiently beside the large henna plant, which towered another four or five feet over the servant's head. The high priest returned his attention to the scroll he was reading until he reached a convenient place to stop. He knew the servant would not speak until Caiaphas acknowledged his presence.

"How does my wife?" Caiaphas asked.

Malchus answered cautiously. "She is resting."

He nodded somberly. Salome had been a virtual invalid since her sister-in-law's death, though Caiaphas knew her sickness was one of the mind, not the body.

"He is come," Malchus said.

"Who?" Caiaphas asked. "Who is come?"

"The rabbi," the servant explained. "The one

you said would not dare to come to the Feast. He is come."

"Where?"

"On the steps and in the courts. Everywhere."

"In plain view," Caiaphas said.

Malchus nodded. "Yes, even teaching on the steps. And the people are saying, 'Isn't this the man the chief priests and scribes are seeking? Here he is, speaking publicly, and they are not saying a word to him.' They are even saying, 'Perhaps the authorities have concluded that he is the Christ!' "

Caiaphas frowned and pinched the bridge of his nose. This teacher, this miracle worker from Nazareth, had produced no end of confusion and frustration for him. When he had first started hearing of the man's appearance, he had felt a twinge of hopeful excitement. He had wondered, Could he be the Anointed One? Even after he had had the audacity to storm into the Temple courts and expel the merchants and money changers, Caiaphas had been more or less willing to suspend judgment until the man could prove—or hang—himself.

But in the many months since then, the rabbi had done nothing to ingratiate himself with the nation's leaders. Sure, he had reportedly performed many impressive miracles . . . out in the villages and towns. And by the time the reports of such wonders reached the chief priests and Pharisees in Jerusalem, they were usually confused and conflated . . . and almost certainly exaggerated. And to make matters worse, when Caiaphas or Gamaliel commissioned parties to witness the man's power, he flatly refused—and sometimes even cursed them for asking for a sign.

Things had recently reached a point where many among the Pharisees, tired of the country rabbi's disregard for them and for the Law, had pushed to have the man arrested and killed before he could gain even more of a following (as it was, some said his followers numbered in the hundreds, and that thousands more were becoming increasingly sympathetic to his teachings). Caiaphas found himself in the awkward position of trying to hold off the Pharisees' extreme plans while trying desperately to make some sense of the controversial man from Galilee. He had lately begun to realize that he was succeeding at neither.

He sighed loudly and looked at Malchus. "Are the crowds so favorable, then? Do they hail this man as Messiah?"

Malchus spoke slowly. "They say, 'When Messiah comes, will he do more miraculous signs than this man?'" Then he shrugged, as if to distance himself from such opinions.

Caiaphas set the scroll carefully on the bench and stood. He rubbed his bearded chin and walked slowly into the house. Malchus shadowed him. Once inside, he stopped and shook his head.

"Summon the captain of the Temple Guard," he said. "Tell him I would speak to him."

84

THE OLD CITY, JERUSALEM

Tracy came out of the Armenian Tavern restroom. On her way back to the table she and Carlos had shared, she noticed that the table was empty. She slowed her pace and quickly scanned the restaurant.

She saw Carlos emerge from the men's room.

Then she saw Miri Sharon standing near the steps at the entrance of the restaurant.

Then she saw her father.

She crossed the few yards to meet Carlos before walking the rest of the way to her father, who wore a strange expression. "Daddy," she said, "what are you doing here?"

Before the sentence was completely out of her mouth, her father stepped forward and punched Carlos in the face like a prizefighter gunning for a championship. Carlos, caught off guard, fell against a chair and upended it before landing on the stone floor with a sickening thud.

"Carlos!" Tracy screamed. She scrambled to grab him, but it had all happened too fast and she was left screaming with hands outstretched toward Carlos's prostrate form. She dropped to her knees and lifted his head. "Carlos, are you okay?"

Without waiting for an answer, she turned and shouted in her father's direction, "What's wrong with you?"

85

ramat rachel

Tracy hadn't spoken to her father since they left the restaurant together. After Rand had thrown the punch at Carlos, Miri Sharon had taken control of the situation. She had apologized to the restaurant staff for everyone, settled Tracy and Carlos's dinner bill, dropped off Carlos where he had parked his Land Rover, and told him the best route to use on his return to Tel Mareshah. Then she had delivered Rand and Tracy back to Ramat Rachel.

Now father and daughter sat alone in the hotel room. Rand had apologized to them all—especially Carlos—for his conduct in the restaurant, and Carlos had asked Rand's forgiveness for causing him so much worry and pain. But Tracy had said nothing, not even to Carlos.

Rand sat on the end of his bed while Tracy gripped a pillow, curled up on her bed, and faced away from Rand. He couldn't tell if her eyes were open or closed. He tried several times to talk to her, to tell her he was sorry, and to describe how frightened he was when he thought he might have lost her. But Tracy never responded, never gave the slightest indication she even heard him.

He stared at the hotel room wall and wished for a minibar so he could have a drink. He'd had nothing stronger than a soft drink since his arrival in Talpiot, and right now he wished he could drink long and hard, and forget what a failure he was as a father. But he was denied even that small comfort. He couldn't leave the room. He couldn't occupy his mind with work. He could only sit and listen to his daughter's disapproving silence.

So he did. He sat. He listened. He remembered.

He had never felt capable as a father. As a student, yes. As an archaeologist, absolutely. Even as a husband, some of the time, he felt reasonably adequate. Of course, he had to consider, maybe that feeling of adequacy as a husband had nothing to do with him; maybe it was simply because Joy was such an incredible wife: patient, understanding, forgiving. But you can't ask an infant to be patient. You can't expect a toddler to understand your lengthy absences. You can't be surprised when a teenage girl has trouble forgiving a father who was never around—and who never knew what to say or how to act on those rare occasions when he was around.

But Tracy wasn't a child any longer. She would be twenty on her next birthday. Maybe it was too late. Maybe she could never forgive him. Maybe he'd messed things up so badly there was no hope of being the kind of father his daughter deserved. But maybe there was enough of her mother in Tracy to give Rand one more chance. Maybe he could start over. Maybe he could salvage something in his relationship with Tracy, enough to start rebuilding things with her.

He dropped his head until his chin rested on his chest. He hadn't prayed in years. He didn't even know if he was really praying now, but he whispered a simple request without closing his eyes: "Help me, please. I don't know what to do. I don't know where to start. I don't even know how to be a father."

He stared at the hotel room carpet and let those words hang in the air. Then a thought appeared, fully formed, in his mind. It didn't feel like something that came from inside him, from his own mind. It felt like it *entered* his mind, from somewhere else. It was as if God had actually spoken to him.

It was as if God had said, "Start there. Start right there. Tell Tracy everything you just told me."

86

*E*leazar wore a murderous expression. "The man must be stopped!" he said with a growl through gritted teeth.

Caiaphas pulled the priest aside, under the porticoes where the festival crowd was sparser. He knew Eleazar referred to Yeshua; the rabbi from Nazareth had been almost the sole topic of conversation through the first seven days of the annual Feast of Tabernacles or, simply, Sukkoth *(Booths)*. The feast took its name from the tents the Jews erected and lived in as temporary shelters in their gardens and courtyards, on the roofs of their homes, in public squares, and all around the Temple, in the courts and porches and along the walls, to commemorate the forty years their ancestors spent wandering in the wilderness of Sinai. It was one of three occasions on which all male Jews were required by the Law to appear in Jerusalem.

The eighth day of the assembly, called Shemini Atzeret, featured the climax of the feast. While the morning sacrifices were being prepared, a priest would lead a procession from the Temple down to the Pool of Siloam, outside the walls of the city.

There he would fill a golden pitcher with water from the pool, while the people shouted and sang with joy. The procession would then return to the Temple, entering the city through the Water Gate, which obtained its name from this ceremony. After three blasts from the priests' trumpets welcomed the priest bearing the water, he would climb the steps and pour out the water (along with an offering of wine) on the altar, accompanied by the shouts and songs of the people.

"He has defiled the offering!" Eleazar continued. "I barely had time to come down from the altar after the pouring of the water, when the man stood up in the crowd and said loudly, 'Whoever is thirsty, let him come to me and drink. And whoever places his trust in me, as the Scriptures promise, streams of living water will flow out from him.' " Eleazar spread his hands in exasperation.

"Yes, I know," Caiaphas said. He had witnessed it himself. Yeshua had stood right in the Nicanor Gate, the broad opening between the Court of the Israelites and the Court of Women, both of which had been overcrowded with worshipers.

"They are saying he is Messiah!" Eleazar reported.

Caiaphas shook his head. "Not all of them," he said.

"You can't believe he is harmless!"

"No. I didn't say that. Don't worry, Eleazar. The guards are under orders to arrest him when the time is right. There is no need to start a riot."

● ● ●

The next day, however, the temporary structures around the city had disappeared, the crowds of pilgrims had dispersed, and the rabbi from Galilee had not been arrested. Caiaphas summoned the captain of the Temple Guard to the Hall of Polished Stones in the Temple. Eleazar was with him, and several Pharisees, including Nicodemus, when the captain arrived with four of the Temple Guard.

"Well?" Caiaphas asked. "Where is the man you were ordered to arrest? Why haven't you brought him in?"

The captain glared at his four subordinates. "Your Excellency," he said, addressing Caiaphas without moving his gaze from the four guards, "these are the men I dispatched to carry out your orders."

The guards looked from Caiaphas to their captain, and back again. "Your Excellency," one of them said, "we tried—"

"You tried?" Caiaphas barked. "You tried? Do I have a guard that tries? Or do I have a guard that performs its duties?"

"Your Excellency," offered another, glancing warily at his captain while he spoke, "we were ordered to arrest the man without a crowd of witnesses around."

"Yes, so?" Caiaphas said.

"Crowds surrounded him constantly. There was no opportunity."

An expression of disgust came over Caiaphas's features. "No opportunity," he said. "You expect me to believe the man was never alone? That he was constantly surrounded by crowds of people?"

"It's true," the guard responded. "No one ever spoke the way this man does."

At that, a young Pharisee named Saul stepped forward. "Has he deceived you also?" he said to the guard, his face purpling with rage. "Tell me, has any of the priests or Pharisees believed in him? Has the Sanhedrin, the rulers of your people, become his talmidim? No! But this rabble, these crowds that know nothing of the Law—there is a curse on them!"

Nicodemus, whom Caiaphas had seldom seen in recent weeks, spread out his hands in a conciliatory gesture. "Men of Israel," he said, "does our law condemn anyone without first giving him a chance to be heard? Who among us has given the Galilean such a chance?"

Saul turned on Nicodemus. "Are you from Galilee, too?" he shouted. "Look into it, and you will see that a prophet does not come out of Galilee. The man is a danger to every one of us! He must be stopped."

87

ramat rachel

Rand stood from his place on the end of his bed and faced Tracy. Her back was still turned to him. Curled up tightly as she was, hugging her pillow against her chest and abdomen, she looked much smaller, much younger than the nineteen-year-old woman she was. He stepped into the space between their beds and sat on the side of his bed, facing her back.

"Tracy," he started, "I don't know what to do. I don't know where to start. And I know right now you're probably so mad at me, you can't think straight, let alone have a conversation with me." He paused, searching for his next words. "So you don't have to say anything. I just hope you'll listen. I hope you'll give me a chance, even though I don't deserve one." Another pause. "I was scared, Tracy. I was so scared. I tried to tell myself that you were okay, and that everything would turn out fine, but I didn't know that, Tracy. I was terrified that you might have gotten lost, or hurt, or—or worse. It's the worst I've ever felt, next to losing your mother."

His eyes filled suddenly with tears and he swallowed hard, struggling to control the emotion that

303

had risen in his voice when he had remembered what it was like to lose his wife.

Tracy had not moved. Rand didn't know whether she was listening, or even awake, but he continued anyway. "When I saw Carlos with you, all that fear and anger erupted, and I hit him because I figured he had put you up to all this. Maybe he did, I don't know, but I could see by your reaction when I hit him that you certainly weren't kidnapped by him or anything like that! I could see you really cared about him, and I was immediately sorry that I'd done that, but it was too late."

He paused and leaned forward, propping his elbows on his knees and clasping his hands in front of him. He felt like he'd lost the focus he started with. *Why was I saying all that?* he asked himself. No good answer came to him.

"I don't even know why I'm saying all this, Tracy. I guess I want you to know that I am so very sorry."

He paused again and watched her back for some sign that she was at least paying attention. He waited for a few moments, but nothing changed.

"I know I've been a disappointment to you as a father. Hell, I've disappointed myself. The fact is, I don't even know *how* to be a father. The only things I learned from my own father were 'Shut up' and 'Don't cry.' So when you came along, I had no idea how to be your father—not when you were little, and definitely not now—now that

304

you're nineteen, and a young woman. An adult.

"But I want to, Tracy. I really do. I want to be the father you need . . . the father you deserve. I just don't know how. I know it sounds ridiculous to say that nineteen years after you were born, but it's true."

His eyes filled again with tears, and he looked around for a tissue. Seeing none, he snuffled and squeezed his nostrils together. "But I'm willing to learn, Tracy. I'm desperate to learn. There's nothing I want more right now than to figure out how to be your father. But I don't think I can figure it out on my own. I'm going to need your help. I know I'm supposed to know all this, right? But I don't. So if you could find it in your heart to forgive me—just enough to help me, tell me how to be a better father, tell me when I'm messing up, and help me do better—I would be so grateful." He stopped to catch the sob that rose in his throat. "And I promise—I promise I will work harder at being your dad than I've ever worked before."

He watched her back for a moment, hoping she would roll over slightly, and maybe smile at him. Maybe there would be tears in her eyes. Maybe she would call him *Daddy*.

When she didn't move, he stood, slowly circled the foot of her bed, and peered carefully at her face.

She was asleep.

88

*S*houted arguments and whispered confidences swirled around Caiaphas like a plague of locusts. The seventy-one members of the Sanhedrin—himself, along with all the chief priests and highest-ranking Pharisees in the nation—had filled the Hall of Polished Stones in response to the reports coming out of Bethany, the little village that lay a mere Sabbath day's walk east of Jerusalem.

The reports came from many sources, and some of them were garbled or contradictory, but all said essentially the same thing: Yeshua, the popular rabbi from Galilee, had arrived in Bethany during the shivah, the seven-day mourning period, for a man named Lazarus . . . and had called the man out of the tomb! Raised him from the dead! The news was spreading, and a great number were openly proclaiming this Galilean as Messiah, prompting this contentious gathering of the Sanhedrin.

As high priest, Caiaphas had called the assembly to order, but very little order prevailed in the room as the debate descended frequently into quarrels and threats. "Rulers of Israel!" he shouted repeatedly, appealing for some decorum. "Let Joseph of Arimathea speak! He was there! Let him speak!"

Joseph of Arimathea stood, and the noise in the room slowly subsided, though a low murmur continued from the various comments and complaints that ebbed and flowed in various places in the room. "There can be no argument about the facts of the case. I was present. I am a witness. Lazarus of Bethany died. He was buried. Yeshua called him from the grave, and he lives today!"

"If he is a miracle worker," shouted one of the priests, "he should have prevented the man from dying! Why did he not heal him?"

At that comment, shouts erupted all over the room, and Joseph of Arimathea shouted repeatedly, "He was not there! He arrived after Lazarus died!" until he grew hoarse from shouting.

But soon the debate shifted entirely away from what had happened in Bethany and became focused on Yeshua himself. Some advised caution; others advocated that he be invited to meet with the council; and still others protested vehemently against conferring any legitimacy, implicit or explicit, on the controversial teacher from Galilee. The Pharisees were divided, but the Sadducees congealed into a unified group.

"He has threatened to destroy this Temple!" said Jonathan, son of Annas. "Many of you have heard his blasphemy with your own ears."

"He says he will rebuild it in three days," one of the Pharisees countered. "A man who can raise the dead, can he not do such a thing?"

"You miss the point entirely!" cried Eleazar. "What do you think you are accomplishing? However he is doing it, this man is performing many miraculous signs, and more and more of the people are flocking to him. If we let this continue, his following will increase until it captures the attention of the governor!"

"Herod already seeks to arrest him in Galilee!" someone shouted.

"Do you think Rome will be as patient as we have been?" Jonathan inserted.

"Of course not," Eleazar said. "You know the Romans will not hesitate, and they will make no differentiation between this man and the rest of the nation, between the Jews who follow him and those like us who are faithful to the Law and the Temple. The Romans will show no mercy. They will come and take away both our place and our nation."

"What if the power of Hashem is on this man?" Nicodemus asked. "What if he has been sent to deliver us from Rome?"

"You don't know what you're saying!" Caiaphas shrieked, his expression becoming apoplectic. "You know nothing at all! You have no idea that it is better for you—for us all—that one man die for the people than that the whole nation perish."

The council rose at Caiaphas's words and

shouted down Nicodemus, Joseph, and a few of the others who had advocated a different course. By the time the group reached a decision, the more moderate members had left the hall. Those who remained agreed, with the Feast of Passover approaching, to let it be known among the Judean populace that if anyone found out where Yeshua was, he should report it to the Sanhedrin, so they might arrest him.

89

ramat rachel

Rand awoke and opened his eyes. Sunlight streamed in the hotel room windows. He closed his eyes for a few moments, and then opened them to confirm the image he thought he had seen moments before.

Tracy was sitting at the table in the corner. She was fully dressed, and seemed to be watching him. He lifted his head from the pillow and waited for his eyes to focus better. It was true; she was looking straight at him.

He raised himself from the bed and propped himself on one elbow. "Hi," he said. "You're up early."

"No," Tracy answered. "You're sleeping late."

He sat. "What time is it?"

"Almost eleven o'clock."

"You're kidding," he said.

"No," she answered, "and you've gotten a bunch of calls and voice mails." She held his phone in her hand and waved it at him.

He lifted both hands to his face and tried to wipe the sleep from his eyes, with only partial success. He still felt groggy. "I can't believe I slept this long."

"Yesterday must have worn you out," she said.

He looked at her. He couldn't tell if she was still mad at him. Something was different about her, he felt sure, but he couldn't figure out what. He sighed. "Yeah," he said. "It's exhausting making a fool of myself."

She didn't respond.

"Who's been calling?" he asked.

She shrugged. "Couple different numbers. One of them is from a Jacques somebody." She tossed the phone to him.

He caught it, scanned the list of recent calls, and then laid the phone next to him on the bed.

"Is it about anything important?" she asked.

He nodded. "Yeah," he said. "It's about the scroll."

"The scroll?" she echoed. "Why don't you call back? Don't you want to know what's going on?"

He inhaled, then exhaled slowly. "Of course," he answered. "But I have more important things to do first."

She pulled her feet up onto the chair and hugged her legs against her chest. "Like what?" she said.

"Tracy, there are some things I want to say to you. I tried to say some of them last night, but—"

"I heard you," she said.

"What?"

"I heard what you said."

"I don't—I thought you were asleep."

She propped her chin on her knees. "I did fall asleep. I think it was while you were still talking." She stopped talking but continued to watch him. Their gazes were fastened on each other while moments of silence passed between them. Finally she dropped her gaze and continued. "I was so mad last night, I—I didn't know what to do. I couldn't think. And I started getting even madder when you started to talk, because talking was the last thing I wanted from you, or I thought it was, anyway, and when you started out it seemed like that just made things worse.

"But when you started talking about how you didn't know how to be a father, I don't know." She paused and looked up at him. "I realized I've never seen you as a real person, you know? I mean, you were my daddy, and you were supposed to know what to do, and what to say, and what I needed. I never thought that maybe you didn't know how. I mean, to a little kid, adults are supposed to know everything, right?

"But I felt like last night was the first time I met *you*." Her eyes brimmed with tears. "It felt like the first time I heard real words coming out of your mouth instead of—I don't know—'Dad words,' you know, the things parents are supposed to say to their kids, like 'I love you,' and 'You're beautiful,' and 'Clean your room.'

"And I was too mad last night to say anything or even to let you know that I was listening. But I was. And so I've been sitting here since I got out of bed and got dressed. I've been doing a lot of thinking." She smiled sheepishly. "Especially for me."

She walked over to the bed and sat down next to her father. Rand watched her, mystified at the momentous change that had occurred, not only in her—though she did seem like a much different person than the girl who had appeared at the excavation site just a few days earlier—but also in him. He felt like he was observing a pivotal moment in time, like the fall of the Berlin Wall, but the events were not only swirling around him, they were also happening inside him. He lowered his head and struggled to control the strange emotions that welled in him.

"I've been a brat," she said. "I've been selfish, and irresponsible, and I'm sorry. I've blamed most of my problems on you and your stupid job. And so what if you haven't been the best dad in the world? You could've done a lot worse. But"—she waved her hand in the air, dismissing those thoughts—"what you said last night meant a lot to me," she said, her voice quivering. "And I don't even know if I can do it, what you want me to do. I don't know if I can help you be a better dad. I don't know if I can be a better daughter. But I've been thinking that maybe . . ." She stopped for a moment, and Rand looked up at her. Tears streamed down her face. "Maybe if we both try to help each other, you can figure out how to be my father, and I—I can figure out how to be your daughter."

He reached his arms around her and pulled her to him, and it seemed like the pent-up emotions of nineteen years poured out from both of them.

90

ramat rachel

Her father's cell phone vibrated on the bed as they embraced and cried together.

"Aren't you going to get that?" she asked. "It's probably important."

He released his grip on her and reached for the phone but didn't glance at it or open it. "I think 'important' has been redefined for me."

She stuck out her bottom lip. "That's so sweet," she said.

He obviously knew he was being mocked. "Yeah, okay," he said. "I just don't want to keep making the same mistakes. With you, I mean."

She shrugged. "I still have to wash up, anyway." She stood and padded to the bathroom, closing the door behind her. She turned on the faucet and stood staring at her reflection in the mirror. She tucked her shoulder-length hair behind her ears. Her cheeks were red and her eyelids were swollen. Finally, without touching the running water, she shook her head, turned off the faucet, and sat down on the toilet seat lid.

She was dazed. She'd never had such an honest moment with her father. And it scared her, now that she had a moment to think about it. She knew he was sincere, there was no doubt about that. But what if sincerity wasn't enough? What if it wasn't just a matter of "not knowing" how to be a father to her? After almost twenty years of being an absentee father, was he even capable of being anything else? It wasn't just the question *Would he change?* but also *Could he?*

And what about her? Could she change how she related to him? Could she let him know when it felt like he was ignoring her or neglecting her, or would she stuff it down like she had for almost two decades? Could she even find ways to express to him what she needed from him? Or would she even know it herself?

The more she thought about it, the more it felt like an unrealistic hope. She wanted to believe in her father. She wanted desperately for him to change. But she definitely didn't want to get her hopes up, because then going back to the way things always were would be even more painful. Devastating.

"I couldn't do it," she said aloud. "I couldn't handle it."

She stood, turned on the faucet, and washed her face.

91

a.D. 31
THe UPPer CITY

The sun waned in the eastern sky over Jerusalem as the chief priests and most influential Sadducees gathered on the roof of Caiaphas's home, where it was cooler. Caiaphas scanned the faces, casually polling the crowd before starting. He preferred not to begin until the key players were present, with the notable exception of his father-in-law, Annas, who had become too fat and too old to ascend the narrow staircase to the roof. His absence didn't bother Caiaphas.

The Pharisees had been purposefully excluded from the latest conference Caiaphas had called to discuss the problem of Yeshua the Nazarene. This was not only because he had noticed several of them—Nicodemus, Joseph of Arimathea, and perhaps one or two others—becoming progressively more sympathetic to the man from Galilee and his inflammatory rhetoric (even to the point, he had learned, of warning the rabbi of Herod's plans to arrest him in Galilee, plans Caiaphas liked to think he had initiated, having communicated with Herod through an intermediary). The other reason this meeting was taking place without the Pharisees on the council was because, for all their nitpicking concerns about Yeshua's disregard for the Law— he healed on the Sabbath, he didn't ceremonially wash his hands before eating, he denigrated the oral law, and so on—some of the more conscientious Pharisees actually seemed inclined to agree with his condemnations of the rampant hypocrisy among both Pharisees and Sadducees. And most of them seemed unconcerned by the actions and words of Yeshua that most offended the priests, which were his repeated statements about the looming destruction of the Temple, as though he were preparing people for a confrontation with Rome—apparently one he would bring about.

In recent days alone, reports had come to Caiaphas that the man had pointed to the gleaming white limestone walls of the Temple and told his followers, "Do you see these impressive buildings? Mark my words: they will be so thoroughly demolished that not one stone will be left balancing on another!"

He had virtually promised that war would break out near and far, and that famines and earthquakes

316

would follow. "But," he was reported to have said, "all these things will be only the beginning of the travail to come." He had even gone so far as to predict a reappearance of the Abomination of Desolation, like that of the Syrian ruler Antiochus Epiphanes almost two hundred years earlier, when he had installed a statue of the Roman god Zeus in the Temple and commanded that sacrifices be made to it.

Such rhetoric had once and for all removed any doubt in Caiaphas's mind about the rabbi from Galilee. The man was obviously deranged, and clearly intended to ignite a war with Rome that no one could doubt would end in the destruction of the nation . . . and the Temple. Perhaps even of the Jewish people themselves.

In any case, Caiaphas considered it prudent to discuss the need for action only with those who could most be trusted. "Rulers of Israel," he said when the group seemed complete, "we have met on numerous occasions to discuss and debate the actions and threats of the rabbi from Galilee. We have let it be known among the people that his activity should be reported to the Sanhedrin. And no one has come forward with information of his whereabouts.

"The time has passed for discussion or debate. The Passover is mere days away, and he is obligated, like all Jews, to come to the feast. He will come, he and his followers. He must be arrested the moment he appears. He cannot be permitted to spread his poisonous teachings any farther than he already has."

"He is too popular now," one of them protested.

"Crowds follow him everywhere," several said.

"If he is arrested in public," Alexander said, "there will be an outcry. His followers may fight back, and they are many."

"It must be done secretly," Jonathan, son of Annas, said.

"No!" Caiaphas shouted. "It must be done at the first opportunity, whether there are crowds around or not. Every moment of delay merely makes matters worse!"

"What difference will a few days make, whether during the feast or after?" Eleazar asked.

"Why don't you tell me, Eleazar?" Caiaphas countered. "Why wasn't he arrested years ago, when he first defiled the Temple courts? Weren't you afraid of the people then, too?"

"The feast brings many to Jerusalem," Jonathan reasoned. "Many . . . from Galilee. Many from the outlying towns. Many who are sympathetic to the rabbi. Arresting him during the feast is inviting trouble we don't need."

Caiaphas turned around and scanned the faces that surrounded him on the roof of his own house. "Are we leaders in Israel? Or have we become the followers?"

Jonathan's voice hardened. "He will certainly be

arrested, my brother. But not during the feast, or there may be a riot among the people."

Caiaphas felt the hair on the back of his neck bristle. His brother-in-law had just addressed him as "my brother" instead of the customary "Your Excellency." He was sure it had been purposeful.

He considered confronting Jonathan at that moment. As his father aged, and Caiaphas's term as high priest stretched into its fourteenth year, the second son of Annas seemed ever more ambitious. But Caiaphas quickly decided to say nothing about Jonathan's choice of words. Some things were more important than his own position as high priest, and certainly the preservation of the nation of Israel—and therefore the response to the rabbi from Galilee—were among those things.

"Your counsel is wise, Jonathan," he said, unsmiling. "We will arrest him when and where the Passover crowds will not interfere. We must be careful of the risks we take when the fate of the nation is at stake."

92

гамат гачеl

According to the log of incoming calls on his cell phone, Rand had received five calls from Dr. Jacques Elon. He pressed the key to check his voice mail and learned that four messages awaited.

The first was from Elon: "Shalom, Dr. Bullock, this is Dr. Jacques Elon at the Center for Conservation and Restoration calling. Shalom. I have analysis ready for you of the ossuaries you excavated. I will hope to speak for you soon. Shalom."

The second message also was from Elon, recorded that morning, a few hours earlier. In a tone that sounded much more urgent than the first message—which Rand knew had been left last night, before he and Miri had left the hotel together—Elon said, "Shalom, shalom, Dr. Bullock, this is Dr. Jacques Elon calling again, I hope to speak for you as the analysis of the ossuaries and the scroll is now permitted for viewing. It is good time to speak for you as soon as you get this message. Thank you, shalom."

The third and fourth voice mails were shorter, simply reiterating Elon's need to hear from Rand. He erased them all and then dialed Elon's number. The call was answered on the first ring.

"Shalom," Rand said. Before he could finish apologizing to Elon for the delay in returning his calls, the doctor had interrupted him and asked when he could come to the center. Rand answered that he planned to come very soon, in the next hour.

"Good, good," Elon answered. "I will see you then."

"Is the scroll well preserved?" Rand asked.

"Mamash tov," Elon answered.

"Excuse me?"

"Mamash tov," he said, before stammering profusely, "yes, yes, of course, very good. The scroll it is very good preserved."

Rand hung up from Dr. Elon as Tracy exited the bathroom. He set his phone beside him on the bed.

"So who was it?" she asked.

"A man from the Center for Conservation and Restoration. About the ossuaries and the scroll."

"What did he say?"

"He said we can come and see them."

"Oh," she said noncommittally.

"Would you like to come with me?"

"That's all right," she said. "You go ahead."

He stood and walked over to her. "I would like us to spend the rest of our time here together. If that's all right with you. I could use your help."

A miniature smile appeared. "How soon do I have to be ready?"

"How much time do you need?" he asked, his

tone surprised. He wasn't even dressed or shaved yet, and Tracy apparently had been dressed for some time, but he still hoped she wouldn't delay him too long.

She picked her cell phone off the table. "I'm ready."

93

GIVAT RAM, WEST JERUSALEM

Tracy noticed the ossuaries immediately upon entering the sterile ten-by-ten-foot room with no windows. A track of recessed fixtures near the ceiling bounced dull light off the ceiling, adding to the claustrophobic effect of the room.

Her father had introduced her only moments earlier to Dr. Jacques Elon, who she immediately decided was a total geek and more than a little creepy. Nonetheless, she had smiled and told him it was nice to meet him. Now the three of them stood side by side and stared at the two intact ossuaries.

"I made it priority," Elon explained, "to analyze these intact ossuaries. The fragments and other portions you brought in to us will come after."

Rand nodded. "What did you find?"

Tracy thought the doctor's smile was too much like the mad scientist in some cheesy movie. She found it hard to take him seriously, but her father wouldn't meet her gaze, so her attempt at an *Is this guy for real?* expression went to waste.

Dr. Elon stroked his goatee and opened the file folder he had carried into the room with him. He consulted it, speaking slowly in his odd mixture of accents. "I examined the stone and the patina under magnification lenses. Upon visual inspection, the patina on the surface of the ossuary appears to being consistent with the geographical area and the cave environment in where you found it."

He looked up from the page and glanced briefly at Rand, then turned back to the page. "Soil particles from the bottom of both ossuaries, along with samples of the patina from various places on the sides and from within the inscription, were studied with a scanning electron microscope. The soil is consistent with the *terra rossa*, the red clay soil that develops around the limestone that is common in this area, and is what one would be expecting for an object excavated in the Silwan area of Jerusalem."

Tracy watched her father, who seemed to be making sense of the man's words. She had no idea what the man was talking about, but she saw her father nodding, and nodded with him, reflexively.

"The patina," Elon continued, "contained no modern elements. It adheres firmly to the stone. No indication of the use of a modern tool or instrument was found. Isotopic analysis produced results that are being consistent with archaeological arti-facts that have been buried in calcareous areas, such as Jerusalem and much of Judea. Also, the isotopic ratios are being consistent with an artifact of two thousand years old."

His delivery reminded Tracy of her dentist at home, a man who could talk constantly while probing her mouth without betraying any sincerity or sensitivity to human emotion.

"And the inscriptions?" Rand asked.

Elon nodded and lifted a page in the folder. "The analysis of the lettering also reveals consistently with the patina of the box. The lettering is certainly original, yes."

"Excellent," Rand said.

"I thought you would be pleased," Elon said.

"Have you performed any paleographic analysis?"

A nod. "Yes, yes, of course," Elon answered. He flipped another leaf in the folder. "The lettering is from Aramaic, which was widely spoken in this region in the Second Temple period. It was the common language, though Greek and Hebrew were also widespread."

"What does the writing say?" Tracy asked.

Elon didn't look at her, but answered her ques-tion by resting a hand on the ossuary nearer to him. "This ossuary belongs to the inscription 'Miryam, the daughter of Shimon.'" He moved his hand to the other bone box and continued. "To this belongs the inscription 'Joseph, son of Caiaphas.'"

94

aiaphas waited for the others to arrive. The clamor of the crowds in the Temple courts was barely a murmur inside the Hall of Polished Stones. He had come early to this place to be alone for a few moments. He wanted time to reflect, to sort out his thoughts, to try to come to some kind of understanding.

He didn't know where things had gone so wrong. He had never wavered in his desire to be a righteous high priest, to restore righteousness to Israel. He had never turned aside from his desire to see the Lord's Messiah, and to see his people freed from Roman oppression and established once more as the people of God, a kingdom of priests, a holy nation, as Hashem had promised to Moses. He had always—and still—wanted that more than anything. But so many of the twists and turns in the road had taken him by surprise. He didn't always know which choice would be the righteous choice, particularly when the expedient conflicted with the important. As in this case.

What was the high priest, the Anointed One of Israel, doing arranging for the arrest of a popular rabbi, a reputed miracle worker? How had it happened that a man who, a few years earlier, had hoped for another Moses to deliver his people from the Romans was now so intent on preventing a popular uprising to prevent his people from being destroyed by the Romans? Would any deliverer become more popular than this man had? Could anyone do the things this man was reportedly doing if God was not with him? Was it possible that Caiaphas, by preventing the man from becoming more popular, was preventing the very thing he'd prayed for all these years?

He sat on one of the stone seats that encircled the room. He lowered his head until his bearded chin touched his chest. There was no way to know. The man from Galilee had confounded the appointed leaders of Israel and frustrated every attempt to draw him out, to make him take action against Rome instead of against the leaders of his people. The Galilean seemed to possess a completely different agenda than Caiaphas. Than the prophets, even.

He heard footsteps outside the hall and knew that his solitude would soon come to an end; Jonathan and Alexander were slated to meet him here, and they would once again commission the captain of the Temple Guard to arrest Yeshua immediately following the Passover, before he could disappear among the towns and villages in the countryside.

The man who entered the hall, however, was nei-

ther Jonathan nor Alexander. Instead of the uni-
form of the Temple Guard, he wore simple clothes,
and his eyes flashed with the look of a caged
animal.

"Who are you?" Caiaphas barked. "What are
you doing here?"

The man seemed to swallow his fear. "Forgive
me, sir," he said. "I see you are a priest."

"Who are you looking for?"

"I am seeking someone on the council," the man
said. "My name is Judas."

95

GIVAT RAM, WEST JERUSALEM

Rand opened the door for his daughter. "Is this too boring for you?" he asked as she passed in front of him on her way out of the room.

"No," she answered.

He felt confident she was lying, but was nonetheless glad she answered as she had. They followed Dr. Elon to another room, identical in size to the first, but even more dimly lit.

Experts at the Center for Conservation and Restoration had carefully treated and unrolled the scroll, which now lay flat between two pieces of specially manufactured glass. It seemed to be roughly the size of an 8½-by-11 sheet of typing paper, maybe a little smaller. Though the edges of the single sheet were ragged, the rest of the page was amazingly preserved.

"A single sheet?" he asked.

"Yes, yes," Elon answered. "A small scroll. Not uncommon."

Uncommon enough, Rand reflected. He knew that papyrus was expensive in the ancient world, and for casual correspondence or temporary records, the *tabula cevata* was used—two wooden tablets framing a surface of colored wax that could be inscribed with a metal stylus, and the wax was simply rubbed or melted in order to be reused. The tablets were bound together with a thong or clasp, like a book. But papyrus sheets were most commonly overlapped and pasted together to form a long roll, or *charta*. Expensive as they were, people used them carefully, so it was not unusual for a person to confine correspondence to a single page. Many scholars believed this was the reason for the brevity of the New Testament letters of Philemon, Second John, Third John, and Jude.

But for a single page of papyrus to be preserved—and discovered in the twenty-first century—*was* unusual. It prompted the question *Why?* What possible reason could someone have had for placing a single-sheet papyrus scroll in the tomb of the high priest Caiaphas?

"It's so small," Tracy whispered.

Rand had been entranced by the document but

now lifted his gaze to his daughter's face. "Do you realize you're looking at words someone wrote two thousand years ago?"

She smiled. "Yeah," she said. "It's pretty cool."

He mirrored her smile and returned his attention to the scroll. "What's the verdict?"

Elon scratched his goatee. "What is that you say?"

Rand looked up. "What's the verdict? Have you analyzed the scroll yet?"

"No, no," Elon said. "It is only beginning, the analysis. We have taken small fragment for particle analysis and dating."

"I see," Rand said. "So how long will that take?"

"Soon."

"Days?"

Elon shrugged. "Not so long."

"All right." He lowered his eyes to study the scroll again. He had hoped for more, but knew from experience that it did no good to try to rush these things. Still, he couldn't help but be disappointed. "I guess I'll anxiously await your report." He looked up to catch Tracy's eye. "Are you ready to go?"

"Sure," she said.

He extended his hand to Dr. Elon. "Thank you very much," he said, shaking the scientist's hand. "I'm grateful to you. You've done great work here in a very short time." He nodded to indicate the file folder in Elon's grasp. "May I have copies of those reports to take with me?"

329

Elon shook Rand's hand, though he wore a puzzled expression. "I do not understand."

"What's that?" Rand released their handshake.

"You are leaving?"

"Yes," he said. "Why? Is something wrong?"

"Do you not wish to know what the scroll says?"

"I don't . . ." Rand blinked. "You mean you have the scroll translated?"

"Yes, yes," Elon said. "I have it here. The paleographer translated the ossuaries and the scroll at the identical time."

96

a.d. 31
THE UPPER CITY

*C*aiaphas heard the footsteps approaching, even over the cacophony of voices inside his house. Many on the council had already responded to Caiaphas's summons, issued after Judas Iscariot, one of the Galilean's talmidim, had come with the promise to lead the Temple Guard to the rabbi's location. Any verdict would of course have to wait for the first hint of daylight, as the Sanhedrin would not officially meet at night, but much had yet to be accomplished before the coming of day. Caiaphas planned to hold the Galilean in the rock-hewn cistern beneath the main floor of his home, while the night was spent arranging testimony and gathering witnesses.

Malchus appeared, breathless, in the doorway. The council sat in a large semicircle, in several rows of benches around the large room. Caiaphas watched the servant search the crowded room with his eyes, and finally caught his gaze and gestured to him.

"They have arrested him," the servant said, panting furiously.

"How soon will they arrive?" Caiaphas asked.

Malchus hesitated. "I—I don't know, Your Excellency."

"What do you mean, you don't know? How far behind you can they be?"

"They"—he dropped his gaze to the floor—"they have taken him to the—the house of Annas."

Caiaphas gripped the servant's shoulder and dragged him from the room. Out in the courtyard, where the air was clear and the night cold, he released his grip and turned his hand over. "Your tunic," he said. "What is all over your tunic?"

Malchus's eyes widened. "I'm sorry, Your Excellency."

Caiaphas wiped his hand off on the man's sleeve. "What is it?"

"It's blood," Malchus answered.

"Blood? Why is there blood on your tunic? Are you hurt?"

"Yes, Your Excellency. I mean, no, Your

Excellency." He lifted a hand to his ear. "That is, I was *hurt*. One of the rabbi's men drew a sword and swung it and—I ducked to avoid the blow but I was not fast enough."

"They attacked you?" Caiaphas scrutinized the man's tunic in the firelight. Nearly the entire left shoulder of the garment was blood-spattered.

"Just one of them. I felt a sharp pain and suddenly blood was everywhere, but then the rabbi, he stepped between me and the man with the sword, and reached out his hand, and before I knew what was happening, the bleeding stopped, and . . ." He rubbed his hand nervously over the side of his head, as if to verify that his ear was still attached.

Caiaphas gripped Malchus's chin in his hand and turned the man's head. It was not like Malchus to lie, but it was clear even in the firelight that wherever that blood had come from, it wasn't from Malchus. He released his grip. "You say they took him to Annas? Why?"

"I—I don't know, Your Excellency. I came straight here to inform you."

Caiaphas thought. He realized that Eleazar had responded to his summons. Alexander also had come. But his brother-in-law Jonathan had not yet arrived. It would be Jonathan, then, who was responsible. Jonathan had taken the rabbi to the house of Annas. What was his motive? Jonathan could be counted on to seize every opportunity to bolster his own power and prestige, but Caiaphas *could not see how taking the prisoner to Annas before bringing him to Caiaphas would accomplish anything. Perhaps it was no more than a show of respect for the old man.*

Whatever Jonathan was thinking, Caiaphas would surprise him. He would welcome the judgment of Annas, whom many in Israel still regarded as the rightful high priest. Well, then, Caiaphas would let his father-in-law share the burden. He would insist that Jonathan relay Annas's opinion to the council. He would make Annas his collaborator in the matter of the rabbi Yeshua.

97

GIVAT RAM, WEST JERUSALEM

Dr. Elon withdrew two sheets of paper from the folder he held and presented them to Rand. "The first page is a photographic print of the scroll, as you see. The Aramaic lettering is being very clear."

Rand nodded. He held the page in front of him so Tracy, standing at his left shoulder, could see. Then he moved the top sheet and tucked it under the other.

"The second page," Elon explained, "is being the translation of the scroll to English."

Rand's mouth was suddenly dry, and he licked his lips. He began reading aloud, slowly.

Nicodemus, servant of Jesus Christ and member of the Council, to Joseph the son of Caiaphas, priest of the Most High,

Peace to you, my friend, and grace from our Lord Jesus Christ. I pray that you may be restored to health and good spirits by my letter.

We both bear the burden of many years, and I do not want you to be unaware that I would come to you without delay if I were not confined to my bed, as I have been for some time now. But though my physical health diminishes, my spirit grows stronger every day, and it is made even stronger by your recent letter.

Your burden has surely been great since that dark Passover when the Lord was sentenced to die. But I rejoice to hear that you have long known the truth—"from the first report of the soldiers," as you wrote to me—and even more so to hear that you desire to become a follower of the Way. Even in ill health, your testimony to the truth of the resurrection—the witness of a Sadducee, and a high priest of Israel!—may be more influential even than that of our esteemed brother, Paul.

As you yourself acknowledged in your letter, you must exercise extreme caution. There are those among the opponents of the Way who will do anything to silence such an influential voice as yours. Therefore, I advise you to be circumspect in all conversation and correspondence, giving no hint of what it is to come. When it is wise and prudent for you to make known your change of heart, it must be done in the most sudden and public way possible. Until then, your safety requires the utmost secrecy.

I am sending my trusted friend, Junias, with this letter, that he may more fully explain the Way to you, and pray for your healing, that the Word of Truth may go forth from you, for the glory of God and the salvation of many.

Peace to you and your household.

No one spoke.

When Rand finished reading, silence reigned in the room, a silence broken only by the whirring of the center's ventilation system coming through the duct overhead.

Rand shook his head like a boxer recovering from a blow. He scanned the translation silently, with Tracy looking over his shoulder, as if he needed to confirm what he had just read with his own eyes and spoken with his own mouth: the astounding possibility that Caiaphas, the high priest who participated in the trial of Jesus, might have become a believer in Jesus and his resurrection. He cleared his throat.

"All right," he said in a breathless voice. "This is certainly a surprise."

He glanced at Tracy. Her eyes seemed wider than usual, but she said nothing.

He turned to Dr. Elon. "Do you have more? Anything about the paleography?"

Elon pulled another single page from the manila folder but did not hand it to Rand. Instead, he scanned the report as he spoke. "She says the writing and grammar is being consistent with what we know of the Second Temple period. The sentence structure is rather lofty, perhaps, compared to most ancient Aramaic sources."

"Maybe that makes sense," Rand proposed, "considering who's doing the writing."

"What do you mean?" Tracy asked.

Rand shrugged. "If the author was Nicodemus, he would have been a highly educated writer. A Pharisee. A member of the Sanhedrin, of course. Someone accustomed to more lofty language. Perhaps."

"Would it mean anything that he was writing to a high priest?" Tracy said.

Rand flashed her an impressed look. "Good point," he said. "He might have been more proper in his language, since he was writing to the highest spiritual and political official in the Jewish hierarchy."

"Being Jewish, though," Tracy asked, "wouldn't Nicodemus have written in Hebrew?"

Rand shook his head. "Not necessarily. Aramaic was the lingua franca of the Jews at the time. For a personal correspondence between two Jews during that period, I would think Aramaic would not have been unusual."

"But wasn't the New Testament written in Greek?"

He smiled at her, letting the fact that he was impressed with her questions show. He thought for a moment before answering. "Yes, but they were intended for circulation. I think Aramaic would have been the more likely choice for a private letter between two people living in or around Jerusalem." He turned to Elon. "Anything else on the paleography?"

Elon shrugged. "Internal and external comparisons indicate consistency with first-century Aramaic forms in both the lettering and the grammar. In short, there is nothing to argue against it as being authentic."

Rand ran a hand over his short brown hair and exhaled slowly. His heart had been beating wildly since reading the translation, and he tried to rein in his racing thoughts. These latest developments were mind-boggling—to find not only the bones of the high priest who presided over the trial that sentenced Jesus to death, but also correspondence between that man and Nicodemus, who Rand remembered had met personally with Jesus on at least one occasion. Not to mention the startling indication that the highest-ranking Jew at the time of Jesus' death later became a believer in his resurrection!

Still, he reminded himself of the famous James ossuary that had surfaced a few years earlier. Initially hailed as the likely burial box of James the brother of Jesus, its authenticity was later called into doubt by an official report of the Israel Antiquities Authority, which said the box had come from Cyprus, not Jerusalem, and the part of the inscription referring to Jesus had been forged. To this day, Rand knew, some believed the box and its inscription to be authentic and some didn't; the whole thing seemed hopelessly tangled in conflicting scholarly opinions and reports.

Of course, Rand reasoned, a key difference distinguished the James ossuary from the Caiaphas scroll and ossuary. Ownership of the James ossuary was claimed by a private collector. If authentic, it would be worth millions of dollars. But the Caiaphas ossuaries and scroll, having been lawfully excavated in Jerusalem, would be owned by the State of Israel. Therefore the provenance of Rand's discovery was established, and the potential for forgery or misrepresentation was greatly diminished. As long as the tests conducted by Elon and his Center for Conservation and Restoration didn't produce any glaring inconsistencies, there was every possibility that Rand had uncovered the first archaeological evidence not only of the existence of Caiaphas and Nicodemus but also of the resurrection of Jesus Christ from the dead.

YOU BELIEVE BECAUSE YOU HAVE SEEN.
BLESSED ARE THOSE WHO BELIEVE WITHOUT SEEING.
—JESUS

98

What do you mean, it's not a story?" Rand was trying not to shout into the phone, with little success. He stood in the cramped living room of the furnished apartment he and Tracy had been living in for the past several months. Two bedrooms, one bath. A kitchen the size of a closet. But the location, just north of Jaffa Road in the Orthodox Jewish neighborhood of Mea She'arim, couldn't be beat. Mea She'arim, a name that means "one hundred gates," was established in 1873 by Orthodox Jews. Only the second neighborhood built outside the Jerusalem city walls, it was initially home to a hundred families and remained a strictly Orthodox neighborhood to this day: dozens of tiny synagogues dotted the neighborhood, barricades prevented cars from entering the neighborhood on the Sabbath, and walls displayed signs reminding passersby that the Torah obligates women to dress appropriately. Though the building they lived in was old, the area was clean, secure, and only a few blocks from the Old City, within walking distance of countless shops and cafés, and just a few miles from the Israel Museum.

The months since the excavation of the Caiaphas tomb had been a blur, but a welcome one in most ways. He hadn't had a drink since he left Tel Mareshah, and almost hadn't craved one since the day he thought Tracy was missing. Every examination and analysis of the Caiaphas ossuaries and the Nicodemus scroll, as he now called it, had pointed in the same direction. Mass spectrometry had dated the scroll to a span of fifty years solidly overlapping Caiaphas's lifetime. Multiple language and writing experts agreed on the authenticity of both the ossuary inscriptions and the epigraphy of the scroll. Several experts even endorsed the osteopathic analysis performed by Nadya Stanishev from Tracy's photographs, pronouncing her findings consistent with other indications that Rand had excavated the two-thousand-year-old bones of the high priest who presided at the trial of Jesus!

With the help of Yigal Havner, Rand had authored a few articles for scholarly journals that would be appearing during the next few months. He had granted several interviews to carefully selected print and broadcast journalists. For several weeks his name and face seemed to appear in nearly every newspaper, magazine, and newscast in the English-speaking world, with the announcement that the tomb of Caiaphas had been discovered by an American archaeologist, and it had contained an ancient letter from Nicodemus to

Caiaphas, offering the first archaeological confirmation of the existence of both men.

And then, suddenly, nothing. As quickly as it had begun, interest had seemed to subside. The initial clamor for information and details about the discovery faded, and journalists, scholars, officials, and colleagues simply stopped calling.

Rand was nonplussed. He carefully reviewed the things he had written and said, wondering if he had somehow failed to express the importance of his discovery beyond the mere facts of the matter. But no, even his scholarly articles and most erudite remarks made clear the extraordinary impact of the tomb and the scroll: if Caiaphas, who had been not only a participant but also a principal in the trial and death of Jesus Christ, had believed in his resurrection, there could remain no reasonable doubt that it had really happened! Yet scholars seemed impressed only with the archaeological confirmation of the existence of Nicodemus and Caiaphas, and journalists seemed to care only to relate the drama of the discovery. Neither seemed the least bit interested in what Rand regarded as the clear implications of the scroll's contents.

So Rand had decided to take the offensive, and approach scholars and reporters with what he regarded as the "real" story. He had tried several already, at the *New York Times*, the *Times* of London, and *Ha'aretz*—names and numbers he had wheeled out of Yigal Havner—and now he spoke to someone named Vandy Burr at the *Washington Post.*

"The resurrection of Jesus is old news," Burr claimed, after telling Rand that he didn't think he had much of a story beyond the initial discovery of the tomb and its contents.

"Old news?" Rand echoed. "To those who already believe it, maybe. But what about the billions of others?"

"I'm a journalist, not an evangelist. You should be calling Billy Graham, not me."

Rand grabbed his forehead with his free hand. He was absolutely stymied, and he wasn't sure where to turn next. The stubborn silence on the other end of the call suggested that Burr was done talking. As he searched his brain for a new tactic, a fresh angle, Tracy appeared in the doorway.

"Dad," she said, "can we talk?"

"Not now, Tracy." He turned toward her so she could see the cell phone he held to his ear.

"Oh, sorry," she said. "I didn't know you were on the phone."

"Are you still there?" he asked the reporter.

"I'm still here, but I really should be going. I'm sorry I can't help you."

"Look, think of it this way," he told the reporter. "If you discovered a signed confession of the gunman on the grassy knoll, wouldn't you want that story?"

"That's different."

"How is that different?"

Vandy Burr sighed loudly into the phone. "The JFK assassination has nothing to do with religious faith. It's history—plain and simple."

"That's exactly what I'm talking about," Rand insisted. "The Caiaphas tomb and the Nicodemus scroll should transform the resurrection story into clear, unmistakable historical fact . . . plain and simple, as you said. That scroll changes everything. In fact, it's infinitely more important than the gunman on the grassy knoll, because it should affect about every person on the planet, don't you think?"

"Afraid not," Burr said. "It's still about faith. You have your faith, I have mine. That's how it is, that's how it's always going to be."

"So let me see if I'm getting it. You're saying that because the earth-shattering discovery I made happens to relate to Jesus, the facts don't matter?"

"Oh, I'm sure it matters to some people," Burr allowed.

"But not to you," Rand said.

"Like I said, I'm a journalist, not an evangelist."

99

*T*hings weren't going well at all.

For the past several hours, Caiaphas and most of the Sanhedrin had presided over a frustrating stream of witnesses who had been summoned during the night by various council members and their servants. Caiaphas became increasingly more sullen as the night wore on.

"You are familiar with Yeshua, the rabbi from Galilee?" Eleazar queried one of the "witnesses," a man who had been roused from sleep by his uncle, one of the council members.

The man nodded. "I have heard his teaching in the Temple."

"And?"

"What do you want me to say?"

"We don't want you to say anything!" Eleazar said with a snarl. *"We are scribes and priests of Israel! We seek only the truth."*

"Then what is it you wish to know? I will tell you only the truth, since that is what you seek."

"Some say he has desecrated the Sabbath," Eleazar prompted.

The man scratched his bearded chin. "I cannot say."

348

"Some say he has healed on the Sabbath."

The man shrugged. "Perhaps he has also pulled an ox from a ditch on Shabbat. I do not know. I have not seen him do either."

Eleazar glared at the man, who obviously saw through the priest's tactics. Doing work on the Sabbath was a capital offense in the Law of Moses, but of course the Law also prescribed mercy toward others, even to livestock. The man used the same wording the rabbi himself had used in refuting—and enraging—the Pharisees. When he had been dismissed, others followed.

Morning approached quickly, and despite careful coaching from some (which turned Caiaphas's stomach), the council had not yet found two reliable witnesses who were able to offer corresponding testimony of a capital offense. One man had been willing to say that the rabbi had shown contempt for the high priest, but no one could corroborate that testimony—and Caiaphas didn't believe it.

"Rulers of Israel," Caiaphas said at last, after a full night of fruitless interviews, "we have nothing with which we can charge this man."

"Nonsense!" said Isaac, a Pharisee. "We know he has done work on the Sabbath and blasphemed the Name! Both are capital offenses!"

"How is it, then," Caiaphas continued, "that of all the witnesses we have examined, no two can make the same accusation?"

"Let me *accuse him, then!*" shouted Benjamin of *Emmaus.*

"*You would be witness* and *judge, then?*" Caiaphas countered. "*Would you transgress right-eousness to defend it, Benjamin?*"

Just then, Caiaphas saw Malchus step in at the door. He nodded to the servant, who came to the priest's side and whispered, "The rabbi is here. They have brought him from the house of Annas and lowered him into the cistern."

Caiaphas nodded. "Stay," he told Malchus. "I will tell you when to send for him."

"Men of Israel, we have heard two witnesses say the same thing," Eleazar offered.

"When was that?" Caiaphas asked.

Eleazar grimaced slightly, to indicate that he granted the weakness of his own argument. "The brother-in-law of Ephraim and the silversmith, Barak. Each said they heard the Galilean say 'I am able to destroy the Temple of God and rebuild it in three days.' "

"If I recall correctly," Caiaphas said, "one of them said only that the rabbi called for the destruction of the Temple."

Eleazar shrugged. "It is a fine point," he admitted. "But the witnesses do not contradict each other."

"And where is it written that such words are deserving of death?" Caiaphas said.

"Not the words alone," injected Benjamin, "but

the rebellion they represent! Moses said 'That dreamer of dreams shall be put to death, because he has preached rebellion against the LORD your God who brought you out of the land of Egypt and redeemed you from slavery. So you shall purge the evil from among you.'"

"Is it not contempt for the Temple and the priesthood," added Eleazar, his voice rising gradually to nearly a shout, "to destroy the Temple, or even to advocate its destruction? Did not Moses say 'The man who shows contempt for the judge or for the priest who serves the LORD your God must be put to death'? Did he not say 'You must purge the evil from Israel'?"

At that, the room erupted into angry shouts and curses aimed at the rabbi from Galilee. Caiaphas saw Jonathan, son of Annas, slipping into the room.

"Silence!" Caiaphas said, holding up his hands. It took several attempts before the room quieted enough for Caiaphas to be heard without shouting. He turned and fastened Jonathan with his gaze. "Jonathan, son of Annas, do you bring news?"

Jonathan appeared startled by Caiaphas's question. "Yes, Your Excellency," he said. "The—the prisoner has arrived."

"And has he been examined by Annas, my father-in-law, as I had hoped?"

Jonathan blinked, clearly surprised at the question. "Mmm—why, yes," he answered. "Yes, Your Excellency, he has."

"And what is the judgment of Annas, my father-in-law, concerning the rabbi from Galilee, Yeshua of Nazareth? Has he committed any transgression deserving of death?"

"Annas the high priest of Israel," Jonathan said, slowly and meaningfully, "advises the council to have nothing to do with Yeshua of Nazareth."

Caiaphas frowned. Jonathan's answer meant nothing, of course. Caiaphas recognized immediately that it was intentionally obscure, preserving Annas's and Jonathan's ability, regardless of which way events may turn, to refer to the wisdom of their counsel. If Yeshua were condemned and his followers sparked a rebellion, Annas and Jonathan could say, "You should have had nothing to do with the man." If Yeshua were condemned and his followers dispersed, Annas and Jonathan also could say, "We were clearly right in advising the council to show no mercy and have nothing to do with the man." And, of course, if Yeshua were released and allowed to continue his inflammatory behavior until it prompted a violent response from the Roman authorities, Annas and Jonathan could likewise say, "The council should have had nothing to do with the man," meaning get rid of him. It was an answer that would serve any contingency.

Caiaphas waited for his brother-in-law to say more, but Jonathan was clearly satisfied with his answer; he folded his arms on his chest and leaned against the wall. "Does he say nothing more?" Caiaphas asked.

"Nothing more, my brother," Jonathan answered. "He believes everyone will act wisely in this important matter."

Caiaphas did nothing to hide his disgust at Jonathan's words. He turned to Malchus. "Have the prisoner brought in." He scanned the room quickly; he had far more than the twenty-three council members the Law called for. But he wanted the entire council, and there were still a handful who had not responded to his summons. He addressed the closer of the two clerks who sat at either end of the semicircle of seats. "Call the roll of the Great Sanhedrin."

As Caiaphas took his seat in the front row of the assemblage, the clerk bent to his task, unrolling a thin scroll and starting with the name Joseph bar Caiaphas. He then proceeded to call the names of the other seventy members of the council, from the youngest to the oldest. In the midst of the roll, the prisoner was escorted into the room by two Temple guards.

Caiaphas watched him as he entered. His striped robe was scuffed and dirty, as though he had fallen face first onto the ground, and his hands were bound in front of him with leather cords. His eyes were bloodshot, and a purple half-moon swelled under his left eye. The guards guided the man from Galilee to the center of the room and turned him to face the half-circle of judges.

When the clerk finished reading and recording the names of those present, Caiaphas stood and faced the prisoner. As the nasi, or president, of the Sanhedrin, it was his task to recite the charge: "Yeshua of Nazareth, you are accused of preaching rebellion against the Lord your God, showing contempt for the Lord's Temple and his priesthood in advocating their destruction, and in blaspheming the Name by proclaiming yourself equal to Hashem."

He turned back to face the Sanhedrin, but addressed the prisoner in a loud voice. "What do you say in your defense?"

The prisoner was silent. He gave no indication that he had heard the high priest's words, but slowly and evenly scanned the faces in the room.

Caiaphas waited, then faced Yeshua and repeated the question. "What do you say in your defense?"

Yeshua's expression showed no distress. He continued his survey of the council and said nothing.

Caiaphas, as required by the Law, gave the accused one more chance to mount a defense. "Aren't you going to answer these charges? What do you have to say for yourself?"

Nothing.

The high priest waited, watching the man's face. Never an imposing figure, he seemed even smaller, less significant now. Caiaphas remembered that his teaching on the Temple steps had been forceful and authoritative; it was hard to believe now that this was the same man.

"Are there any witnesses to speak for the accused?" His voice rang in the marble-floored hall and dissolved into silence. He waited. No one spoke.

He cast another glance at the prisoner, then sat and nodded to Eleazar, who called the witnesses, one at a time. Each of them repeated an account of having heard the rabbi saying he would destroy the Temple and rebuild it in three days. As each one spoke, various members of the council stood to shout their shock and disapproval. When the second had finished, Caiaphas stood again and stepped closer to the prisoner.

"Will you say nothing in your defense?" he asked, peering into the Galilean's eyes. Yeshua met his gaze with eyes that showed weariness but no fear, and no anger, before turning his head to look past the high priest.

Voices began to rise behind Caiaphas as he and the rabbi studied each other. "Tell us if you are the Messiah," someone said.

"Are you the Son of God?" another shouted.

The questions increased, and soon the room devolved into a clamor. Without turning around to face the council, Caiaphas raised a hand in the air, still watching the prisoner carefully. If you are sent from God, *he found himself thinking, while he waited for the room to quiet,* now would be the time to make it known.

The shouting ceased then, and Yeshua slowly turned and fastened his gaze on Caiaphas, as though he had read the priest's thoughts. "If I tell you," he said without raising his voice, "you will not believe. And if I ask you your thoughts, you will not answer."

Caiaphas felt his face flush, as though the prisoner's words had been a direct challenge to him personally. He searched the man's face but could not detect whether the words had been intended for the council or for the high priest, but he suddenly had the sense that this unsophisticated rabbi was being clever with him. He suddenly felt all the sleeplessness and frustration of the past twenty-four hours coalescing in him, and he stepped to the side, in front of the guard, so the whole council could see the Galilean's face as he issued the challenge that no righteous Jew could refuse.

"I adjure you in the name of the living God," he said. "Tell us if you are the Messiah, the Son of God!"

Yeshua nodded, as though he had just gotten what he had wanted. "It is," he said, turning his head to address the entire room, "exactly as you say. And in the future you will see me, the Son of Man, sitting at God's right hand in the place of power and riding on the clouds of heaven."

The entire room seemed to emit a gasp, and time froze. Caiaphas, in that instant, saw clearly the impossible choice that lay before him. This man, this miracle worker, this doer of wonders, had explicitly and undeniably claimed before all the assembled rulers of Israel that he was the promised Mashiach, *the Anointed One, the deliverer they had long awaited. At the moment when silence was no longer an option, when refusal to answer would have violated the Law of Moses, this Galilean rabbi named himself the Son of David, the Root of Jesse, the Righteous Branch, the Star out of Jacob, and the Sun of righteousness, the Deliverer of his people, Israel.*

In what could not have been more than a few seconds, but that seemed to contain an eternity of decision, Caiaphas had to weigh: He must either accept this Galilean's testimony concerning himself and here, before all the scribes and chief priests of his people, acknowledge that Yeshua was who he claimed to be—or judge his words as blasphemy, a crime committed in the very presence of the council, making the testimony of any other witness unnecessary and irrelevant.

In that instant he felt the tables turn. He was the prisoner, not Yeshua. He was condemned. He was sentenced.

No! he thought. *This Galilean—this Nazarene, of all things!—had put him in an utterly unreasonable situation. It was unjust. Insane. In a mere fleck of time, to be expected to believe the nearly impossible? I will not!*

He lifted both hands to the collar of his expensive garment, gripped it tightly, and pulled it violently down and away from his neck, ripping it down the middle. "Blasphemy!" he shouted, his eyes filling with tears of anger and regret. "Blasphemy! Why do we need any witnesses? You have all heard his blasphemy. His crime has been committed before your very faces." He was screaming hysterically. "What is your verdict?"

"Guilty!" someone shouted. Someone else stood and ripped his robes as Caiaphas had done. "Blasphemy!" he screamed.

Others followed suit, and soon the stone walls of the room shook with the ruling.

"He is condemned by his own words!"

"He is guilty!"

"He is a blasphemer!"

"He must die!"

Hysteria took over then, and several of the council members leaped up from their seats and advanced on Yeshua. Several spit in his face. Some slapped him. One even punched him viciously in the face. Caiaphas backed away, breathing heavily, sobbing uncontrollably. He sat and buried his face in his hands.

100

Tracy returned to her room, leaving the door open so she could hear when her dad's conversation ended. She frowned at her reflection in the mirror, wishing there was something more she could do with her hair, something special, something Carlos had not seen before.

She and Carlos had continued to see each other after that enchanting and disastrous evening at the Armenian Tavern in the Old City, when her father had spoiled the best day of her life with a right cross to Carlos's jaw. For the first few days after the incident, Tracy had to content herself with occasional phone calls from Carlos, taken or returned only when she was out of her father's presence. Since then, however, on Carlos's days off from the work at Tel Mareshah, as well as on an occasional evening, they had sunbathed on the beach at Tel Aviv, floated in the Dead Sea, and climbed the heights of Masada, the last stronghold of Jewish loyalists against the Roman armies after the destruction of Jerusalem and the Temple in A.D. 70. He had proudly showed her the magnificent array of discoveries and restorations at Tel Mareshah, where he worked with the great Yigal

Havner. They both contracted a serious bout of food poisoning after eating together, reclining on large cushions, at a roadside restaurant not far from Jericho.

But Tracy's favorite times were their returns to the Old City of Jerusalem, and especially their frequent forays through the shops and cafés in the upscale Jewish Quarter. He had first held her hand as they strolled along the paving stones of the Cardo, the ancient "Main Street" of Jerusalem. Their first kiss had been atop the wall near the Citadel of David, when she had just climbed a short flight of steps to a high point in the wall, and he helped her up, pulled her into an embrace, and kissed her gently but passionately while it seemed the whole city of Jerusalem spun in circles beneath her feet. And he had confessed that he had fallen in love with her as they sat in an outdoor café near Herod's Gate.

Today, however, was a mystery. Carlos had called a few minutes earlier to tell her he had his first time off in more than a week, and ask her if he could take her to dinner. She agreed, of course, and went immediately to tell her father about her plans. That was when she had interrupted his phone conversation.

As she fumbled with her hair, tying it, untying it, tousling it, combing it, she thought she heard her dad say good-bye. She made it no farther than the door of her room when she heard him talking and assumed she had been mistaken. But as the minutes passed, and her hair seemed less and less willing to cooperate, she was sure her dad had finished several conversations.

Maybe he just forgot, she told herself. She stood in the doorway of the living room and waited. He was pacing the floor and gesturing. Frustration showed on his face as he spoke, then listened, then apparently tried to interrupt the other person, without success. When he saw her standing in the doorway, he tossed her an exasperated look that clearly communicated, *Don't bother me.*

She went back to her room, disappointed. Things between them had been better since they had cried together in the room at Ramat Rachel, but Tracy still didn't feel like they had much of a relationship. From time to time Rand told her about his work, and she would occasionally tell her father about the trips she had taken with Carlos. Occasionally he would ask her if she wanted to eat out somewhere for dinner, and sometimes she would offer to help him with his work. But that was about the extent of their interaction. She still didn't really know him, and she was sure he didn't know her.

When she heard him say good-bye in the next room and immediately begin another call, she pulled out a pen and a piece of paper. She would have to leave a note in case he even noticed she was gone.

101

Carlos held the chair for her, and Tracy sat at the same table they had shared months before in the Armenian Tavern. The waiter greeted them enthusiastically and asked if they desired water with their meals. Carlos said yes, then ordered the same meals the two of them had eaten on that earlier occasion.

He reached for her hand and held it. He kissed her softly on the lips. Tracy closed her eyes as they kissed, and left them closed for a long moment afterward.

"Are you happy?" he asked.

She opened her eyes and nodded at him, smiling.

"I am happy also." He paused for a moment. He seemed to be thinking. Then he said, "I do not think I could be any happier, except for one thing."

She blinked. She hadn't expected that. "What's that?"

"We have enjoyed many, many happy times together," he said. "And I hope we will enjoy many happy times in the future." He paused, and perhaps for the first time since she had known Carlos, he seemed uncertain, undecided.

Suddenly, in an instant, she knew what was hap-

362

pening, and her heart began to flutter uncontrollably. She should have seen it coming: the mystery about this day, the return to the Armenian Tavern, the repetition of the first meal they had ordered here. He was going to propose to her!

A thousand thoughts seemed to crowd her mind at the same moment. Was she too young to get married? Where would they get married? Where would they live? Would it mean not going back to college? What would Rochelle say? What would her father say? Would she need his permission? Would he give it? Could she even get married in Israel? Who would perform the ceremony?

She felt suddenly emotional. She gazed at Carlos's earnest expression as he seemed to search for the right words, and she loved him even more than before. Of course she would say yes; that wasn't in doubt at all. The rest, she supposed, they would just have to figure out together. She wrestled with her mind, trying to bring her focus back to the moment at hand. Carlos had begun to speak again, and she wanted more than anything to handle this important occasion well. She wanted to stop him and just say *yes* before he went any further, but she forced herself to listen and tried to smile as calmly as possible.

"I do not know how to ask this, but I have wanted to for a very long time, almost from the first moment we met. I have waited, however, because I do not want to do anything that will make you uncomfortable. But as happy as you have made me already, I would be even happier to know that your heart is beating with the same love as mine is beating."

She nodded, wishing he'd just get on with it.

"I know I have told you many times how my heart belongs to Jesus Christ," he said.

She blinked, trying not to let her confusion show. He was making this a lot harder than it had to be.

"And I have learned from you that you were raised by a mother who followed Jesus Christ as I do."

She stopped smiling. The waiter arrived with their food at that moment, and neither Carlos nor Tracy spoke as the seemingly countless platters were set on the table. He took her hand, bowed his head, and gave thanks for the food, but Tracy didn't listen to a word of his prayer. Her mind was fastened on the last few things he had said, and his repeated mention of Jesus Christ, and the bewildering direction the conversation had taken. This was nowhere near the kind of proposal she had hoped for.

But with the food on the table and the prayer finished, Carlos continued down the path he had started on. "I have too long hesitated to speak to you of this, because for some time we were getting to know each other. Now I feel that I know you, and I love you, more than I have loved anyone on earth."

She relaxed slightly, smoothing her napkin on her lap and lifting her fork. He seemed to be back on track, and she braced herself for the words that would change her life.

"And so I wish to ask you," he said, "if you follow Jesus Christ with your whole heart, as I do? It will give me much joy to know that."

Her fork froze in midair over her plate. She blinked at him. "What—what did you say?"

"I ask if you follow Jesus Christ."

She felt her face flush, and emotion welled inside her. Her eyes filled instantly with tears. She set her fork on the table as calmly as she could, and opened her mouth to speak, but no words would come out. She suddenly wanted to be somewhere else, anywhere else but here. She couldn't believe she had thought he was going to propose, and now that she knew that wasn't his purpose, she couldn't control the disappointment that flooded her and filled her and threatened to come pouring out of her in waves of tears and sobs.

She was trembling, she knew that. But she couldn't seem to stop the emotions. She knew if she tried to say anything, she would only start crying uncontrollably. So she stood as calmly as she knew how, laid her napkin on the table, and left the restaurant as quickly as possible.

102

*C*aiaphas felt numb.
Within moments of the watchman's words from the pinnacle of the Temple and the trumpet blasts of the priests announcing that the sun had risen on the first morning of Pesach, the great feast of Passover, the Sanhedrin had convened the formal trial of Yeshua of Nazareth in the Hall of Polished Stones. It was over quickly.

Caiaphas presided without once looking at the prisoner, whom he had seen as he entered the hall, looking even more bruised and bloody than he had appeared at the palace. Caiaphas dutifully presented the charge and reminded the body that the prisoner had pronounced his own guilt before their very eyes. All that remained was for the clerk to call the roll. He called seventy-one names—as always, from the youngest to the oldest. Only three names lacked a response: Annas, Nicodemus, and Joseph of Arimathea. The sixty-eight men who answered the roll each pronounced the prisoner guilty.

The clerk then recorded the inscriptio, *the formal record of the name of the accused, the charge* against him, and the verdict and sentence that had been issued by the Sanhedrin. Because the crime necessitated the death sentence, the *inscriptio*, along with the accused himself, would have to be relayed to the governor, Pontius Pilate, for the confirmation and carrying out of the sentence, since the Sanhedrin lacked the authority under Roman law to execute criminals.

The Sanhedrin dispersed into the Court of the Gentiles, already crowded with priests, Temple servants, worshipers, animals, and merchants. As if he were sleepwalking, Caiaphas commissioned Jonathan and Eleazar to remand the prisoner to the governor.

"I assumed you would do so yourself," Jonathan said.

"I will remain in the Temple," Caiaphas replied with a growl.

"What if the governor does not accept our verdict?" Eleazar asked. Everyone knew the governor's reputation for capricious, even irrational, behavior. If Pilate was inclined to vent his thinly veiled contempt for the Jews, the Sanhedrin's verdict would amount to nothing.

He fastened his gaze on Jonathan, son of Annas. "Then we can only hope that 'relief and deliverance for the Jews will arise from another place,' " he said, knowing that both of them would recognize Mordecai's words to Queen Esther. He led them out of the Hall of Polished Stones and into the sunlight of the new morning, leaving the prisoner behind in the custody of the Temple guards.

"We must rally supporters from among the Sanhedrin and the Temple servants," Jonathan suggested.

Eleazar nodded enthusiastically. "Yes, and they must surround the prisoner on the march to the Praetorium. The rabbi's followers may be watching."

At that moment, as they crossed the Court of the Gentiles, a man with a tortured expression appeared in their path. He fell to his knees at Caiaphas's feet. The high priest realized with amazement that this was the man who had agreed to lead the Temple authorities to Yeshua. He was hardly recognizable as the same man, with his face deformed by the twin horrors of guilt and regret.

"I have sinned," the man said. "I have betrayed an innocent man."

Caiaphas ignored him and addressed Eleazar and Jonathan. "What you are about to do," he told them, "do it quickly."

"No!" the man screamed, prompting Caiaphas to step around him and stride away as quickly as he could, while Eleazar and Jonathan went to fulfill their commission. He passed through the Eastern Gate and into the Court of the Women before the man caught up to him again on the half-circle of steps leading to the Nicanor Gate.

"Please," he begged, blocking the priest's way, "I was wrong. It's all a horrible mistake." He untied his money bag from his belt and emptied it into his open palm. Several coins clattered to the steps at his feet, but he extended the rest toward the priest. "See? I'm returning the money."

"You are a fool," Caiaphas said. "And you are too late."

"No, I beg you." His voice was a mere whimper now. He still held out his handful of silver shekels to Caiaphas. "You have to do something."

Caiaphas moved so close to the man he could smell the sweat on his lip. He spoke in a fierce whisper. "Oh, I have," he said. "I have done something. And soon enough, I will know what I have done. So why should I care what you have done? That's your problem." He stepped around the man once more and walked through the ornate Nicanor Gate and into the Court of the Priests. Once through, he heard the jangle of coins landing on the smooth marble floor around him, and knew the rabbi's betrayer had flung his blood money into the Temple.

Caiaphas looked back through the gate, but there was no sign of the man. He turned to his left, and immediately his gaze settled on Alexander, the treasurer of the Temple. He gestured to him.

"Take care of this," he told him, pointing to the scattered coins on the stones at his feet.

"Of course," Alexander answered. He immediately summoned several Levites and set them to picking up the coins. "I will add it to the treasury."

"No," Caiaphas said. "We can't put it in the Temple treasury. It is blood money."

The treasurer's eyes widened. "What shall I do with it, then?"

Caiaphas closed his eyes and sighed. He thought he might never escape the problem of the rabbi from Galilee. "Do something good," he said. He opened his eyes. "Find a use for this money that will not add guilt to guilt."

103

MEA SHE'ARIM, JERUSALEM

Yigal, my friend," Rand pleaded, "you have to help me. Please." He stood over the sink in the tiny kitchen of his Mea She'arim apartment, eating a juicy tomato sandwich with one hand while holding his cell phone to his ear with the other hand.

"I will do whatever I can," Yigal Havner said. "You know that."

"I can't get anyone to return my phone calls. No one seems the least bit interested in the significance of the Nicodemus scroll."

"No one?"

Rand sighed loudly. "Not the people who should be interested."

Havner simply echoed Rand's words. "Not the people who should be interested."

"Oh, I'm having to fight off some people who want the rights to the whole story. But they're not the ones who should be most interested."

"I do not understand," Havner said. "Like whom?"

Another frustrated sigh. More like a grunt. "Like the Vatican, for one, okay? Some guy with a long Italian name calls me every day and he won't take no for an answer."

"You are surprised that the Vatican is interested?"

"No, I'm not surprised. I'm not surprised that some outfit called Agapé Broadcasting Corporation won't leave me alone, either. I've heard from a dozen different Christian magazines or companies of one kind or another, and none of that surprises me. That's not the point."

"What *is* the point?"

"The point is, now that the discovery has been confirmed and announced, and the bare facts of the find are on record, no one seems interested in what it all means, in the possible significance of the discovery."

"I thought you said dozens of people are interested?"

"But that's just it, Yigal," Rand said, setting down the remains of his sandwich and switching the cell phone to the other hand. "The only people who seem interested in the scroll's significance, in what it says, as opposed to the mere fact of its discovery, are the very people who need it least. The Vatican and the Agapé network are interested because the scroll seems to prove what they already believe."

"You can hardly blame them for that," Havner said.

"Of course not! I don't blame them for that." Rand wondered if Havner was even listening to him. "But I don't understand why *everyone else* is so uninterested. For God's sake, Yigal, you know what that scroll says! Wouldn't you think somebody in the world besides those who already believe in the resurrection would want to hear— would want to report, for crying out loud—the most definitive evidence yet found that the accounts of the Bible are actually true? That Jesus actually did rise from the dead? That an honest-to-God high priest of Israel admitted it?"

The other end of the conversation fell silent for a few moments until Rand said, "Are you still there?"

"Yes, I am still here," he answered. "I think you just answered your own question."

"How?" Rand asked. "How did I answer my own question?"

"When you said your discovery seems to con-firm—compellingly so—what the Bible has said for the past two thousand years."

"Yeah," he said. "So?"

"Rand, my friend," Havner said in a tone that

resembled a teacher giving a favorite student a good-natured scolding, "think of all you know of this world wc live in, and the news media, and the academic world. Do you see anything around you to justify your expectations?"

He sat on a kitchen chair. "What do you mean?"

"Think of our own field of archaeology," he said. "No one makes a name for himself as an archaeologist by merely confirming what people already believe."

"You're not listening, Yigal. I'm not interested in merely confirming what people already believe. That's why I've said 'no' to the Vatican and Agapé and the rest. I'm interested in getting the word out to people who *don't* already believe. People who haven't even considered the possibility of believing, maybe, who think the stories of Jesus and his crucifixion and resurrection are just fictions or fables, as I did. People who wouldn't pay the least bit of attention if the Vatican or the Agapé network told the story, but who might look into it if it was Manuel Garcia at the *Times* or Vandy Burr at the *Post* telling it. That's what I'm trying to do."

A moment of silence followed Rand's outburst until Havner said, "I wish you luck, then."

"You wish me luck?"

"Yes, absolutely."

"But can you help me?"

"I don't think so," Havner said.

"Why not?"

"Because I think you are wrong."

"You think I'm wrong?" Rand said. He couldn't believe what he was hearing from his old friend. "You think I'm wrong to want to inform people of the significance of an important archaeological discovery?"

"No," Havner answered. "I think you are wrong to believe people simply need more convincing information."

104

THE OLD CITY, JERUSALEM

Tracy dashed up the steps of the Armenian Tavern and out onto the street. She had no plan, no idea where she would go; she only knew she had to be alone, she had to find someplace private, because she knew a mountain of tears would soon erupt from her, and she didn't want anyone to see it happen.

She turned at first toward the Jaffa Gate, but there were too many people around, and she knew that whether she turned down the narrow street one way or toward the gate the other way, there would be no escaping the crowds. So she turned back toward the restaurant, determined to find someplace on the other side of the Armenian Tavern to be alone. As she did, she saw Carlos racing up the steps from the restaurant, and she whirled and ran toward the shops and crowds of King David Street.

She heard Carlos's voice calling behind her. She hastened, and shouldered her way through the shoppers and merchants of the narrow stone-paved lane until she was practically running. He kept calling, and gaining on her, until she felt his hand on her shoulder and she turned and buried her face into his chest and let herself cry, while he put his arms around her and held her there in the middle of the busy lane.

"What is wrong?" he asked gently. "What have I done? Why do you cry?"

She shook her head back and forth while one wave of tears after another washed through her, until they slowed, then stopped. Her sobs turned to sniffles, and her groans to sighs. He still held her. He hadn't spoken since the first questions he had asked after catching up to her.

"Can we go somewhere?" he asked.

She nodded, wiping her cheeks with her hands.

He led her back the way they had come. They rounded a corner and he motioned to a set of stone steps at a doorway. They sat down together. She hadn't looked at him since leaving the restaurant.

"What is wrong?" he asked. "Please tell me what I have done to make you cry."

She couldn't tell him. How could she explain that she had expected a proposal, and so was disappointed when he asked a different question instead? She shook her head, and her dilemma prompted fresh tears, and she began to cry again, softly this time.

Finally she looked at him. His guileless face, and his patient suffering while he waited for some explanation from her, melted her heart.

"I'm sorry," she said. She made several attempts at starting an explanation, but each attempt died on her lips.

"Did I offend you?" he asked.

She shook her head.

"Did I say something wrong?"

She shook her head, then reconsidered. Shrugged.

Carlos kept asking, patiently prodding her, and periodically indicating his willingness to make things right if she would explain what had caused her such pain. While this was going on, however, Tracy wrestled with her fears and doubts. What would he think of her if she confessed that she had expected a proposal? How would he react? Would he think she was more in love with him than he was with her? Would he believe that she was silly, or that she was rushing things?

They had talked about the future many times, and always with the assumption that they would be a part of each other's future. But neither of them had broached the subject of marriage, except in the most general, harmless terms. So how could he be anything but surprised at her wild assumptions back in the restaurant, and the crushing disappointment that had followed?

None of this is his fault, she saw. *He had no way of knowing what I was thinking. Everything he said in the restaurant was so kind and—and romantic. Except when he got to saying all that stuff about Jesus. But I wasn't offended. Was I? I don't think so. No, I just thought he was talking about one thing, when he was really talking about something else. If I hadn't ruined everything with my silly hopes and dreams, it would have been different.*

It would have been different, she thought. *How would it have been different? What would I have said? If I hadn't gotten all emotional because he wasn't asking me to marry him, what would I have said when he asked me if I followed Christ? I would have said yes, of course. Right? I'm a Christian. I believe in God and Jesus and all that stuff. But . . . that's not what he asked, was it? Maybe that was what he meant. Maybe he just puts it differently.*

She lifted her gaze and looked at him. He wasn't looking at her. He had been sitting next to her on the steps for—how long? She had no idea how much time had passed. But he had been so patient and so kind. He would occasionally ask her a question or two and then he would wait, watch the people passing by, sometimes turning back to watch her for a while as she thought things through. But never once did he show any sign of frustration or irritation. She found herself smiling slightly as she watched him, and then he turned and saw her watching him.

She still smiled. "What you asked me, back in the restaurant . . ."

"Yes?" he said.

"You didn't ask me if I believe in Jesus."

"No."

"You asked me if I follow him."

"Yes," he said, nodding.

"Why?"

"Why?" he echoed.

She nodded. "No one has ever asked me that before. At least, not like that."

"Is that how I upset you?"

"No," she said, shaking her head briskly. "No, it's just . . . I've always believed in Jesus, ever since I was a little girl." She explained that her mother had raised her not only to believe in Jesus but also to love him, pray to him, and trust him for forgiveness and salvation.

He seemed to be studying her as she spoke. "Do you think believing in Jesus is the same as following Jesus?"

"I was going to ask you that question," she said.

He smiled broadly. "I think many, many people 'believe' in Jesus Christ. They believe he lived and died and rose from the grave. They believe he is the Messiah of the Jews and the Savior of the world. They believe his death provided for the salvation of everyone who comes to him."

"But that's different from following him?"

He nodded, still smiling. "That is why I asked you if you *follow* Jesus Christ. When Jesus walked on the Earth, there was no difference between a person who believed in him and a person who followed him. To believe in Jesus was the same as to follow him. Once a person made the enormous step of faith to believe that this man from Nazareth was truly the Son of God, the Savior of the world, there was only one logical, reasonable way for that person to respond: to devote his or her life to following him—learning what he taught, obeying what he commanded, fulfilling the mission for which he gave his life.

"Today, of course, it is not this way," he continued. "I do not know how it is possible, but there are many people who think it is possible to believe that Jesus was born of a virgin, lived a sinless life, died for the sins of the world, and even that he rose from the dead, and yet not devote their lives to intentionally and wholeheartedly following him."

"Well," she said, "when you put it like that—"

He laughed. "Is there another way to put it?"

She smiled shyly. "I guess not."

They fell silent then, and watched the stream of merchants and shoppers that flowed past the busy corner of King David and Armenian Patriarchate streets—tourists; a pair of policemen; a man guiding a pushcart; a woman carrying an oversized tray of freshly baked bread; Armenian Catholic priests; and a Hasidic family, probably on their way to the Western Wall. Finally Tracy turned to Carlos.

"You're right," she said.

"I am right?"

"I've known all my life who Jesus is, and all he did for me. For us." She turned on the step so she no longer sat shoulder to shoulder with him, but faced him as much as possible. "But I don't know why I thought that was enough, considering—well, everything. Know what I mean?"

"I think I do," he said, smiling broadly.

"So," she said, "will you help me?"

"Help you?"

She nodded. "Yeah, you know. You've been doing this for a while now, right? If you could help me, I would like to follow him, too."

He said nothing, but his eyes roamed over her face for a few long moments until he took her head into his hands and kissed her more passionately than he ever had before.

105

*C*aiaphas, sitting on a low couch in the high priest's quarters in the Temple complex, initially feared the approach of an army. The ground rumbled beneath his feet as if thousands of infantry were marching and shaking the whole structure in which he sat. He held on to his seat and watched the walls and ceiling of the room tremble around him. The room swayed, dust flew through the air, and the stones beneath his feet seemed to rise and fall like tidewaters.

By the time the trembling ended, he knew it was not caused by an approaching army but by an earthquake. He exited his quarters into the Court of the Gentiles to a scene both frightening and surreal. The afternoon sky was dark, and the crowds of worshipers on the busiest day of the year at the Temple cowered and whispered and watched the sky. A dull hush seemed to fall even on the merchants and caged animals in the court, and people flowed uncertainly away from the Temple as though they might at any moment bolt for the exits.

He weaved his way through the bewildered throng, crossed the Court of the Women, and

381

passed through the Nicanor Gate into the Court of the Priests. The atmosphere was nothing like a festival. Even the priests and the Levites seemed anxious to leave. A middle-aged Levite hastened toward Caiaphas and greeted him with a slight deferential bow. Caiaphas remembered that the man's name was Shimon.

"The veil," Shimon said. "It has been . . . damaged."

"Damaged?" Caiaphas knew, of course, that Shimon spoke of the massive curtains that separated the Holy of Holies from the rest of the Holy Place, the inner sanctuary of the Temple. "How?"

Shimon shook his head. "It has been torn in two . . . starting from the top."

Caiaphas stared at the man. "In two? How?" Caiaphas repeated.

"The earthquake," he said, as if it should have been obvious.

Caiaphas looked around the shadowy scene. First the earthquake, then the darkness, now this. He suppressed a shudder. What was happening? Something momentous, he knew, but he strained to absorb it all. The veil of separation that marked off the safety of the Holy Place from the awesome presence of Hashem—it had been torn. What did it mean? What should be done? And what would happen next? He started to tremble. The ground seemed to swell beneath his feet, until he feared it might open and swallow him. At last, and with *great effort, he shook himself, and did his best to focus on the Levite's face. "We will see to it later."*

"Later?" Shimon echoed.

"The Sabbath is coming."

"But shouldn't we—"

"It is finished!" he said. "We must prepare for Shabbat. See to it."

As Caiaphas exited the Temple and strode toward the exit that would take him over the Tyropean Valley on the great staircase, his servant Malchus appeared at his side, wide-eyed and trembling. Caiaphas stopped. "What is it?"

"You told me," he said, panting heavily, "to inform you when the execution was finished."

"So it is finished?"

Malchus seemed startled by the priest's words. He nodded slowly. "He died as the ground shook."

Caiaphas turned and gazed toward the north-western corner of the Temple, where Fortress Antonia stood and, beyond it, the place of cruci-fixion. He peered up at the ashen sky before turning his attention back to Malchus. "You saw it all?"

"Yes, Your Excellency," he answered. He seemed to be fighting back tears. "He is being taken down from the cross now."

"He did not try to fight?"

Malchus shook his head.

"He did not resist?"

"No," he said.

"He just . . . let them kill him?"

A slow nod. "Like—like a lamb being offered."

The priest inhaled sharply at his servant's depiction. "Like a lamb," he said.

Malchus nodded, and tears did come then, rolling down his face in the dim light of that dark afternoon.

"Go," Caiaphas said. Malchus's tears unnerved him even more. He turned again to face the Temple, remembering the strange words of the Immerser that Nicodemus had reported to him those—what was it?—three years ago? "Behold, the Lamb of God."

The smoke and smell of the day's sacrifices still hung over the Temple, causing Caiaphas to wonder at himself, and at the seeming confluence of events that swirled around him. He felt confident that he had made a colossal mistake. He should long ago have acted on his suspicion—hope?— that the Galilean rabbi had been sent from God. Only now, he knew, it was too late. He had never felt such dread.

106

Rand had heard a voice mail message ring in while he was talking to Yigal Havner, so after finishing his call to his old friend, he pressed the key to check his voice mail as he walked into Tracy's room.

She wasn't there. He saw a scrap of paper on her unmade bed and picked it up. The note said she was going out with Carlos and would keep her cell phone on. Well, that was progress.

He ended the call to his voice mail, dialed Tracy's number, and was surprised when she answered on the second ring.

"Tracy, hi," he said. "I got your note."

"Oh, good," she answered. "Carlos wanted to take me to lunch in the Old City again."

"Well, thanks for leaving the note."

"Sure."

An awkward silence filled the receiver for a moment. Rand didn't know how to say what he had in mind, but he decided to try. "I was on my phone a lot before you left," he said. "I—I don't think I paid attention to you the way I should have. I—I'm sorry."

Rand sensed hesitation on the other end of the

line, but he couldn't tell whether Tracy was touched . . . or upset.

"Thanks, Dad," she said finally. "I've got to go, but I'll talk to you later, okay?"

The call ended. Rand stood for a moment, looking around Tracy's bedroom. He and Tracy had gotten along well enough in the past couple of months, but he wasn't sure they'd become any closer, or that he had done any better at being a father to her. In fact, he reflected, he still didn't have much more of an idea of what it meant to be a father to her.

He remembered that he still hadn't checked his voice mail, so he pressed the key again and listened to the message. The caller identified himself as David Bernstein from the *Jerusalem Post*, and said he wanted to talk to Rand about his discovery. Rand had left multiple messages for *Post* reporters in recent weeks and didn't recall a Bernstein, but maybe so; he could check his notes later. When the man started rapidly reciting his phone number, Rand darted into the living room to find a pen and paper, but wasn't quick enough; he had to replay the message to get the number.

Finally, he thought as he dialed the number, *someone is willing to report on the earth-shattering importance of the Caiaphas tomb and the Nicodemus scroll.* His call was answered on the third ring. "Shalom," he said. "This is Dr. Rand

Bullock calling for David Bernstein." He pronounced "Bernstein" to rhyme with *vine*.

"Yes, Dr. Bullock, thank you for returning my call. This is David Bernstein," pronouncing it to rhyme with *keen*. "I would like to speak with you concerning your discovery of the so-called Caiaphas ossuary."

So-called? Rand thought the reporter's phrase was a little strange but let it slide. "Yes," he said, "I'm glad you called. Of course, the tomb and the ossuary are important, as they help to establish the authenticity of the discovery, but it's the scroll and what the scroll contains that are far more significant."

"Ken," the man said, using the Hebrew word for "yes." "But I am mainly interested in the ossuary, the one bearing the name of Caiaphas, particularly considering the news of Russan Aziza's announcement."

"I'm sorry, what?"

"Would you like to make a response?"

"A response to what?" Rand said. "I'm afraid I don't understand."

"So you are saying the news has taken you by surprise?"

"What news are you talking about?"

"You deny any knowledge of his claim?"

"Mr. Bernstein, I don't know what you're talking about. Can you fill me in? Can you kind of give me a little background. I'm—I'm totally lost here."

"Nu," he answered, using a Hebrew term that could be rendered, "Whatever." "You are Dr. Randall Bullock, correct?"

"Yes," Rand said.

"And you excavated the tomb in Talpiot that is said to have contained the bones of Caiaphas the high priest?"

"Yes."

"And one of the ossuaries you claim to have found was an intricately decorated limestone box with the name of Caiaphas inscribed on two sides. Is that right?"

"I didn't *claim* to find it," he answered. "I actually did find it. And the inscription was 'Joseph son of Caiaphas,' but otherwise what you said is true, yes."

"And are you aware that Russan Aziza, a prominent antiquities collector, has come forward to claim he sold you the Caiaphas ossuary?"

"What?" Rand said.

"And are you aware that Aziza claims there were no inscriptions on the ossuary when he owned it, only the intricate decorative patterns you observed?"

Rand felt disoriented. "Is this some kind of prank?"

"I beg your pardon?"

"Are you sure you're talking to the right person? There must be some mistake."

"No, sir, I don't think so. The IAA is reevaluating the case based on Mr. Aziza's evidence."

"You can't be serious. Who's this Aziz guy?"

"Aziza. Russan Aziza. He's an antiquities collector. Been around for years—decades, actually."

"And he says he *sold* me the Caiaphas ossuary?"

"Yes, sir, he says he has a bill of sale, signed by you."

"Well, that's impossible."

"So you are saying he is a liar?"

"No, I'm not saying that, I don't even know the guy—never even heard of him before you mentioned his name."

"You deny knowing him?"

This was feeling more like an interrogation than an interview. "You can cut the *Law & Order* crap," he said. "Whoever this guy is and whatever he's saying, I'm just telling you that the Caiaphas ossuary was discovered in situ in the tomb in Talpiot, with the decorative pattern *and* the inscriptions at the time of excavation. I have the photographs to prove it. I can e-mail them to you right away."

"These photographs," Bernstein said. "They were taken—when?"

"During the two days of excavation."

"Aziza claims he sold you the ossuary last year. Would your photographs disprove that?"

He was dumbfounded. *Of course not,* he realized. His and Tracy's photos would merely show the ossuary and the inscriptions in the tomb. There was no way to prove they had been there when Rand entered the tomb. "No," he answered. "I guess not."

"Do you have a statement to make?"

Rand dearly wanted to cuss the guy out loud and long, but he said, instead, "Yes. I do have a statement. Are you ready?"

"Yes, sir, go ahead."

"I do not know Russan Aziza. I have never met him. I found the Caiaphas ossuary in the Talpiot cave and have made no alterations to it, nor to the scroll that was discovered inside it. How's that?"

"Excellent," the reporter answered.

"Is that all you need? Because, if it is, I have some questions for—"

"I do have another question."

"Go ahead."

"Do you have a comment about the *Post* report that you have been under investigation by the Israel Police?"

"What?" This was becoming more absurd and outrageous by the second. Rand wondered momentarily if the reporter's next question would have something to do with extraterrestrials.

"The story reveals you've been investigated by the Israel National Police since your discovery of the Talpiot tomb."

Rand switched the phone to his other ear. "Look, I don't know what's going on or where these crazy stories are coming from—"

"You deny that you've been the target of an investigation?"

"Yes, of course," he said. "I've spent the months since—"

"Have you engaged in illegal activity?"

"No!" He let out a string of profanity, then made a decision. "Look, if you would like to talk about the significance of my discovery—especially the enormous importance of the scroll and what it says—I would be more than happy to talk to you. But otherwise, this conversation is over."

"Thank you, Dr. Bullock," Bernstein said. "I think I have what I need."

He hung up.

107

a.d. 31
THE UPPER CITY, JERUSALEM

It was the gloomiest Sabbath imaginable for Caiaphas. Malchus's incessant crying had become so annoying that he had dismissed the servant and forbidden him to show his face to his master, at least until the Sabbath had passed. Then, at the Sabbath meal he shared that Friday evening at his father-in-law's palace, the talk had returned repeatedly to the trial and death of the Galilean rabbi—the last subject Caiaphas wanted to hear about.

Jonathan and Eleazar, of course, had steered the

series of hearings—before Pilate, then Herod, then the final inquiry by Pilate—through to completion, and also had been present for the crucifixion. Annas's younger sons, Theophilus, Matthias, and Annias, had carried out various assignments given to them by Jonathan and their father. Each had his own perspectives to report, and his own victories to celebrate, all of which sickened Caiaphas.

"You are silent, Caiaphas," Jonathan said during the meal. "Does something trouble you?"

He considered ignoring the comment completely but said, "No, my brother, I rejoice when the priests of Hashem put a Jew to death."

"A rebel," Eleazar said. "A blasphemer. You should rejoice."

Jonathan chewed and swallowed. "I don't understand your unhappiness, Caiaphas. It was you who said that it is better that one man die than for the whole nation to perish. The man was arrested, tried, and executed with a minimum of trouble. The peace was preserved, and our nation is once again saved from catastrophe. You, of all people, should be proud."

"I am not," he said.

"I am!" said Theophilus. "May all blasphemers share his fate!"

"And what do you make of the darkness that fell on our land?" Caiaphas asked.

Jonathan shrugged. "Have you not seen a dust storm before?"

"This was no dust storm," Caiaphas answered, "and you know it."

"What other explanation is there?"

"And the earthquake that shook the earth—and tore the veil in the Most Holy Place? What caused that, my brother?"

"We have all experienced such things before, have we not? Except Annias; he may be too young!"

Annias started to protest, but his older brothers mocked him until he threw up his hands and became quiet.

In a wheezing voice, Annas, the former high priest, asked, "What are you suggesting is the meaning of such things?" He flashed an almost toothless and utterly insincere smile at Caiaphas.

"I am suggesting nothing," he answered.

"Nothing?" Annas said. "Then you probably make nothing of Nicodemus and Joseph claiming the Galilean's corpse."

Caiaphas looked sharply at his father-in-law, then mentally kicked himself for letting the old man see his surprise. Apparently the surprise on Caiaphas's face had gratified him. "I assume you do," he answered.

Annas shrugged, then coughed. "It doesn't matter," he said when his coughing fit ceased. "But it would be wise to call on the governor tomorrow to ask for a guard to be posted at the tomb."

"A guard?" Caiaphas scratched his bearded chin. "To keep a dead man in?"

"To keep living men out," Annas retorted. "Some say the Galilean promised to rise after three days, like Jonah coming out of the whale. A detachment of soldiers would simply prevent his followers from stealing his body and claiming he rose from the dead."

"Why involve the Romans again?" Matthias asked. "Why not post Temple guards at the tomb?"

"If the tomb is secured by Temple guards," Jonathan interjected, clearly anxious to endorse his father's reasoning, "the Galilean's followers could simply steal the body after the three days are over and the guard is withdrawn. They could claim the Temple guards had fallen asleep—or that they'd never been there—and it would be only the word of the priests and the soldiers in their pay saying otherwise. But if the Romans post the guard, and if the tomb remains secure after three days, that is a different matter."

"If the tomb remains secure?" Caiaphas said.

"When the tomb is still secure," Jonathan answered, scowling. "No one, not even the most rabid Zealots, are insane enough to challenge a Roman guard. More important, however, the people will recognize that the Romans have no agenda, and therefore a Roman guard is better than a Jewish guard. No one will believe the Galilean's followers, no matter what claims they

394

make." He shot his father an obsequious glance.
"Very wise, Father."

Annas nodded appreciatively.

"Very wise, indeed," Caiaphas said. He lifted his
wineglass and tipped it in Annas's direction. "Not
only are we collaborators with the Romans; they
have become our witnesses as well."

Annas's aged eyes narrowed. "Does this course
of action not please Caiaphas the high priest?"

He set down his wineglass. "Nothing about this
pleases me."

"I see," said Annas, stifling a cough.

"I will do it," Jonathan said. "I will assemble a
delegation to Pilate. I will make sure it is done."

Caiaphas fastened a humorless gaze on
Jonathan and said nothing.

108

THE OLD CITY, JERUSALEM

Tracy ended the phone call from her father and
resumed walking arm in arm with Carlos on their
way to where he had parked the Land Rover. She
felt amazingly lighthearted, even giddy. She was in
love; that was a large part of it. But she also felt the
force of a new affection, and a new intention to go
beyond the "mere belief" she had harbored for
most of her life and actually become a committed

follower of Jesus Christ, as Carlos followed him.

She laughed aloud as they walked along the bustling Jaffa Road outside the walls of the Old City.

"What is funny?" Carlos asked.

"I'm just happy," she said.

"I am happy, too," he said.

They walked in silence for a few moments until Carlos asked, "Will I ever learn how I made you cry in the restaurant?"

She laid her head lightly on his shoulder as they walked. "It seems so silly now."

"Then let us laugh about it together."

She lifted her head off his shoulder and glanced sideways at him. "It's embarrassing."

He shrugged. "I will survive being embarrassed."

"No, I mean it's embarrassing for me." She stopped walking. "Promise not to think I'm stupid?"

"I could never think you are stupid." He smiled fondly at her.

She lowered her gaze. "I started crying," she said, "because I thought you were about to . . . ask me to marry you." She looked up at him shyly.

He stopped smiling.

"What's wrong?" she asked.

"You . . . did not want me to ask you?"

"No," she said, "that's not it. I meant I was disappointed because I thought you were about to propose, and then you didn't, and I started crying because I'd gotten my hopes up."

"So you are not disappointed anymore?"

She felt herself blush. "A little, I guess."

He gripped her hand. "Come," he said. He led her back up the sidewalk to an opening in the wall of the Old City. They climbed a stone staircase to the narrow walkway along the top of the wall. He pointed to the structure behind them. "That is called David's Tower. It was not built by David, but the column was one of three towers built by King Herod, and the minaret on the top was added more than three hundred years ago."

He turned and pointed northeast. "Those domes are the Church of the Holy Sepulchre, on the site of Calvary." He draped an arm over her shoulders and pulled her close to him, turning her to the east. "That gold dome is the Dome of the Rock, of course, on the site of the Temple, and beyond it is the Mount of Olives." He turned her a little more to the right. "And below us is the City of David, and the Kidron Valley, and in the distance, the hills of Ephrata, where Bethlehem lies."

"Why are you showing me all this?" she asked.

He looked at her. "It is very beautiful, yes?"

"Yes," she said. "But why are you showing it to me?"

He released his hold on her shoulders and turned. Using both hands, he squared her shoulders to face

397

him. She peered up, curious, into his obsidian eyes.

"I agree with King David that this city is the most beautiful on earth. It has inspired poets and prophets for thousands of years. And it becomes more beautiful every time I visit. But it pales beside the beauty of the woman I wish to marry." He removed one hand from her shoulders and withdrew a small envelope from the pocket of his jeans. He fumbled for a moment before extracting a ring and shoving the envelope back into his pocket.

Tracy felt her eyes filling with tears.

"I did not plan to do this today, because I have not yet spoken to your father, and I do not know if he will give me his blessing. But I do not wish for you to be disappointed for one minute more." He knelt on the stone beneath their feet. "Tracy, I love you. I cannot live without you. I don't want to spend a single moment apart from you. I want to spend my life trying to make you as happy as you make me. Will you be my wife?"

She tried frantically to wipe the tears from her eyes so she could see his face as he spoke, but she finally gave up. She knelt with him, threw her arms around him, and said, "Yes!" She hugged him more passionately than she ever had before, and cried unreservedly in his arms.

109

a.d. 31
THE UPPER CITY, JERUSALEM

*E*arly the next morning, Malchus escorted Jonathan son of Annas into the courtyard garden of Caiaphas's palace. The high priest reclined on a padded bench next to a table overflowing with cucumbers, tomatoes, onions, and olives, but the food was untouched. His appetite had utterly deserted him. "I did not expect the company of Jonathan bar Annas on this day," he said. He motioned to the couch next to his.

Jonathan smiled nervously. "Thank you," he said. "I'm afraid I cannot stay."

Caiaphas recognized in Jonathan's expression an attempt to mask the desperation inside. He propped himself up on one elbow. "What have you done?"

"I represent my father in asking you to convene the council."

"Why?"

Jonathan shuffled his feet and answered without looking at Caiaphas. "It's the soldiers."

"What soldiers?"

"The detachment the governor gave me to—to secure the Galilean's tomb."

Caiaphas nearly upended the table in his effort to stand up. "What about them?" he snapped.

Jonathan clearly hated the words he had to speak. "They—they came to me this morning, terrified."

"Of what?" Caiaphas shouted the question through gritted teeth. He wanted to strangle his brother-in-law for his dawdling manner of getting to the point.

"Pilate granted us a watch," he said, which Caiaphas understood to mean sixteen soldiers, which would have guarded the tomb in four quaternions of four soldiers each, rotating every three hours. "The entire first watch came to me this morning. They—they described feeling an earthquake, and seeing—"

"Seeing what?" Caiaphas insisted.

Jonathan returned a look that said he didn't fully expect to be believed. "An angel. They said an angel appeared in the garden and they saw him move to the tomb, roll the stone away from the door, and—and sit down on the stone."

Caiaphas was speechless. He inspected Jonathan's face and saw no trace of mockery. In fact, the only emotion he could be sure he recognized was misery, pure and complete despair. He sat down on the bench and stared at the stony soil beneath his feet. "The—the Roman guard," he said, emphasizing the word "Roman," "said they saw an angel."

He felt rather than saw Jonathan shaking his

400

head. "Yes," he answered. "They said they all collapsed in fear at the sight." He cleared his throat. "When they came to, the angel was gone. The tomb was empty. The grave clothes were left behind, but the body was gone. They came to the Temple, found me, and asked what they should do. They are terrified, of course."

"Of course," Caiaphas answered. The penalty for their dereliction of duty would certainly be death if their superiors were to find out. He lifted his gaze to Jonathan's tortured face. "Do you believe the soldiers' story?"

"I am a Sadducee," he answered wryly. "We don't believe in stories of angels."

"No, of course we don't," Caiaphas said.

"But we have to do something."

"Yes," Caiaphas agreed. "I assume you consulted your father. What did he say?"

He started to speak, then apparently reconsidered what he had intended to say. He spoke without taking his eyes off Caiaphas. "He reminded me that you are the high priest of Israel."

Caiaphas emitted a single syllable: "hah." He stood and walked a few yards away, while Jonathan waited. Caiaphas's heart beat rapidly, and he thought for a moment he might lose his balance. He wished he had time to think. There were too many questions. Too much to consider. He couldn't even slow down his racing thoughts to a manageable quantity.

Finally, he shook his head and gestured to Malchus, who had been standing nearby, wide-eyed, through the entire conversation. "Alert the clerks, tell them to assemble the council. We will convene at the sixth hour."

110

a.d. 31
THE HALL OF POLISHED STONES, JERUSALEM

The places usually occupied by Joseph of Arimathea and Nicodemus were empty when the Sanhedrin convened in the Hall of Polished Stones at the southwestern corner of the Temple complex.

By the time Caiaphas, as the nasi, the president of the council, had instructed the clerks to call the roll, nearly everyone knew why they had gathered.

"Why do you call the names?" one of the men protested. "Is someone on trial?"

"Proceed," Caiaphas told the clerk nearest to him. He would insist on recording those who took counsel in the decision.

When the roll was complete, Caiaphas reiterated the report Jonathan received from the soldiers, and then called on the council to devise a solution.

"Solution?" protested Simon of Hebron. "What solution? The soldiers failed in their duty. They must face the consequences. We have no responsi-

bility to protect Gentile dogs—much less our Roman oppressors!"

Zechariah stood and pounded the floor with his staff. "Shall we let the soldiers' story spread through Jerusalem, and Judea, and all of Israel then? That an angel came and delivered the Galilean rabbi from the grave?"

"Do we know that is not what happened?" Gamaliel asked.

A shocked silence seized the room until Eleazar son of Annas responded, "Have you become one of them?"

Gamaliel seemed unruffled. "I am simply pointing out that it may be worth asking if the soldiers' story is credible."

Silence fell on the room again. A few of the council members exchanged puzzled glances, while others stared at their feet, or at the stone floor.

"Gamaliel asks us to believe in angels and spirits, and the dead coming to life," said Eleazar. "Those are the superstitions of Pharisees!"

Immediately the room erupted into shouting and cursing and insults between Sadducees and Pharisees, priests and rabbis. Caiaphas watched it all with a weary eye and eventually caught the gaze of Gamaliel, who looked at him as if to say, I should have known better.

"Silence!" Caiaphas shouted. He repeated the command until the council members settled down, and most took their seats again. "We will get nowhere if we argue among ourselves. We must focus our efforts on what to do. We must put the interests of our nation and our people above our own differences."

Joseph of Bethany stood. "If the soldiers who guarded the Galilean's tomb are executed, the story will circulate among the people. There will be no way to stop it."

"The soldiers must say nothing," said someone else. "They should simply return to barracks and report that nothing unusual occurred during their assignment."

"You forget," another countered, "that the stone has been rolled away, and the Roman seal on the tomb has been broken. They can't just claim nothing happened!"

"The Romans impose a penalty of death for breaking a seal!" someone shouted.

"How can they execute an angel?" an old Pharisee on the front row of seats countered, prompting a few chuckles from those around him.

"We should pay the soldiers to keep silent." It was Jonathan son of Annas.

"They have no interest in spreading the news," someone agreed.

"That's quite an understatement," another added.

Jonathan faced the semicircle of council members. "We could offer them money to spread the news that the Galilean's followers came during the night and stole the body. That explains the location of the stone, the breaking of the seal, and the empty tomb."

Eleazar nodded. "Yes, and it makes every follower of the Galilean a suspect . . . in the eyes of Rome."

"That will never work," someone countered. "The guards could be executed for sleeping on their watch just as surely as for passing out."

"Yes," Caiaphas said, sure that the edge in his voice betrayed his revulsion with the whole discussion, "but their story does not supply the 'facts' we need. Jonathan son of Annas has crafted a solution that makes the truth irrelevant."

Jonathan shot his brother-in-law an irritated look. "We will have to assure the guards that we will talk to the prefect if the report ever reaches him. Just as he granted us the guard because our interests and his intersected in the first place, we will show him how neither he nor we benefit from the story of Roman soldiers fainting and angels appearing and Galilean healers coming out of the tomb."

"Does any of us know," Gamaliel interjected again, "what has become of the body? If the tomb is empty, and we are supplying the story of his followers stealing the body, where is the Galilean?"

Caiaphas scanned the face of his old friend and occasional adversary. The Pharisee had finally expressed what had been nagging Caiaphas since he had heard the soldiers' report.

111

Rand ended his cell phone call and cursed under his breath. Every attempt to reach Sergeant Major Miri Sharon had failed. He had left a voice mail for her at the police station, but they refused to give him a cell number or tell her where he could reach her.

He found a phone book in a kitchen drawer, but the listings were in Hebrew. He called the police station again, asked for the street address, wrote it on a slip of paper, and shoved it into his pocket. He picked up his car keys and headed for the front door. He opened it to a surprised Miri Sharon, whose fist seemed poised to knock at that very moment.

"What are you doing here?" he said. "I've been trying to get in touch with you."

"It was not me," she said.

"What?"

"I came to tell you," she said, "I am not the source of that story."

"So it's true?" he said. "I'm under investigation by the police?"

She shook her head. "No."

"But the newspapers say I am."

"Yes," she said.

"I don't understand."

"I do not understand either, but—may I come in?" she asked.

"Yes," he said, flustered. "Yeah, sure." He backed out of the doorway and held it open for her. As she entered, he suddenly saw his living room as she would be seeing it: it was an embarrassment. Papers, books, and boxes littered the room, and he apologized awkwardly for the mess.

She sat on the only uncluttered section of the old couch and crossed her legs. "I learned of the story only today. I came straight here to explain to you that I had nothing to do with it."

"Then who did?"

She shook her head. "I am sorry. I do not know. I assume the reporter simply found your name in the police records from the night we searched for Tracy."

"So that's the 'police investigation' the reporter was talking about?"

"I am not aware of any other investigation."

"I don't understand what's going on."

"Is there any reason for someone to say things about you that are not true?" she asked.

He stood, arms akimbo, shaking his head. "No, of course not." He shook his head vigorously, then stopped suddenly.

She noticed. "Did you just think of something?"

He shrugged slightly. "It's crazy, really. I mean,

I've pestered enough reporters in the past couple of weeks, I guess I've made a nuisance of myself to some. But nothing that would prompt anyone to start spreading lies about me."

"Why have you—what did you say—'pestered' reporters?"

He struggled to know where to start and what to say. So he sat next to her on the couch and decided to attempt a more or less chronological account of all that had happened since they had turned over the bones of Caiaphas to the hevrat kadisha. The identity of the bones in the tomb, which she probably knew from the initial news accounts, though he hadn't told her while they were still at the excavation site. The discovery of the scroll. The authentication of the ossuaries and the scroll. The translation. And the subsequent reports of the discovery, which emphasized the archaeological significance while generally ignoring the spiritual impact of the words in the scroll.

"By the time all apparent interest in reporting on my discovery started to wane," he explained, "what I regarded as the *real* story still hadn't really been reported by the press."

"The *real* story?" she said.

"Yes!" he said. "The real story isn't the discovery of the high priest's tomb or his bones or anything so academic as all that. The real story is the two-thousand-year-old testimony of a high priest of Israel to the resurrection of Jesus Christ from the dead!"

"But I thought you said the scroll was written *to* the high priest, not *by* him."

"Yes, but it—it refers to Caiaphas's belief in the resurrection. In no uncertain terms."

"But," Miri said, "even if it is evidence that the high priest believed in the resurrection, it does not mean it happened."

Rand stood again, and his voice rose. "Would the high priest of Israel—the high priest who presided at Jesus' trial—possibly have been persuaded to believe in the resurrection if it never happened? If he was less than one hundred percent sure? If there were any way to doubt it or refute it?"

Miri's expression was flat, unyielding, but not hostile. She met Rand's gaze without flinching . . . and without answering.

"Don't you see?" he finally continued. "This is the closest anyone has ever come to proving the resurrection of Jesus Christ! The only thing closer to absolute proof would be the discovery of two-thousand-year-old videotapes of the event itself!"

Miri's nostrils flared momentarily. Then she answered, "Don't *you* see what that would mean? To the world?"

"Yes, I think I do—" Rand started to say, but she interrupted him.

"No, I do not think so." It was her turn to gesture; she held a single finger in the air like a politician preparing to make a point. "The State of Israel—much of the world, in fact—is kept from destruction only because there's a tenuous balance among the various religions of the world. Have you been to the Western Wall, Dr. Bullock?"

He nodded. "Yes, of course."

"Have you seen the armed guards who stand on the wall and watch over every entrance and exit? They are not there to protect the wall alone. They are also protecting the Temple Mount, or Al-Haram al-Qudsi al-Sharif, as the Muslims call it. Why do Israeli forces protect a Muslim holy site? Because we know that an attack on the Western Wall or an attack on the Al-Aqsa Mosque would cause an explosion of violence that would make all previous wars look small. So you will forgive me, please, if I do not get excited about a discovery that you hope will make all religions of the world come around to your way of thinking.

"Do you think the hevrat kadisha are as fanatical as they are because they lack enough information about Jesus Christ? Do you think Muslims have chosen their religion because they do not know the right things? Do you think that if the world could learn of your discovery it would change things? I hope that is not what you think, because if it is, I believe you are fooling yourself."

Rand stared at her, stunned. Though he had always known, of course, that he and Miri

410

Sharon came from much different backgrounds, he suddenly saw with greater clarity than ever before the yawning gulf that separated the two of them. After a few moments he spoke again, his tone softer. "That *is* what I believe," he said. "I *have* to believe it. I'm an archaeologist; most of the time we deal in the tiniest increments of understanding, rejoicing over discoveries that add the slightest sliver of knowledge to our understanding of cultures and civilizations. I'd have to be crazy to spend my life digging in the dirt and cataloging pieces of pottery if I thought truth didn't matter.

"So yes, I have to believe that something as big as this—this discovery of mine, this two-thousand-year-old scroll, can change things, maybe not for everyone, not even for most. And sure, I know the most died-in-the-wool Muslims and Buddhists and Jews aren't going to pay any attention. But what about all the rest? What about all those who aren't fanatical in their devotion to this religion or that? What about people who feel lost or confused? Who don't know what to believe? What about people who are *looking* for truth? For something that would help them make some sense of their world? So maybe I am a fool for believing it, but I think truth matters. I think it matters a lot. I think it can change people . . . and if it can change people, maybe it can change other things as well."

411

She smiled at him, as if she were impressed. Then the smile disappeared. "May I ask you a question before I go?" She stood and pulled a ring of keys from the pocket of her shorts.

"Of course," he answered.

"Has the truth changed *you?*"

112

a.d. 31
THE HALL OF POLISHED STONES, JERUSALEM

The council had adjourned. The arrangements had been made. The hall had emptied. Only Caiaphas remained in the chambers of the Great Sanhedrin.

He was alone. In this moment of agony and decision, he felt his aloneness keenly. Things had gone horribly wrong in the matter of the Galilean rabbi, but even now he couldn't think clearly enough to pinpoint exactly what . . . or why. He felt like every turn he and the council had made had been woefully wrong, but he couldn't imagine taking any other course. He couldn't comprehend how things had gotten so hopelessly off beam, nor could he discern what to do now. Even if he knew what to do, he felt certain it was too late. The only course left to him was to make the best of a bad situation and hope that someday things would return to normal. What else could he do? He had no one he could trust, no one he could ask for counsel, no one to whom he could unburden his heart.

He was alone.

113

Mea She'arim, Jerusalem

Tracy and Carlos saw Miri Sharon's car leaving as they approached the apartment in Carlos's Land Rover. Tracy lowered her window and called to her, but Miri apparently didn't hear her. A few minutes later they had found a parking space on the street only a block away, and entered through the front door of the apartment.

"Dad?" Her father was seated on the floor in front of the couch, his face buried in his hands. He gave no indication that he had heard her. She crossed the room and knelt beside him. "Dad, are you all right?"

He lifted his head slowly and looked at her through eyes rimmed with tears.

"What's wrong?" she asked. "What's going on?" She felt Carlos standing behind her.

Rand shook his head slowly. "I'm sorry," he said before he broke down into sobs and buried his face in his hands again.

"Dad," Tracy begged, "what's wrong?" She

turned and cast a helpless glance at Carlos, who gingerly stepped around them both and sat on the couch at Rand's shoulder without moving books and papers that covered the cushions.

Great, heaving sobs racked Rand's body. Tracy trembled as she watched him, and soon she was crying, too, though she had no idea what was producing her father's tears. Finally he seemed to gather himself, with great effort, and he looked at her with eyes full of pain and sorrow. "I don't know where to start," he confessed. Slowly at first, and then with gathering momentum, he related the events of the past few months, and his growing frustration in recent weeks at not being able to get out the story of what he believed made the Nicodemus scroll so important. He recounted his conversations with reporters, and his phone calls that day with Yigal Havner and the reporter from the *Post*. He told them about Miri showing up at the apartment and the discussion between them, and then, most important, her parting question: "Has the truth changed you?"

He leaned his head back on the seat cushion of the couch and stared at the ceiling. "I told her it had," he said. "I told her the truth *had* changed me, but it was a lie. It was just a reflex. I knew what the 'right' answer was, but as soon as I said it, I knew it was a lie." He lowered his head and fastened his gaze on Tracy. "The truth is, I haven't changed at all. Have I?"

She blinked, casting about for some kind of reassuring answer, but he continued speaking before she could respond.

"I mean, I feel like a lot has changed in these past few months, but none of it has been in me. I—I look at the stories of the Bible totally differently now; they seem to have the ring of truth to me now, because I've actually seen the bones of Caiaphas, I know he was a real person. I've actually looked at Nicodemus's handwriting! And I've come to believe in the fact of Jesus' resurrection from the dead, based on hard evidence, you know? I didn't believe any of this stuff a few months ago, but now I don't just believe it, I also want everyone to know how incredibly strong the evidence is for it all! That's why I've been such a pain in the neck to so many reporters these past few weeks, because my mind has been changed and I've got to believe that there are other people out there who are at least willing to consider the evidence, the facts, in coming to conclusions about their own worlds and their own lives and their own faith systems.

"But that's just it. I realized, when Miri asked me that question—'Has the truth changed *you?*'—that my beliefs may have changed as a result of these discoveries . . . but *I* haven't." His brow wrinkled and his eyes rimmed with tears again. "I know we've done better these past few months, Tracy," he said, "but I know I'm still not the father you deserve. And I'm sorry for that. I don't know how to change. I don't know how to be this new person I want to be. I feel like my beliefs have changed considerably. I feel like I know the truth, but I don't feel like it's changed me at all."

Tracy reached out and grabbed her father's hand. She sat cross-legged next to him and held his hand between both of her palms. "Daddy, you *have* changed, but I think I know what you mean, too." She looked at Carlos, who smiled and nodded encouragingly to her. "Carlos was just explaining to me, not more than a couple of hours ago, I guess, that there is a difference between believing the truth about Jesus and following him."

Rand looked at her and nodded thoughtfully.

"Lots of people believe that Jesus lived and died and rose from the grave, but that doesn't mean they've committed their lives to following him."

"Of course," Rand said.

"But when Caiaphas and Nicodemus were alive, there was little difference between believing in Jesus and following him. Anyone who came to actually accept that Jesus was really who he said he was pretty much followed him. They didn't just say they accepted the truth of his teachings or the fact of his resurrection, and they didn't just go to church, either." Tracy flashed Carlos a look, as if to ask how she was doing.

Carlos jumped in. "Tracy is right," he said. "To follow Jesus meant a great deal more than that. It meant to reorient their whole lives around Jesus. It meant to turn away from the way they used to live and accept Jesus as their rabbi—and then learn a whole new way of life as a result of his living presence at work in their lives."

"That's what your mother always talked about," Rand said, speaking to Tracy.

"Yeah," she said, "but I don't think I ever understood it quite the way Carlos put it."

"And you think that's what I'm missing," he said. "You think that will really change me."

"Daddy," she said, releasing his hand and changing to a kneeling position, "I think this is what Jesus meant when he said, 'You will know the truth, and the truth will set you free.' I don't think he meant just knowing something intellectually—or archaeologically." She smiled. "I think he meant something much more personal than that. I think he was talking about knowing the truth the way a person knows another person, you know? Not just an assortment of facts, but a relationship, in which the truth isn't a 'what' but a 'who.'" She paused and looked at Carlos. "I'm not saying it very well."

"I think you are doing just fine," Carlos answered. He turned to Rand, who looked up at him over his shoulder. "Tracy has said it well. Becoming a true follower of Jesus means also that Jesus, through his Holy Spirit, comes to live inside of you, and changes you from the inside to the outside. Perhaps that is the change you were talking about earlier."

417

"I think it is," Rand said.

"It is something you wish to do?" Carlos asked.

Rand furrowed his brow and looked solemnly at Carlos. He wondered silently at the turn things had taken. The discovery of the Caiaphas tomb had ignited a chain of events that had brought him to this point, but was that discovery the source of the faith he had previously lacked? At what point did he become willing to believe? At what point had he started believing? Was the scroll the thing that had done it? Or did the tomb and the scroll simply drive him to the Bible, with fresh eyes and a willing heart?

All these questions popped in Rand's mind in the space of a few seconds, like firecrackers on a string. He saw clearly that it didn't matter how many people came to believe in the truth of the resurrection because of the scroll, unless their eyes were opened as his had been. As it was, he supposed, millions of people had accepted the truth of the resurrection without ever experiencing an awakening of faith like what was happening inside him. He wasn't merely prepared to accept an assortment of facts; he also was prepared to change the direction of his life. He didn't know where that faith had come from, or when it had taken root, but he suspected that it hadn't been solely a result of the evidence he found in the Caiaphas tomb. That might have triggered his faith—it sure hadn't hurt—but Rand imagined that he'd always had enough evidence . . . but he only recently had the eyes of faith to see it. He was sure that's what had made the difference.

He suddenly realized that Carlos and Tracy still awaited an answer. He glanced from one to the other and then snapped his head in a determined nod. "Yeah," he said. "That is something I want to do."

Carlos slipped off the couch and knelt on one knee beside Rand. He placed his left hand on Rand's shoulder. "Do you confess that you are a sinner, and that your sins have separated you from God?"

"Absolutely, yes," he said.

Carlos nodded, and the hint of a smile flickered on his face before he continued. "Do you repent of your sin? In other words, are you willing to turn your back on all your sins and learn a new way of living from your rabbi, Jesus?"

"Yes."

"Do you understand that because Jesus died on the cross, you need only to ask him to receive forgiveness of all your sins, freedom from the guilt and punishment your sins deserve, and eternal life?"

"Yes."

"Do you intend to follow Jesus Christ in every area of life and serve him wholeheartedly as your rabbi and Lord?"

"Yes," he answered, even more vehemently than at first.

"Do you think you are able to say all that in a prayer, asking God to accept the offering of your heart and life?"

"You mean right now?" Rand said.

Carlos smiled. "Yes, that is what I mean."

He looked from Carlos to Tracy. "I'm not much for praying," he said.

"You will not be talking to us," Carlos said.

"Do I—am I supposed to close my eyes?"

"If you wish," Carlos said. "It helps some people concentrate better."

"Okay then," Rand said. He closed his eyes and inhaled deeply. "Jesus, you know I'm not very good at this. But I do believe you rose from the dead. I believe you are who you said you were. So I guess I'm ready to put my money where my mouth is." He paused. "Let's see. I may not be doing this right, but I am sorry for my sins, especially for the kind of father I've been. I hate that I haven't been what Tracy needed in a father all these years." His voice quivered with emotion. "I've been a jackass, and I know that just scratches the surface. I'm sorry. Forgive me, please. Come into my heart and make me new, like Carlos said, from the inside out. I give you my life. Whatever it means, I'll follow you from here on out."

He opened his eyes. Tracy looked back and forth from him to Carlos. She was smiling broadly, and there were tears in her eyes.

"Amen," Carlos said.

"Yeah," Rand said. "Right. Amen. I forgot that part." He started laughing, and crying, and the others joined in the laughter until it seemed they'd never stop.

114

a.d. 31
THE UPPER CITY, JERUSALEM

*T*he past few weeks had been a nightmare for *Caiaphas. Reports had begun to surface that Yeshua, the rabbi from Nazareth, had actually been seen, alive, not only by individuals but also by entire crowds in Galilee. The reports had been relayed to Caiaphas primarily through Malchus, whose countenance had changed significantly in the weeks since Passover. He seemed to have grown up suddenly, and the previously expressionless servant now went about his duties smiling, sometimes singing.*

As the Feast of Firstfruits approached, Caiaphas was a mess. He hadn't enjoyed a meal or a good night of sleep since Passover. He found it extremely difficult to concentrate. He had several times been engaged in conversation with someone but his attention had just wandered off while his companion was still speaking. For days now he had suffered from a severe rumbling in his chest that made it hard to breathe, and he began to fear that the curse of God had fallen on him.

Finally, as he reclined on a low couch beneath an olive tree in the courtyard, he summoned Malchus. "I have questions to ask you, Malchus," he said.

The servant nodded agreeably.

"Questions about the Galilean," he added, closely watching his servant's face.

Malchus nodded. Smiled.

"You seem to be much informed," Caiaphas said, stopping to cough violently for a few moments. After the coughing fit ceased, he gathered himself and continued. "You seem to be much informed about the events of the past few weeks. Have you become one of them?"

"One of them?" Malchus echoed.

"A follower of the Galilean."

Malchus hesitated only slightly before answering. "Yes," he said.

"You saw him arrested."

"Yes."

"You saw him hanged on a tree."

"Yes."

"You know he died and was buried."

"Yes."

"And yet you are one of the dead rabbi's talmidim?"

"No," Malchus answered.

"No?" Caiaphas echoed. "But you said—"

"I do not follow a dead rabbi. I have seen the resurrected Messiah with my own eyes."

Caiaphas blinked. His mouth felt impossibly dry. "You have seen him?"

Malchus nodded.

"Tell me."

An eager smile spread across Malchus's face. "I traveled to Mount Tabor with Andronicus and Junias. Hundreds of others had gathered there at Yeshua's instruction. He sat down and taught us, and told us that all authority in heaven and on Earth had been given to him and that we were to spread his teachings and make people from all nations into his talmidim."

"When was this?"

"Two weeks ago."

"And you saw him? You saw him."

He nodded. "With these eyes. In the company of more than five hundred others who saw him, too."

"Where is he now?"

"They say—the Eleven—that he was taken up into Heaven before their very eyes just days ago."

Another coughing fit rose in Caiaphas's chest, and he writhed in pain on his couch. After several minutes of coughing, he recaptured his breath and asked, "How can it be?"

"We have always known that when Mashiach comes, he will perform many signs and wonders. Could he do something greater than this: to rise from the dead?"

"But he was hanged on a tree," Caiaphas said. He did not have to explain his statement; he and Malchus both knew the words of Moses' Law stating, "Anyone who is hung on a tree is under God's curse."

"Like the serpent in the wilderness," Malchus countered. "He was lifted up for the healing of his people . . . and of the world."

Caiaphas laid his head back on his bench and closed his eyes. "It is too much," he said. "It is too hard to accept." Caiaphas's wheezing threatened several times to erupt into more coughing, but he lay as still as he could. "It is just too hard," he repeated.

"Naaman almost refused healing because it seemed too easy. Perhaps 'too hard' is a blessing."

Caiaphas opened his eyes and stared at Malchus as if he were seeing him for the first time. "When did you become wise?"

He smiled. "I am only a servant," he said, "of a wise master."

Caiaphas inspected the man's face but saw no trace of irony or mockery. He couldn't tell if he referred to Caiaphas . . . or someone else. The Galilean, probably. "It would be absurd for the Kohen HaGadol of Israel to become the follower of a simple country rabbi."

"Perhaps . . . but it would be fitting for the high priest of Israel to acknowledge the Messiah of God, the Anointed One."

"Do you"—a cough erupted suddenly, but Caiaphas managed to control it quickly—"do you try to make me believe?"

Malchus's smile disappeared. He leveled his gaze at the priest. "I do not have to. I think you believe already, though you have not started to follow."

"How can I do that, Malchus?" Caiaphas's tone was sincere, even pleading. "I am Kohen HaGadol. I cannot do as you have done. It is not that simple for me."

"Perhaps not. But who knows," he answered, using a phrase that was familiar and significant to them both, "whether you have been made Kohen HaGadol for such a time as this?"

Caiaphas studied the face of his faithful servant. Oddly, he thought of the bloodstained tunic Malchus wore on the day of the Galilean's arrest, and suddenly realized he had been telling the truth about the events of that night. He sighed heavily. "I wish I had someone to talk to," he said. Malchus was a mere servant. He needed someone . . . "Like Nicodemus." He sat up. "Yes, Nicodemus. I will go to his house. You will go before me, to announce my visit."

Something in the servant's reaction arrested Caiaphas. "What is it?"

"They say he is not well. He has not been out of his house for weeks, and they say he may die."

"Nicodemus?"

Malchus nodded.

"What afflicts him?"

Something in the servant's manner told Caiaphas he didn't wish to answer. The priest let it go for the moment. "Joseph, then," he said. "You will take me to Joseph of Arimathea."

Again, Caiaphas thought he detected some hesitation in Malchus.

"What is it?" he demanded. "What's wrong?"

"Joseph," he answered. "They say he has fled the city."

"Fled the city? What does that mean?"

"It may not be safe to say."

A fierce coughing fit shook Caiaphas's body until he had to sit again on the couch. "You will tell me," he commanded. "Why has Joseph fled the city?"

Malchus flashed an anxious look at Caiaphas. He grimaced, then obeyed. "He believes his life is in danger," he said.

"From whom?"

"Some say it is the same people who have caused Nicodemus's illness."

"Caused his illness?" Caiaphas said. "You mean from poison?"

Malchus barely nodded.

"Who?" Caiaphas said through a hacking cough.

Malchus dropped his gaze and waited for the priest to stop coughing. Even then, however, his answer was barely audible. "The family of the high priest," he said.

115

When the laughter subsided, the joy and energy remained. Rand practically leaped up from his seat on the couch and paced the floor. "This is fantastic," he said. "This is what the whole world needs. Everybody should feel this way."

Tracy's beaming face brought even more joy to his heart. She looked as though she might explode with happiness, and it made him even happier to see her so happy. Carlos stood next to her, beaming almost as brightly.

"Maybe I've been going about this the wrong way," Rand said, still pacing. "I've been more or less expecting the newspapers and magazines of the world to get the news out about the Nicodemus scroll. But they don't understand its significance, and when I think about it, why should they? They haven't experienced what I'm experiencing right now—right? So maybe I've been wrong to expect them to understand how important all this is. Maybe I've been wrong to put off the Vatican and the Agapé network and all the rest. Maybe I just need to get the word out, through as many outlets as I can, and not worry about the rest."

"Even Jesus," Carlos added, "addressed many of his words to 'those who have ears to hear.'"

Rand shot him a quizzical look. "What's that mean?"

Carlos shrugged. "I think Jesus used that phrase as a way to acknowledge that not everyone who heard his words would be able or willing to understand them. But he spoke them anyway."

"I see," Rand said. "You're saying that I don't have to choose or manage who I tell the story to."

"Yes, correct. Because I believe you are supposed to tell the story to everyone."

"Right," he agreed. "Of course. Just get the story out. Every which way I can. Right?" Then his eyes narrowed slightly as he thought he detected something, some odd communication between Tracy and Carlos. "Are we still talking about the scroll?"

Carlos smiled broadly. "Yes."

"But . . . we're talking about more than that."

"Yes." Carlos glanced at Tracy, and they exchanged smiles.

"Daddy," she said, "Carlos helped me commit to following Jesus, too."

He looked back and forth from his daughter's face to Carlos's face. "No kidding," he said.

"It happened just a little while ago," she said. "Right after lunch. Right before we came home."

"No kidding," Rand repeated. He stepped over to her, wrapped her in his arms, and twirled her in a circle. "That's amazing!"

Laughter enveloped the trio again, and when it subsided, Rand clapped a hand on Carlos's shoulder. "I don't know what to say," Rand said. "You've—for both my daughter and for me, you've—I don't know what to say. I can't thank you enough."

Carlos glanced briefly at Tracy, then back to Rand. "I hope that is true," Carlos said, a nervous laugh punctuating his words. "Because I have something else to tell you."

Rand released his grip on Carlos's shoulder. "Okay," he said, still smiling. "What's that?"

"I love your daughter very much, and I ask your permission to make her my wife."

116

a.d. 31
The Upper City, Jerusalem

Joseph of Arimathea had disappeared.
Nicodemus was gravely ill.

According to Malchus, the Galilean's followers, though they had seen the risen Yeshua with their own eyes, cowered behind closed doors and locked gates, afraid of the high priest's family.

But I am the high priest! *Caiaphas reasoned as he watched the sun set from his couch in the courtyard. But lately, he knew, a shift had taken place.*

His aging father-in-law, Annas, had summoned enough strength to return, at least partially, to prominence among the leaders of the nation. And Jonathan, son of Annas, had obviously been positioning himself to become high priest . . . whenever the necessity—or even the opportunity, Caiaphas was sure—presented itself.

The Feast of Firstfruits hadn't even arrived, and Annas and Jonathan apparently had begun tightening the noose on the small body of people who claimed to have seen the risen rabbi, starting with the worst offenders—Nicodemus and Joseph, the members of the Great Sanhedrin who had displayed their loyalty to the Galilean at the moment of his greatest humiliation. Caiaphas knew they would not rest until every professed witness to the resurrection of Yeshua had been silenced. He knew, even if Joseph fled to Damascus or Antioch—or Rome itself—they would send delegations to find him and arrest him.

If it was true—and he knew it was—how would Annas and Jonathan react if it became known that Joseph bar Caiaphas, the Kohen HaGadol and nasi of the Sanhedrin, had actually accepted the truth of the Galilean's resurrection from the dead? For Malchus had been right. Caiaphas had already begun to believe, though he had not yet begun to follow. But he would. He would repent of his previous unbelief—and the horrible results, for him and for the nation. And then he would produce *fruit in keeping with repentance. He would be a true follower of the risen rabbi.*

But he would have to be extremely careful and exceedingly patient. He was in a precarious position. The coming weeks and months would certainly require more caution and cunning than anything else he had ever faced as high priest. But he would do it. He would find a way. He would somehow lead his nation to acknowledge their Messiah, and the Earth would be filled with the knowledge of the glory of the Lord, as the waters cover the sea.

117

MEA SHE'ARIM, JERUSALEM

Your wife?" Rand echoed Carlos's question. His smile disappeared, and he looked at Tracy. "What—what is he talking about?"

Tracy leveled her gaze. When she spoke, her voice was soft but firm. "Daddy, Carlos has asked me to marry him, and I said yes."

Rand blinked. He sat down. He suddenly remembered that day several months ago when he thought he had lost Tracy, when he had vowed never to lose her again. "I've just—I haven't even gotten started," he said to no one in particular.

"What?" Tracy asked.

"I promised you," he said, "that I would work hard at being your dad, and learning how to be the kind of father you need. But I feel like I haven't even gotten started. I've wasted most of the past few months, and I know that's my fault . . . but now I'm supposed to give permission for you to get married?"

Tracy sat next to him on the couch. "You also asked me to help you, remember?"

He frowned and nodded.

"You said you wanted me to help you be a better father, to tell you what I needed from you, right?"

Another nod.

"I haven't done that very well these past few months," she said. "But right now I don't need you to tell me how young I am or that Carlos and I have only known each other a few months, or that we come from very different backgrounds; I know all that. I don't need you to tell me it won't be easy, or that we'll have to figure out things like visas and citizenships and where to get married and where we're going to live. Or that I can't give up on college. I know all that, too. *We* know all that.

"I guess what I'm saying is, I don't need you to *tell* me anything, I need you to *show* me your support, show me you love me and trust me, show me you'll be there when I have questions or need help."

She stood from the couch, put her arm through Carlos's, and wrapped his arm in a hug. "But

Daddy, I love this man, and I want to marry him more than anything else in the world right now. And the thing I want most after that—the thing I *need* most from my father—is the love and support that will make me believe that I can handle all the decisions and obstacles and difficulties we may face in the coming months because my father will be there to help me . . . and my fiancé." Her voice quivered, and her eyes welled with tears. "You asked me to tell you, and so I'm telling you: that's what I need from my dad right now."

Carlos slipped his arm from Tracy's grip and wrapped it around her waist. Rand stood slowly. He knew this was the same girl he and Joy brought home from the hospital, but it seemed impossible. He wished from the bottom of his heart that he could reverse all his foolishness and neglect over the years, and relive her first steps, her first day of school, her softball games, her prom dates. He wished he could read her a story again, or buy her cotton candy. He longed with all his heart to redeem his many failures as a father, and be able to start over with the only daughter he would ever have.

Then, much as it had that night at Ramat Rachel, a thought formed in his mind. This time, however, it seemed to come from somewhere inside him, as though it came from God. It said, "Start here. Start right now."

He got up from the couch and stepped over to

where Carlos and Tracy stood. He gripped Tracy's shoulder in one hand and Carlos's in the other. He peered into his daughter's eyes. "Are you sure that's what you need from me?"

She smiled and nodded as tears spilled from her eyes.

He felt his eyes filling with tears, too. "Are you sure this is the man you want to marry?"

She met his gaze, still tearful, still nodding.

He turned to Carlos. "Will you take much better care of my daughter than I have? Will you be the man she deserves?"

He answered with steel in his trembling voice. "She deserves more than I can be, but I will give to her my everything."

It took a moment for Rand to compose himself. A man never knows when he rises in the morning what the coming day may bring—of sorrow or joy, pain or healing, guilt or salvation, regret or hope. Much less can he know that a single day may bring all those things . . . or how he will respond.

Rand wasn't sure he could do it, until he did. He embraced them both, his daughter and his future son-in-law. He swallowed hard, and wrestled with his emotions for a few moments before answering, "Okay, then. Yes. You have my blessing."

118

Malchus waited patiently for the high priest's latest coughing fit to subside.

"I think I'm getting better," Caiaphas joked. He tried to laugh, which caused a new round of convulsions. Finally he extended a thin scroll, encased in a leather sheath, to his servant.

Malchus gripped the scroll, but the priest didn't let go. Each held on to one end as Caiaphas said, "You must take great care. No one but Nicodemus may see this. Do you understand?"

"Yes," Malchus said, and his expression told Caiaphas that he understood fully.

"You must wait for his response, and bring it immediately to me, and only to me. Do you understand?"

"Yes."

Caiaphas released his grip on the scroll and watched as Malchus tucked it inside his tunic. "Go," Caiaphas said.

Malchus turned to leave. Caiaphas groaned, and reclined once more on the couch that had been his bed during the past several days. Before

435

he closed his eyes, he saw his wife, the daughter of Annas, watching him with obvious interest from the window of their home.

EPILOGUE

a.d. 37
HINNOM VaLLeY, JerusaLem

Malchus *waited for the women—the wives of Theophilus and Matthias, two of Annas's sons— to complete the ritual of reburial that had been practiced by Jews in the Jerusalem area for more than a hundred years. Approximately a year after burial, enough time for the flesh to thoroughly decompose, a tomb would be reopened and the bones of the deceased would be gathered into an ossuary, making the burial niches available for more burials.*

They stood silently in the elaborate family tomb where Annas's entire family—including sons-in-law and daughters-in-law—would be buried. One by one, the women unwrapped the bones of Caiaphas from the grave clothes he had been buried in, wiped them off, and placed them into the elaborate ossuary, starting with the leg bones and finishing with the skull.

Much had changed in the years since the death of Yeshua Mashiach. His master, Joseph bar

Caiaphas, had corresponded briefly with Nicodemus before the Pharisee's death. Malchus knew that Caiaphas believed Nicodemus's death had not been accidental, any more than Stephen's illegal stoning outside the city walls had been spontaneous. In fact, according to Caiaphas, his wife's family—Annas, who still lived, and his sons—had repeatedly (though unsuccessfully) plotted the death of Saul the Pharisee, who had become a follower of Yeshua.

After Nicodemus died, only Malchus and Junias knew the truth of the high priest's faith in Yeshua. But Malchus believed the family of Annas had found out somehow; he suspected that the sickness that incapacitated Caiaphas for the last several years—and perhaps even his death almost a year ago—had been related to his hope in Yeshua. All of Caiaphas's caution and patience had failed to save his life, and now that his brother-in-law Jonathan had been appointed high priest in his place, there seemed no possibility that his change of heart would ever be known. The truth would, quite literally, be buried with Caiaphas.

So when the women had finished placing the bones in the box, and reached for the heavy limestone lid, Malchus stepped forward.

"I will do that," he said. "I will put on the lid for you and place the box in the niche."

The women exchanged agreeable glances and stepped toward the door of the tomb. Malchus, with his back to the women, reached into the folds of his tunic and pulled out the scroll, the dangerous document Caiaphas had kept hidden these past few years. He tucked it against the inside wall of the ossuary and then slowly lifted the lid, placed it on top, and slid the ossuary deep into the arched niche in the wall.

HISTORICAL NOTES

Prologue
The discovery of the Talpiot burial cave during construction of the Peace Forest occurred in 1990.

Chapter 1
Tel Mareshah is an actual archaeological site that is now part of the 1,250-acre Beit Guvrin National Park, which lies in the Judean plain an hour southwest of Jerusalem.

Chapter 5
Valerius Gratus was the Roman governor of Judea who removed Annas from his position as high priest, and in A.D. 18 appointed Caiaphas to that post.

Chapter 7
Both Shimon and Gamaliel (son and grandson, respectively, of the Great Hillel) were on the Sanhedrin during Caiaphas's tenure as high priest.

The Hebrew word Hashem (the Name) is used by Jews as a synonym for the name of God, which is considered too holy to pronounce.

Scholars differ on whether high priests after the exile were anointed.

CHAPTER 9

The physical descriptions of the tomb are factual.

CHAPTER 11

The descriptions of Caesarea, here and elsewhere, are based on historical and archaeological evidence.

CHAPTER 12

The laws in Israel concerning reburial of human remains change frequently, as the authorities seek an acceptable balance between religious and scientific considerations.

CHAPTER 14

The New Deli at 44 Efek Refaim is one of two locations for the store in Jerusalem. The other is on Hillel Street.

CHAPTER 15

The Jewish historian Josephus records that the high priest's vestments were kept in Fortress Antonia, first under Herod's authority and then in Rome's keeping. According to Josephus, the vestments were returned to Jewish custodianship by Vitellius, the governor of Syria from A.D. 35 to 39.

CHAPTER 17

According to Alfred Edersheim in his book *The Temple: Its Ministry and Services*, the great

Jewish philosopher Maimonides (among others) enumerated 140 circumstances or conditions that permanently disqualified a person from the priesthood (and 22 temporary disqualifications from service).

Edersheim cites the practice of anointing the high priest in the pattern of the Greek letter χ in *The Temple.* "The coincidence," he writes, "is certainly curious."

CHAPTER 25

Lucius Aelius Sejanus, as prefect, was the most powerful man in Rome during Emperor Tiberius's self-imposed exile on the island of Capri.

Marcus Ambivulus and Annius Rufus were the predecessors of Valerius Gratus as procurators of Judea. Marcus Ambivulus was in office from A.D. 9 to 12, and Annius Rufus from A.D. 12 to 15.

Pontius Pilate, who succeeded Valerius Gratus as procurator, was accompanied to Judea by his wife, Claudia Procula, granddaughter of Augustus and daughter of Claudia, Tiberius's third wife. It was unusual for a procurator's wife to accompany him to the province; wives usually preferred to stay in the luxury of their Roman estates.

CHAPTER 27

The physical descriptions of the two ossuaries in this chapter and elsewhere correspond to the two most important ossuaries found in the Talpiot tomb.

CHAPTER 29

As described in this chapter, one of Pilate's first acts as governor of the province of Judea was to transfer the Augustan cohort—and their iconic standards—to Jerusalem, where the Jewish residents and authorities were sure to consider them idolatrous (see Josephus: *Antiquities* XVIII, III, 1 and *Wars* II, IX, 2–3). Historians are not sure whether Pilate did this out of ignorance or arrogance.

CHAPTER 34

The inscriptions described in this chapter are the actual inscriptions on two of the ossuaries found in the Talpiot tomb. Though not mentioned in this novel, there also were ossuaries found in the tomb bearing the inscribed names "Shimon" and "Salome," as well as another with the apparent family name "Qafa," or Caiaphas.

CHAPTER 36

The Gospel of John matter-of-factly reports an incident involving a servant of the high priest whose name was Malchus.

The account of Hanun's shameful treatment of David's delegation to the Ammonite king is recorded in 1 Chronicles 19.

CHAPTER 37

The coin described in this chapter was found in the

skull of the skeleton inside the Miryam ossuary in the Talpiot tomb.

Chapter 44

The account of the bronze serpent (cited by Caiaphas in this chapter) is recorded in Numbers 21:4–8; the account of Hezekiah's destruction of the bronze serpent appears in 2 Kings 18:4.

Herod the Great's erection of the golden eagle over the entrance to the Temple is recorded in Josephus (*Antiquities* XVII, VI, 2–3).

Josephus records the incident of the ensigns, including Pilate's threat in the theater to slaughter the crowds who had traveled there to protest the ensigns, as well as their willingness to die, as the reasons for his decision to relent and remove the ensigns from Jerusalem (see *Antiquities* XVIII, III, 1, and *Wars* II, IX, 2–3). There is no historical evidence, however, that Caiaphas paid such a call on Pilate.

Chapter 45

Levanon's Catalogue of Jewish Ossuaries is a fictional name. However, other listings of ossuaries (and their contents and inscriptions) discovered in Israel do exist.

Chapter 51

The English translation of *"Hinei Ma Tov,"* the song Tracy heard, is "How good and pleasant when friends live together in peace." The song is taken from Psalm 133.

CHAPTER 55

The events and dialogue in this chapter and in Chapter 58 are based on descriptions in the Gospels.

CHAPTER 64

The rebellion of Judas the Galilean is mentioned in the Gospel of Luke and in the works of Josephus.

CHAPTER 71

Long-standing tradition marks the site of the Roman Catholic church St. Peter in Gallicantu as the site of Caiaphas's house. An alternative site nearby, a more recent discovery, was discovered along the stone lane that would have traversed Jerusalem's Upper City.

CHAPTER 73

The Armenian Tavern, at 79 Armenian Orthodox Patriarchate Road, is indeed one of the finest places to eat in Jerusalem's Old City.

CHAPTER 75

The healing of the man at the Pool of Bethesda is recorded in John 5:1–16.

Chapter 80

The words of Yeshua in this chapter are based loosely on John 5:17–47 from the New Living Translation.

Chapter 86

The events of this chapter and in some of the dialogue are based on John 7:37–52.

While the Pharisee named Saul is not mentioned in the biblical accounts of this scene, Acts 22 reveals that Saul (later called Paul) was raised in Jerusalem and was a protégé of Gamaliel. In addition, Paul himself says in Philippians 3:5–6 that not only was he a Pharisee, but that he zealously persecuted the Church. Though the words Saul speaks in this chapter are taken directly from John's Gospel account, and there is no evidence that Saul was the person who spoke those words (other than Nicodemus, the words of the Pharisees in John 7:37–52 are not attributed to any individual), the zeal Paul displayed in persecuting the Church (and later in defending the Gospel) is certainly consistent with the words I attribute to him in this chapter.

Chapter 88

The events of this chapter and some of the debate among the Sanhedrin are drawn from John 11:45–57.

Chapter 91

The events of this chapter are based on a short passage in Matthew 26:3–5.

Chapter 96

All four Gospels record the arrest of Jesus and the attack on the high priest's servant, whom John names as Malchus (John 18:10).

Chapter 99

The events of this chapter and some of the debate among the Sanhedrin are drawn primarily from the Gospels of Matthew and Luke.

The words of the Law Benjamin quotes are from Deuteronomy 13:5.

The words of the Law Eleazar quotes are from Deuteronomy 17:12.

When the high priest "adjured" Jesus to answer his question, as recorded in Matthew 26:63, a refusal to answer would have transgressed the commandment recorded in Leviticus 5:1. Thus many scholars believe Jesus was obligated to answer the question.

Chapter 102

The Gospels do not specify Caiaphas's involvement in any of the events of Jesus' trial and crucifixion after the trial in Caiaphas's house.

The words of Mordecai to Queen Esther are found in Esther 4:14. There is no evidence, of course, that Caiaphas ever used this phrase, but he certainly would have known it.

Judas's change of heart and attempt to return the thirty pieces of silver to the priests is recorded in Matthew 27:3–10.

CHapTer 105

The synoptic Gospels (Matthew, Mark, and Luke) all record the veil of the Temple being split; Matthew records the earthquake.

CHapTer 110

The events of this chapter are drawn from events described in Matthew 28:11–15.

CHapTer 115

The New Testament reports (in 1 Corinthians 15:6) that Jesus once appeared to more than five hundred people at once, after his resurrection. It is not recorded where this took place, but Mount Tabor is a reasonable guess.

CHapTer 116

There is no scriptural mention of Nicodemus or Joseph of Arimathea after Jesus' burial. Tradition says Nicodemus was martyred in the first century, and various legends tell of Joseph traveling to England after the resurrection. It is at least curious that neither man is mentioned as being among the Sanhedrin or involved in the early Church after the resurrection.

The final words of this chapter are a quote from Habakkuk 2:14: "For the earth will be filled with the knowledge of the glory of the LORD, as the waters cover the sea" (NIV).

epilogue

The only biblical mention of Caiaphas after the trial of Jesus occurs in Acts 4, where he is described as present (with John, Alexander, and others in Annas's family) at the trial of Peter and John before the Sanhedrin. This trial resulted in the release of Peter and John.

Joseph bar Caiaphas was deposed as high priest in A.D. 36 or 37, and was replaced by his brother-in-law Jonathan, son of Annas. It is not known when or how he died.

Center Point Publishing
600 Brooks Road • PO Box 1
Thorndike ME 04986-0001 USA

(207) 568-3717

US & Canada:
1 800 929-9108
www.centerpointlargeprint.com